QABBALISTIC MAGIC

Talismans, Psalms, Amulets, and the Practice of High Ritual

SALOMO BAAL-SHEM

Destiny Books
Rochester, Vermont • Toronto, Canada

Destiny Books
One Park Street
Rochester, Vermont 05767
www.DestinyBooks.com

Destiny Books is a division of Inner Traditions International

Library of Congress Cataloging-in-Publication Data

Baal-Shem, Salomo.
 Qabbalistic magic : talismans, psalms, amulets, and the practice of high ritual / Salomo Baal-Shem.
     p. cm.
 Includes bibliographical references and index.
 ISBN 978-1-59477-358-7 (pbk.)
 1. Cabala. 2. Magic. I. Title.
 BF1623.C2.B23 2010
 135'.47—dc22

                                                                    2010028147

Printed and bound in the United States by Lake Book Manufacturing

10 9 8 7 6 5 4 3 2 1

Text design and layout by Priscilla Baker
This book was typeset in Garamond Premier Pro with Parma Petit used as a display typeface

To send correspondence to the author of this book, mail a first-class letter to the author c/o Inner Traditions • Bear & Company, One Park Street, Rochester, VT 05767, and we will forward the communication, or contact the author at his website **www.qabbalah.org** (English) or **www.qabbalah.de** (German).

To Marita in Love

Woodcut of Ezekiel's vision

Contents

Foreword

During the course of more than forty years in the world of the Western Mysteries, I have read my way through countless books, always searching for those that I can truly praise.

As a teacher and the Director of Studies for the Servants of the Light School of Occult Science, I need to be able to recommend books that I think will offer students the most accurate and the most carefully researched material. There are books aplenty on magic and its many side paths, but there are only a few of which I can truly say, "this is unique, this is something you must have on your shelf, this is a book you will turn to again and again." You are holding one such book in your hands now. The sheer scale of knowledge and the depth of research contained in these pages astounds me. I have lived with the Qabbalah for more than forty years and thought that for a non-Jewish person I was fairly well informed. Then I read this book and found I was wrong. What you have here is the result of many years of patient work and painstaking attention to detail. I know of no other book that even comes near to the scholarship you will find in these pages.

There is little if anything in print today that speaks so openly and so eloquently to the subject of Judaic lore of this kind. The author has spent the greater part of his life working with this knowledge and is now ready to share it with the world.

Those who study the mysteries will find it a treasure house of information; those who simply want to read and enjoy a book pertaining to their own ancient racial belief system will be amazed and even disturbed at what is revealed here. Historians will pore over its meticulous attention to detail, and scholars will envy the ease with which the subject is handled.

I have been privileged to watch this book grow to completion and to know its author. What has been achieved here is a masterpiece of research and love of the subject itself. As a teacher, I give it my highest recommendation; as a reader and lover of history, I will return to it again and again; as an author myself, I marvel at the dedication and scholarship that has gone into it. For those who study the Qabbalah it should be considered essential to their studies. It will become required reading for my students, and I predict that in the future it will become the definitive book on Qabbalistic magic.

DOLORES ASHCROFT-NOWICKI,
DIRECTOR OF STUDIES, SERVANTS OF THE
LIGHT SCHOOL OF OCCULT SCIENCE

Acknowledgments

My everlasting thankfulness to Dolores Ashcroft-Nowicki, my beloved teacher, the greatest teacher a student of the mysteries could hope to find. Without her advice, help, encouragement, and friendship, this book would not exist.

Thanks also to Mike Haynes, whose help and advice in proofreading was immensely valuable.

Further, thanks to Christina Shrewsbury, who helped as the second proofreader for several chapters; to Andrea Geller, the third proofreader; and to Oliver Kraft, who helped edit several images.

My thanks also to the syndics of Cambridge University Library for granting permission to publish fragments from the Genizah, and to Hebrew University Magnes Press, Taylor and Francis Books, and Red Wheel Weiser for various image permissions.

. . . And to all those who walk the spiritual path with me.

This book contains Divine Names. Please treat the book with respect, and do not take it into a bathroom or any other unclean place.

Note to the Reader on Spoken Rituals

Throughout the book you will find passages typeset in bold. This is an indication that these words are to be spoken out loud. These passages have also been placed within gray boxes so they can quickly be located.

Within these bolded passages you will also find words appearing within brackets or parentheses. If the words within these brackets or parentheses are also bolded then they are likewise to be said out loud.

However, if the words within the brackets or parentheses appear in a lighter face, they are either a translation, alternate Hebrew or English wording, or a reference for the text, or they represent instructions of something you should do. These lightface translations or instructions are not said out loud. In some cases, you may prefer to substitute the alternate word(s) appearing in parentheses. This is entirely up to you, since the words mean the same thing.

On a few occasions the author needed to fill in wording within the rituals or prayers where the ancient text was not readable or where words may have been missing. These clarifications appear within brackets. As stated above, if these bracketed words are part of a spoken prayer or ritual and they are in boldface type, they should be spoken out loud as part of the passage in which they appear.

Introduction

B"H[1]

The Qabbalah[2] (pronounced ka-ba-LA, stressing the last syllable) is the Jewish mystical, spiritual, and occult tradition that has existed under various names and in various forms since the time of the early prophets, when the mysteries were taught to Abraham by the priest Malkizedek. (I am aware that some scientists say the Qabbalah has its origin in the Middle Ages, but this is a simplification based only on that which was written down. The term Qabbalah has been used only since the twelfth century, but long before this time, there was a living spiritual tradition handed down from teacher to student over the ages.)[3]

Many Jews are totally unaware of the rich magical tradition that exists in the Qabbalah. Many (non-Jewish) people believe that Qabbalistic magic can be performed only in a temple with black and white squares. Nothing could be further from the truth. The temple with black and white squares is a Masonic symbol, and even though this tradition was greatly influenced by

---

[1] B"H is an abbreviation of Be-Ezrat HaShem and means "With the help of HaShem."

[2] I use the spelling Qabbalah because it is closest to the Hebraic spelling (קבלה), for the letter Q is related to the Hebrew letter Qof, and the double B indicates that the Bet in the middle is "geminated or doubled," according to linguistic terminology. The H at the end is the Heh in the Hebraic spelling. (Other common ways of spelling it are: Qabalah, Qabbala, Qabala, Kabbalah, Kabalah, Kabbala, Kabala, Cabbalah, Cabalah, Cabbala, and Cabala.)

[3] In Genesis 17:5 Abraham's name was changed from Abram to Abraham. Would we say that he existed only from that moment on? We certainly do not find the name Abraham in the Bible before Genesis 17:5. The same is true of the Qabbalah. The term *Qabbalah* has been used since the Middle Ages, but the tradition is much older.

the Qabbalah (via the Hermetic tradition), it is mainly a Christian tradition originating in the lodges of the free stonemasons, or freemasons, who built the medieval churches. In the Jewish tradition, there is only one Temple: the Temple of Solomon. (Under certain circumstances, however, the Jewish home is called *Miqdash Me'at,* the "miniature sanctuary.")

It is nevertheless true that some rituals were to be performed in a special room prepared for this work. Even in early talmudic times, the Qabbalist was instructed to "sit in a chamber or roof, where he will be alone" in order to perform his rituals and invocations. In one text this special room in which the magician works is actually called his *Miqdash,* "Temple."[4] To have such a place permanently reserved for spiritual work is a good thing, but it is certainly not necessary.

The Qabbalah is certainly not an "indoor only" tradition with no connection to nature or the elements. In this book you will find rituals to be performed both inside and outside (in one case, even standing up to your loins in a river or lake—can you be closer to the elements?).

I will describe all aspects of traditional Qabbalistic and Jewish magic, from the earliest sources to the (relatively recent) developments in Eastern Chassidism. You will find both simple techniques for use in everyday life, and the most difficult and advanced techniques of high magic.

I hope to reach both Jews and non-Jewish people with this book. In the ancient world, the Jewish occult tradition was used as an important source of wisdom by the surrounding peoples, such as the ancient Greeks, and in the Middle Ages both Christians and Muslims benefited from studying the Qabbalah and were not afraid to learn from a Jewish tradition. The magical knowledge of the Jews had a very high reputation throughout the Middle East and Europe. It is my wish that both Jews and non-Jews benefit from this book, and that they regard each other with religious tolerance.[5]

---

[4] Literally, *Miqdashecha,* "thy Temple," or *Beit Miqdashecha* (since the magician is addressed directly in the instruction). Ms. Cambridge, Add 647, fol. 18a, Ms Bologna University Lib. 2914, fol. 178b–80b; Ms Oxford, 1638, fol. 59a, see "Golem," Moshe Idel (p. 60*ff*).

[5] Note that the Jewish faith is probably the first that formulated a concept of religious tolerance. It was the first to say that every nation should worship their gods as long as each keeps in mind that there is only one Creative Source. In fact, in the Jewish faith, there is a very strict rule of never discouraging other people from worshipping the Divine in their own way. Jews believe that God has created every nation for a purpose; therefore, Judaism has never attempted to impose its ways on other nations.

Some rituals in this book can be dangerous if performed by inexperienced beginners, in particular the Invocation of the Prince of the Countenance, the Ritual of the Golem, and the Vision of the Merkavah. Others, such as the Ritual of the Robe of Righteousness, require a special purification of the soul. I definitely advise the reader to observe very carefully the instructions given in this book. Certainly, no one should consider himself experienced enough to approach these rituals unless he has studied practical Qabbalah and ritual magic under a competent expert and master of the tradition for at least five (better, ten) years. In some cases, such as in the case of the Vision of the Merkavah, a less-experienced person can perform the technique if guided by a master of the tradition. To those who are new to this type of work, there are many easier techniques in this book to start with and to use to gain experience.

This book is not written for scientists, but for those who intend actually to practice Qabbalistic magic. Nevertheless, I have kept all the translations as close as possible to the original, although every language has its own magic. A literal translation of a Hebrew invocation will not always work in English—at least, not very well. In those cases I have made very minor changes. For example, I have translated the phrase *mashbia ani alecha* as "I invoke thee." Literally, the root *shava* (שבע) means "to swear," or in the form Hifil, "to adjure." Yet I have changed this slightly due to the way angelic beings are approached in our times by those who serve the Light—that is, with respect and not by binding them with an oath. The ancient Hebrew word *mashbia* did have both meanings, but there is no doubt that even in ancient times it was used mainly to "invoke" rather than to bind by an oath those who truly served God. This is most obvious in the Invocation of the Prince of the Countenance, in which the phrase *mashbia ani alecha* alternates with *ani qore le-cha,* meaning "I call upon thee." Here, both phrases were used with the same meaning.[6]

In some original texts, the phrase Ploni ben Plonit appears. Literally this means "So-and-so, son/daughter of So-and-so." Note that in magical

---

[6] Nevertheless, it cannot be denied that there were those who tried to bind evil spirits by using dark arts, and they would have used the same phrase with the meaning "I conjure thee." Those, however, were not true Qabbalistic magicians, but sorcerers who did not follow the path of the Qabbalah. (For the difference between Qabbalists and sorcerers, see chapter 1, Magic and Qabbalah.)

work, a person was identified by his name and the name of his mother.[7] For texts in which another person is concerned, I have written: [Insert name], son/daughter of [Insert name of mother] for the magician to fill in as appropriate. In contexts where the magician speaks of himself, I have replaced this phrase with [Insert your magical name], for in modern magic, many Qabbalists use a magical name that identifies their magical personality, and in this case the magical name is the appropriate one to use. If you do not have a magical name, use your first name and the name of your mother.

To make it easier for the reader to use this book, text to be recited is printed in bold. Text in brackets is not to be recited, but simply serves as a translation, an explanation, or an instruction.

I hope that this book will help to keep alive the tradition of my forefathers, and that it will inspire modern people with the wisdom and knowledge of the ancient times.

---

[7] This is in accordance with the Jewish tradition, in which the lineage follows the maternal line, because no one could be absolutely sure about the father, but the mother was certain. In the same way, individuals were careful not to affect the wrong person with a magical invocation or spell. In our times, however (considering modern methods of proving parentship), many rabbis believe that it no longer matters if the lineage follows the line of the mother or the father.

Magic and Qabbalah

In the Bible we find several passages that seem to forbid any kind of magic, so how is it possible that a spiritual tradition based on the Bible includes magic? The Bible mentions that certain acts of magic are forbidden, and those who practice them are subject to the death penalty: "Thou shalt not suffer a sorceress (Mechashefah) to live" (Exodus 22:17).

Sorcerers or black magicians are called *kashafim* or *mechashefim*. Mechashefah is the female singular form. (The female form is used because sorceresses were considered to be more common than sorcerers. Even today, more women than men are engaged in the occult.)

Both kashafim and mechashefim come from the verb *kashaf,* meaning "to enchant or bewitch," and thus describe a person who undertakes acts of evil or dark magic, for to enchant or bewitch someone means either to manipulate someone against their free will or to cause harm to someone. These acts of magic are clearly forbidden in the Bible, and those who perform them are to be punished. In the Talmud we find a more philosophical clarification of what makes sorcerers evil: "Rabbi Yochanan said: Why are they called sorcerers (kashafim/mechashefim)?—Because they oppose the Heavenly Agencies" (Babylonian Talmud, Sanhedrin 67b).

5

A sorcerer is someone who acts against the Powers of Heaven, and thus in direct conflict with the Divine Plan and the Will of God. It is only logical to condemn every act—magical or not—that is directed against the Will of God. In all of this, however, we do not find every act of magic forbidden. Did not the prophets and priests have magical powers? Did not Moses and Aaron perform the same acts as the magicians of Egypt?

> And YHVH spoke unto Moses and unto Aaron, saying: When Pharaoh shall speak unto thee, saying: Show a wonder for thee; then thou shalt say unto Aaron: Take thy rod, and cast it down before Pharaoh, that it become a serpent. And Moses and Aaron went in unto Pharaoh, and they did so, as YHVH had commanded; and Aaron cast down his rod before Pharaoh and before his servants, and it became a serpent. Then Pharaoh also called for the wise men (chachamim) and the sorcerers (mechashefim); and they also, the scribe-magicians (chartumim, literally, "scribes," i.e., lecture priests)[1] of Egypt, did in like manner with their secret arts. For they cast down every man his rod, and they became serpents; but Aaron's rod swallowed up their rods.[2]
>
> And YHVH said unto Moses: Say unto Aaron: Take thy rod, and stretch out thy hand over the waters of Egypt, over their rivers, over their streams, and over their pools, and over all their ponds of water, that they may become blood; and there shall be blood throughout all the land of Egypt, both in vessels of wood and in vessels of stone. And Moses and Aaron did so, as YHVH commanded; and he lifted up the rod, and smote the waters that were in the river, in the sight of Pharaoh, and in the sight of his servants; and all the waters that were in the river were turned to blood. And the fish that were in the river died; and the river became foul, and the Egyptians could not drink water from the river; and the blood was throughout all the land of Egypt. And the scribe-magicians (chartumim) of Egypt did in like manner with their secret arts.[3]

---

[1] This term refers to a certain class of priest called *cheri-hebet* in Egyptian. The cheri-hebet was the lecture priest who was the master of ceremonies and the reciter of magical chants and invocations. Thus he had the function of a magician in the Egyptian priesthood system.

[2] Exodus 7:10–12.

[3] Exodus 7:19–22.

Moses's Staff Becomes a Snake *by Julius Schnoor von Carolsfeld*

And YHVH said unto Moses: Say unto Aaron: Stretch forth thy hand with thy rod over the rivers, over the canals, and over the pools, and cause frogs to come up upon the land of Egypt. And Aaron stretched out his hand over the waters of Egypt; and the frogs came up, and covered the land of Egypt. And the scribe-magicians (Chartumim) did in like manner with their secret arts, and brought up frogs upon the land of Egypt.[4]

And YHVH said unto Moses: Say unto Aaron: Stretch out thy rod, and smite the dust of the earth, that it may become gnats throughout all the land of Egypt. And they did so; and Aaron stretched out his hand with his rod, and smote the dust of the earth, and there were gnats upon man, and upon beast; all the dust of the earth became gnats throughout all the land of Egypt. And the scribe-magicians (Chartumim) did so with their secret arts to bring forth gnats, but

---

[4] Exodus 8:1–3.

they could not; and there were gnats upon man, and upon beast. Then the scribe-magicians (Chartumim) said unto Pharaoh: This is the Finger of God (Elohim).[5]

You will notice that there is no difference in what Moses and Aaron did to the magicians and sorcerers, except that Moses and Aaron acted on behalf of God, while the sorcerers tried to act against the Divine Will. Consequently, Moses and Aaron were superior.

Thus we learn that magic is not forbidden in general, but only if it is not in harmony with the Divine Will. This view is also supported by the Talmud:

Abaye said: The laws (Hilchot; i.e., rabinical laws) of sorcerers (kashafim) are like the laws of the Shabbat: There are among them [certain actions which are to be punished] by stoning, and there are among them [certain actions] which are exempt [from punishment], yet forbidden, and there are among them [certain actions] which are permitted from the outset. He who performs [black magic] work (Maasseh) is [to be punished] by stoning, he who merely affects the eyes (i.e, an illusionist or stage magician) is exempt [from punishment], yet it is forbidden; permitted from the outset are [white magic works] such as those [performed] by Rav Chanina and Rav Oshaaya on the eve of every Shabbat; they studied "Rules of Formation" (Hilchot Yetzirah; i.e., the *Sefer Yetzirah*) and created a small (literally, "third-grown") calf and ate it.[6]

The Talmud distinguishes between three types of magic.

1. Black magic: This is forbidden, and the sorcerer who performs this kind of magic has committed a major crime and will be punished severely.[7]

---

[5] Exodus 8:12–15.
[6] Babylonian Talmud, Sanhedrin 67b. See chapter 21, Creating a Golem with the *Sefer Yetzirah* (Book of Formation).
[7] The death penalty is actually not (only) the earthly punishment, but it is also an analogy for *Karet,* which means to be "cut off" and refers to the cutting off (that is, heavenly eradication) of the entire soul—and in some cases, immediate physical death by God's hand. This is seen as the Divine Punishment for dark magic such as necromancy. It is actually very rare, but if a person has completely handed over his soul to the dark side, this is his fate, for the forces of darkness are the forces of destruction.

2. Illusion (stage magic): This is not real magic at all, but an illusion mistaken for magic. The charlatan who performs a trick or an illusion and pretends that this is an occult act has committed the minor crime of misleading others.[8] He will not, however, be punished. (If he did not pretend to do real magic, it would not be a crime at all, but merely entertainment.) Seekers on the occult path sometimes look for great physical phenomena. These will always be misleading, for magic happens not on the physical plane, but on the astral plane or higher. Magic may, however, affect the physical plane, but if a magician heals by magic, the patient will often recover much faster than expected, but he will still recover naturally; a broken bone will not heal instantly. If a magician causes it to rain, it will rain after a while, but according to the laws of nature—that is, if there are no clouds in the sky, the clouds have to appear first, and then it can rain. It will not rain out of a blue sky. If any phenomenon looks like the physical "stage magic" type, this is what it will be—illusion and not magic. If the person who demonstrates it claims to be performing magic, he is a charlatan.

3. White magic: This is magic applied for spiritual purposes, such as to understand the Mystery of Creation. It can also be used to heal or help when used in harmony with the Divine Will. (Note that whenever you heal or help someone with magic, you must first have their permission, for otherwise you act against their free will, which was given to humans by God—thus you act against God.)

Magical powers were usually seen as a sign of spiritual understanding and achievement, as in the case of Moses, who was invested with the power to perform miracles as an outer sign of his inner spiritual authority (Exodus 4:1–9), or in the case of Rav Chanina and Rav Oshaaya, whose knowledge and understanding of the *Sefer Yetzirah* (which is one of the foundations of theoretical Qabbalah) enabled them to perform practical magic.

The term *magic*, however, was not used in order to avoid confusion with *sorcery*, which is not a sign of spirituality at all. Because white magic was seen as the result of true understanding and mastery of the Qabbalah, the magical application of this knowledge was called Practical Qabbalah. A Qabbalistic magician is called a *Baal-Shem* (plural: *Baaley-Shem*), meaning

---

[8] In India, many false gurus use stage magic to convince their disciples (*chelas*) of their superior magical powers. The same was also true in Talmudic times.

a "Master of the Name." In other words, he is one who knows how to apply Divine Names[9] to cause magical effects. This term for a Qabbalistic magician has been in use since the Middle Ages, and it was applicable to both rabbis and nonrabbis alike. One of the most famous Baaley-Shem is Israel Baal-Shem-Tov, the founder of Eastern European Chassidism.

Some more mystically inclined Qabbalists (usually influenced by Isaak Luria) have tried to separate Qabbalah from Practical Qabbalah (magic), but magic has always been a part of the tradition of the Qabbalah. It was used by the early prophets and by the sages who ascended to the Merkavah—and who were often identical with the Rabbis of the Talmud, about whom there abound stories of their occult knowledge and use. Even in the Zohar you can find a spell against Lilith. Many magical invocations were used by the Chassidey Ashkenaz,[10] and it is also well known that the great Israel Baal-Shem-Tov and his followers made use of spells and amulets, and they were proud of their profound knowledge and skill in practical Qabbalah. Magic was, and is, a part of the Qabbalah.

---

[9] The Name especially refers to the Tetragrammaton. A *Baal-Shem(-Tov)* is one to whom the true pronunciation of the Divine Name has been revealed either by his teacher or in meditation (by an Inner Plane Teacher).

[10] For more information on the Chassidey Ashkenaz, see chapter 19, Revelation of the Secret Name.

Who May Study
the Qabbalah?

Very often, we hear that we are not permitted to study the Qabbalah before the age of forty. This is, however, not true. Isaak Luria (1534–1572), often seen as one of the greatest Qabbalists of all times, began studying the Qabbalah at seventeen. His teacher Moses Qordovero[1] (1522–1570) began to study the Qabbalah when he was twenty.

In fact, some of the most famous Qabbalists left this world before the age of forty. Isaak Luria lived only until age thirty-eight, Moses Chaim Luzzatto (1707–1746) reached thirty-nine, and Nachman of Breslov (1772–1810) also died at thirty-eight.

The age limit of forty is actually a very late development. In the early days of the mystical tradition, it seems to have been a rule that the secrets of the Merkavah could be studied only by someone who was thirty years old. But this may have had more to do with the fact that a Jewish scholar of that age would have had a very good basic knowledge of the scriptures,

---

[1] Sometimes written Cordovero.

which in those days was seen as a basis for further studies. As we will see in chapter 12, The Vision of the Merkavah, however, even these age rules were not hard and fast.

Originally, the rule that an individual should be forty to be permitted to study the Qabbalah was introduced by the Ashkenazim (Middle European and East European Jews). The Sefardim (Middle Eastern Jews) never knew of this rule, and it consequently did not apply to them.

In the seventeenth century, the false messiah Shabbatai Tzevi (1626–1676) misused Qabbalistic symbolism to mislead those who were overcredulous. He convinced a large number of Jews to follow him to the Holy Land. On the way, he was threatened by the Turkish sultan—and under threat of being killed (and unwilling to die for his beliefs), he converted to Islam. Obviously, he became very unpopular.

The age rule was made to prevent history from ever repeating itself. It was believed that this would successfully restrict the study of the Qabbalah to those who would have the maturity not to fall for another false messiah. Even today, most rabbis consider the study of Qabbalah a dubious subject, because in their eyes it is connected to false messianism and superstition.

Yet the number forty may have been chosen for a deeper reason. I have always been surprised that the age limit of forty has never been understood to have a numerological significance. Forty is the number of years Israel wandered through the desert and the number of days Moses spent on Mount Zion to receive the Commandments. It is also generally the number that must be passed in order to receive higher knowledge, vision, salvation, or enlightenment.[2]

---

[2] Forty is *chevel* (חבל), which means "pain"—in particular, the pain of childbirth. Thus it represents the pain that must be overcome before a spiritual initiation. This pain must be endured in order to let the soul mature to the point at which higher wisdom can be understood. Also note that the letters of the word *chevel* (חבל) are very similar to those in *qabbal* (קבל), which is the root of the word Qabbalah (קבלה). A saying by Yehudah ben Teyma in the Mishnah may have influenced the choice for the age of forty:

> A person is ready to study the Scriptures (the Bible) at five years, at ten years to study the Mishnah, at thirteen for the commandments, at fifteen for the Talmud, at eighteen for the bridechamber (wedding), at twenty for one's life pursuit, at thirty for power (authority), at forty for Understanding (Binah), at fifty for advice, at sixty to be an elder (Zaqen), at seventy for venerability, at eighty for [inner] strength (Psalm 90:10), at ninety for bending down (i.e., turning away), and at a hundred a man is as one who has died for he has gone beyond and has ceased acting in the affairs of this world. (Mishnah Avot 5:24)

The deeper levels of the Qabbalah can be understood only by someone who has walked the path of life (which is called by occultists the "Path of the Hearth-Fire") for a certain amount of time. Only those who have experienced the good and the bad sides of life have gained the maturity to understand the higher mysteries. But this maturity is not a matter of a fixed age limit, even though most people do not reach a certain level of maturity before a certain age. According to my experience, nowadays no student of the Western Mysteries has ever reached the higher levels of the mysteries before thirty, and most people need much longer than this. But the few who have reached these levels by this age have already been study-ing the mysteries for many years, and they obviously started their studies much earlier than thirty. Thus I believe Qabbalistic study should be denied no one, no matter how young they are, as long as they are of religious matu-rity. In the Jewish tradition, this maturity is signified by the Bar Mitzvah or Bat Mitzvah (for young adults who are thirteen years old). Yet young students should be taught only in a way that is appropriate for their age. I generally believe that the practice of magic should not be approached in any form before the age of eighteen.[3]

---

[3] Eighteen is the number of life in the Jewish tradition.

3

Women in the Qabbalah

The spiritual tradition of the West is closely related to the teachings hidden in the Bible. Unfortunately, these teachings are often interpreted by those who have no deeper understanding of them or who misuse them for their own ideology. Many misconceptions have therefore come into being. It may seem that the Creation myth in the Bible is dominated by the male aspect, and, indeed, most people think that God created man before he created woman. On closer examination of the text, however, you will see that the first human being that God created was male *and* female, just as the Creator himself is both male and female while being beyond both: "And Elohim created man in His own image, in the image of Elohim He created him; male and female He created them" (Genesis 1:27).[1]

---

[1] Please note that even though both Elohim and man are called *he,* this does not describe a spiritual concept, but rather reflects the limits of translation. In the Hebrew language, there is no neutral gender. In fact, strictly speaking, men do not have a gender of their own, but share it with mixed or neutral subjects. Therefore, something consisting of both male and female aspects will be described as male. Only subjects that are purely female were seen as special, and therefore are honored by having a gender of their own.

Thus the first human being was created in the perfect image of God. But where is the female side of God? Many people think of the biblical God as male, a belief that is incorrect. In the Qabbalah, the Divine is described by the Sefirot of the Tree of Life. Keter is beyond concepts of male or female.[2] Chochmah is the Divine Father, and Binah is the Divine Mother. In Tiferet we find another male aspect called the Holy One, blessed be He, and in Malchut the female side of God is known as the Shechinah, the Presence of God.

We see that the Divine has a female side, but what about mortal women? Where is their place in spiritual life? In ancient times, the most important ceremonies in the Temple were performed by the High Priest on Yom Kippur (the Day of Atonement). The High Priest—in fact, every priest—would always have been a man. It may seem that Judaism does not think much of women with regard to religious service and spiritual work, but this again is not true! The most holy day in the Jewish religion is not Yom Kippur, but the Shabbat. The Shabbat is the first thing God made holy, and it is celebrated in the Jewish home. The celebrant, however, is not a man, but the wife, the lady of the house. The Jewish home is called Miqdash Me'at (miniature sanctuary), for every home is a holy place. In fact, the home is more important than the synagogue, which is not a sanctuary at all.[3] The task of a woman—to bring down the Shechinah into the Jewish home—was considered so important that women were freed from other spiritual duties such as the study of the Holy Scriptures and many other religious tasks in order to do this. "When a man is at home, the root of his house is the lady of the house, because of her the Shechinah does not leave the house. As we have learned: 'Isaak brought her [Rebbeka, his wife] into the tent of his mother Sarah.'[4] The Light (candle) was lit[5] for the Shechinah came to the house." (Zohar 50a)

The lady of the house is the High Priestess of her miniature sanctuary.

---

[2] The magical image of Keter is an elderly bearded man shown from the side. What is not often said is that the image is androgynous, not male. One side is male, looking toward manifestation; the other is female and looking toward the Unmanifest aspect of God (Ayin Sof). The female side is receptive, accepting the influx from the Ayin Sof, and the male side is creative, using the influx to create the world.

[3] Neither does the synagogue have a *Mezuzah* (a sign of blessing fixed on a doorpost to indicate that a person is entering a holy place).

[4] Genesis 24:67.

[5] For more details on the lighting of candles at Shabbat, see chapter 22, Shabbat.

Thus, in the Qabbalistic view of the world, every woman is a priestess. The most holy celebrations in the Jewish tradition are performed by women, not men. Women have always had their place in the Jewish tradition. It is not commonly known that there were also female prophets. The Talmud mentions seven: Sarah, Miriam, Deborah, Hannah (mother of Samuel), Abigail (who became a wife of King David), Huldah (from the time of Yirmiyahu), and Esther.

Magic has always been practiced by Jewish women—probably even more so than by men. It is only because women seldom learned to write that we do not have many documents by female magicians. The Talmud, however, mentions quite a few women skilled in the magical arts,[6] not least the daughters of R. Nachman (Babylonian Talmud, Gittin 45a). In fact, the Babylonian Talmud states that "most women practice magic" (Sanhedrin 67a).

The female side is very important in Qabbalistic magic. If a person is influenced by magic, either by using it himself or by it being used on him, he is identified as Ploni Ben Plonit in magical manuscripts. This means he was called by his name and by the name of his mother.[7]

What exactly is the position of women in the Qabbalah? It is often said that traditional Qabbalistic teachings were not accessible to women, yet this is simply more misinformation—several cases of female Qabbalists are known to us.

One example is Francesa Sarah, who lived in Safed in the sixteenth century. We know about her because she was mentioned in one of Chaim Vital's books, the *Sefer ha-Chezyonot*. She was an extraordinary woman, a mediator in full contact with a *Maggid* (an Inner Plane Teacher or Master). She was very respected among the rabbis who consulted her for advice in

---

[6] It is true that female magic was often viewed with disdain. I believe this was meant to discourage black magic practices such as love charms and curses, which were quite common, rather than that it meant that magic was generally seen as a bad thing. R. Simeon bar Yochai, who is quoted as warning that the Jewish daughters are flagrantly involved in witchcraft (Erubin 64b), is also known to have practiced magic himself. He exorcised a demon from the emperor's daughter (Me'ilah 17b), and, in another case, he used the power of his magical eye (the Evil Eye) to turn his opponent into a heap of bones (Talmud Yerushalmi, Shevi'it 9:1, 38d). It seems that he knew very well what he was talking about.

[7] As I mention in the introduction, the female lineage was always seen as very important in the Jewish tradition, because though it might not be clear who a child's father was, people could be absolutely sure who his or her mother was.

spiritual matters. She was also blessed with the gift of prophecy. In one case, she predicted the precise day on which one of the rabbis would die as atonement for the sins of his congregation.

Another example of a female Qabbalist is Fioretta of Modena, who emigrated from Italy to Safed. Fioretta not only studied the Holy Scriptures and rabbinic literature, but was also deeply devoted to the study of the wisdom of the Zohar (seen by many as the most important source of Qabbalistic teachings). She passed on her wisdom and knowledge to her grandson, the Qabbalist Aaron Berechiah of Modena (who died in 1639). It is only from his writings that we know of Fioretta, for he paid tribute to her in two of his books[8] and called her a rabbi.

Because women seldom wrote books of their own in those days, we know only about those female Qabbalists who are mentioned in the books of others. Further, because we do not know much of their teachings, even the names of these women are seldom heard. It would, however, be foolish to believe that the few we know about are the only ones. There were many other great women who studied and practiced the spiritual tradition of the Qabbalah. Those women who were mentioned in books were only the tip of the iceberg. As we have seen, there is no reason for a woman not to study the Qabbalah.

---

[8] *Seder Ashmoret ha-Boqer* (also published as *Me'eirey ha-Shachar*), Mantua: 1624; and *Maavar Yabboq*, Venice: 1626.

4

The Names of God

The Divine Names are essential in Qabbalistic magic; therefore, it is important to understand their usage. The Name of God is not just a way to identify God. It is an expression of His nature and His power, for God and His Name are One. God is often simply called HaShem (The Name).

The most Holy Name of God consists of the four consonants *YOD HEH VAV HEH.*

יהוה

This is why it is sometimes called the Tetragrammaton (Greek τετραγράμματον, or "word with four letters"). Some believe it originates in the verb *havah,* "to be," and thus it would mean "He will be," but whether this is the true meaning or not is one of the great mysteries of the Qabbalah.[1]

The Name of God was (and still is) seen as being so holy that the rab-

---

[1] Two versions of this verb are also used as Divine Names HAYAH (היה), "He was," and HOVEH (הוה), "He is." In later texts we also find HAVAYAH (הויה), "Existence."

bis considered it ineffable. It was pronounced only once a year by the High Priest. After the destruction of the Temple, its proper pronunciation was lost and soon became a mystery. When the Torah is read, Jews say Adonai, "My Lord,"[2] instead (except in the constellation of Adonai YHVH, which is spoken as Adonai Elohim). Therefore, if the Divine Name is part of biblical quotations written in this book, I have transliterated it as YHVH, and it should be pronounced Adonai. YHVH is *not* pronounced Yehovah. In Hebrew Bibles and prayer books, the vowels of Adonai are written below the Tetragrammaton to remind the reader to say Adonai.

The vowels of Adonai:

are written here—YHVH:[3]

Because not every reader of this book is able to read Hebrew, I shall explain [why it is not pronounced Yehovah] using roman letters instead. The consonants will be replaced by capital letters: A D N Y for Adonai and Y H V H for the Name of God. The vowels will be written as noncapital letters:

A e D o N a Y

Now if we transfer the vowels of Adonai to YHVH, this is what we get:

Y e H o V a H

But all it means is: "Remember not to say the Name of God; say 'Adonai' instead." It was *never* pronounced Yehovah! Unfortunately, when the Bible

---

[2] This is actually a plural form. Literally, it means "My Lords." This is usually interpreted as a sign of respect, however according to the mystical interpretation, it is plural because it refers to both God and the Shechinah—that is, the male and female aspects of God.

[3] You may have noted that there is a patach below the *Alef* in Adonai, while below the *Yod* in YHVH there is a sheva. This is so because according to Hebrew grammar, a sheva cannot be written below an *Alef* (or below any other guttural sounds such as *Heh, Chet,* or *Ayin*). For this reason, it is replaced by a chataf-patach -ː.

was translated into Latin by the church, the translator did not fully understand the meaning of the masoretic text (the Hebrew Bible with vowels), so he misread the Name, and when Martin Luther translated the Bible from Latin to German, he adopted this reading mistake—and now many people believe Yehovah to be the Name of God.[4]

Outside of prayer or Torah reading, pious Jews do not even say Adonai, but instead use the HaShem in order to avoid using the Name of God in vain (Exodus 20:7).

The true pronunciation of YHVH is a mystery, though several Hebrew names such as Eliyahu (Elijah, which means My God is Yahu) include the Divine Name. This suggests the pronunciation Yahu, which would fit with the Greek transliteration IAO (IAΩ).[5]

My advice to the Qabbalistic magician is not to engage in unprovable speculation,[6] but to use the power of the Four Holy Letters and say: YOD HEH VAV HEH whenever the Divine Name is needed in ritual. (Many great Qabbalists of the past have followed this method in one way or another.)[7]

It is forbidden to erase or destroy the Name of God.[8] Therefore, Jews do not write it down in order to prevent it from being erased or treated in an inappropriate way. The only exceptions are holy books (or prayer books), which may not be destroyed—but when they are not used anymore, they must be kept in a special room in a synagogue called a *genizah* or must be buried in a Jewish graveyard.

If the Name of God is written incorrectly in a Torah scroll, it cannot be erased or corrected; the entire page must be written anew. A professional

---

[4] If you ever want to end a Jehovah's Witnesses' visit to your door, explain to them that the name Jehovah is actually a reading mistake. They will leave instantly.

[5] Many scholars believe that Yahu is a short form of Yahueh or Yahuveh (also written Yahveh).

[6] Meditation on the true pronunciation of the Divine Name may in fact be a very rewarding exercise, but for the purpose of this book, I encourage the reader to use the pronunciation given here.

[7] Sometimes, however, they added various combinations of vowels to each of the four holy letters, as in the case of Abraham Abulafia's system. In other cases they added the vowels assigned to the Sefirah they wanted to work with (Keter = Qamatz *a*, Chochmah = Patach *a*, Binah = Tzereh *e*, Chesed = Segol *e*, Gevurah = Sheva short *e*, Tiferet = Cholem *o*, Netzach = Chireq *i*, Hod = Qubbutz *u*, Yesod = Shuruq *u*, Malchut = no vowel) or they meditated on the spelled-out form of the letters, as in Luria's system.

[8] Based on Deuteronomy 12:3–4.

scribe (called a *sofer*) who writes the Name of God does make a special effort to prepare himself mentally in order to sanctify the Name.[9] According to tradition, once the scribe starts writing the Name, he must not stop or let himself be interrupted—not even to greet a king (because God is the King in Heaven, and writing His Name is meant to show respect to Him and must not be interrupted to show respect to any lesser being).

In order to avoid writing the Name of God in other texts, various abbreviations such as the letter *Heh* or (two or three) *Yod*(s) were used. Or the names were slightly changed. For example, Eloqim was written instead of Elohim. (Some even say Eloqim in spoken language in order to avoid using this name in vain.) Many very pious Jews expand this rule to include non-Hebrew languages. Thus God will be written G-d or G'd. Because this book may, to a certain degree, be seen as a Qabbalistic prayer book, and because it is impossible to teach the correct pronunciation of the Holy Names used by the ancient Qabbalists to invoke the Divine Power without writing down the necessary information, I have no choice but to write even the most Holy Names in this book. This being the case, if I do write the most Holy Names with their vowels, it makes very little sense not to write the vowels of the English word God. Therefore, I have decided to write God with its vowel—and because this book is meant to reach both Jews and non-Jewish people, this spelling will also make it easier to read.

Other Names of God

The number of Divine Names in the Qabbalah is too great to give a complete list here, but I will at least explain the most common ones. (Some long invocations in this book consist mainly of Divine Names and magical Words of Power.)[10]

Adonai

Explanations for this name appear in the first part if this chapter.

---

[9] There are seven Divine Names in the Jewish tradition that require special attention of the sofer (scribe). These are: YHVH, Ehiyeh asher Ehiyeh, Elohim, El, Shaddai, Adonai, and Tzevaot.

[10] We would need at least another book to try to explain the meaning of all of them. In addition, the meaning of some of them is hidden in mysteries. If you wish to find out more about them, use them in meditation or apply one of the many methods explained in this book to gather information from the inner planes.

Yah

Yah is an abbreviation of YHVH.

Ehiyeh asher Ehiyeh

Ehiyeh asher Ehiyeh means "I am that I am." It can be interpreted as "I am pure Existence" or "I am the ever existing One" or even "I am the ever-becoming One," for grammatically it implies a neverending process.[11] In the Bible, it is the Name God himself reveals to Moses (Exodus 3:14). In the Qabbalah, it belongs to Keter, the highest aspect of God.

Elohim

Like Adonai, the name Elohim is a plural form.[12] According to the mystical interpretation, it is plural because it refers to the higher union of God and the Shechinah—that is, the male and the female aspects of God (Chochmah and Binah)—as opposed to Adonai, which refers to the lower union (Tiferet and Malchut).

El

El means simply God. It is the oldest and most universal name for God. It can be used for the Creator or for any lesser god. It often appears with certain attributes, such as: El Yisrael (God of Israel), El Eliyon (Most High God), El Olam (God of the Universe/Everlasting God), El Gibbor (God of Strength/Power), El Shaddai (Almighty God), or El Chai (Living God). El is sometimes also translated as "strong one," "mighty one," or "hero," or as "strength," "might," or "power"—for example, in Genesis 31:29.

Eloah

Eloah is a poetic version of El. Unlike El, Eloah is used only for the Creator and never for any lesser gods.

Shaddai

Shaddai means "Almighty." According to Exodus, this was the name known

---

[11] This is due to the fact that biblical grammar does not have a past, present, or future tense. Rather, it differentiates between a process that has ended and one that has not ended.

[12] This is commonly interpreted as *pluralis majestatis* or *pluralis excellentiae*.

[13] It is possible that in early times, God was simply named after those who were his servants. Thus he was called "the God of Abraham, the God of Isaac, and the God of Jacob" (Exodus 3:6) or "God of your fathers" (Exodus 3:15–16).

to the patriarchs:[13] "And Elohim spoke unto Moses, and said unto him: 'I am YHVH; and I appeared unto Abraham, unto Isaac, and unto Jacob, as El Shaddai (God Almighty), but by My name YHVH I made Me not known to them'" (Exodus, 6:2–3).

Tzevaot

Tzevaot means simply "Hosts" or "of Hosts." It is never used alone; it is used only as an attribute for either YHVH or Elohim. It often originally refers to human armies based on the book Samuel: "Then said David to the Philistine: 'Thou comest to me with a sword, and with a spear, and with a javelin; but I come to thee in the Name of the YHVH Tzevaot, the God of the armies of Israel, whom thou hast taunted'" (1 Samuel 17:45).

In Qabbalistic explanation, however, it is interpreted as referring to the Hosts of Heaven—that is, the angels.

Ha-Qadosh Baruch Hu

Ha-Qadosh Baruch Hu means "The Holy One blessed be He." This title usually refers to the Bridegroom of the Shechinah (the female side of God)[14]—that is, God in Tiferet.

The Pronunciation

I have tried to transliterate the Hebrew words in such a way that it is as easy as possible for an English-speaking person to pronounce them correctly. I would like to explain some details.

In ancient magical manuscripts, the Divine Names and magical words have often been marked by writing them inside a square, or they have been overlined (the Hebrew equivalent of underlining) or have been marked with dots written above them. In this book, magical names and Divine Names are marked by writing them in capitals. Thus the name of the angel Michael will be written here as MICHAEL. This will apply only when these names must be pronounced in ritual. Outside of ritual, they will be written in the normal way. Further, in ritual texts I have written names in such a way that they are close to the original Hebrew pronunciation, thus Gabriel appears as GAVRIEL. You may decide to actually "chant" or "vibrate" these names, which is a special way of speaking them that resembles a deep humming voice and that causes a vibratory resonance in both the magician's body and the room in which he performs the magic. (This

---

[14] See chapter 22, Shabbat.

HEBREW CONSONANTS

Hebrew Letter		Transcribed Sound
Alef	א	Has no sound of its own
Ayin	ע	Has no sound of its own
Bet	ב	B (with dagesh/hard sound—pronounced as b in but) and V (without dagesh/soft sound—pronounced as v in have)
Gimel	ג	G (pronounced as g in go)
Dalet	ד	D (pronounced as d in do)
Heh	ה	H (pronounced as h in hammer)[15]
Vav	ו	V (pronounced as v in voice. Where Vav is a semivowel, it is either o or u; see Hebrew Vowels, p. 25)
Zayin	ז	Z (pronounced as z in zoo)
Chet	ח	CH (pronounced as in the Scottish pronunciation of the word loch)
Tet	ט	T (pronounced as t in two)
Yod	י	Y (pronounced as y in yes)
Kaf	כ	K (with dagesh/hard sound—pronounced as k in kid) and CH (without dagesh/soft sound—pronounced as in the Scottish pronunciation of the word loch)
Lamed	ל	L (pronounced as l in left)
Mem	מ	M (pronounced as m in man)
Nun	נ	N (pronounced as n in no)
Samech	ס	S or sometimes SS (pronounced as s in see)
Peh	פ	P (with dagesh/hard sound—pronounced as p in pen) and F (without dagesh/soft sound—pronounced as f in leaf)
Tzadde	צ	TZ (pronounced as t in tip and z in zip)
Qof	ק	Q (pronounced as c in cat)
Resh	ר	R (pronounced as r in rib)
Shin	ש	SH (shin, pronounced as sh in she) and SS or sometimes just S (sin, pronounced as s in sin or ss in pass)
Tav	ת	T (pronounced as t in two)

[15] The chart of the *International Phonetic Alphabet for English*, which I used, suggests *ham*, but I felt *hammer* would be more kosher.

HEBREW VOWELS

Hebrew Letter		Transcribed Sound
Qamatz	ָ	A or O (pronounced as *a* in *car* or as *o* in *horn*)
Patach	ַ	A (pronounced as *a* in *car*)
Tzereh	ֵ	E (pronounced as *e* in *great* or *they*)
Segol	ֶ	E (pronounced as *e* in *set*)
Sheva	ְ	E (pronounced as a very short *e*, as in *synthesis*)
Cholem	וֹ	O (pronounced as *o* in *horn*)
Chireq	ִ	I (pronounced as *i* in *machine*)
Qubbutz	ֻ	U (pronounced as *oo* in *room*)
Shuruq	וּ	U (pronounced as *oo* in *room*)

method is easy to teach but very hard to describe in a book.) Speaking them this way will add quite a bit of power to your voice, because vibration is energy, and the power and meaning of a Divine Name also comes from its vibration. For example, the sound of Ehiyeh describes a wave of "involution and evolution" or "creation and perfection." To use the method of vibration, however, is advisable only if the passages with magical names are not too long; otherwise, it will strain the vocal cords.

5

The Mysteries of the Soul

The knowledge of the soul is called "the secret of secrets" in the Zohar,[1] given only "to those who are wise in their hearts."[2] The importance of the understanding of the nature of the soul can not be overemphasized, for it is the foundation of all spiritual work. According to the Qabbalah, there are three levels of the soul, and these are connected to each other: the *Nefesh,* the *Ruach,* and the *Neshamah.*[3]

> Rabbi Shimon was walking along the way, and with him were his son,
> Rabbi Eleazar, Rabbi Abba, and Rabbi Yehudah. As they were walk-

---

[1] The *Sefer ha-Zohar* (Book of Splendor) is the most central Qabbalistic work, written in the form of a commentary on the Torah. It is supposed to have been composed by Simeon ben Yochai, who lived during a time of Roman persecution, which forced him to hide in a cave for thirteen years. During this time, he studied the Torah with his son Eleazar, and, according to tradition, this was when he was inspired by God to write the Zohar. (Modern scholars ascribe the Zohar to Moses de Leon, who lived in Spain in the thirteenth century.)

[2] Zohar I:81a.

[3] Ibid.

ing, Rabbi Shimon said: I am perplexed that the children of this world (i.e., ordinary people) do not pay attention to the words of Bible or to the reason for their own existence. He opened [the discussion] by saying: "With my Nefesh have I desired Thee in the night; with my Ruach within me will I seek Thee early; for when Thy judgments are in the earth, the inhabitants of the world learn righteousness" (Isaiah 26:9). This verse has already been explained and I have explained it [too]. But come and behold: The Nefesh of the son of a man (i.e., human being) goes out from him and rises upwards when he goes to bed. And if thou sayest that they all rise upwards, [know that] not each and every one sees the Countenance of the King. Yet the Nefesh rises, and leaves behind a particle of it in the presence of the body (Guf); one impression for minimum life of the heart. And the Nefesh leaves (wanders around) and seeks to rise. And there are many levels to rise. It drifts about and it meets in them bright essences of impurity (Qlippot). If it is pure and has not been defiled during the day, then it rises upward. But if it is not pure then it is defiled among them and becomes attached to them, and rises no further. And there are made known to it promises. And there it becomes attached to those promises of coming times. And sometimes they cast it aside and make known to it false promises. And thus it leaves (wanders around) in such a manner all the night, until the son of man wakes up and it returns to its place. Happy are the righteous ones (Tzaddiqim) for the Holy One, blessed be He, reveals His secrets to them in dreams, so that they may guard themselves from Judgement (Din, Gevurah). Woe to the sinners who defile themselves and their Nefesh. Come and behold: Those who have not defiled themselves, when they go to bed, their Nefesh rises and first enters into all those levels, and rises and does not become attached to them, and after [that] it leaves (wanders) and drifts [upward], and therefore rises on its way. The Nefesh that deserves to rise may appear before the Countenance of the Days (Afey Yomin; i.e., Keter) and becomes attached to the ambition to see—and the desire to ascend to the sight of the pleasantness of the King and to visit His Palace (Hechal). This is the son of man who shall ever have a share in the world to come. And this is a Nefesh that yearns to reach the Holy One, blessed be He; and does not become attached to other bright essences (Qlippot); and leaves to its own holy kind; and seeks the place from which it came (went out).

Therefore it is written: "With my Nefesh have I desired Thee in the night," in order to pursue Thee, and not be tempted by other gentile (idolatrous) kinds. Come and behold: "My Nefesh." This is the one that dominates at night and pursues its own level: Ruach [is the one that dominates] during the day. As it is written: "With my Nefesh have I desired Thee in the night." This is the Nefesh that dominates during the night. "With my Ruach within me will I seek Thee early." This is the Ruach that dominates during the day. And if thou sayest that [they are] two separated levels, this is not so! For they are one level and they are two connected [as] one. And [there is] one higher [level of the soul] that dominates over them. And it is attached to them and they to it, and it is called Neshamah. And all these levels rise in the mystery of the wisdom (Chochmah; aram. Raza de-Chochmeta), [The Zohar is not written in Hebrew but in Aramaic. Raza de-Cochmeta is the original Aramaic term, but the classical Qabbalistic Term is Chochmah.] for if a son of man sees these levels, he sees with the wisdom on High. And this Neshamah enters into them and they become attached to it. And if it dominates, then the son of man is called holy, perfected and totally devoted to the Holy One, blessed be He. The Nefesh is the lower wakefulness, and this is [the one] closest to the body (Guf) and feeds it (i.e., the body). And the body is connected to it, and it is connected to the body. Eventually it is refined (i.e., spiritually healed),[4] and becomes a throne on which the Ruach resides. This is due to the awakening of the Nefesh which is connected to the body. As it is written: "Until the Ruach be poured upon us from on high" (Isaiah 32:15). Afterward, when both are refined, they are ready to receive (le-qabbla) the Neshamah. Thus, the Ruach becomes a throne for the Neshamah to reside upon. And the Neshamah is concealed high over all, most hidden and unattainable. Thus there is a throne upon a throne, and a throne for the highest. And when thou see (observe) these levels, thou will find the mystery of wisdom (Chochmah; aram. Raza de-Chochmeta) in this matter. And all this is wisdom (Chochmah) to be attached [to thy soul] in this manner to [perceive/achieve] these concealed things. Come and behold: the Nefesh is the lower wakefulness, for it is attached to the body (Guf). In the same manner as a flame (light) is [attached to] a

---

[4] Compare chapter 27, Tiqqun ha-Olam: Healing the World.

candle. The lower flame is black (dark, dull), attached to the wick and is never [totally] separated from it. And is not refined except through it. And when it is refined through the wick it becomes a throne for the upper white (pale) flame that dwells on the black (dark, dull) light. Eventually, when both are refined, the white (pale) flame becomes a throne for the concealed flame that can neither be seen nor known; for it rests on the white (pale) flame and thus they are a perfect (complete) flame. And so a son of man reaches complete perfection (inner peace). And thus he is called "holy," as it is said: "As for the Holy Ones that are on the earth, they are the excellent in whom is all my delight" (Psalm 16:3). It is similar with the mystery on High.[5]

Everything in our spiritual work—in fact, everything in our life—depends on the proper understanding of the soul. It is important not only to know the theory, but also to be able to apply it to yourself. Let us look at each part of the soul in more detail.

The Nefesh (Emotional Soul, Lower Self)

Nefesh means "soul," "breath," "scent," "emotion," "desire," "person," "life." The Nefesh is that part of the soul that dominates when we are asleep, especially when we dream. It contains our subconscious mind and all our desires, including our drives that are connected with it.[6] It also contains our emotions that cause the contents of our subconscious mind. It is interesting to note that "scent" is one of the meanings of the word, for more than any other sense, scent affects directly the subconscious mind. The Nefesh belongs to the astral level, and the word *Nefesh* is also used for the astral body.[7] The Nefesh is also related to the moon, the symbol of the upper Nefesh.[8] The Nefesh also is vital for our sexuality: "Nefesh is the force (Cheyla) from which the body is built. When a man is aroused in this world to mate with his wife, all parts of the sum are prepared to receive enjoyment from it. Then the Nefesh and the desire of these agree upon that act" (Zohar 1:81a).

Our emotional state has an enormous influence on the body. We say

---

[5] Zohar I:83a–b.

[6] In modern psychology the subconscious mind is seen as the source of our dreams, as Freud (a Jew!) rediscovered. This knowledge was no secret to the ancient Qabbalists.

[7] See chapter 24, Contacting the Maggid: The Inner Plane Teacher.

[8] Zohar II:142b.

"that makes me sick" if we feel bad, for emotional imbalance can make us sick, just as positive emotions can benefit our health. The body is controlled and formed according to the influence of the Nefesh.

We must understand that the Nefesh, our lower soul, is very powerful, either for good or bad. Due to its involvement with the body, it is often unjustly condemned, but in the Qabbalah even the Nefesh is considered to be (potentially) holy. It is, indeed, lower than the other aspects of our soul, but nevertheless, it has a very important function. To emphasize this fact, my teacher Dolores Ashcroft-Nowicki sometimes calls it the Power Self, for it gives us the power we need in every aspect of life. This is quite in accordance with the view of the Zohar, which says that the Nefesh of the body (Guf) is called "strengthening power" (*koach ha-machaziq*), for it strengthens the body.[9]

The Ruach (Mental Soul, Conscious Self)

Ruach means "mind," "spirit," "soul," "breath," "wind," "air," "inspiration," "direction." The Ruach dominates by day, meaning it is the part of our soul that gives us our conscious mind used in the normal waking state. It is the source of the intellect and of our ability to study and learn.[10] "Ruach is the 'voice,' and it is called 'Knowledge' (Daat). And it is connected to a person who raises his voice in the study of the Torah. And it is called the 'Written Torah' and the 'Mental Soul' (or 'Intellectual Soul'). From it come good deeds" (Zohar I:79b).

Certainly, no one in his right mind would consider his own intellect "most hidden and unattainable." Neither would anyone be called holy just because his intellect is the dominant part of his soul.

The Ruach rules over the Nefesh.[11] By the awareness and self-control of our mind, we can tame our emotions. Ruach and Nefesh are connected, and together they form the mortal personality that we inhabit in this incarnation. When this incarnation ends, the Nefesh sooner or later goes to Gehinom/Purgatory to purify itself from earthly desires and the Evil Urge. (After our earthly life, an imprint of our earthly lives—loosely con-

---

9 Zohar I:110a.

10 Some people consider the Nefesh to be the subconscious mind (controlling the body), the Ruach to be the emotions, and the Neshamah to be the intellect. This view is found especially in later times. It definitely contradicts the view of the Zohar that describes the Neshamah as "concealed high over all, most hidden and unattainable" (see above).

11 Zohar I:206a.

nected to the grave—is said to remain on the astral level.) Eventually, our emotional experiences may be assimilated (as memories) by the Ruach.[12] The Ruach is partially immortal, because the contents of the mind—memories—are absorbed into the higher realms (symbolized by the Garden of Eden), for otherwise we could not recall past lives. When we try to do so, a momentary connection is made. Yet only the Neshamah is totally immortal and lives in the higher realms.[13]

> Come and behold: For seven days [after a person died] the Nefesh leaves the house to the grave, and from the grave to the house, and mourns him. Three times a day, the Nefesh and the body (Guf) are judged together, though there is none in the world who knows it or watches it to awaken the heart. Afterwards, the body (Guf) is expelled and the Nefesh leaves to cleanse [itself] in Gehinom (Hell, Purgatory); And [then it] goes out and leaves into the world to visit the grave, until it wears that which it wears. After twelve months all is fixed (settled). [The] body (Guf) is discarded in the dust. [The] Nefesh is bound and enlightened by the Ruach, enclosed in that which it wears. [The] Ruach enjoys itself in the Garden of Eden. [The] Neshamah rises to the delight of delights. All of them are connected to each other at certain times.[14]

The Neshamah (Spiritual Soul, Higher Self)

Neshamah means "soul," "spirit," "breath." The Neshamah is a part of our soul that is so high that it is concealed and unattainable for the ordinary man, and even the seeker on the spiritual path finds it the most difficult to access. This is so because it is not a part of our incarnate personality, but is instead part of our immortal soul that dwells in the higher regions. It nevertheless influences our life once we purify our personality to such a degree that we are ready to receive its influence.

The Neshamah rules over Ruach and Nefesh,[15] for the higher always rules over the lower. It guides us throughout our life and our spiritual

---

[12] Elsewhere in the Zohar, it is said: "And when a man dies in this world, that Nefesh never leaves the grave. And because of this power, the dead know and talk with each other" (Zohar I:81a).
[13] Compare to Zohar II:141b–142b.
[14] Zohar I:226a–b.
[15] Zohar I:206a.

work. In its higher aspect it gives us wisdom and inspires us with awe of God. In its lower aspect it gives us understanding and inspires in us repentance (*Teshuvah*).[16] If the Neshamah dominates our self, we become totally devoted to God. According to the Zohar, this is the definition of a holy man. In fact, to make the Neshamah the dominating influence in your life (and be guided by its wisdom) is the central goal of all spiritual work.

Why is it so difficult to become aware of the Neshamah? Let me explain with an analogy: Imagine you are in a beautiful forest with a radio playing at full volume. Due to the radio, you cannot hear the birdsong. This does not, however, mean they the birds are not there. Once you silence your worldly and selfish craving for entertainment (symbolized by the radio), you will be able to hear the beautiful singing of the birds (symbolizing the Higher Self).

The terminology of the Zohar indicates that a man gains a certain soul at a specific point in his spiritual development. This means that not all aspects of the soul are equally accessible to everybody. Every human being has emotions, and therefore, access to the Nefesh is very easy. But we are able to access the Ruach only if we have refined and purified the emotions to a certain degree. The majority of people in the present time form their opinions and decisions through emotions and feelings rather than by the use of reason. Thus their decisions depend to a great deal on fear, anger, or craving and other unbalanced (*Qlippotic*) influences. In the terminology of the Zohar, they have not yet earned the gift to be given a Ruach. There are few who are led by reason, but even fewer are led by wisdom, altruistic love, awe of God, and the selfless desire to serve the Light. Such people are indeed very rare. The Zohar calls them the ones who have attained contact to the Neshamah and are dominated by its influence.

The Evil Urge (Yetzer ha-Ra)

What is it that prevents us from receiving the influence of the Neshamah? According to the terminology of the Zohar, this is the Evil Urge (*Yetzer ha-Ra*), symbolized by Samael and the snake. "The Evil Urge (Yetzer ha-Ra) is the Ruach of the beast (animal). And concerning this King Solomon said in his wisdom, 'Who knoweth the Ruach of man whether it goeth upward, and the Ruach of the beast whether it goeth downward to the earth?'

---

[16] Zohar I:79b.

(Ecclesiastes 3:21). The Nefesh of the beast is the Nefesh that comes from the side of the Evil Urge (Yetzer ha-Ra)."[17]

Both Nefesh and Ruach can be influenced by the Evil Urge. The Nefesh is the main subject for the Evil Urge, for if a man follows his selfish craving and anger, he defiles his Nefesh. The Ruach is the intellect, and, consequently, it is not subject to anger or craving, but it can be defiled by pride and arrogance, for here resides the ego. The Ruach is to rule over the Nefesh, and thus it should be free of its influence. But if it allows itself to be affected by the desires of the body, it loses its rulership and becomes a slave to the lower self. This is why we must take care to keep our soul as pure as possible. A small sin may lead to a bigger sin, and so on. Therefore, we must make an effort to minimize the influence of the Evil Urge by reducing the amount of anger, jealousy, greed, craving, and egoism in ourselves.

> And it has been taught: R. Shimon ben Eleazar says in the name of Halfa bar Agra in R. Yochanan ben Nuri's name: He who tears his garments in anger, he who breaks his vessels (ha-meshaver Kelav)[18] in anger, and he who scatters his coins in anger, in thy eyes he will be an idolater, because such are the wiles of the Evil Urge (Yetzer ha-Ra): To-day he says to him, "Do this!"; and tomorrow he tells him, "Do that!" until he bids him "Go and serve idols," and he goes and serves [them]. R. Abin said: What verse [intimates this]? "There shall no strange god be in thee; neither shalt thou worship any foreign god" (Psalm 81:10). Who is the strange god that resides in man himself (literally, "in his body")? Say, that is the Evil Urge (Yetzer ha-Ra)![19]

Even small things matter, for over a length of time, they will have a powerful influence on our character. This process works both ways. The counteracting principle to the Evil Urge (Yetzer ha-Ra) is the Good Urge (*Yetzer Tov*) that comes from the influence of the Neshamah. If we continue to perform good deeds, this will eventually become second nature to us: "Ben Azzai says: 'Rush (i.e., be eager) to perform even a minor Mitzvah (i.e., religious duty, commandment, good deed), and flee from sin; for one Mitzvah leads to another Mitzvah, and one sin leads to another sin; for

---

[17] Zohar I:79b.

[18] Compare to the Shevirat ha-Kelim, the Breaking of the Vessels in Lurianic Qabbalah.

[19] Babylonian Talmud, Shabbat 105b.

the reward of a Mitzvah is a Mitzvah, and the reward of a sin is a sin'" (Mishnah [Pirqey] Avot 4:2).

We become attached to that which is within us.[20] If we refine[21] and purify the lesser aspects of our soul, we attract that which is holy—in other words, the Neshamah. And furthermore, by overcoming the Evil Urge in ourselves, we lessen the evil in the world, and thus we heal the world.

The Soul in All Its Aspects

There are more aspects of man that must be considered at least briefly: The physical body is called *Guf* (meaning "body," "person," "substance," "surface"). It consists of the four elements—that is, the four philosophical principles: "And in this pattern He (God) created the body (Guf) from [the] four elements: Fire, Air, Earth and Water" (Zohar I:80a).

Then there is the *Tzelem* (meaning "shadow," "picture," "image"). This is the etheric body[22] or etheric double, as it is called sometimes. The Tzelem is the pattern after which the shape of the physical body is formed, which is why it looks like a double or shadow of the physical body. When a child is conceived, the Tzelem causes the body of the child to grow and take shape. "When he (man) goes out [into the physical world]: Through the Tzelem he grows [and] by the Tzelem he walks. This is the meaning of 'Surely man walketh in a *Tzelem*'"[23] (Zohar III:104b).

The Tzelem is the intermediary between the Nefesh and body, belonging to the body, but not to the Nefesh, for it consists of very fine physical matter. The Tzelem is also responsible for the health of the body. When a man becomes very ill (or if he departs from this world), the appearance and shape of the Tzelem changes beforehand.[24]

Body (Guf) and Tzelem are the two material parts of man. The immaterial parts—that is, the parts of the soul—are fivefold:[25] "'And thou shalt

---

[20] See above.

[21] This process is called *Tiqqun* in the Qabbalah. (See chapter 27, Tiqqun ha-Olam: Healing the World.)

[22] The Tzelem is not the astral body—even though the two are often confused. If, in meditation, we rise to the astral plane, the term *Nefesh* is used in the ancient texts (see chapter 24, Contacting the Maggid: The Inner Plane Teacher).

[23] Psalm 39:7.

[24] Zohar I:217b and Zohar I:227a.

[25] This means seven parts altogether. Note that seven is a number with great significance. The five names of the soul are first found in Midrash Bereshit Rabbah 14:9.

love the YHVH thy Elohim with all thy heart' (Deuteronomy 6:5), it corresponds the body 'and with all thy soul' it corresponds the [different aspects of the] soul (Nishmeta, i.e., Neshamah). For there are five names to it: Neshamah, Ruach, Nefesh, Chayah, Yechidah" (Zohar II:158b).

The *Chayah* (living one) is the Primal Spark or divine life force from which we come. It is sometimes called Neshamah of Neshamah.[26]

The Yechidah (single one) is the highest level of the soul. As the name single one indicates, there is only one Yechidah for all beings—that is, on the level of the Yechidah, we are all one. Thus, my Yechidah is the very same as your Yechidah. The level of the Yechidah is the level of the total unity of all beings, both with each other and with God.[27]

Each of the aspects of the soul is connected to the Tree of Life: The Yechidah belongs to Keter, the Chayah to Chochmah, the Neshamah to Binah, the Ruach to Tiferet[28] (often seen as including the surrounding Sefirot Chesed, Gevurah, Netzach, and Hod), the Nefesh belongs to Yesod, and the body (Guf) to Malchut (as does the Tzelem, which is the finer aspect of the body). Some believe that the Nefesh belongs to Malchut, due to its connection to the body.[29]

---

[26] Chayah and *Yechidah* are often included in the Neshamah and are seen as more subtle levels of the Neshamah.

[27] Some say that this level could be attained only in messianic times or even only by the Messiah himself. Yet it has been attained in the past and can still be attained, but once it is attained, the individual himself becomes a Messiah (the level reached by Henoch—Hebrew: Chanoch, also known as Enoch—when he became Metatron).

[28] Very occasionally Ruach is related to Daat.

[29] In this case, the body is usually seen as a level of its own.

6

Kavvanah

Magical Intention

Intention is all in the art of ritual magic.

DOLORES ASHCROFT-NOWICKI

In the following chapters you will find many spells, charms, and instructions for making amulets and talismans, and later in this book you will find advanced invocations and rituals. To activate this ancient magic, however, it is not enough to recite the words and perform the actions described. In order to cause a magical effect you must recite and perform with *Kavvanah*.

Kavvanah (כוונה) is the fundamental principle of Qabbalistic magic, although it is not easy to translate into English. The dictionary definitions are "intention," "meaning," "concentration," "devotion." In Qabbalistic literature, Kavvanah means all of them.

In order to cause any magical effect, you must create a thought-form and do so with a specific intention and concentration. You then must empower it with emotion and devotion. The secret of magic is not to do the most complex rituals, but to bring forth from within you the emotion and feeling of magical power when it is needed.[1]

To be able to direct your intention with concentration and devotion onto a specific aim and call down Divine Power is what the ancient Qabbalists called Kavvanah. There is an ancient text called *Chapter about the Kavvanah According to the Ancient Qabbalists,* written at the end of the thirteenth century, describing the development and use of Kavvanah.[2]

Chapter about the Kavvanah According to the Ancient Qabbalists[3] (with Commentary)[4]

Whoever fixes something in his mind with perfect fixation, [will find that] the essence will turn to him.

If you are able to concentrate on one thing to the exclusion of everything else, you will attract the essence of this thing,[5] and if you make a connection with it, you will be able to change it. Most people cannot direct their thoughts, and they cannot keep one thing at a time in their mind. They want one thing and its opposite, and therefore, they achieve nothing.

---

[1] If this is so, why do we need rituals at all? One of the reasons is that it is much easier to learn to activate magical power by the use of powerful rituals. We do need rituals to learn the art of magic, but ritual is a matter of beauty and worship of the Divine. The relationship between God and Israel has often been described in erotic language (for example, in the Song of Songs). Sex is just another expression of the creative power. I will therefore use sexuality as an analogy: Magic without ritual is like sex without foreplay. If a situation is urgent and if you do not have much time, it can be done without ritual. As in the case of sex, the creative power depends not on the length of time you invest, but whether you are willing to celebrate the divine Creative Power and treat it with dedication. Such celebration will make a difference.

[2] See also Chaim Vital, *Shaarey Qedushah,* part IV, chapter 2:12.

[3] Shaar ha-Kavvanah le-Mequbalim ha-rishon

[4] Because the text may be difficult to understand, after a portion of text, I have inserted comments that explain its inner meaning.

[5] Compare: "Having circumscribed the task you have set yourself, see it in relation to the Cosmos. By seeing the Cosmic Archtype you will draw in the force of that ideal and by seeing the circumscribed form, which it is desired to manifest, you will focus that force" (Dion Fortune, *The Cosmic Doctrine,* Chapter XXVI. "The Law of Limitation").

Therefore, if thou prayest or speakest a blessing or if thou want to focus on something in its truth, visualize with thy mind that thou art Light and everything around thee [is Light] and from every corner and from every side shines Light. And inside the Light is a Throne [of Light] and on it is the Or Nogah (Glowing Light)[6] and opposed to it is another Throne of Light and on it is the Or Tov (Good Light) and [it will be like] thou art between them.

To avenge turn to the Nogah and to be compassionate turn to the Tov. And the words that come from your lips (literally, "that which comes from your lips") shall face its countenance. And turn thyself to thy right and you will find Light. This is the Or Bahir (Bright Light).[7] And at thy left thou wilt find splendour. This is the Or Mazhir (Shining Light). And between them and above them is the Or Ha-Kavod (Light of the Glory). And around it is the Or Chayim (Light of Life). And above it is the Keter Ha-Or (Crown of Light) that crowns the objects of the thoughts, and enlightens the ways of the visualisations, who makes the shininess (Zohar) of the visions shine. And there is no fathom nor limit to this Light.

The Or Nogah (Glowing Light) corresponds to Gevurah and the Or Tov (Good Light) corresponds to Chesed. Thus Nogah gives revenge and Tov gives compassion. The Or Bahir (Bright Light) is Netzach and the Or Mazhir (Shining Light) is Hod. Netzach is right and Hod is left. (The ancient Qabbalists saw both the body of man and of Adam Qadmon with the pillar of strength on the left and the pillar of mercy on the right side.)[8] The Or Ha-Kavod (Light of the Glory) corresponds to Tiferet, which is between and above Netzach and Hod. The Or Chayim (Light of Life) relates to Yesod and the Keter Ha-Or (Crown of Light) corresponds to the Sefirah Keter.

And from its perfect Glory comes will, blessing, peace, life, and all good to those who keep the way of its unification. But those who

---

[6] But the path of the righteous (Tzaddiqim) is as the *Or Nogah* (here: light of dawn), that shineth more and more unto the perfect day (Proverbs 4:18).

[7] And now men see not the Or Bahir (here: light [which is] bright) in the skies; but the wind passeth, and cleanseth them (Job 37:21).

[8] Modern Qabbalists agree concerning the body of Adam Qadmon, but concerning mortal humans, they believe that strength is found on the right side and mercy on the left.

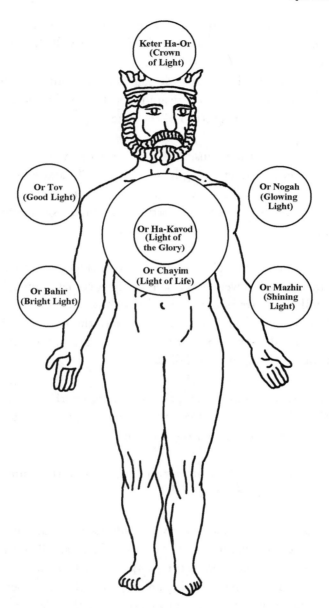

stray from its way the Light is hidden [from them] and turns over to
the opposite way and appears as rebuke and reproof.

But the upright way is performed according to the Kavvanah of
him who knows to concentrate on its truth with devotion (Devequt,
literally, "attachment") of thought and will that emanates with full
strength from the Unfathomable.

Only if you know how to concentrate on the truth of the Path of Light through the devotion of your thought and of your will that connects you to the Divine will you be able to perform this miracle. Both thought and will must be applied. This means you must create a suitable thought-form and have enough willpower to activate it. Both thought and will must be connected to the everlasting truth of the One.

> For according to the intensity of the power of the Kavvanah [one may be able] to attract strength through its will, and will through its mind, and visualization through its thought and power through its [spiritual] achievement and fortitude through its contemplation (Iyun).

There can be no thought or desire that distracts you if the power of the Kavvanah is well developed. Inner strength comes from a strong will. A strong will comes from a clear mind that has a definite idea of what it wants. Clear visualization is created by precise thought and observation. Magical power is developed by spiritual achievement and fortitude is developed by contemplating the Light of the One.

> When there is no passing thought and desire interfering with it, it (the Kavvanah) intensifies through the might that directs it to draw [down] Emanation coming from the Ayin Sof.

The more you are able to attract the influence of the Unmanifest, the stronger the Kavvanah becomes.

> It fulfills everything and every work (maasseh) [according] to his mind and to his will, if he knows how to differentiate (literally, encircle) the edges of the limited things and the will of their thoughts from the essence from which they are, and he will ascend above them through the power of his Kavvanah. And he will go deeper in order to counteract his sterile way and he can [create] a new way [according] to his will by the power of his Kavvanah, that comes from the perfect Glory of the hidden (literally, ignored) Light, that has neither figure nor image, neither measure nor size, neither estimation nor limit, neither account nor ending and no fathom and no number and no end in any regard.

By the power of the Kavvanah, everything and every work can be accomplished according to the will of the Qabbalist. Note that the text describes the interaction of will (power) and mind (form). In order to do so, you must learn to differentiate between that which comes from the limited world and that which comes from the Divine Source. This means you must learn to differentiate between the needs, desires, thoughts, and limitations of your mortal self and the Divine from which all things come. In this way, you can ascend above these limitations and reach a level of spiritual depth that enables you to neutralize these limitations by connecting to the Light of the One, which is beyond human understanding.

> And he ascends by the power of his Kavvanah from one thing to the next until he reaches the Ayin Sof. He needs to direct his Kavvanah in a way that is suitable for [attaining] his [spiritual] perfection, so that the Highest Will (Ratzon Ha-Eliyon) clothes itself in his will, and not that only his will clothes itself in the Highest Will.

We must ascend by striving—step by step up Jacob's Ladder—until we reach a point at which we can unite our intentions with the Divine Source. We must turn our will into a garment or vessel for the Highest Will that is the Will of the One. We must not just try to use the Highest Will as an instrument or garment for our own lower desires.

> For indeed, the Shefa (Divine Influx) is like a strong fount that never ceases [to flow], but only if he is careful in his approach to the Highest Will in the matter that he clothes the Highest Will in the will of his aspiration. By union of the Highest Will and the lower will, by its identification, and by devotion (*Devequt,* literally, "attachment") to the Unity he draws [down] the Shefa in order to [attain] his [spiritual] perfection.

The Divine Influx is unlimited. In order to attract this unlimited power, we must unite our conscious intentions with the Highest Will by devotion to the One. Thus we can attain spiritual perfection and accomplish our aims, for then they are identical with the aims of the One.

> And there is no perfection of the lower will if his approach is for its own needs, only if in his approach [to the Highest Will] he clothes it in [his]

desires and [lower] will to reveal the identification sufficiently enough, that [otherwise] is concealed in mystery (i.e., the identification).

If you try to use this method to fulfill your own selfish or egoistic desires, you will fail. If you try to connect yourself to the Divine in order to serve your egoistic wishes, the attempt cannot succeed. You will succeed only if you manage to identify your will with the Highest Will in such a way that your desires are purified of everything that is not in harmony with the Highest Will. The identification of the lower will with the Highest Will is a mystery to all those who are motivated by their ego. Only those who are led by their Higher Self are able to understand this secret.

> And if he approaches in this way, then also the Highest Will comes close to him and adds fortitude to his power and desire to his will to accomplish and complete anything, and even for the things he wants for himself (literally, even for the will of his soul) in which the Highest Will has no portion.

If, however, you try to connect to the Divine in a truly selfless way, the Divine will approach and meet you halfway. And in this case, the Divine Will adds its power to yours, and your will shall become stronger, and everything you do will become more perfect. And even personal aims that are not a direct part of the Highest Will may be accomplished, providing they do not contradict the Highest Will.

> And regarding this it is written: "He that strives for good seeketh Will" (Proverbs 11:27).

This proverb means that he who strives for the highest aims also seeks to fulfill the Will of the One, for both are the same.

> For in so far as his will is attached to a matter suitable to the Highest Will, the [Divine] Wish (i.e., the Highest Will) will clothe itself in it (i.e., his lower will) and draw [to him] any object according to his will. For thus it becomes stronger in it through the power of his Kavvanah, and draws down the Shefa that crowns the secrets of the things and essences in the way of Chochmah (Wisdom) and in the spirit (Ruach) of Binah (Understanding) and in the fortitude of Daat (Gnosis).

If your will is united with the Will of the Creator and directed onto a matter suitable to be subject to the Divine Influx, then the Divine Power will cause a change according to your will. This will happen because the Divine Power will be added to your power and your Kavvanah will draw down the Divine Influx. The Shefa comes from Keter and descends through Chochmah, Binah, and Daat.

> And according to how he clothes himself with Spirit (Ruach) and expresses his Kavvanah through his words and performs signs in his actions he will draw down the Shefa from power to power and from cause to cause until his deeds are completed according to his will.

In order to draw down the Divine Power into manifestation, you must follow three steps.[9] First, you must focus your magical intention on the level of the spirit. The Shefa itself comes to us from the level of Atzilut. The act of focusing the intention brings it down to the level of Beriah. Beriah is the level of the Divine Plan, and this is where your intention must become a vessel for the Shefa. Your magical intention then must be expressed in a suitable form, which is done by using an appropriate Word of Power or Holy Name to provide a form through which the power can be directed. This brings the power to Yetzirah, the World of Formation. Finally, you must perform a symbolic act—such as writing a talisman, drawing a symbol in the air, or any other magical act—in order to bring the power into Assiah, the World of Making.

> And in this way the ancient ones used to spend a while before prayer, to remove remaining thoughts and to focus on the way of the Kavvanah and the power of its direction.
> And [they spend] a while in prayer to express the Kavvanah in verbal speech.
> And [they spend] a while after the prayer contemplating how to direct the power of the Kavvanah, that is completed in the speech, in the way of visible work.
> And because they were Chassidim[10] their Torah (i.e., the recitation

---

[9] The three principles of *Machshavah* (thought), *Dibbur* (speech), and *Maaseh* (deed) are called *Levushim* (Garments of the Soul) in the Qabbalistic tradition. They are also known in the Eastern Mysteries as *Sanmitsu,* the three-part secret of spirit, word, and action.

[10] The Chassidim are the pious ones; see chapter 26, Chassidut and Hishtavvut: Mystical Devotion and Equanimity.

of the passages from the Bible) turned into action and their work was blessed.

This principle was applied by the ancient sages to every religious act. First, they cleared their mind and focused themselves on the intention of prayer. Then, they directed all their intention, devotion, and emotional power into the prayer. And finally, they found a way to bring the intention of their prayer into manifestation. Their recitation of biblical verses therefore brought about magical changes, as will be described in the following chapters of this book.[11]

This is the way of the ways of prophecy, that he who acquaints himself with it will rise to the level of prophecy.

In other words, if you follow this path, you will have the magical powers of the prophets.

The Technique

This is what you must do in order to make use of this ancient method to activate the power of Kavvanah.

1. Visualize that you are light, everything around you is light, and light is shining from every corner and every side. See and feel the light around you and within you. You must be one with the light, and the light must flow through you, filling you with divine energy. This is very important—do not rush this step!

2. On your left (at shoulder level), visualize a Throne of Light and on it a golden-red glowing light called the Or Nogah. Feel the intense power of Divine Justice, and vibrate OR NOGAH and ELOHIM.

3. On your right, visualize another Throne of Light and on it a warm, beneficent, silvery-white light called the Or Tov. Feel the warmth and loving power of Divine Mercy, and vibrate OR TOV and EL.

4. On your right, below the Or Tov, visualize a bright pink light. This is the Or Bahir. Feel the eternal victorious power of the Divine, and vibrate OR BAHIR and YOD HEH VAV HEH TZEVAOT.

5. On your left, below the Or Nogah, visualize a deep radiant pink light. This is the Or Mazhir. Feel the splendor of the Divine,

---

[11] Especially in chapter 8, Shimmushey Tehillim: The Magical Use of Psalms.

and vibrate OR MAZHIR and ELOHIM TZEVAOT.

6. Then, above your head, visualize an infinitely brilliant-white light in the shape of a crown. This is the Keter Ha-Or, the Crown of Light. It is the source of all and nothing is equal to it. It is far beyond human understanding. Feel the endless potential of the Divine, and vibrate KETER HA-OR and EHIYEH ASHER EHIYEH.

7. Below Keter (around your solar plexus), and above and between the Or Bahir and the Or Mazhir, visualize a beautiful light that has the yellow of the sun itself. This is the Or Ha-Kavod (Light of the Glory). It is the light of true harmony. Feel the glory and harmony of the Divine, and vibrate OR HA-KAVOD and YOD HEH VAV HEH.

8. Around the Or Ha-Kavod is the Or Chayim (Light of Life). It has a beautiful orange color. Feel the divine life energy circulating through your body, and vibrate OR CHAYIM and EL CHAI.

9. Now focus on the intention of the magical work you want to perform. Make absolutely sure that there is nothing in it that is not in harmony with the Highest Will. You must concentrate on your aims very clearly before you proceed to the following step.

10. Now perform any magical work you desire. If someone has done wrong and you must call upon Divine Justice, turn to the Nogah and direct your intention toward Divine Justice. To do so, you must build—or rather, bring forth—a very clear idea of the concept of Divine Justice. (If you find yourself trembling in awe and respect, you probably have the right feeling.) If you want to send blessings or help to someone, turn to the Tov and direct your intention toward Divine Mercy. To do so, you must build—or rather, bring forth—a very clear idea of the concept of Divine Mercy. (Here you can expect a feeling of deep love and compassion filling your heart.) In any magical work you perform, make sure you use the three principles of intention, word, and action. (Because you have already fulfilled the first of these three principles in the previous stage, you now must find an appropriate verbal expression, and eventually, you must manifest the work by a suitable symbolic act. The following chapters of this book will offer you plenty of techniques for doing so.)

By using this method it will not take long for you to see your magical effects, if (and only IF) you have taken care to work in harmony with the Higher Will.

7

Segullot
Spells and Charms

Segullot (singular: *segullah*) are small but very powerful spells or charms or magical invocations. Some involve a physical action (such as writing), while many are simply spoken.

The use of segullot is not high magic, but they were seen as an important help in overcoming the problems of everyday life. In everyday life, we encounter problems and difficulties that we cannot influence, or that we can influence only to a limited degree. Through the ages, this is when people have asked for the help of the Divine, and those who knew about the ancient mysteries have used their knowledge of the Holy Names and magical formulas to find help, blessing, guidance, and healing in matters both mundane and spiritual—both for themselves and for those they loved.

Segullot are such a help. In times when technology did not make life as easy as today, magic was used to aid. But even today, many problems of life are beyond our influence, and now there is as much reason to use the ancient secrets as there was in the past.

Ethics

Some people hesitate to use magic for personal benefit, but we know from scripture that both the prophets and the ancient sages used their powers to help and heal those they loved, doing so with the blessing of God. Why should we not do the same? As long as we observe the rules of ethics, there is no reason why we should not make life better if we have the power to do so.

First, you must never use magic to fulfill the desires of the Evil Urge (yetzer ha-ra)—that is, the part in all of us that tempts us to act against Divine Law. In other words: You must NEVER use magic to harm anyone or to be the agent of your hate, malevolence, or jealousy.

Second, you must understand that because God gave free will to humanity, it is not for you to take it away. Therefore, you must NEVER try to use magic in order to interfere with anyone's free will, even if you think it is for the better of the person concerned. This means that it is unacceptable even to heal someone without their permission. (I believe, however, that parents may decide this issue for children, who are not of the age to make such a decision themselves. If, however, they are old enough to make a decision, even their parents must accept what they decide.)

Third, ALWAYS try to act in such a way that your actions are in harmony with the Divine Will and make the world become a better place. (The process of trying to turn evil and imbalance in the world into harmony and goodness is what is called *Tiqqun ha-Olam*—healing the world. We will learn more about this in chapter 27.) Furthermore, NEVER get involved with the powers or beings of the Qlippot (unbalanced forces), as nothing good will ever come from them.

These are the basic rules you must observe in every magical act. If you break any of these rules, you will eventually have to face the Angels of Severity and Justice (*Din*) and be subject to their judgment.

Segullah for Fishing

Take a shard of pottery from the sea and write on it:

And the Angel of God, who went before the camp of Israel, removed and went behind them; and the pillar of cloud removed from before them, and stood behind them; and it came between the camp of Egypt and the camp of Israel; and there was the cloud and the darkness here, yet gave it light by night there; and the one came not near the other all the night.

And Moses stretched out his hand over the sea; and YHVH caused the sea to go back by a strong east wind all the night, and made the sea dry land, and the waters were divided." (Exodus 14:19–21)

Ye Holy Names, by Your great power, bring to me a fish
that weighs [Insert amount].
Amen Amen Selah

Write this on the third day of the week (Tuesday) after the ninth hour of the day (nine hours after sunset). Then go out of the city and say seventy-two times:

Baruch Shem Kavod Malchuto Le-Olam Va-ed.
(Blessed be the Name of His Majesty's Glory for ever and ever.)

Then say seventy-two times:

Blessed be the Glory of YHVH from His Place. (Ezekiel 3:12)

And then throw the shard into the water with all your strength, and cover your face for a short time. Then go fishing.

Segullah against Danger

In a place where there is danger, say these Names three times with a loud (and/or firm) voice:

YOD HEH VAV HEH
YOD HEH VAV HEH
YOD HEH VAV HEH
TAFTAFIYAH
decree fear (awe) to those men
that they cannot harm me or my body or my wealth (possessions).
Amen Amen

Segullah for Path Jumping (Qefitzat ha-Derech)

In the traditional Hebrew scriptures, many descriptions of fast travel, teleportation, or out-of-body journeys are described. The traditional term for such techniques is Qefitzat ha-Derech, "path jumping."

Rabbi Hai Gaon wrote in the eleventh century that one of the Baaley-Shem (magicians) was seen on the eve of Shabbat in one place and, at the same time, in another place, several days' travel from the first. Another legend describes how old Rabbi Eleazar of Worms transported himself from Germany to Spain in order to teach the Qabbalah to Nachmanides.

The following technique is described in many different manuscripts and in various forms. Unfortunately, many of them are either incomplete or corrupt. Most instructions agree that you need a reed with seven knots and a scarf for this segullah. I have combined information from various texts for this technique.

To prepare yourself, five days of immersion, fasting, and sexual abstinence are required.

In order to travel one month's distance in one moment, take a reed with seven knots and a parchment made from a male calf. Some say the reed should be short, while others say it should be six feet long.

Write on the parchment:

ADBARIEL the Great
TAGRIEL the Great
QAFTZIEL the Great
ALBAS the Great
TAFTAHARIEL the Great
KETUSHIEL the Great
AKATRIEL the Great
QADOSH QADOSH QADOSH (Holy Holy Holy)
YOD HEH VAV HEH TZEVAOT
His Glory fills the entire earth. (Isaiah 6:3)
RABBAN HA-OLAM (Master of the Universe)

An alternative text to be written on the parchment is this:

And he came to a certain place and stayed there
overnight because the sun had set.
And he took a stone from the place and put it beside his head
and went to sleep at this place. (Genesis 28:11)
I invoke thee SAASIYAH the princely angel,
serving under the princely angel PORIHIEL
In the name of
SHAASHIEL
AVEYRIEL
SHAMASHIEL
YARHIEL

SHAMIEL
METATRON
MAYEMIEL
that thou shalt bring me to a [designated] place,
in the accompaniment of the fiery angel LAEHAROF
quickly and without any pain or discomfort, and without any fear.
AMEN AMEN AMEN
SELAH SELAH SELAH

Place the parchment in the reed. Some texts advise boring a hole into the middle knot and placing it into the hole. Others tell us to make seven holes, with seven parchments inside.

On the third day of the month, when the new moon is clearly visible, go outside the city boundaries and place the scarf on your face. With complete concentration, strike the reed to the east, west, north, and south. To travel, ride on the reed and hasten to the desired destination. Some say that you should also recite the names on the parchment while riding.[1]

Segullah to Be Heard

Sometimes we find it difficult to get the attention of those to whom we have to speak. These may be officials, the boss at work, or just the people in the town in which we live. If you wish to be heard by people, or by a man of authority or a judge, say this:

Give ear, O ye heavens, and I will speak; and hear,
O earth, the words of my mouth.
My doctrine shall drop as the rain, my speech shall distill as the dew,
as the small rain upon the tender herb, and as the showers upon the
grass: Because I will proclaim the Name of YOD HEH VAV HEH:
ascribe ye greatness unto our God. (Deuteronomy 32:1–3)

I invoke You, Shemot ha-Qadoshim (Holy Names) **for with You**
Moses admonished the children of Israel in the desert, that
You cause my words to be heard by [Insert the name of the person or
the group of people by whom you want to be heard] **and that my words**
should be acceptable.

---

[1] The aim of this technique is to exhaust the body and create a state of trance in order to experience an ethereal or astral projection.

In the Name of
HI AF ZAY YAR NAS VA HATZ SAR MA YAH MA
VAS ESH DAT BO RAH

And in the Name of
YAY AT DAR PAS KA MAL TAT RAV LAL QAZ
CHAYIT KAVAR SHASH SA YAD DAL KAM MA AM
LI YAV DI SHAV AR ZAV

And in the Name of
KO YAZ SHAY MAH YOD HEH VAV HEH EL QA
DAL EL HAD BOG

I cried unto **EL YOD HEH VAV HEH** with my voice, and
He heard me out of His holy hill. Selah. (Psalm 3:4)
Baruch Shem Kavod Malchuto Le-Olam Va-ed
(Blessed be the Name of His Majesty's Glory for ever and ever.)
Amen Amen Amen
Selah Selah Selah
Hallelujah

Segullah for Entering the Presence of a Mighty Man

If you want to be heard, you must be permitted to have an audience first.
Speaking to a sultan (as intended by the original spell) or any other person
of authority was not, and still may not be, easy.

Say seven times:

And **YHVH** helpeth them, and delivereth them;
He delivereth them from the wicked, and saveth them,
because they have taken refuge in Him. (Psalms 37:40)
The Lion roars and the ruler subdues
ASAN ASA UVISA
MALKIEL BALOM
Amen Amen Selah

Segullah for Shutting Someone's Mouth

This Segullah is designed to help if someone speaks falsely about you. The
power of this Segullah comes from the Holy Letters of the Hebrew alphabet that cannot be used for evil.

I adjure and bind and obstruct and shut and block the
hearts of all sons of Adam and daughters of Eve that they
may not harm me [Insert magical name]!
LAHAQIEL is the great angel who is appointed over love.
May he have consideration over [Insert magical name],
when he goes out and when he comes in,
When he lays down and when he arises.
In the Name of the great Name
AGUQAT TAGAT PAGAT who is one
And whose Name is written ATEN ATZ His Name ELA
Alef Bet Gimel Dalet Heh Vav Zayin Chet Tet Yod Kaf Lamed
Mem Nun Samech Ayin Peh Tzadde Qof Resh Shin Tav

Segullah for Love

There are a many ancient formulas for love, but these methods often did
not respect the free will of the desired person. The ancient sorcerers would
have used a piece of unbaked clay (probably in the shape of a heart), thrown
it into the fire, and said that the heart shall burn (enflame) in desire in the
same way as the clay. In other spells, the same technique (throwing clay
into the fire) would be used for a magical attack to cause harm. Thus we
see that such methods are deeply unethical. The fact that such formulas
called for the invocation of the names not only of several angels, but also
evil princes, is a clear sign that, according to our ethical standards, this is
black magic.

The following charm calls for the Will and help of God to ensure that
no harm is done to the beloved. This is done by using traditional formulas
(abbreviations) such as: K.Y.R. (Ken Yehi Razon, thus may it be Thy Will);
B.H.N.V. (Be-Ezrat Ha-Shem Naasseh Ve-Natzliach, with the help of God
we shall act and succeed). Such formulas are quite common. The abbreviations Y.Y. (*Yod Yod*, or YHVH) and A.A.A. (Amen Amen Amen) are also
found in this charm.

This segullah offers love and brings the loving one to the attention
of the beloved. Thus, if the beloved has never noticed what a wonderful
person the loving one is, this segullah will help. In this respect, it is like
perfume on a spiritual level, for it helps to start a relationship and endows
love (which should always be given freely), but does not force the beloved
into a relationship. He or she still has the free choice to begin a loving
relationship or not.

Mix ink with saffron, and on the fifth day (Thursday) at noon, write the following charm on the parchment of a gazelle:

דריאל שדיאל אמריאל פוסה
אפום היפצום אור מיתא
משמיא דו אסס קיא טיאל²

Ye art the names ruling
over all unions of lovers in the name of Y.Y.
and over the star signs (mazalot) of the
children of Adam—who descended.
Offer great love from [Insert name of lover]
son/daughter of [Insert name of mother]
to the heart of [Insert name of beloved]
son/daughter of [Insert name of mother] **K.Y.R.**
Soon soon soon quickly quickly quickly
good good good
A.A.A. Selah
Grace and love between Adam and Eve
B.H.N.V.

Then put seven pieces of coal in a new clay vessel, and take a piece of the garment of your beloved (the one you love), and write on it, burning frankincense (and aloe), and also burn the writing in the fire. Do not extinguish the fire with water, and when the fire has burned down, pound the coals, putting them between the feet of your beloved (i.e., disperse them where he or she is likely to walk).

Segullah for Finding Hidden Money

Segullot that are of a divinatory nature are sometimes called goralot (lots). This divinatory method is supposed to be good for finding hidden—that is, buried—treasures. (Of course, such a method will work only if there are any treasures hidden!)

Take a white cock and feed it for seven days with old wine. Then write the following names on a (copper) plate and suspend it from the right wing of the cock:

In the name of MICHAEL GAVRIEL QADOSHIEL MEDABNIEL

---

² Dariel, Shadiel, Amriel, Poseh, Afum, Hiftzum, Ur, Mita, Meshamia, Do, Asas, Qia, Tiel—the angelic names in roman letters.

**MEDANIEL UCHSHMIEL BERACHIEL MUGIEL
TAQFIEL MARIUT YAH YAH YAH**
Amen Amen Amen Selah

Then let it go. Wherever it goes and scrabbles [where the cock digs] on the ground, hidden treasure will be found.

Segullah for a Lost Thing

This is for someone who has lost something and does not know where and how he lost it.

Seven times on a piece of paper, write the name of the item together with the name of the person who lost it and the name of his mother: [Insert name] son/daughter of [Insert name of mother]. Then say:

> **This mystery is on (for) the name of** [Insert name],
> **son/daughter of** [Insert name of mother]
> **NATAR YEMEYNATAR ASGINTAL YEMEYNATAR**

For three nights, place it under your head (i.e., pillow), and you will remember where the lost item is.

Segullah for Protection on a Journey

A name for protection on a journey, called the name of the lap:

Write this name on parchment of deer, and suspend it from the right lap of your garment.[3] The name is צמרכד (*Tzamrakad*). If you see robbers, touch the lap and they will not harm you.

Segullah for a Sick Person

If you wish to know whether a sick person will recover soon, say, seven times:

> **ALAMON ALAMON ALAMON ALAMON
> ALAMON ALAMON ALAMON**

If the ill person looks at you, smiling, he will recover soon. If he turns away to the wall, this is not a good sign, and if he lies on his back, his illness will last long, but he will eventually recover.[4]

---

[3] This would probably have been rolled together and enclosed in a little container. Suitable containers can be made easily from thin copper pipe or bamboo. (Alternatively, the parchment might be sewn into the lap.)

[4] Note that there is much psychology and common sense involved in this oracle.

Segullah for Healing

Segullot for healing are sometimes called *refuot* (healings). Supposedly, there is no spell better than this for effective healing.

Write the following (with food coloring) on the inside of a cup, and speak the words over the cup. Then let the sick person drink (wine or water) from the cup, thus absorbing the healing power. Finally, write it on a talisman, and suspend it from his neck.

**In the Name of
YAH YAH YAH YAH YAH YAH
YHVH TZEVAOT, who sitteth upon the Keruvim.[5]
With these names that are written** [literally, engraved],
rebuke this [name the illness][6]
from the body of [Insert name], **son/daughter of**
[Insert name of mother] **and from the
bodies of his/her sons and daughters
Amen Amen Selah
RAPHAEL will make it succeed**

Finished and completed

Segullah against a Headache

To cure a headache, say:

**ABALAH BALAH ABALAH BALAH BALAH
ABALAH LO BALAH
ABALAH ABALAH BALAH ABALAH LO ABALAH
ABALAH ABALAH ABALAH to** [Insert name],
son/daughter of [Insert name of mother]. **Selah**

Segullah for Overcoming Difficulties during Childbirth

Speak over the woman:

**And all these thy servants shall come down unto me, and bow down
unto me, saying: "Get thee out, and all the people that follow thee;**

---

[5] 1 Samuel 4:4 and 2 Samuel 6:2.

[6] The original is unclear. Probably scabies.

> and after that I will go out." And he went out. (Exodus 11:8)
> Go out! I will go out and he went out.

Segullah against a Scorpion

Scorpions were a serious problem in ancient times. If a scorpion was seen in the house, everybody feared being stung. To expel a scorpion, the following spell could be used.[7]

Scorpion, scorpion, male or female
EL SHADDAI over your stings
GAVRIEL over your horns
MICHAEL over your loins
From now until eternity
Amen Amen Selah

Segullah against a Sting of a Scorpion

If you have been stung by a scorpion, write over the painful spot, and the pain will diminish like the word:

אקרוס
קרוס
רוס
וס
ס

Segullah for Solving Sexual Problems

I hesitated to include this segullah, but to give a correct picture of the spectrum of ancient spells, I must include a spell against sexual problems. Sexual difficulties were often seen as the result of the interference of the demoness Lilith (in other words, the influence of imbalanced forces).[8] This segullah is designed to solve the bindings of the demoness (here called Norea),[9] thus permitting man and woman to enjoy their sexual relationship. Speak this over wine and sesame oil:[10]

---

[7] You may find that this spell can be adapted to a mosquito.

[8] Health is often seen as a result of balance; therefore, illness must be the result of imbalance. Thus the concept of the ancients is much wiser than it may seem at first to the modern reader.

[9] Norea is Noah's bride, and sometimes the daughter of Eve. She is sometimes seen as an equivalent of Lilith.

[10] Wine and oil are symbols for the sexual fluids of husband and wife.

A good word cometh forth from before God (Elaha) that breaks laws of copper and laws of lead, with which Norea, the bride of Noah, brought sin. I call upon the Angels of Compassion to dissolve the magical bindings of the evildoers who in the days of Adam and Eve were not there to do evil sorcery and deeds of hate. Those shall also not exist for [Insert name], **son of** [Insert name of mother] **and** [Insert name], **daughter of** [Insert name of mother] his wife. Not in the vascular system of his body, and not in the vascular system of his great limb that is called penis. He shall ejaculate and emit semen. In the name of SATMIEL ACHIEL GAVRIEL HECHLIMIEL HERMES RAPHAEL. In the name of these six angels who solve and do not bind, shall he [Insert name], **son of** [Insert name of mother] be unbound. By the wine from the vine and the oil of sesame.
Amen Selah

Segullah to Remove a Curse

If someone has been the victim of black magic, use this segullah to annul the effect of the curse. This segullah is well tried.

Write (with food coloring) on the inside of a cup:

That frustrateth the tokens of the imposters, and maketh diviners mad; that turneth wise men backward, and maketh their knowledge foolish. (Isaiah 44:25)

אחסיה יחוש זא יפף
אחסיה יחוש כבנז
אחסיה יחוש ⟋ ✗ ⟋
אחסיה יחוש ڢ غد ڂ

Then say over the cup:

That frustrateth the tokens of the imposters, and maketh diviners mad; that turneth wise men backward, and maketh their knowledge foolish. (Isaiah 44:25)

ACHSIYAH YACHUSH ZO YAFOF
ACHSIYAH YACHUSH KAVGAZ
ACHSIYAH YACHUSH
ACHSIYAH YACHUSH

Then wash the writing away with water from the cup, and let the victim drink a little from the water (that has absorbed the spell). Then wash his face and body with the rest of the water.

Finally, write it again, making it into an amulet that will be suspended from his neck.

The Emergency Call

This segullah is for those situations in which help is needed quickly. If you are in distress or trouble at any time, say:

> **RABBAN HA-OLAMIM** (Master of the worlds)
> **Thou hast Strength (Koach) and Power (Gevurah).**
> **Save me from this distress**
> **ATAH GIBOR LE-OLAM ADONAI**
> **AGLA**
> **UMI HA-SHEM AKOPIATON UQITZEY**

And help will come.

8

Shimmushey Tehillim
The Magical Use of Psalms

Very often, psalms were part of magical spells and incantations, although psalms are more magical chants in themselves. Each psalm has a specific application for a certain effect. Shimmushey Tehillim is the magical use of psalms.

Currently, there is available only a translation of this magical use of psalms by the German theologian Godfrey Selig, who was not a Qabbalist and who did not always understand what he translated. Furthermore, some of the magical names and procedures in his translation differ considerably from the ancient texts available to me. Sometimes, he even changed the meaning of psalms to fit his own religious beliefs; for example, Psalm 95, used "against compulsory baptism," was changed into a prayer of the pious for his erring and unbelieving brethren. A psalm that was meant against proselytizing to others (which is a very un-Jewish thing to do) was turned into a psalm for those who need to be proselytized to because, according to the Christian view, they are erring. He therefore turned it into the exact opposite.

In this chapter, you will find the use of the psalms as they appear in the ancient manuscripts. The manuscripts available to me were not always complete, so I had to fill in the gaps based on Selig's translation.

How to Use the Magical Power of a Psalm

Every psalm has a Divine Name assigned to it. The Name is composed of letters taken from different words and verses of the particular psalm, and are seen as the key that unlocks its power. If you therefore wish to use a psalm for magic, the first thing to do is to read the psalm and learn which letters from which words and verses compose its Holy Name. When you recite the psalm, always concentrate on its name, keeping your mind focused on it all the time.

Psalms are very powerful magic spells and incantations whose power multiplies considerably if spoken in Hebrew. Some psalms are also known to have special prayers assigned to them to cause certain specific results. These prayers are supposed to be spoken immediately after the recitation of the psalm.

I advise the reader to open the quarters[1] (the four cardinal directions) before applying the power of the psalm. To do so, draw the sign of the Magen David (Star of David), because the psalms are ascribed to King David. Say: "I open the [east, south, west, or north] in the Name of [the Holy Name of the psalm]." If you open the quarters, do not forget to close them after the work is done.

If your request has been granted, pray Psalm 150 to thank the Holy One, blessed be He.

Images and Amulets

Very often, psalms were not only spoken, but also were used in amulets. (We will deal with Qabbalistic amulets in detail in chapter 9.) Sometimes, such an amulet was written not simply line by line, but with the words arranged in a special way.

Special significance was given to Psalm 91. There were supposed to be forty-one Names as keys to the power of this psalm:[2]

---

[1] The four quarters are the four cardinal directions as used in ritual. We sometimes speak of "Nominal East" when we define East in a room whose four walls do not exactly match the cardinal directions, since we prefer not to work toward the corners of a room.

[2] Psalm 91 was often combined with the last verse of Psalm 90, called the Vihi Noam.

וני אעו יכע ויכ יבע בשי אלם ואא
בכה ימי מהב ילו כתצ ואל תמל מיי
מבי מיצ ימא ומא ליר בתו רתכ אים
עשמ לתא רול יבכ מול לכר עכי
פתכ רעש ותת כוכ בחו אכי שיו עאב
אוא יאוב

VENIY EAU YACHE VICH YAVE BASHIY ALAM VAA
BACHAH YAMIY MAHAV YALU KARATZ VAAL TAMAL MEY
MAVIY MITZ YAMA VAMA LIR BATU RATACH IYM
ASHAM LATA RUL YAVACH MUL LACHAR ACHIY
PARACH RAASH VATAT KUCH BACHU ACHIY SHIU AAV
AVA YAUV

Each of the 41 Names is a notarikon (a kind of acronym) consisting of the first letters of the words of the psalm.[3] When these Names were used to write a protective amulet, they were sometimes arranged in the form of a menorah:

---

[3] וני is a notarikon of the first letters of ויהי נעם יי.

אעו is a notarikon of the first letters of אלהינו עלינו ומעשה.

יכע is a notarikon of the first letters of ידינו כוננה עלינו.

ויכ is a notarikon of the first letters of ומעשה ידינו כוננהו.

יבע is a notarikon of the first letters of בסתר עליון ישב.

This is another example of an amulet on which the words are arranged to form a specific pattern:

Amulet from Sepher Schimmusch Tehillim
by Gottfried Selig (1788)

This amulet is designed to help and protect a woman and her child during childbirth. It must be written on parchment and placed on the navel of the pregnant woman while speaking a prayer.

In the center of the amulet are permutations[4] of the Tetragrammanton.

---

[4] Permutation (Hebrew: Temurah) is a method to exchange the Hebrew letters of a word to create another word. The most common methods are called: At-bash, Ab-gad (Avgad), Al-bam, and Aiq-Beqar. The name of each of these methods actually describes the method: For each name consisting of two parts, the first part tells you which letter Alef is changed into and the second part tells you which letter Bet (or any other letter) is changed into. From this information the entire method can be deduced. The method at-bash is described in chapter 14, The Work of Wisdom and Understanding. In the method Ab-gad, Alef is exchanged with Bet and Gimel with Dalet. In the method Al-bam, Alef is exchanged with Lamed and Bet with Mem. In the method Aiq-Beqar, Alef is exchanged with Yod or Qof (and vice versa) and Bet with Kaf or Resh (and vice versa). Aiq-Beqar is often used to reduce numbers to one digit.

The next square consists of Psalm 142:8: "Bring my soul out of prison, that I may give thanks unto Thy name; the righteous shall crown themselves because of me; for Thou wilt deal bountifully with me." In the third square are written the names of the four holy creatures, and in the outer square the words Anneni Yah, "Answer to me [o God] YAH," are written sixteen times.

This is the prayer that must be spoken:

May it be Thy Will, God of Heaven and earth, God of our forefathers. Hear my words, O mighty, great, and adorable God. Hear my prayer for the sake of Thy most Holy Name EHIYEH ASHER EHIYEH YAH YOD HEH VAV HEH EL ELOHIM YOD HEH VAV HEH TZEVAOT SHADDAI ADONAI compassionate and merciful Father. In the time of need Thou hearest the plea of those who fear Thee. Accept my prayer as the prayer of the entire nation. Accept it for the sake of all peoples prayers, and look with compassion on the woman whose womb is closed and who cries in the pain of birth. Answer our prayers and help [Insert name of woman]. Have mercy upon her and her child, and keep them alive and healthy. King of Kings, Holy of Holies, hear her cries and accept her prayers, as Thou accepted the prayers of Hannah. Let her hope not be in vain, and fulfill the request of Thy maidservant, and let her prayer be like an offering of frankincense, and let her fearful heart be like Thy altar. Hear me, I plea to Thee, hear me O Lord. Amen Selah

THE INDIVIDUAL PSALMS AND THEIR USE IN MAGIC

Psalm	Purpose	Holy Name	Words
1	**To find grace and favor:** Pray the psalm seven times in the morning and in the evening. **Against miscarriage:** Write the psalm and the name on parchment made from deer (or on paper, according to another instruction), and let it be suspended on her body (in a bag and under the clothes). **Prayer (also to be written):** May it be Thy Will,[5] EL CHAD, that this [Insert name], daughter of [Insert name of mother] shall not have a miscarriage. Let her and her child be healthy. And remove her pain and suffering from her. From now and forever. Amen Amen Amen Selah Selah Selah. **To halt menstrual flow:** Write on a shard of pottery and throw it in a dovecote until it breaks.	EL CHAD (One God)	(אשרי) verse 1; (לא) verse 1; (יצליח) verse 4; (ודרך) verse 6
2	**To gain favor:** Say the psalm seven times in the night over olive oil, and anoint your hands and feet. **Against a storm at sea:** Speak the psalm and the prayer, and write both on a shard of pottery. Throw it into the sea and the waves will be calm. **Prayer:** May it be Thy holy and benevolent Will to stop the rage of the storm and booming of the waves and let them calm down. O benevolent Father, bring us safely to our destination, for only Thou hast the power and might to help us, and Thou willst do so to honor Thy Holy Name. Amen Selah. **If a mob is against you:** Speak it to the four quarters before dawn. **Against a headache, write verses 1–8 and say:** May it be Thy Will, compassionate and merciful God, to spare this [Insert name], son of [Insert name of mother] and healest him from every disease he may have in his head for now and forever.	SHADDAI (Almighty One)	(רגשו) verse 1; (נוסדו) verse 2; (יוצר) verse 9

---

[5] Yehi Ratzon mi-l(e)-Fanecha (a very common formula).

Psalm	Purpose	Holy Name	Words
3	**Against headache and pain in the shoulders:** Speak it over olive oil, add salt, and salve the victim. **Prayer:** ADON HA-OLAMIM (Lord of the Worlds), may it be Thy Will to be my healer and helper and heal me from my head- and shoulder ache, for I can find help only in Thee, and only from thee comes advice and action. Amen Selah. **Against being hated:** Murmur it over water, and pour it over the head of the victim.	ADON (Lord)	(וְאַתָּה) verse 4; (בַּעֲדִי) verse 4; (הֲקִיצוֹתִי) verse 6; (הוֹשִׁיעֵנִי) verse 8
4	**Against bad luck:** Speak this psalm three times before dawn. **Prayer (say each time):** May it be Thy Will, YEHIYEH, the great, mighty, and awesome Name, that I shall be successful on my way and in my deeds. And fulfill what I request in the best possible way, and do as I desire on this very day. Amen Amen Amen Selah Selah Selah. **To find favor:** Do as above, but change the Prayer: May it be Thy Will, YEHIYEH, the great, mighty, and awesome Name, that I shall find grace and compassion in the eyes of [Insert name], son of [Insert name of mother]. And may he fulfill what I request on this very day. Amen Amen Amen Selah Selah Selah. Or pray this psalm in the morning and evening or seven times if you need something from someone. Do this while concentrating on the name, and you will succeed.	YEHIYEH (He Will Be)	(תְּפִלָּתִי) verse 2; (סֶלָה) verse 5; (יְהֹוָה) verse 6; (תּוֹשִׁיבֵנִי) verse 9
5	**To find favor:** Speak it during the night seven times over olive oil, and anoint your hands and feet. **Prayer:** Have grace for me for the sake of Thy great, honorable, and Holy Name CHANANYAH, and guide the heart of my ruler in the best way, and grant that he will look upon me with merciful eyes and let me find mercy and favor in him. Amen Selah.	CHANANYAH (Grace of God)	(חָפֵץ) verse 5; (נְחֵנִי) verse 9; (נְכוֹנָה) verse 10; (הַדִּיחֵמוֹ) verse 11; (כַצִּנָּה) verse 13

Psalm	Purpose	Holy Name	Words
6	**Against diseases of the eye:** Speak the psalm seven times (some say for three days). **Prayer:** YHVH my Father, may it be Thy Will for the sake of thy great, honorable, and Holy Name, YESHAYAH Baal ha-Teshuvah, (Master of Salvation) that is within this psalm, that Thou healest me from illness, disease, and pain of my eyes, for Thine is the power and the salvation, and only Thou hast the power to help. In Thee I trust. Amen Selah.	YESHAYAH (Salvation of God)	(יהוה) verse 2; (שובה) verse 5; (עשׁשׁה) verse 8; (יבשׁו) verse 11; (ויבהלו) verse 11
7	**Against enemies and persecutors:** If enemies try to cause you trouble or make you unhappy, take earth or dust from the ground, speak this psalm over it, throw it behind you or where your enemies or persecutors are or from where they will come, and be able to go wherever you want. **Prayer:** May it be Thy Will, EL ELIYON, that Thou turnest the heart of my enemies as Thou turned the enemies of Abraham, our forefather, when he called upon the Name (HaShem). Amen Selah. **Against an enemy:** Fill a new pot or cauldron with water from a spring and recite verses 7–18 four times. Then pour it on the place where your enemy lives or passes, and you will be victorious. **Say each time:** May it be Thy Will, EL ELIYON, that Thou throwest down and subduest [Insert name], son/daughter of [Insert name of mother], my enemy. Amen Amen Amen Selah Selah Selah. **In a court of law to be said before the trial:** May it be Thy Will, EL ELIYON, that Thou grantest me to depart acquitted and a free man.	EL ELIYON (Highest God)	(אשׁר) verse 1; (אודה) verse 18;[6] (הושׁיעני) verse 2; (אלי) verse 7; (ידון) verse 9; (ישׁוב) verse 13; (עליון) verse 18
8	**To gain favor for your business:** Speak this psalm seven times over olive oil, and anoint your face, hands, and feet. Do this for three days after sunset. **Prayer:** May it be Thy Will, RACHMIEL, to grant me grace and favor in the eyes of people for thou guidest the hearts of people according to Thy Holy Will. Amen Selah.	RACHMIEL (Compassion of God)	(אדיר) verse 2; (ירח) verse 4; (אדם) verse 5; (מאלהים) verse 6; (תמשׁילהו) verse 7

---

6 By Al-bam.

Psalm	Purpose	Holy Name	Words
9	**Against diseases in a male child:** Write the psalm on paper, and suspend it from the child's neck. **Prayer:** May it be Thy Will, EHIYEH ASHER EHIYEH, for the sake of Thy Name, that Thou removest the disease from this boy [Insert name], son of [Insert name of mother] and ease his pain. Heal his body and soul, and keep him safe from all illness and danger all his life. Amen. **Against enemies:** Say this psalm. **Prayer:** May it be Thy Will, EHIYEH ASHER EHIYEH, for the sake of Thy Name, that Thou withdrawest me from the influence of my enemies and protectest me from my persecutors, as Thou protectest the psalmist from the harassment of his many enemies. Amen.	EHIYEH	(אודה) verse 2; (האויב) verse 7; (רגלם) verse 16;[7] (סלה) verse 21
10	**Against possession by a demon:** Fill a new vessel with water and olive oil, and murmur the psalm over it (nine times). **Prayer (to be added each time):** May it be Thy most Holy Will, EL METZ, to heal this [Insert name], son/daughter of [Insert name of mother], who is ill in body and soul from all plagues and oppressions, to strengthen the powers of his body and soul, and to deliver him from all evil. Amen Selah.	EL METZ (God of the Oppressed)	(אלה) verse 7; (למה) verse 1; (ענוים) verse 12; (הארץ) verse 17
11	**Against persecutors and harm:** Speak this psalm. **Prayer:** May it be Thy Will, PELE, to protect me from all enemies and persecutors and from all evil for the sake of Thy Holy Name. Amen Selah.	PELE (Miraculous One)	(אפל) verse 2; (פעל) verse 3; (אדם) verse 4;
12	**Against persecutors and harm:** Speak this psalm. **Prayer:** May it be Thy Will, AVIEL, my father, that all plans against me shall fail, and that Thou shalt protectest me from all danger and harm, for Thou art my Father and Thine is the kingdom and the power. Amen Selah.	AVIEL (My Father Is God)	(אביונים) verse 6; (אקום) verse 6; (לו) verse 6

[7] By At-bash.

Psalm	Purpose	Holy Name	Words
13	**Against unnatural death:** Pray this psalm to be protected from lethal dangers. **Prayer:** May it be Thy Will that Thou shalt protectest me from an evil, fast, or unnatural death. Save me from lethal accidents, for Thou art my help and my God, and Thine is the Power and the Glory. Amen Selah. **Against diseases of the eye:** Speak this psalm over an herb (or medicine) that cures the eye. Then bind it over the eye.	AZRIEL (My Help Is God)[8]	(עֲצוֹת) verse 3; (מִזְמוֹר) verse 1; (יָרוּם) verse 3; (עֲנֵנִי) verse 4; (אֹיְבִי) verse 5; (יָגֵל) verse 6
14	**Against defamation and mistrust:** Speak this psalm. **Prayer:** May it be Thy Will, EL EMET, to grant me that people have favor and mercy for me, that they trust and believe my words, and may no defamation cause mistrust of me. Thou canst help me, for Thou guidest the hearts of men, and liars or slanderers are an abomination unto Thee. Save me for the sake of Thy Name. Amen Selah.	EL EMET (God of Truth)	(אֱלֹהִים) verse 1; (מַשְׂכִּיל) verse 2; (אֶחָד) verse 3; (עַמִּי) verse 4; (עֲצַת) verse 6
15	**Against obsession by an evil spirit or melancholy:** Pray this psalm over a new pot filled with water from a spring, and then cleanse the body of the patient with the water. **Prayer:** May it be Thy Will, merciful God, to heal this [Insert name], son/daughter of [Insert name of mother], who is bereft of his senses and plagued by an evil spirit. Heal him from all evil, and enlighten his mind for the sake of Thy Holy Name YALI. Amen Selah.	YALI	(יָגוּר) verse 1; (רֶגֶל) verse 3; (יִמּוֹט) verse 5
16	**To discover a thief:** Take clay from a potter (or mix mud from a river and sand from the sea), and write all the names of the suspects on pieces of paper. Form pieces from the clay or mud with the papers inside (or stuck to it). Then fill a vessel with fresh water (from the river). Carefully, one by one, place inside the vessel the pieces with the names inside them, and speak the psalm over the vessel eleven times. The paper of the thief will rise to the surface of the water. **Say each time:** May it be Thy Will, CHAY, to make known to me who is the thief who stole [Insert the name of the stolen object] from me, and let the name of the thief come to the surface. Amen Selah.	CHAY (Living One)	(חֲבָלִים) verse 6; (עָלַי) verse 6

[8] Azriel is the name of the Angel of Death. (Also note that 13 is the number of this psalm and the number of Death in the Tarot.)

Psalm	Purpose	Holy Name	Words
17	**For a safe journey:** If you are attacked on a journey, take a handful of dust and speak this psalm over it. Then throw it into the face (or direction) of your enemy, and you will be saved from his grasp. **Prayer:** May it be Thy benevolent Will, YAH YHVH, to give luck to my journey, lead me on a straight way, guard me from all evil, and bring me safe and happy to the people, for the sake of Thy mighty and honorable Name. Amen.	YAH	(עלי) verse 9; (מרמה) verse 1
18	**Against robbers:** Speak this psalm and you will be saved from their grasp (and the robbers will lose their way). **Prayer:** May it be Thy most Holy Will, EL YAH, to guard me mightily from these robbers and from all enemies, opponents, and evil encounters. For Thine is the power and Thou canst help. Hear me for the sake of Thy most Holy Names EL YAH. Amen Selah. **Against sickness:** Speak this psalm over water and oil, and apply it to the patient.	EL YAH (Elijah, My God is Yah)	(אשר) verse 1; (שאול) verse 1; (תמים) verse 33; (האל) verse 48
19	**Against a spirit:** Say this psalm (seven times), and the spirit will flee. **Then say:** May it be Thy Will, YAH, the great and awesome Name (HaShem), that thee makest flee the evil spirit from this [Insert name] son/daughter of [Insert name of mother], and write it down and suspend it from his neck. **Against fever:** Say this psalm. **Against a difficult birth:** Write verses 1–5 on a shard of pottery from a road junction. Then say the psalm seven times. When the woman gives birth, remove the shard immediately. **To open the heart (to learn the Torah and the Talmud):** Purify yourself from all that is impure, take a cup of wine with honey, and speak the psalm (and the name) over it for seven days. **Then drink it and say:** May it be Thy Will, YAH, great and Name (HaShem), that thou openest my heart (or the heart of [Insert name], son/daughter of [Insert name of mother], for thy Torah with all its wisdom, and do not let me (or him/her) forget what I (he/she) learned forever. Amen Amen Amen Selah Selah Selah.	YAH	(וגאלי) verse 2; (השמים) verse 15

Psalm	Purpose	Holy Name	Words
20	**If you go to a mighty man:** Fill a new vessel with water, add myrrh and bay leaves, and speak this psalm and Psalms 23, 24, 92, 94, and 100 three times over it during the night. Then wash your face with it and anoint yourself with balsam, praying to God, and you will succeed. **In a court of law:** Murmur this psalm over rose oil and oil (and water and salt). Mix them and wash your face, hands, and feet. **Prayer:** Lord and Judge of the world, Thou hast power over the hearts of men and Thou guidest them according to Thy Will. Grant that I find mercy and favor in the eyes of my judges, those who have power over me, and guide their hearts in my best interest. Let them speak a fair and favorable judgment, that I can go as a free man. Hear me, oh merciful Father, and fulfill my request for the sake of Thy honorable Name. YHVH. Amen Selah.	YHVH	(יַעַנְךָ) verse 2; (סֶלָה) verse 4; (יְמִינוֹ) verse 7; (קָרְאֵנוּ) verse 10. (The last word must be permutated according to At-ba.)
21	**If you go to a mighty man (with a petition):** Say this psalm seven times over olive oil, and anoint your face, hands, and feet. Afterward, write verses 1–4, and suspend them from the neck. **Against a storm at sea:** Mix rose oil, water, salt, and resin, and speak this psalm over it. Pour the mixture into the raging sea, and the water will be calmed. **Say, then:** May it be Thy Will, YHVH, by the great, holy, and awesome Name (HaShem) that comest forth from this psalm, that thou calmest the raging sea, for thou rulest over the tides of the sea and the crashing waves. Amen Amen Amen Selah Selah Selah.	YAH	(יְהֹוָה בְּעֻזְּךָ) verse 2; (רוֹמָה) verse 14
22	**To pass a harbor or travel safely on sea:** Speak this psalm (seven times a day), and you need not fear anything. (Also used for safe travel on land.)	AH	(אֱלֹהַי) verse 3; (עָשָׂה) verse 32

Psalm	Purpose	Holy Name	Words
23	**For a (prophetic) dream:** Purify yourself and fast for one day. Speak the psalm seven times before going to bed. **Prayer (to be spoken after each repetition):** Lord of the worlds, by Thy unspeakable power, might, majesty, and glory, hear the prayer of a humble petitioner, and fulfill my request, my Father. May it be Thy Will to reveal to me [Insert the question] as Thou hast revealed to our ancestors when Thou revealed their destinies to them in their dreams. Fulfill my request for the sake of Thy adorable Name, YAH. Amen Selah.	YAH	(יהוה רעי) verse 1; (בבית יהוה) verse 6
24	**To receive an answer from the creator:** Speak this psalm, and you will receive an answer.	MEZ	(ליהוה)[9] verse 2; (הארץ) verse 2; (ומלואה) verse 2
25	**For success:** Pray this psalm in the morning, and you will have success.	ALAH	(אליך)[10] verse 1; (יעלצו) verse 1; (הדריכני) verse 5
26	**Against danger or imprisonment:** Pray this psalm.	ELOHI (My God)	(אשר) verse 10; (לשמע) verse 7; (לא) verse 4;[11] (חטאים) verse 9
27	**To conquer a city or to be welcome in a city:** Pray this psalm.		
28	**To appease an enemy:** To bring about peace between you and your enemy, speak this psalm.	HEY	(לדוד) verse 1;[12] (עולם) verse 51[13]
29	**Against an evil spirit:** Take water that has not seen the sun, seven willow rods from the desert, and seven leaves of the (date) palm tree that has not yet brought forth fruit, and put them into a large pot or cauldron filled with water. Murmur over them ten times in the evening, and place the pot below the stars on the earth, and then pour out the contents at the gate of the house.	AH	(יהוה) verse 1;[14] (הבו) verse 2

9 *Mem* from *Lamed* and *Ayin* from *Heh* by Al-bam, and *Zayin* from *Vav* by Ab-gad.

10 The text is unclear. The words are my suggestion, according to the traditional name.

11 By permutation.

12 By permutation.

13 By At-bash.

14 By Aiq-Beqar.

Psalm	Purpose	Holy Name	Words
30	**For protection from all evil:** Pray this psalm every day. **Against pain in the body:** Speak this psalm and Psalms 13, 16, and 45.	EL	(אֲרוֹמִמְךָ) verse 2; (לְמַעַן) verse 12
31	**Against diseases of the eye:** Speak this psalm over water, and wash the eye with it. **Against headache and pain in the body:** Speak this psalm over olive oil, and salve the affected person. **Against the Evil Eye and against slander:** Speak this psalm over olive oil, and salve your hands and face.	YAH	(פַּלְּטֵנִי) verse 2; (הַמְּיַחֲלִים) verse 25
32	**To gain grace and protection from the Evil Eye:** Speak this psalm.		
33	**For a woman whose children die and to exorcise a spirit:** Write this psalm, and suspend it from her neck (with the Name YHVH). Murmur it over olive oil, and anoint the patient.	YHVH	(לַיהוה) verse 2; (הוֹדוּ) verse 2; (עֲצַת) verse 10; (הַיֹּצֵר) verse 15
34	**To gain the favor of nobles or governments (or to free a friend from suppression):** Say this psalm (and the previous one).	PELE (Miraculous One)	(פָּדָה) verse 23; (לִפְנֵי) verse 1; (קָרָא) verse 7
35	**If a man hates or hassles you:** Pray this psalm for three days, three times a day.	YAH	(לְחֻמִּי) verse 1; (וְצֵנָה) verse 2
36	**Against slander:** Pray this psalm, and no damage will be done to your reputation.	EMET (Truth)	(אָוֶן) verse 5; (מִשְׁפָּטֶיךָ) verse 7; (תְּהוֹם) verse 7
37	**Against drunkenness:** Speak this psalm over a cup of water with some salt. Let the affected person drink a bit, pour the rest on his head, and wash his face with it. **Against severe illness:** Speak this psalm seven times over oil, and the patient will be healed.	AHEY	(אַל-תִּתְחַר) verse 1; (מְהֵרָה) verse 2;[15] (וִיעַזְּרֵם) verse 40
38	**Against great misfortune:** At dawn, go outdoors, pray this psalm and the next one to heaven, and you will be answered. **Against slander:** If someone has defamed you in such a way that the authorities have turned against you, go outside early in the morning and pray this psalm (and the next one) seven times. Then fast for the remainder of the day.	AH	

---

15 The text is unclear. The word is my suggestion, according to the traditional name.

Psalm	Purpose	Holy Name	Words
39	See above.	HEY	(הֹשַׁע) verse 14; (אָמַרְתִּי) verse 2
40	**Against evil spirits:** Pray this psalm every day.	YAH	(שִׁוַּעְתִּי) verse 2; (חוּשָׁה) verse 14
41	**If you are dismissed from your job:** If your position has been given to someone else, speak this psalm and the next two psalms for three days, three times a day, and you will experience a miracle.	EMET (Truth)	(אַשְׁרֵי) verse 2; (אָמֵן) verse 14; (תְּמַכְתָּ) verse 13
42	**For a (prophetic) dream:** Fast for one day, and get up on the ninth hour (after sunset). Speak the psalm seven times, and then go to bed. While you sleep [get up and] speak it once. Then purify yourself, and speak it three times.	TZEVA	(כְּאַיָּל) verse 2;[16] (מַה-תִּשְׁתּוֹחֲחִי) verse 12;[17] (אֱלֹהַי) verse 7
43	**Against blindness:** Make a pen from new wood, and write this psalm twice. Bind it to the head, and the blindness will become better.		
44	**Against debts:** Speak this psalm before the night [begins].	CHAY (Life)	(קוּמָה) verse 27;[18] (אֱלֹהִים) verse 2
45	**If you have a wicked wife:** Speak this psalm seven times over olive oil and anoint your face, and she will be much nicer.	REM	(רָחַשׁ)[19] verse 2; (וָעֶד) verse 18
46	**If a man hates his wife:** Placing a hair of hers under the door hinge, say this psalm seven times over rose oil. Anoint the face of the woman, and he will love her. And she shall drink from the oil. (Then read Psalm 47.) **If a woman hates her husband:** Take balsam oil and say this psalm and the next two psalms. He shall anoint his right hand, his foot, and her right hand, and they will be reconciled.	EHIYEH	(אֱלֹהִים) verse 2; (מְאֹד) verse 2;[20] (יְהוָה צְבָאוֹת) verse 12; (סֶלָה) verse 12
47	**To win favor of neighbors:** Pray this psalm seven times every day.	YAH	(כֹּל) verse 2;[21] (נְדִיבֵי עַמִּים) verse 10[22]

16 Tzadde by gematriah (Ach-bat) from *Kaf*.
17 Bet by gematria (Al-bam).
18 Chet by gematria (Al-bam) from *Qof*.
19 Letters by gematria.
20 Heh by permutation (At-ba) from *Dalet*.
21 Yod by permutation (At-ba) from *Kaf*.
22 By permutation.

Psalm	Purpose	Holy Name	Words
48	**To frighten your enemies:** Pray this psalm, and your enemies will be frightened and terrified, and thus they will not dare to cause you trouble.	ZACH	(קדשו)[23] verse 2; (יכ זה תאלהים) verse 15
49	**Against fever:** Write this psalm, and suspend it from the neck. (Some say also add verses 1–5 of Psalm 50.)	SHADDAI (Almighty One)	(שמעו) verse 2; (קרבם) verse 12;[24] (אדם ב'קר) verse 21
50	**Against enemies and robbers:** Write this psalm, and suspend it from the neck.	CHAY (Life)	(זבח) verse 5; (אנכי) verse 7
51	**If you have committed a severe sin:** Speak the psalm for seven days over sesame oil, seven times in the morning, seven times at noon, and seven times in the evening. Then anoint your body with the oil and purify yourself, and your request (to be atoned) will be answered.	REM	(פרים) verse 21;[25] (בבוא-אליו נתן) verse 2[26]
52	**To retaliate against your enemies:** Speak this psalm together with Psalms 53 and 54.		
53	**To frighten your enemies:** Pray this psalm, and your enemies will be frightened and terrified and thus will not dare to cause you trouble. (If you further want to retaliate against your enemies, speak the next two psalms as well.)	EL	(אמר נבל) verse 2; (ישראל) verse 7
54	**If you want to make something or do an important work:** Pray this psalm and the next psalm in the synagogue.	YAH	(ראתה עינ') verse 9; (מסתתר עמנו) verse 2[27]
55	See above.	VAH	(ואתה אלהים) verse 24; (האזינה) verse 2
56	**If you need goods:** Pray this psalm and the next one secretly in the synagogue. **When in chains or in prison:** Pray this psalm. **Against the Evil Urge:** If you want to resist an evil desire, pray this psalm.		

[23] By permutation.
[24] By permutation.
[25] *Resh* by gematria (*Vav Mem Resh = Vav* to *Mem* and *Mem* to *Resh = Ach-bat*) from *Mem*.
[26] By permutation (Al-bam).
[27] By permutation.

Psalm	Purpose	Holy Name	Words
57	**For good fortune:** Pray this psalm after the morning prayer, and you will be lucky in all your deeds.	CHAY (Life)	(חָנֵּנִי אֱלֹהִים) verse 2; (רֻמָּה) verse 12[28]
58	**Against a snappish dog:** Pray this psalm, and you will not be harmed.	VAH	(אָדָם) verse 2; (הַאֻמְנָם) verse 2
59	**Against the Evil Urge and against evil magic (pray this before dawn):** Speak it for three days, three times a day. **After each time, say:** May it be Thy Will, YHVH ELOHIM, the Great and Holy Name that emerges from this psalm [song], that Thou savest me from the Evil Urge (Yetzer ha-Ra) and from evil [magic] words and evil imagination and evil thoughts, as Thou have saved him who prayed this psalm (song) before Thee. (This is also supposed to work on driving away evil neighbors.)	YHVH ELOHIM	(יְשׁוּבוּ לָעֶרֶב) verse 7; (הַצִּילֵנִי) verse 2; (וַאֲנִי אָשִׁיר עֻזֶּךָ) verse 17; (חַסְדִּי) verse 18[29]
60	**Before a battle:** Pray this psalm, and you will not be harmed.	VAH	(צָרֵינוּ) verse 14; (לְלַמֵּד) verse 1[30]
61	**On entering a new home:** Speak this psalm when you move in, and you will have fortune.	SHADDAI (Almighty One)	(שִׁמְעָה) verse 2; (כִּי) verse 9;[31] (יוֹם) verse 9[32]
62	**To be saved from need and debts:** Pray this psalm. **For forgiveness of sins:** Speak this psalm on Sunday after the evening prayer, and after the *Minchah* (afternoon prayer service) on Monday. **After you have finished the psalm, say:** May it be Thy Will, EL ECHAD, that Thou forgivest and pardonest and releasest me from my sins, as thou hast forgiven and pardoned and released him who has spoken this psalm before. Amen Selah.	YAH	(יְשׁוּעָתִי) verse 2; (כְּמַעֲשֵׂהוּ) verse 13[33]
63	**If you have a business partner and want to separate without a conflict:** Speak this psalm, and you will get a good share.	VAH	(הַמֶּלֶךְ) verse 12; (יְהוּדָה) verse 1

[28] By permutation (*Resh Yod* = Am-ban).

[29] We have *Yod Heh Vav* and another *Yod* where there should be a *Heh* to complete the Tetragramaton. Instead, we have a *Yod* = 10. Therefore, 5 represents the *Heh,* and the remaining five represent the five letters of Elohim.

[30] By permutation (At-ba).

[31] By permutation (*Dalet Kaf Tzadde* = Achbat).

[32] By permutation (At-bash).

[33] By permutation (At-ba).

Psalm	Purpose	Holy Name	Words
64	**If you want to request something from someone:** Speak this psalm and Psalms 65–67 on the way to him, and you will succeed. **On fording a river:** Speak this psalm, and you will be safe.	SHEM	(שמע אלהים) verse 2; (ישמח צדיק) verse 11[34]
65	**If you want to request something from someone:** Speak this psalm and Psalms 66–67, and you will succeed.	YAH	(ישירו) verse 14; (דמיה) verse 2
66	**Against possession by a spirit:** Write this psalm and murmur it over the writing, then suspend it from the neck of the possessed person.	YAH	
67	**Against continuous fever or for a prisoner:** Say this psalm. (This psalm, written in the form of a menorah, is often found printed in prayer books. It consists of seven verses and forty-nine words—7 × 7. The fifth verse consists of forty-nine letters, counting the double *Mem* as two.)	YAH	(יברכנו אלהים) verse 8; (סלה) verse 2
68	**Against a spirit:** Use water that has not seen the sun and murmur the psalm over it. Pour it out before dawn.	YAH	(יקום) verse 2; (נורא) verse 36[35]
69	**Against debts:** Speak this psalm over water, and then drink the water.	VAH	(וזרע) verse 37; (הושיעני) verse 2
70	**For a fight:** Speak this psalm before the fight and you will be victorious.	CHAY (Life)	(אלהים) verse 2;[36] (תאחר) verse 6[37]
71	**To be freed from prison:** Speak this psalm twenty-one times in the morning, seven times at noon, and seven times in the evening for a period of time, and you will be free.	PELE (Miraculous One)	(גוזי) verse 6;[38] (לעולם) verse 1; and Alef by permutation
72	**For favor (of a mighty person):** Write this psalm on parchment, and suspend it from your neck.	AH	(אלהים) verse 1; (וימלא כבודו) verse 19[39]

[34] By permutation (At-bash).

[35] By permutation (*Heh Nun* = Ai-bach).

[36] By permutation (*Alef Chet Samech* = Ach-bat).

[37] By permutation (*Resh Yod* = Am-ban).

[38] By permutation (*Gimel Yod Peh* = Ach-bat).

[39] By permutation (The text is corrupt; probably *Kaf Samech Qof* = Ahbu).

Psalm	Purpose	Holy Name	Words
73	**For favor:** Write this psalm on parchment, and suspend it from the neck. **Against compulsory baptism:** Pray this psalm seven times each day.	EMET (Truth)	(אַךְ טוֹב) verse 1; the rest are unclear
74	**Against enemies and oppressors:** Pray this psalm regularly, and you will experience a miracle, ending your problems.	REM	(מַרְעִיתֶךָ) verse 1; (תָּמִיד) verse 23[40]
75	**For forgiveness of sins:** Pray this psalm.	CHAD (One)	(צַדִּיק) verse 11; (הוֹדִינוּ) verse 2
76	**To exorcise a spirit from a mother of a baby:** Write the psalm and suspend it from her neck (or from the baby's neck if the baby is already born). **Against (danger of) flood and fire:** Pray this psalm.	YAH	(נִבְצַר) verse 13; (נוֹדַע) verse 2[41]
77	**If people who hate you are troubling you, or if spirits frighten you:** Speak this psalm and Psalms 78–80, and you will experience a miracle. **Against all manner of distress:** Speak this psalm.		
78	**If people hate you or spirits trouble you:** Speak this psalm and the next two, and you will experience a great miracle. **To win grace at court:** Speak this psalm.	YAH	(יְנַחֵם) verse 72;[42] (הַאֲזִינָה) verse 1
79	**To be rid of your enemies:** Speak this psalm regularly.	YAH	(תְּהִלָּתֶךָ)[43] verse 13; (וַאֲנַחְנוּ עַמְּךָ) verse 12
80	**Against the temptation of idolatry:** Speak this psalm and the next one.	YAH	(רְעֵה) verse 2;[44] יהוה אלהים צבאות) verse 20
81	See above.	VAH	(יַאֲכִילֵהוּ) verse 17; (הַרְנִינוּ) verse 2

40 By permutation (*Dalet Mem Tav* = Ai-bach).

41 By permutation (*Heh Nun End-Kaf* = Aiq-Bekar = 50 exchanged for 5).

42 By gematria (*Yod Mem* = At-bash).

43 By permutation.

44 By permutation (*Heh Resh* = Aa-baf).

Psalm	Purpose	Holy Name	Words
82	**If you are sent on a mission:** Speak this psalm, and you will arrive quickly, be successful, and return soon.	AH	(אלהים) verse 1; (קומה) verse 8[45]
83	**For a fight:** Write this psalm and suspend it from your neck, and no one will harm you or be victorious over you.	YAH	(אלהים) verse 2;[46] (נשמדו) verse 11
84	**For someone who is ill:** Speak this psalm over a pot of water that has not seen the sun (i.e., that is fresh), and pour it over the ill person or wash him with the water. (Make sure the temperature is comfortable.)	EL	(צבאות) verse 2; (בך) verse 13[47]
85	**If a man is angry or troubles you:** Go outdoors and pray this psalm to heaven, facing his direction (or to the south), and then go to him and you will be accepted benevolently.	VAH	(תתן-לנו) verse 8; (הראנו יהוה) verse 8
86	**Against an evil spirit:** Speak this psalm (uncertain).	YAH	(אני) verse 1; (הטה) verse 1
87	**To free a man from prison:** Speak this psalm (uncertain).	EL	(אהב יהוה) verse 2; (מעיני בך) verse 7[48]
88	**To free a man from prison:** Go outdoors at night, and pray this psalm (and the next one) to heaven. **To save a city or a community:** Speak this psalm.	YAH	(יהוה אלהי ישועתי) verse 2; (הרחקת) verse 19
89	**Against broken bones:** Speak this psalm over olive oil. (Some say also speak Psalm 88 after it.) Put some oil on wool and make a bandage from it. **For love:** Speak this psalm (uncertain).	CHAY (Life)	(חסדי) verse 2; (אמונתך בפי) verse 2
90	**Against lions or evil spirits:** Speak this psalm. It is considered even more powerful in connection with the next one.	SHADDAI (Almighty One)	(תפלה למשה) verse 1; (אדני) verse 1; (אדני--מעון) verse 1

45 By gematria (*Heh Lamed Qof* = Ach-bat).
46 By permutation (*Alef Yod Qof, Heh Nun End-Kaf* = Aiq-Bekar).
47 By gematria (*Kaf Lamed* = At-ba).
48 By gematria (*Bet Lamed* = Ach-bal).

Psalm	Purpose	Holy Name	Words
91	*Against a lion or a spirit:* Speak this psalm, and he will move away. *After you have spoken this psalm and the previous one, say:* May it be Thy Will, EL SHADDAI, the great One, the mighty One, and the awesome One, (ha-Gadol ha-Gibbor ve-ha-Nora) that Thou castest aside the evil spirit that came upon [Insert name], son/daughter of [Insert name of mother], and Thou soon sendest to him healing and peace; and Thou returnest him to health. And Thou answerest him as Thou hast answered to Moshe [Moses], Thy servant, when he spoke this psalm before Thee. And Thou let rise his prayer before Thee as the fragrance of the incense rose before Thee on the altar. Amen Amen Amen Selah Selah Selah. *To protect your house from evil:* Write the entire psalm backward and hide it over or behind the door, and you will be saved from every evil misfortune. (Some say add the last verse of Psalm 90, for then you will get what is called the Vihi Noam.)	EL	(בִּישׁוּעָתִי) verse 16;[49] (אֹמַר--לַיהוָה) verse 2[50]
92	*If you want to go to a Lord or a mighty man:*[51] Fill a new vessel with water and add myrtle and bay leaves; speak this psalm over it and Psalms 94, 100, 20, 23, and 24; and drink it three times in one night. Wash yourself with this water in one night. Then salve yourself with balsam. Then pray the psalms again. *Then say:* May it be Thy Will, jealous God, that Thou will throw down and humiliate [Insert name of person] and show me miracles as Thou hast thrown down and humiliated opponents and shown miracles to the one who prayed these psalms before. And let my prayer rise before Thee as the pleasant odor of frankincense on the altar.	YAH	(לְהַגִּיד) verse 16;[52] (עֶלְיוֹן) verse 2[53]
93	*In a court of law:* Speak this psalm.		

49 By gematria (*Alef Yod Qof* = Aiq-Bekar).

50 By gematria (*Heh Lamed Qof* = Ach-bat).

51 To understand this psalm, remember that Jews were seldom treated fairly, so this formula may call upon the memory of Moses going before the pharaoh.

52 The text is unclear. The word is my suggestion, according to the traditional name.

53 By permutation (*Heh Nun End-Kaf* = Aiq-Bekar).

Psalm	Purpose	Holy Name	Words
94	*If a person who hates you is troubling you:* Purify yourself, go outside at dawn, put a bit of frankincense in your mouth, and face east. Then pray this psalm and Psalm 100, and you will see great miracles. (Some say go on Monday and face northeast). *And after you have spoken these psalms, say:* May it be Thy Will, EL QANO TOV, that Thou bringest down and oppressest [Insert name], son/daughter of [Insert name of mother], my enemy. And so demonstrate miracles to me, like those Thou hast performed to oppress and bring down the enemies of Moses, our teacher, peace be upon him [Moshe rabenu alav ha-shalom], for he prayed to Thee with these psalms. And let my prayer rise before Thee as the pleasant odor of frankincense on the altar.	EL QANO TOV (Good zealous God)	
95	*Against compulsory baptism:* Pray this psalm.	EL	(אשר-נשבעתי) verse 11; (לכו נרננה) verse 1
96	*To make your family happy:* Pray this psalm.	YAH	(שׁ"רו) verse 1; (באמונתו) verse 13[54]
97	Same as above. (Also against theft.)	YAH	(יהוה מלך) verse 1; (והודו) verse 12[55]
98	*To make peace between enemies:* Pray this psalm.	YAH	(שׁ"רו) verse 9[56] (לפני יהוה) verse 9[57]
99	*To become pious:* Pray this psalm.	VAH	(אלהינו) verse 9; (הארץ) verse 1[58]
100	*To be victorious over your enemies:* Pray this psalm seven times.	YAH	(כל-טוב) verse 5; (עבדו-את-יהוה) verse 2
101	*Against evil spirits or evil people:* Write this psalm and Psalm 68 on a parchment, and suspend it from the neck.		

54 By permutation.
55 The text is unclear. The word is my suggestion, according to the traditional name.
56 The text is unclear. The word is my suggestion, according to the traditional name.
57 By gematria (*Heh Lamed Qof* = Ach-bat).
58 By gematria (At-bash).

Psalm	Purpose	Holy Name	Words
102	**Against childlessness:** Pray this psalm and the next one.	YAH	יהוה שמעה (' תפלתי) verse 2; (יכון ') verse 29[59]
103	See above.	AH	
104	**Against a destructive enemy or demon (maziq):** Pray this psalm.		
105	**Against a tertian fever:** Pray this psalm. (Some say pray this psalm against the quatrain fever[60] and the next one against the tertian fever.)	YAH	(לי'עקב) verse 10; (הודו ') verse 1
106	**Against the quatrain fever:** Pray this psalm. (Some say pray this psalm against the tertian fever and the previous one against the quatrain fever.)	VAH	(הודו ליהוה) verse 1;[61] (הללו-יה) verse 4
107	**Against daily fever:** Pray this psalm.	YAH	(ישלח ') verse 20; (ברנה ') verse 22
108	**For a blessing in your house:** Write this psalm (and its name) on a piece of parchment, hide it behind the door, and you will be blessed in your coming and in your going and in all your undertakings.	VAH	(צרינו ') verse 14; (וכנוד ') verse 3[62]
109	**If a hater hassles you:** Take a handful of mustard and put it in a new vessel, add spring water (not wine, as is misinterpreted in some texts!), and speak this psalm over it for three days. Then pour out the water in front of your hater's house, and beware that you are spattered by no drop of the water.	EL	(אלהי ') verse 1; (כי-יעמד ') verse 31[63]
110	**For peace (between enemies):** Pray this psalm.	YAH	
111	**To gain new friends:** Pray this psalm.		
112	**To increase your power:** Pray this psalm.		
113	**Against idolatry:** Pray this psalm.		
114	**For a merchant:** Write down the psalm, and place it inside the shop. (Or carry it with you.)	AH	(ישראל ') verse 1; (יהודה ') verse 2

59 By permutation (*Heh Nun End-Kaf* = Aiq-Bekar).

60 A fever that has a cycle of seventy-two hours.

61 By permutation.

62 By permutation (*Heh Nun End-Kaf* = Aiq-Bekar).

63 By permutation.

Psalm	Purpose	Holy Name	Words
115	**For a (religious) debate:** Pray this psalm.		
116	**Against an unnatural or sudden death:** Pray this psalm every day.		
117	**For protection and mercy (of a mighty man):** Speak this psalm, concentrating on the name YAFEL before and after, and wear clean and beautiful garments, and you shall succeed with your request. *If you broke an oath:* Pray this psalm with repentance in your heart.	YAFEL	
118	**For a (religious) debate:** Pray this psalm.		
119	**For one who wishes to perform a Mitzvah (a sacred duty):** Verses 1–8 (*Alef*). Speak the entire passage. **Against spasm of the body:** Verses 1–8 (*Alef*). Speak the entire passage twice. **Against forgetfulness and to open the heart (to learn the Torah):** Verses 9–16 (*Bet*). Speak the entire passage. Write on a boiled and peeled egg verses 9–16 and: Moses commanded us a law, an inheritance of the congregation of Jacob (Deuteronomy 33:4) and This book of the law shall not depart out of thy mouth, but thou shalt meditate therein day and night, that thou mayest observe to do according to all that is written therein; for then thou shalt make thy ways prosperous, and then thou shalt have good success (Yoshuah 1:8). Also write on it the holy names corresponding to this passage: CHAFNIEL (חפניאל, Cover of God), SHUVNIEL (שובניאל, Repetition of God), MUPIEL (מופיאל, From the Mouth of God). And write: Open my heart for Thy Torah and all I learn be remembered. Do this in the hour of the Minchah (afternoon prayer service) during fasting on Thursday. Eat the egg immediately in one piece, and say verses 9–12 three times. **If you wish to complete a deal:** Speak verses 17–24 (*Gimel*) ten times, and you will have success.		

Psalm	Purpose	Holy Name	Words
119 cont'd	**To heal the right eye:** Speak verses 17–24 (*Gimel*) seven times.		
	If you want to hold a speech in public: Speak verses 25–32 (*Dalet*) eleven times.		
	To heal the left eye: Speak verses 25–32 (*Dalet*) seven times.		
	To make a decision: Speak verses 25–32 (*Dalet*) seven times.		
	If your heart desires a sinful thing: Speak verses 33–40 (*Heh*) fifteen times, and the Evil Urge (Yetzer ha-Ra) will flee. (Or write it on deer parchment and suspend it from the neck.)		
	If you want to go before a lord or a mighty person: Speak verses 41–48 (*Vav*) twenty-one times.		
	To make your subordinates obey you: Speak verses 41–48 (*Vav*) over water, and let them drink it.		
	If someone tries to seduce you to do something wrong: Speak verses 49–56 (*Zayin*) twenty-five times, and you will return to your good aims.		
	Against anthrax: Write verses 49–56 (*Zayin*) on pure parchment, and place it at the patient's bed		
	If you want to learn the Torah: Speak verses 57–64 (*Chet*) eight times, and your heart will be opened to the Torah.		
	Against pain in the upper body: Speak verses 57–64 (*Chet*) seven times over wine, and let the patient drink it.		
	Against pain in the spleen, kidneys, or hips (lower body): Speak verses 65–72 (*Tet*) over the patient's drink.		
	If someone is suffering: Speak verses 73–80 (*Yod*) twenty-six times.		
	For favor of God and men: Speak verses 73–80 (*Yod*) after the morning prayer.		

Psalm	Purpose	Holy Name	Words
119 cont'd	**If someone has evil plans against you:** Speak verses 81–88 (*Kaf*) seven times, and the plans will be rendered ineffective.		
	Against a furuncle on the right side of the nose: Speak verses 81–88 (*Kaf*).		
	To win in court: Speak verses 89–96 (*Lamed*) twelve times.		
	To open the heart (i.e., learn the scriptures): Speak verses 97–104 (*Mem*) forty times, and then write them three times on an apple or an etrog (citron). Eat the apple or the etrog, and then speak them for another forty times (40 is the number of *Mem*).		
	Against pain in the right arm or hand: Speak verses 97–104 (*Mem*).		
	Against forgetfulness: Speak verses 105–12 (*Nun*) seven times.		
	For a safe journey: Speak verses 105–12 (*Nun*) for a few days before and after the morning and evening prayer.		
	To frustrate someone's evil plans: Speak verses 113–20 (*Samech*) seven times.		
	If you want to fast: Speak verses 121–28 (*Ayin*) seventeen times in the evening.		
	Against someone who wants to do you injustice: Speak verses 121–28 (*Ayin*) nine times.		
	Against pain in the left arm or hand: Speak verses 121–28 (*Ayin*).		
	Against a furuncle on the left side of the nose: Speak verses 129–36 (*Peh*).		
	For a victory at court: Speak verses 137–44 (*Tzadde*) twenty-four times in front of the judge while he sits on his seat.		
	If you want your prayer to be heard: Speak verses 145–52 (*Qof*) twelve times.		
	To make your persecutor return: Speak verses 153–60 (*Resh*) seven times.		
	To create peace: Speak verses 161–68 (*Shin*) eight times.		

Psalm	Purpose	Holy Name	Words
119 cont'd	**Against forgetfulness:** Speak verses 169–76 (*Tav*) seven times. (Furthermore, there seems to be a practice of knot magic connected to the last passage. If someone has pain in the loins, after saying the psalm, tie knots in water for him and say: Adam, Seth, Enosh, Kenan, Mahallalel, Yared, Jared, Henoch, Methuselah, Lamech, Noah, Sem.)		
120	**Against snakes or scorpions:** If you see a snake or a scorpion on a journey, speak this psalm seven times, and you may continue your journey safely. **For justice in court:** Pray this psalm.		
121	**For safely traveling alone at night:** Speak this psalm seven times.		
122	**For going to a great man:** Speak this psalm thirteen times, and he will welcome you in a friendly way. (Further, speak this psalm in the synagogue, and you will be blessed.)		
123	**When a servant has run away:** Write this psalm and your name and his name on a foil of lead or tin, and he will come back.		
124	**On fording a river or traveling in a boat:** Pray this psalm, and you will be safe.		
125	**For a journey into the lands of enemies:** Speak this psalm over salt and scatter it in all four directions before you enter the land, and you will be safe.		
126	**For a woman whose children die:** Write on four pieces of parchment this psalm along with these angelic names: SANVAI (סנוי) SANSANVAI (סנסנוי) SEMAN-GLOF (סמנגלוף). Then hide them in the four walls (or corners) of your house, and the children will live. These angels also appear in unusual shapes on an amulet in *Sefer Raziel* (see page 87 for a full picture of the amulet).		
127	**For protection of a newborn child:** Write this psalm on parchment, and suspend it from the neck.		
128	**For an expectant mother:** Write this psalm on parchment, and suspend it from the neck.		
129	**For virtue:** Pray this psalm every day after the morning prayer.		

Psalm	Purpose	Holy Name	Words
130	**To escape from a city in which guards patrol:** Speak this psalm four times to the four quarters of the world. A deep sleep will fall upon the guards, and they will not be able to see you when you pass in front of them.		
131	**Against arrogance:** If you wish to gain modesty, speak this verse three times a day.		
132	**On fulfilling a vow:** If you have not fulfilled a vow, praying this psalm will help you to do so.		
133	**For love and friendship:** Speak this psalm (daily), and you will receive both.		
134	**For studying:** Speak this psalm.		
135	**For repentance and refinement (of the soul):** Pray this psalm three times a day.		
136	**To confess your sins:** Pray this psalm.		
137	**Against enmity, hate, or envy:** Pray this psalm.		
138	**For love and friendship:** Speak this psalm.		
139	**For love between a man and a woman (husband and wife):** Speak this psalm.		
140	**Against enmity between husband and wife:** Speak this psalm.		
141	**Against fear (of the heart):** Speak this psalm. (This can also be used against heart disease.)		
142	**Against lumbago:** Speak this psalm.		
143	**Against pain in the hips or arm:** Speak this psalm.		
144	**Against broken bones:** Speak this psalm.		
145	**Against evil spirits:** Speak this psalm in connection with the previous one.		
146	**Against stabbing or cutting wounds:** Speak this psalm daily.		
147	**Against bites of serpents or stings from scorpions, spiders, or insects:** Speak this psalm.		
148	**Against fire:** Speak this psalm.		
149	**Against fire:** Speak this psalm. (This can also be used against nocturnal emission.)		
150	**Thanking God:** Pray this psalm to thank God if you have been saved from danger or if your requests have been fulfilled.		

Amulet from Sefer Raziel *(see Psalm 126)*

Other Verses

In addition to the psalms, many other verses were used for specific magical purposes. On amulets a notarikon (an anagram) would have been used. For example, "Heal her now, O God, I beseech Thee" (Numbers 12:13) has been used against fever. In this case, the first letters were turned into the magical word A.N.R.N.L.[64] (אנרנ״ל = אל נא רפא נא לה).

Following, you will find an overview of the most common verses used in magic. Sometimes, only the beginning of a verse was used. In such cases, the number of the rest of the verse is written in parentheses.

Against Fever

Numbers 12:13   Heal her now, O God, I beseech Thee . . .

Numbers 12:13   And Moses cried unto YHVH, saying: Heal her now, O God, I beseech Thee . . .

Deuteronomy 7:15   And YHVH will take away from thee all sickness; and He will put none of the evil diseases of Egypt, which thou knowest . . .

---

[64] Probably pronounced "Anranel."

Against Bleeding

Exodus 17:16   And he said: The hand upon the throne of YHVH: YHVH will have war with Amalek from generation to generation.

Psalm 51:3   Be gracious unto me, O God, according to Thy mercy; according to the multitude of Thy compassions blot out my transgressions.

For Protection at Night

Genesis 49:18   I wait for Thy salvation, O YHVH.

Against the Evil Eye

Numbers 11:12   Have I conceived all this people? Have I brought them forth . . .

Numbers 21:17(–20)   Spring up, O well—sing ye unto it . . .

Against Black Magic

Isaiah 41:24   Behold, ye are nothing, and your work a thing of nought; an abomination is he that chooseth you.

Numbers 23:22   God who brought them forth out of Egypt is for them like the lofty horns of the wild-ox.

Exodus 22:17   Thou shalt not suffer a sorceress to live.

Exodus 30:34   And YHVH said unto Moses: Take unto thee sweet spices, stacte, and onycha, and galbanum; sweet spices with pure frankincense; of each shall there be a like weight.

Exodus 33:23   And I will take away My hand, and thou shalt see My back; but My face shall not be seen.

Leviticus 1:1   And YHVH called unto Moses, and spoke unto him out of the tent of meeting, saying . . .

Against Evil Spirits

Psalm 5:8   But as for me, in the abundance of Thy loving kindness will I come into Thy house; I will bow down toward Thy holy temple in the fear of Thee.

Psalm 110:6   He will judge among the nations; He filleth it with dead bodies, He crusheth the head over a wide land.

To Exorcise Demons

Deuteronomy 32:10(–12)   He found him in a desert land, and in the waste, a howling wilderness; He compassed him about, He cared for him, He kept him as the apple of His eye. (As an eagle that stirreth up her nest, hovereth over her young, spreadeth abroad her wings, taketh them, beareth them on her pinions—YHVH alone did lead him, and there was no strange god with Him.)

To Exorcise Demons from an Infant

Numbers 6:24(–27)   YHVH bless thee, and keep thee; YHVH make His face to shine upon thee, and be gracious unto thee; YHVH lift up His countenance upon thee, and give thee peace. (So shall they put My name upon the children of Israel, and I will bless them.)

To Dissipate a Mirage or Hallucination

Exodus 15:6   Terror and dread falleth upon them; by the greatness of Thine arm they are as still as a stone; till Thy people pass over, O YHVH, till the people pass over that Thou hast gotten.

Against Robbers

Exodus 15:15   Then were the chiefs of Edom affrighted; the mighty men of Moab, trembling taketh hold upon them; all the inhabitants of Canaan are melted away.

Song of Songs 2:15   Take us the foxes, the little foxes, that spoil the vineyards; for our vineyards are in blossom.

Genesis 32:2(–3)   And Jacob went on his way, and the angels of God met him.

Deuteronomy 11:25   There shall no man be able to stand against thee: YHVH thy God shall lay the fear of thee and the dread of thee upon all the land . . .

Against Theft

Psalm 97:2   Clouds and darkness are round about Him; righteousness and justice are the foundation of His throne.

Against an Enemy

Exodus 19:9   The enemy said: I will pursue, I will overtake, I will divide the spoil; my lust shall be satisfied upon them; I will draw my sword, my hand shall destroy them.

Exodus 15:6   Thy right hand, O YHVH, glorious in power, Thy right hand, O YHVH, dasheth in pieces the enemy.

Exodus 15:18   YHVH shall reign forever and ever.

Proverbs 1:17   For in vain the net is spread in the eyes of any bird . . .

In War

Psalm 83:14   O my God, make them like the whirling dust; as stubble before the wind.

Exodus 15:3   YHVH is a man of war, YHVH is His Name.

Deteronomy 21:10   When thou goest forth to battle against thine enemies, and YHVH thy God delivereth them into thy hands, and thou carriest them away captive . . .

Against Slander

Exodus 15:7   And in the greatness of Thine excellency Thou overthrowest them that rise up against Thee; Thou sendest forth Thy wrath, it consumeth them as stubble.

Against Pursuers

Exodus 15:4   Pharaoh's chariots and his host hath He cast into the sea, and his chosen captains are sunk in the Red Sea.

Against Fire

Numbers 11:2   And the people cried unto Moses; and Moses prayed unto YHVH, and the fire abated.

In Times of Trouble

Song of Songs 5:2   I sleep, but my heart waketh; Hark! my beloved knocketh: Open to me . . .

Song of Songs 2:14   O my dove, that art in the clefts of the rock, in the covert of the cliff, let me see thy countenance . . .

For Safety on a Journey

Numbers 10:35(–36)   And it came to pass, when the ark set forward, that Moses said: Rise up, O YHVH, and let Thine enemies be scattered; and let them that hate Thee flee before Thee.

Genesis 32:31   And Jacob called the name of the place Peniel: for I have seen God face to face, and my life is preserved.

Song of Songs 7:12   Come, my beloved, let us go forth into the field; let us lodge in the villages.

Exodus 15:13   Thou in Thy love hast led the people that Thou hast redeemed; Thou hast guided them in Thy strength to Thy holy habitation.

At Sea

Psalm 114:2   My loving-kindness, and my fortress, my high tower, and my deliverer; my shield, and He in whom I take refuge; who subdueth my people under me.

Isaiah 43:14   Thus saith YHVH, your Redeemer, The Holy One of Israel: For your sake I have sent to Babylon, and I will bring down all of them as fugitives, even the Chaldeans, in the ships of their shouting.

Isaiah 43:2   When thou passest through the waters, I will be with thee, and through the rivers, they shall not overflow thee . . .

To Be Saved from Danger

Exodus 6:6(–7)   Wherefore say unto the children of Israel: I am YHVH, and I will bring you out from under the burdens of the Egyptians, and I will deliver you from their bondage, and I will redeem you with an outstretched arm, and with great judgments . . .

To Obtain Invisibility

Genesis 19:11   And they smote the men that were at the door of the house with blindness, both small and great; so that they wearied themselves to find the door.

Genesis 1:2   Now the earth was unformed and void, and darkness was upon the face of the deep . . .

To Begin a New Piece of Work

Exodus 36:8   And every wise-hearted man among them that wrought the work . . .

For Success

Genesis 39:2   And YHVH was with Joseph, and he was a prosperous man; and he was in the house of his master the Egyptian.

Exodus 15:11   Who is like unto Thee, O YHVH, among the mighty? Who is like unto Thee, glorious in holiness, fearful in praises, doing wonders?

For Profitable Trade

Genesis 44:12   And he searched, beginning at the eldest, and leaving off at the youngest; and the goblet was found in Benjamin's sack.

Genesis 31:42   Except the God of my father, the God of Abraham, and the Fear of Isaac, had been on my side, surely now hadst thou sent me away empty.

To Win a Good Name

Song of Songs 1:15–16   Behold, thou art fair, my love; behold, thou art fair; thine eyes are as doves. Behold, thou art fair, my beloved, yea, pleasant; also our couch is leafy.

To Win Favor

Genesis 46:17   And the sons of Asher: Imnah, and Ishvah, and Ishvi, and Beriah, and Serah their sister . . .

Numbers 26:46   And the name of the daughter of Asher was Serah.

Song of Songs 6:4   Thou art beautiful, O my love, as Tirzah, comely as Jerusalem, terrible as an army with banners.

Proverbs 18:10   The name of YHVH is a strong tower: the righteous runneth into it, and is set up on high.

For a Sweet Voice

Exodus 15:1   Then sang Moses and the children of Israel this song unto YHVH, and spoke, saying: I will sing unto YHVH, for He is highly exalted; the horse and his rider hath He thrown into the sea.

Song of Songs 1:1   The song of songs, which is Solomon's . . .

To Make Rams Thrive

Proverbs 27:26(–27)   The lambs will be for thy clothing, and the goats the price for a field.

Against Nocturnal Emission

Psalm 49:6   Wherefore should I fear in the days of evil, when the iniquity of my supplanters compasseth me about . . .

To Halt Menstrual Flow

Leviticus 15:28   But if she be cleansed of her issue, then she shall number to herself seven days, and after that she shall be clean.

To Arouse Love

Song of Songs 1:3   Thine ointments have a goodly fragrance; thy name is as ointment poured forth . . .

At a Betrothal

Song of Songs 4:1(–5)   Behold, thou art fair, my love; behold, thou art fair; thine eyes are as doves behind thy veil . . .

Blessing for a Newly Married Couple

Genesis 27:28   So God give thee of the dew of heaven, and of the fat places of the earth, and plenty of corn and wine.

Numbers 24:5(–7)   How goodly are thy tents, O Jacob, thy dwellings, O Israel!

To Make Peace and Harmony between Husband and Wife

Song of Songs 8:5   Who is this that cometh up from the wilderness, leaning upon her beloved?

To Cure Sterility

Deuteronomy 7:12   And it shall come to pass, because ye hearken to these ordinances, and keep, and do them . . .

For Easy Childbirth

Exodus 11:8   Get thee out, and all the people that follow thee . . .

Exodus 11:8   And all these thy servants shall come down unto me, and bow down unto me, saying: Get thee out, and all the people that follow thee."

Genesis 21:1   "And YHVH remembered Sarah as He had said, and YHVH did unto Sarah as He had spoken.

For a Newly Circumcised Infant

Genesis 48:20   And he blessed them that day, saying: "By thee shall Israel bless, saying: God make thee as Ephraim and as Manasseh." And he set Ephraim before Manasseh.

For Crying Children

Genesis 25:14   [A]nd Mishma, and Dumah, and Massa . . .

Jeremiah 31:15   Thus saith YHVH: Refrain thy voice from weeping, and thine eyes from tears . . .

On Entering a New Home

Exodus 40:2   On the first day of the first month shalt thou rear up the tabernacle of the tent of meeting.

Genesis 37:1   And Jacob dwelt in the land of his father's sojournings, in the land of Canaan.

Genesis 47:27   And Israel dwelt in the land of Egypt, in the land of Goshen; and they got them possessions therein, and were fruitful, and multiplied exceedingly.

To Study and to Strengthen Memory

Psalm 119:49   Remember the word unto Thy servant, because Thou hast made me to hope.

Proverbs 15:1   A soft answer turneth away wrath; but a grievous word stirreth up anger.

Proverbs 16:1   The preparations of the heart are man's, but the answer of the tongue is from YHVH.

Job 32:9   It is not the great that are wise, nor the aged that discern judgment.

Yoshuah 1:4   From the wilderness, and this Lebanon, even unto the great river, the river Euphrates.

Isaiah 26:1   We have a strong city; walls and bulwarks doth He appoint for salvation.

To Have Prayers Answered

Exodus 34:6(–7)   And YHVH passed by before him, and proclaimed: YHVH, YHVH, God, merciful and gracious, long-suffering, and abundant in goodness and truth . . .

Exodus 15:2   The YHVH is my strength and song, and He is become my salvation; this is my God, and I will glorify Him; my father's God, and I will exalt Him.

Dream Divination

Deuteronomy 29:28   The secret things belong unto YHVH our God; but the things that are revealed belong unto us and to our children forever . . .

Song of Songs 1:7   Tell me, O thou whom my soul loveth, where thou feedest, where thou makest thy flock to rest at noon . . .

9

Qameot

Talismans and Amulets

Talismanic magic is a very important part of ancient Hebrew magic. In the Qabbalistic tradition, a talisman is called a *qamea* (plural: *qameot*). The word *qamea* comes from *qama,* "to bind or knot," because this type of talisman is bound to the body.

The ancient talismans were mainly segullot (spells or charms) that were written down, allowing people to carry the power of the segullah on the body. It is the most common magical way to deal with mundane problems in Qabbalistic magic.

The most common aims of qameot were: to win or keep love, to gain favor, for success in business, to gain or keep health, for easy childbirth, for protection against demons or black magic or on journeys, and to defend against enemies or slanderers.

These talismans were often made by Qabbalistic magicians for their clients to help them with all kinds of problems. Yet some authorities, especially those who came from the Order of the Golden Dawn, warned against making talismans for many clients.

Detail from an amulet against Lilith in Sefer Raziel *(Amsterdam: 1701)*

Another point that beginners are apt to run away with, is that Talismans can be made wholesale. Suppose a dozen Talismans were made to do good to as many different people, a ray from yourself must charge each Talisman. You have sent out a sort of spiral from your aura which goes on to the Talisman and attracts a like force from the atmosphere—that is, if you have learned to excite the like force in yourself at the moment of consecration. So that, in the case supposed, you would have a dozen links connecting with you, like so many wires in a telegraph office, and whenever the force which any of these Talismans was designed to combat becomes too strong for the force centred therein, there is an instantaneous communication with you—so that the loss of force to which you would be continually liable might be such as to deplete you of vitality and cause you to faint.[1]

It is very obvious that the Qabbalistic qameot were used often, and were probably sold to clients. Even the great Israel Baal-Shem-Tov, the founder of modern Chassidism, made a living from selling qameot.

---

[1] Israel Regardie, *The Golden Dawn* (Woodbury, Minn.: Llewellyn, 1994), 480.

Jewish magicians were famous for being experts in the magical arts. (Even in nations with a strong magical tradition of their own, people came to Jewish magicians to ask for help because of the Jewish magician's reputation for magical knowledge.) I have always wondered—keeping in mind what has been said—how it is possible that Jewish magicians could do something that the magicians of the Golden Dawn deemed impossible (to accomplish without negative consequences). It is very unlikely that all of them could have made a beginner's mistake. Of course, it is likely that there were some charlatans among these magicians, but I do not believe that this could be true for all of them—certainly not for sages such as Israel Baal-Shem-Tov. But how could they do what they did—and how did they empower the qameot? What rites did they use?

In fact, it is very likely that the original Qabbalistic magicians never used any special ritual method to empower their talismans. In his very useful book *How to Make and Use Talismans,* Israel Regardie writes: "I would say that merely having completed the mechanical drawing of the talisman, in the best manner possible and with concentration, would invest it with a good deal of force. How much energy is involved depends entirely on the skill and development of the student. If he has the 'know-how' the talisman can be charged or consecrated all the way through the process of drawing it."[2]

The problem described above can be solved if the qamea is not charged with your own energy, but with the energy of the Divine. This is possible because there is always an unlimited source of energy available to anybody who knows how to draw upon it.

Agrippa of Nettesheim, who was much closer to the ancient Qabbalists than to the Golden Dawn, knew about the old secrets upon which was based the ancient art of making talismans. He explains that if a piece of matter is properly prepared in a way that corresponds to the heavenly principles, and if nothing stands in the way, the matter will receive a heavenly influence that will animate and empower it.[3]

The well-prepared form will attract the corresponding force; the form will create a vacuum that will be filled by the appropriate force.

Magic works because Nature cannot abide a vacuum . . .
DOLORES ASHCROFT-NOWICKI,
THE RITUAL MAGIC WORKBOOK, 22

---

[2] Israel Regardie, *How to Make and Use Talismans* (London: Aquarian Press, 1970), 47.
[3] Agrippa of Nettesheim, *De Occulta Philosophia,* book I, chapter 36).

This secret seems to have been lost by the Hermetic magicians. Magicians trained in the Golden Dawn tradition are told that the only way to empower a talisman is to charge it with your own energy. Some of them believe that a talisman must be charged; that otherwise it will be be inert. This belief closes them as channels, preventing them from creating the vacuum that draws the necessary energies into the qamea. (To avoid misunderstanding: I do not wish to reject the method of charging a talisman with your own power, but merely to open the mind of my readers to other possibilities.)

Today, ready-made talismans can be bought at occult suppliers. These are created by machines or by a silversmith who is not a magician. Such a talisman will not have any effect at all. No power was invested in it during the process of its making. It will be empty—and no vacuum has been created that is able to attract any useful energies. (As an analogy: Inside an empty box there is no vacuum; there is only emptiness.)

Types of Qameot

Qameot were made from paper or parchment and also from gold, silver, bronze, copper, or lead. The material depended both on the wealth of the person and on the purpose of the talisman. For example, lead, a poisonous metal, was often used for magical attacks.

It seems that paper and parchment were more common than metal. This may be because they are easier to work with. Paper was the most common material, probably because it was the cheapest.

Most qameot were rectangular—and thin, metal foil qameot were usually 4 to 12 centimeters long and 2.5 to 6 centimeters wide. Most are usually longer than wide. Some are square, however, and a very few are wider than long. For parchment, the size could be up to 21 centimeters long and 9 cemtimeters wide.

Parchment and metal qameot were usually long, thin strips that could be rolled together and were often worn in a metal, leather, or wooden case. Paper qameot could be any size and were often bigger, because the material was much cheaper. They either took the form of a long, thin strip, up to 47 centimeters long and 6.5 centimeters wide (in this case, they would be rolled together as described above), or they were up to 25 centimeters long and 16 centimeters wide, and would be folded to enable them to be carried on a person.

Some silver qameot were made of thicker material (0.5 to 1 millimeter) and were worn like ordinary amulets. These were usually square, rectangular, circular, hexagonal, heart- or hand-shaped, or pointed. They were worn by loops attached to the qameot, and their size usually measured about 5 centimeters × 5 centimeters, although some were as large as 9 centimeters × 6 centimeters or as small as 3 centimeters in diameter.

To make a parchment qamea, you can buy some inexpensive strips of parchment from a bookbinder (these are normally left over from his work). To make a metal qamea, you can buy some thin, metal foil of copper or brass. An art supply shop or a supplier for professional silversmiths may sell this material. To engrave it easily, it should be about 0.1 to 0.2 millimeters thick. If you cannot get thin, metal foil, you can still do what was done in the old times: Hammer it until it is thin enough. Use a small anvil and a plain hammer, which can be bought for a small sum at a silversmith supplier. Obtain silver of 0.5 millimeter and start hammering it. After a while, heat it with a blow torch until it glows red or orange, in order to keep it smooth. Think of the purpose of the qamea while hammering it into the metal, thus investing it with extra power.

An amulet case can be made of brass or copper, reed or bamboo, or any other material. Even a leather or linen tube will do.

Magical Alphabets, Sigils, and Symbols

Various magical alphabets were used to add extra power to the qamea. Included here are some examples of very common magical alphabets (i.e., the Celestial Alphabet or the Alphabet of the Angels).

How to Make a Qamea

I. Decide on the Aim of the Qamea

First, decide what you want the qamea to do. Be specific; you may get what you ask for! Most qameot take great care to describe and occasionally repeat in other words what the magician wants to happen. If you want to set a time limit, think about what is realistic and what is needed. Some qameot were designed to work as fast as possible—phrases such as "hurry and do not delay" are used in these cases. Do not rush this step! Once you have completed step 1, you have done half the work.[4]

2. Ask the Higher Forces for Help

Next, prepare the place of working. It may also be a good idea to open the quarters. (This is not absolutely necessary, but it may add to the power.) Then invoke the powers with which you want to work. This may be one or more of the Sefirot, one or more angels, or the Holy Letters themselves. It is very powerful and very traditional to invoke directly the Holy Letters of the Hebrew alphabet. Invocations such as "O ye Holy Letters" are not uncommon because the letters are the Divine Principles that bestow magical power to the writing or engraving of qameot. They are very pure and cannot be used for any work that is not in harmony with the Will of the Creator. (If you follow their instructions, you are quite safe from doing something wrong.)

Make sure you feel connected to the powers you work with before you go onto the next step!

3. Meditate on the Formula of the Qamea

Close your eyes and meet the Sefirah, angel, or the letters of the Hebrew alphabet with which you will work. Let them tell and show you what the qamea should look like. You will see the qamea as it will be when it is finished. (The letters or the angel may lead you to a place on the astral plane where you can see the finished qamea, or sometimes the letters may turn themselves into the qamea. It is also possible that the qamea appears in the corresponding Sefirah.) It is very traditional to make magical or sacred implements according to an image seen in a meditative state or inner vision. Such was the case when Moses made the implements of the Temple.[5] As it is written: "And look that thou make them after their pattern, which was shewed thee in the mount" (Exodus 25:40).

Note the material, text, and symbols used. Maybe you will be told to use one of the traditional formulas for talismans, or maybe you will be given a new one specially designed for your purpose.

Sometimes strange symbols or sigils will be used. Some of them will come from magical alphabets such as the Alphabet of the Angels; some

---

[4] "Thorough preparation means quick completion. In these matters, insufficient time is usually given to the preparation, and therefore the achievement is incomplete" (Dion Fortune, *The Cosmic Doctrine* [London: SIL, 1995], chapter 26, 153).

[5] To be more precise, Betzalel made them according to Moses's instructions.

will be combinations of different letters of one alphabet, while others may be received in meditation without even the magician knowing what their origin is. Do not worry if some of the symbols do not make sense to you, especially if the qamea is not for you. The symbols were designed to affect another person, and to him or her they will be of service (but do not expect him or her to explain their meaning). The result does not have to be very complicated. Sometimes, it is enough just to write down what you want to happen and add the magical names and biblical verses that correspond, or to use a traditional formula for talisman-making, changing it for your purpose if needed.

You may also be told or shown how to use the talisman, where to place it, and so forth. It is also possible that you will get further instructions on how to make or empower the qamea. Maybe you will be asked to add the powder of some special herbs to the ink or to hallow the qamea in a special incense. Do not be surprised if the instructions are quite detailed and you receive a precise recipe to follow.

Sometimes the Guardian Angel of the person concerned will appear, either in meditation or during the work. If this is the case, listen to his advice and accept his help. In some cases, you may be told that the kind of help you have asked for cannot be given because a karmic task must first be performed. If this is the case, simply accept it! You may also, however, be given instructions for the creation of a qamea that may help solve the karmic problem.

If you are experienced with this kind of work, the need to meditate before making the qamea may decrease. You may be able to receive most of the information you need in the process of the making. I advise, however, that you not omit the meditation; you may always get additional information, and you will avoid becoming overconfident and subject to hubris. Nevertheless, if you have already developed a strong contact with these forces, you may receive a great deal of information in the waking state once you start to think about the qamea.

This method of designing a talisman in a meditative state works best if the subconscious mind of the magician contains a multitude of symbols, formulas, and correspondences. A deep knowledge of Qabbalistic symbolism will therefore be very helpful for this exercise. For the same reason, I advise the reader to study the examples of qameot and formulas described in the remainder of this chapter. This pool of formulas and symbols is useful because communication with higher powers must be accomplished through the symbols already found in the subconscious mind of the magician. (More information about this can be found in chapter 24, Contacting the Maggid: The Inner Plane Teacher.)

4. Make the Qamea in a Meditative State

Unless the presence is still felt, call upon these for assistance: the Sefirah, the angel, the letters of the Hebrew alphabet, and any other helpers (such as the Guardian Angel of the client). When you feel their presence, start to make the qamea.

In order to write, use a new pen, pencil, or slate pencil (a book about calligraphy may show you how to make one). Alternatively, you could have one specially made for magical work. To engrave, use a nail (or better, cut the nail into two pieces and place the sharp end in a wooden handle), or in some cases you may even wish to use a crystal with a sharp end.

Some qameot look as if they were written without much care or skill, yet we know that those who made them were mainly rabbis or highly trained scribes. The reason for the apparent careless appearance of these qameot is neither lack of skill nor lack of care. The most likely reason is that these qameot were written in a state of deep meditative trance.

It is very important to write or engrave the qamea in such a state. Always start this work by entering a deep meditative state of consciousness. If you find yourself thinking rationally about the qamea—its design or function or whether it will work or not—then stop your work and bring yourself back into a meditative state. This may be done by reciting Divine Names or permutations of the Hebrew letters (for example, as is done in the Golem ritual; see chapter 21, Creating a Golem with the *Sefer Yetzirah*). In order to fall into a meditative state, you may also repeat, like a mantra, the purpose of the qamea. Make the qamea with a deep awareness that writing or engraving the letters is a powerful and creative magical act.

Offer yourself as a channel for the letters, Divine Powers, or angels with which you are working. Try not to use your own energy; just let their energy flow through you. You may not even be interested in the result; you may be interested only in following the instructions you have received. Just do what the Divine Forces have asked you to do. Forget the idea of performing anything; you are only the channel. You may even feel that these powers are moving your hand.

There is no need to add any energy of your own, because the act of writing or engraving the Divine Letters or symbols is creative in itself, and you may also rely on the energy of the powers you called upon. The amount of energy invested in the qamea depends only on your ability to be a channel.

Sometimes, you will get more information during the process of making the qamea. This may appear as a feeling that you should add a certain symbol or change a certain phrase. If so, follow the instructions. As in all kinds of meditation, some realizations need more time to come through.

If you have done the work correctly, you will feel vitalized after completing it. If you feel weak, something went wrong. Perhaps you used your own energy instead of acting as a channel for the higher powers.

Examples and Formulas

Examples and formulas are important material to give to the subconscious mind so that from this material, it can create and compose a new qamea. The following qameas may give you inspiration for your own.

Various abbreviations are used in most qameot. *Amen* is often abbreviated as 'א, *Selah* as 'ס, and *Hallelujah* as 'ה. Thus א'א'א'ס'ה' would mean *Amen Amen Amen Selah Hallelujah.*

A very useful technique is to diminish or expand the letters and, therefore, the power or influence of a word and what it represents.

To manifest the power of the Tetragrammaton, this formula can be used:

$$
\begin{array}{c}
\text{י} \\
\text{ה י} \\
\text{י ה ו} \\
\text{ה ו ה י}
\end{array}
$$

A very well-known formula to diminish fever is ABRAKADABRA, from the Aramaic *abra ke-dabra* (which means "diminish as the word"). Thus the fever will fade away like the word:

$$
\begin{array}{c}
\text{א ר ב ד כ א ר ב א} \\
\text{ר ב ד כ א ר ב א} \\
\text{ב ד כ א ר ב א} \\
\text{ד כ א ר ב א} \\
\text{כ א ר ב א} \\
\text{א ר ב א} \\
\text{ר ב א} \\
\text{ב א} \\
\text{א}
\end{array}
$$

A Qamea Formula to Gain Success and to Understand the Mysteries

In Thy Name, RACHUM (Compassionate One), in the Name of YAH YAH YAH EHIEH ASHER EHIEH, Melech Malki Melachim (The highest King over Kings of Kings), may He be blessed, I ask thee, METATRON, prince of the host of YOD HEH VAV HEH, to do all that I want (need) and to cut down all my enemies. In this Name and with thee, I have invoked the glowing star whose name is Mercury, and the angel, the prince, who is over it, whose name is [Insert name of angel that rules the matter] In this Name I have invoked you, that you give me all that I ask for and reveal to me all secrets of the world, and incline the whole world toward me and turn everyone in the world to love me.

A Qamea to Gain Favor

This qamea was made in the eleventh century in order for Abusad ben Baldin to gain favor. It was written on paper, and its dimensions are 18 centimeters × 26 centimeters. This is a typical example of a long talisman. The formula has been used for many purposes, including love magic.

(front page)

In the Name of YOD HEH VAV HEH we will act and succeed. May it be favorable before thee that thee suspend all thoughts of men, which are directed against Abusad ben Baldin, and all evil plans that his enemies have planned, and those that hate him and who quarrel with him. Suspend all evil thoughts and all plans and all intrigues of their hearts, and may their hearts be repressed and their mouths be silenced and their evilness be destroyed and their face be put to shame. And when they look at me—me, Abusad ben Baldin—they shall be filled with love for me, and their hearts shall be turned to love and all their hate shall be forgotten and not be remembered, and may I, Abusad ben Baldin, find grace and mercy and compassion in their eyes. In the name of YACHSIEL, the angel RAHUEL, and AVVABAZBARIEL ALTASPAM PENO MURIEL AD BECHALIEL SMO SHEALU UHHIEL and ANANIEL RAFPIEL PESPUA ⲨⲀⲋⲟⳆⲟⳞⲟⲟⲟⲒⲨ From today until eternity, Amen Amen Selah Selah. "Arise for our help, and redeem us for Thy mercies' sake."[6] In Thy Name, ELAHA CHAYAYA

WE-QAYAMA (Living and Existing God), for Thou art heroic, free this Abusad ben Baldin, BEHARSIM ARIRIM YE'USHUT TZEVAOT AVIM MUMIM and SISONIM STEY ADIM, you Holy Names, I invoke you with those holy and mighty Names, save this Abusad ben Baldin from all who seek evil for him and all who make plans against him and who think of evil plans. They shall not move and shall not turn their eyes to the right or to the left and shall not open their lips to speak an evil word about me, Abusad ben Baldin, and not have authority or ability to do evil to him. And bind their tongues that they cannot think of an evil plan against me, Abusad ben Baldin. ᴆᴆᴆᴆᴆᴆᴆᴆ ᴣᴣᴣᴣᴣᴣᴣ In the Name of ANAQTAM PASTAM PASPASIM and DIONISIS. And the LORD called unto Moses, and spake unto him out of the tabernacle of the congregation, saying, "And YOD HEH VAV HEH called unto Moses, and spake unto him out of the tabernacle of the congregation, saying,"[7] out of the tabernacle to him YOD HEH VAV HEH and spoke to Moses and called. ✂ 𐤀 𐤉 "A strong tower is the Name of YOD HEH VAV HEH, with Him hurries the righteous one and is saved."[8] May it be YOD HEH VAV HEH that Abusad ben Baldin will act successfully, and may YOD HEH VAV HEH be with him, and may YOD HEH VAV HEH turn mercy (love) and grace to Abusad ben Baldin in the eyes of all who see him, in the Name of YOD HEH VAV HEH TZEVAOT. May it be favorable before Thee, Melech Malki Melachim (The highest King over Kings of Kings), the Holy One, blessed be He who sits in 390 firmaments (390 = Shamaim = heaven), in the name of the angels that are set over each and every firmament. In the name of the four chayot who carry the high and exalted Throne, I invoke you with the great invocation with which Josef has invoked Gavriel, who has taught to him seventy languages, and Gavriel has transmitted to him this Name, YAH, for He 𐤉 is among the seventy names of the Holy One, blessed be He. And in him is grace and mercy (love) and honor and greatness and glory for Abusad ben Baldin.

---

[6] Psalm 44:27.

[7] Leviticus 1:1.

[8] Proverbs 18:10.

(back page)

> In the eyes of the princes and judges and in the eyes of all who see
> him, they shall help him in all things and hurry for his desires and
> not be late for an hour, and ye shall suspend all their hate that is in
> their heart and turn it into love in the Name of HEHA HEHA HEHA
> AHEH AHEH YAH EHIEH ASHER EHIEH has sent me to you (Exodux
> 3:14) from now forever and eternity Amen Amen Amen Selah Selah
> Selah Halelujah 𝖄 AH VE-YAHA YAHU HEHA AAH BABU MAV
> Amen Amen Selah TAFIEL PAR AFRESHNITA SHANTIEL SHANTIEL
> TZEVAOT Amen Amen Selah.

A Qamea to Be Successful

This qamea was made to make the shop of Abu Aliz ben Baqa successful. It
was written on paper, and its dimensions are 25 centimeters × 16 centimeters.
Note the direct invocation of the Holy Letters show in the original below.

Original invocation of the Holy Letters

In the Name of YOD HEH VAV HEH YISRAEL
we will act and succeed. For Abu Aliz ben Baqa by
whatever name he may be known. May the Lord
come forth in a blessing upon thy store houses
and upon all the work of your hands, and may He
bless the land which YOD HEH VAV HEH
ELOHEYCHA has given
to thee. In the Name of
TZEVAOT TZEVAOT TZEVAOT TZEVAOT
QADOSH QADOSH
QADOSH לליל QADOSH חחח טטט
Amen Selah Selah Selah. I have
invoked You all Holy Letters, that You gather the feet
of every man and woman and every merchant into
the shop of Abu Aliz ben Baqa. May they buy
from him of their own free will, Amen Amen
Amen Selah.

A Qamea to Cure

This qamea was made to cure Rabbi Eleazar, son of Esther. It is 7.5 centimeters × 5 centimeters and was made from a copper sheet.

A song of praise for MELECH OLAM (King of the World)
YAH YAH YAH YAHISH OLAMIM EHIEH ASHER EHIEH,
King who speaks the enfolded mystery to every evil and
stinking spirit not to cause pain to Rabbi Eleazar,
son of Esther, the servant of ELA SHEMAYAH (God of Heaven) CHAZAQ
VE-GER SHARAD U-PARAT TARGIN ASTAD U-
BAQTAH SALSALYARHA QALALQAM YAQIFAS
SURIEL RAPHAEL AVIEL ANAEL NAHARIEL NAGDIEL
AFHAPAHEL and ANANEL MAS PAS YAQRANDIRAS
YAHU KARMASIS ELHA RABBA TAHTAH GAHGAH
TAHTAH MARMAR PASPAS YOD HEH VAV HEH
QADOSH. In every place where this qamea will be seen, you
shall not detain him, Eleazar, son of Esther. And if you detain
him in this moment, you will be cast into a fiery burning furnace

(Daniel 3:6). Blessed art Thou, ADONNU, the Healer of the whole world send healing and cure to Eleazar. BUBRIT TABRIT BASHTARUT, the angels that are appointed over fever and shivering, cure Elazar. By a holy command!

A Qamea to Exorcise a Spirit

This qamea was made to exorcise a spirit from Klara, daughter of Kiranah. It was made from gold, and its dimensions are 4.3 centimeters × 11 centimeters. Note the combination of Hebrew and Greek letters.

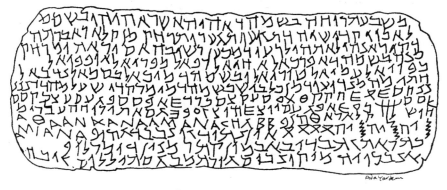

A copy of a qamea to exorcise a spirit

I adjure thee, spirit, in the Name of EHIYEH ASHER EHIYEH and in the name of his holy angels that thee move away and be rebuked[9] and be far away from Klara berata (daughter of) Kiranah, and from now on thou will not have still power over her; be bound and be banished from her. In the name of AFRACHAEL, ACHIEL, RAPHAEL, MAFRIEL, OFAFIEL, KAPUIEL, AMIEL TURIEL, and in the name of MICHAEL, BESAMEL, NEDVAEL. May she be sealed from thee and further from all evil. In the Name of the holy Logos of the World דד נגנ

ננ חס EΩE חקק OXΘ סעקצסכרדE אפפסס פגע סעצכקסס

ǮΦOIΣ ו πΕצτου עסיוצצו כואΑΕOΓ ס OΣK And also the signs of the Hebrew spirit who causes pain to Klara.

AΘA ANIXANAΛMANACHABB חנם Θ

AMIANAΦ בבדגחוΦ S תודזו S אין ΩΩΩΩ יה יה יה יה

כתראת זתבדי אב במון קתר מנין דימר ליפ

אנברויה מיקונכוס גור תמב גסת יללום זובה

A Qamea for Protection

This qamea was made to protect Yehudah ben Simchah. The qamea was made from parchment and is 4.3 centimeters × 11 centimeters (the original is on page 111, left column; the translation is on page 110). Note the diminishing letters and words on the left side of Solomon's Seal.

Abbreviations

- H.Y.V. (Ha-SHEM yishmarhu ve-jechihu) = "May God guard him and may he live"
- B.Sh.K.M.L.V. (Baruch Shem Kavod Malchuto Le-Olam Va-ed) = "Blessed be the Name of the Glory of His Majesty forever and eternally"
- S.H.P. (Sar ha-Panim) = "Prince of the Countenance"
- Y.Ch.Sh.L. (Yechi Shemo Le-Olam) = "May His Name live forever"
- A.A.S.V. (Amen Amen Selah Ve-Ad) = "Amen Amen Selah forever"

A Qamea to Ensure Health

This qamea to ensure health was made from thick silver, and its dimensions are 9 centimeters × 4 centimeters (see page 111). The translation appears below the image of the original qamea.

Abbreviations

- E.D.M.E. (ELHA De-Rabbi Meir Anenu) = "God of Rabbi Meir answer us!"
- K.Y.R.A. (Ken Yehi Razon Amen) = "Thus may it be Thy Will Amen"
- A.G.L.A. (Atah Gibor Le-Olam ADONAI) = "Thou art mighty forever Adonai"

May it be Thy Will, YOD YOD [YHVH] AVA AHUAH
EHIYEH ASHER EHIYEH,
That Thou Will do this for Thy sake and for the sake of Thy Holy Name,
That Thou will guard Yehudah ben Simchah H.Y.V.
from the Evil Eye and evil spirits and from every enemy and adversary and from fear
and trembling and fright and shaking and horror and from pain and shuddering and
headache and heart attack and heartache.
By the power of the forty-two-letter Name, AVAG YATATZ QARA
SHATAN NEGED YACHASH BATAR TZATAG
CHAQAV TANA YAGAL PAZAQ SHAQUTZIT
B.Sh.K.M.L.V.
In the Name of ZERAF ZERAF MITZ BAMUN ELOM
TITANER TISBER SABRA
APSEY UN METATRON S.H.P.
ELIYAHU HA-NAVI (Elijah, the prophet) YOHECH RAGLA
AHAVONIM EL SHADDAI, guard
Yehudah ben Simchah H.Y.V. Y.Ch.Sh.L.
from every kind of Evil Eye and from every enemy and misfortune and from fear and
trembling and fright and shaking and horror and from every devil or devils and liliths
(succubi) and evil spirits and from pestilence and from plague, and may no evil thing
have control over him hence and forever by the power of the Name
ARIMAH BARIMAH GARIMAH
DARIMAH HARIMAH VARIMAH
ZARIMAH CHARIMAH TARIMAH
YARIMAH KARIMAH LARIMAH
MARIMAH NARIMAH SARIMAH
ARIMAH PARIMAH TZARIMAH
QARIMAH RARIMAH SHARIMAH
TARIMAH[10] ANCHTAM PESTAM
PESPASIM DIONYSIM[11]
B.Sh.K.M.L.V.
SANVAI ve-SANSANVAI
Ve-SEMANGLOF
LALECH   LALECH

I beseech Thee ELOHEY YISRAEL (God of Israel) save the son of Thy maidservant from
all headache and pain in the head and from all disease hence and forever
A.A.S.V.

---

[10] Note that the first letters of these names are in alphabetical order.
[11] Maybe a permutation of Dionysos.

יהי רצון מלפניך זו אנא אהוה

אהיה אשר אדיה

שעשא לשמים ולשמים ולך הכל

שעשא את יהוה בן שמחה הזו

...

אלהנה בליהמה גרימה

דרימה הרימה ורימה

דרימה חלגמה פגרימה

דגרימה בריגה לרגמה

מרימה נדרגמה סדרגמא

עדרומה פהרומה צרדרגמה

קרימה רלימה שרדגמה

תלרימה אנקתם פסתם

פספסים דיונסיס

בשלשמלו

סנרי וסנסני

וסמנגלוף

ללה

עזכתריאל

פהצץ

FS.KI.94

Left: A qamea for protection

A qamea for health

בשם אהיה

In the Name of
EHIEH EHIEH ANTIEL
SHUSHIEL, and in the Name
of SANVAI SANSANVAI
SEMANGLOF HUTZ
LILITH and the first EVE.
In the Name of ANAQTAM
PASTAM PASPASIM
DIONISIS. In the Name of
MICHAEL and RAPHAEL
URIEL ARGAMAM
GAVRIEL E.D.M.E.
SHALMIEL YAHU Health
K.Y.R.A. A.G.L.A. ᛏ ᛏ

10

The Magic Bowl

The magic bowl (Aramaic: *kasa;* Hebrew: *kos*) is a very common item in Jewish magic and is a special type of amulet or talisman. (Theoretically, any object could be made into an amulet, even though some objects are not very useful for this purpose and some materials are not very good at holding the power invested in them.) The fact that magic bowls were seen as a type of amulet is documented in the bowl texts themselves, for in some of them the bowl is called a qamea (amulet). Not all amulets have to be hung or worn on the body. If a talisman is meant to protect a place or the people therein, it is wise to choose a shape that fits this purpose. In many ways, the magic bowl is to the house, dwelling, or family what the amulet is to the body or individual person.

There are some similarities between the magic bowls and the later spell bottles (also called witch bottles), which have been used since the 1600s, especially in Britain, and which are also well known in Voodoo. The earliest spell bottles were used for protecting the home against black magic, which was also the most common use of magic bowls. Both were often buried in the earth under the house of the person to be protected. Thus it is possible that the magic bowl is a more ancient version of spell bottles. The earliest magic bowls are at least more than one millennium older than the earliest spell bottles. In fact, there is evidence that the practice of using magic bowls in this way goes back as far as ancient Mesopotamia.

Many magic bowls have been found by archaeologists at sites of late antiquity, and they are mainly of Babylonian origin. These bowls are usually found buried upside-down in the corners of houses or rooms—in some cases, two of them facing each other to make a sphere.

There has been much speculation on how the bowls were used. Some scientists believe they were some kind of demon trap, a kind of magical mousetrap. This idea was described by J. A. Montgomery and is mainly based on two bowls (numbers 4 and 6 in his description). In the first case, he translates the beginning of the text: "Covers to hold in sacred Angels and all evil Spirits and the tongue of impious Amulet-spirits. [. . .]"[1]

This translation, however, is a bit dubious (although I have no better alternative to offer). Furthermore, the text seems to be written by somebody who did not entirely understand the principles involved, otherwise he would not have used the bowls against sacred angels (literally, holy angels) and evil spirits alike. The maker of the bowl could not have been a master of Jewish magic, but someone who tried to copy this type of work. (Similarly, there are people in our time who use magical formulas they do not fully understand.) Therefore, it cannot serve as evidence for this type of magic.

The second bowl that he uses as an example of his theory is indeed a true magic bowl. His translation starts: "A press [כיבשא] which is pressed down upon Demons and Satans and impious Amulet-spirits and Familiars [רוחי בישתא, literally evil spirits] and counter-charms and Liliths male and female [. . .]." I do not see any reason why J. A. Montgomery translates רוחי בישתא as "Familiars," as this is a specific form of spirit invested in an animal. The text ends: "[. . .] And whoever will transgress against this press and does not accept these rites, shall split asunder violently and burst in the midst [. . .] and his abode shall be in the seventh hell of the sea, from this day and forever. Amen, Amen, Selah."[2]

We see that the demons, devils, satans, and evil spirits are not kept under the "press," but are sent away to hell. I do not deny that it is generally

---

[1] *Aramaic Incantation Texts from Nippur* by J. A. Montgomery, Philadelphia: University Museum, 1913, (p. 133).

[2] Ibid. (p. 141).

possible that demons may have been captured with such methods, but it was not the main purpose of magic bowls. Such uses were undoubtedly exceptions. If his translation of the text of the first bowl is correct, it might be such an exception (and such methods may well be the origin of the legends of the genie in a bottle).

There might be also a misinterpretation of some passages that describe how the demons are bound. Furthermore, images of bound demons have been drawn in the middle of many bowls. Yet the idea of a demon bound is mainly a symbolic way of expressing that the demon has been disarmed or rendered harmless. As shown in the following example, this terminology is often found together with the command to go out or to be removed from the house. "Thoroughly bound, sealed, tied and charmed [are you] by the Name. May you be bound and sealed and removed from the house and dwelling of Dabarah son of Shelam and of Ima daughter of [. . .] and of Sharshay daughter of Ima and of Ikuma son of Ima and of all their house, and of all their dwelling, [you] all evil liliths and all devils (Shedim), demons, bindings, idols, [oaths], curses, misfortunes, mishaps, spells, evil sorceries, mighty deeds and all hateful things. [. . .]"[3]

Thus it is obvious that the demon is not kept inside the bowl, but instead is banished from the place protected by the bowl. No magician in his right mind would trap a demon in his own house or in the house of his client, thereby creating a magical time bomb.

One of the main reasons for the shape of the magic bowls is the principle of analogy. The bowl is shaped like a sphere because it creates a sphere of protection around the house and seals it against all evil. The bowl buried in the earth below the house creates an aura of protection similar to its own shape.

Occasionally, in the bowl texts, such a protective shield is seen as a

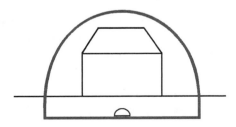

[3] Fiorella Cottier-Angeli Collection, Geneva. See: Joseph Naveh and Shaul Shaked, *Magic Spells and Formulae* (Jerusalem: Magnes Press, 1993), 113.

wall. In one text, the bowl describes "a wall of pure diamond (or steel),"[4] and in the text of another bowl, the house is " . . . sealed and countersealed by three large walls. . . ."[5]

If the bowl is actually buried in the earth, it will be connected to the great power of the earth and will absorb and transform negative energy. This is sometimes called the Mystery of the Earth in the terminology of ancient bowl magic. This is also the reason why the bowl is sometimes called a press (כישא), because it presses or drags the negative energies down into the earth to be absorbed. Even if the bowl is not buried in the earth, an astral connection to the earth can be made so that all negative energies are absorbed by the earth. In fact, the astral connection is even more important, so do not worry if it is impossible for you to bury the bowl because you live in an apartment. The bowl will adjust to your needs, and if you place it on the floor of your dwelling, it will have some connection to the earth. "The Mystery of Heaven is buried in the Heaven, and the Mystery of the Earth is buried in the earth."[6] Note that there is also a Mystery of the Heaven—the power to overcome evil that comes from "above." It refers to the fact that no evil force can stand against the Divine, just like no shadow can overpower the light.

In the ancient times the bowl would have been buried in the corner of the house or room, and occasionally four bowls were buried in four corners of the room to create an extra-strong protection from all four directions, as illustrated by a picture found at the center of one bowl:

Copy of an image from a magic bowl, Kelsey Museum 19502. (Seleucia-on-Tigris, sixth or seventh century CE, clay)

The square symbolizes the room, the four circles represent the four bowls, and the circle is the protective sphere created by the bowls. This picture, however, is merely to show how the bowls would have worked. This is not actually an example of such a set of four bowls. Here, one lone bowl

---

[4] Formerly in the possesion of V. Barakat, Jerusalem. See: Naveh J., and S. Shaked. *Amulets and Magic Bowls* (Leiden and Jerusalem: E. J. Brill/ Magnes Press, 1985), 124.

[5] Fiorella Cottier-Angeli Collection, Geneva. See: Naveh J., and S. Shaked. *Magic Spells and Formulae* (Jerusalem: Magnes Press, 1993), 113.

[6] Formerly in the possesion of V. Barakat, Jerusalem. See: Naveh J., and S. Shaked. *Amulets and Magic Bowls* (Leiden and Jerusalem: E. J. Brill/Magnes Press, 1985), 124.

gives protection from all four directions. The effect of four bowls could also be achieved with a single bowl, and in fact single bowls were probably much more common. What is important is the intention. If you intend one bowl to have a certain effect, this will be so—that is, if you are a well-trained magician. Even if you are not, you would be well advised to try to make a single bowl work as well as you can rather than to try four bowls at once. Most of the bowls described in this chapter have been created to protect the owner in such a way. There will be one example of a set of four bowls. (Other examples of how to symbolize protection from the four directions will be shown later in this chapter.)

There is also another way of using a magic bowl, and this method is still employed in the Near East: It is based on filling a bowl with water or other liquids in order to charge them with a specific type of power. Methods of charging water or other liquids are very ancient, and some uses of this kind are explained in other chapters of this book.

How to Make a Magic Bowl

To make a magic bowl, the magician formed a bowl from clay and wrote the magical text inside the bowl before hardening it in the fire. The process of baking clay in the fire was often considered a way to empower the item, thus perfecting the process of charging.

Bowls were usually inscribed on the inside and in a spiral shape, beginning from the bowl's center and moving toward the rim in clockwise (deosil) fashion. (The spiral writing creates a whirl that repels all evil.) If the space in the bowl was too small, writing was continued on the outside (beginning at the rim and going clockwise again).

The average size of a magical bowl is about 16 centimeters in diameter at the top and about 5 centimeters deep. The biggest bowl ever found, however, measures about 34 centimeters in diameter and is about 15 centimeters deep.

A method that can be used today involves either making a bowl from clay or buying a new china bowl that has not been used before. Write on the inside of the bowl with thermo-hardening water-based paint for porcelain or clay. This is a type of color that will not be washed away after the bowl has been baked in an ordinary oven.

In old times the floor of a house itself was probably earthen. Only very rich people would have had a proper floor. In any case, it would have been easy to bury the bowl under the floor. This may, however, be a problem in a modern apartment. If you cannot bury your magic bowl, place it under your bed or under any piece of furniture. (Many modern cupboards or bookshelves, for example, have a small space that keeps the lowest board from the ground—just large enough for a bowl.)

Make sure you direct your intention on connecting the bowl to the earth. It may help to take some real earth (soil) from the garden, and place it around the bowl. You may, for example, place the bowl inside a shoebox filled with earth.

The Design of a Magic Bowl

The basic procedure of designing the bowl is the same as described for the qamea (talisman) in chapter 9.

Some (though not all) magic bowls have a central symbol. This is either an image of the demon, usually drawn bound or defeated, or a protective symbol. The most common protective symbol is the cross within the circle.

In modern magic, this is considered to be a symbol of Malchut. It is also related to the ancient way of writing the letter *Tet.* (Interesting—for this letter means "snake," and in some bowls, a snake in the shape of a circle was used as a symbol for protection from demons or to defeat the demon.) In one case, this symbol was drawn over the whole bowl, and the text was written into the created four quarters—as was usual, from the center of the quarter to the rim. This division corresponded to the four directions.

Variations of this arrangement include four smaller crosses (the ancient form of the letter *Tav,* which is related to the earth).

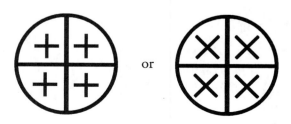

or

But there are other possibilities as well. There might have been a simple square as a center symbol, or much more complex images. Here are a few other examples:

A snake in the shape of a protective circle

Here, the snake surrounds, seals, and binds.

The spiked spiral is also used as a protective symbol.

Here, the spiked spiral appears as a protection on the right and left side of a demon drawn in a rather abstract way.

Another spiral-shaped protective symbol

Here is another symbol that reminds us of a snail's shell. The text belonging to this bowl starts with the Shma Yisrael—"Hear Israel"— the same text also found in the mezuzot, the "house phylacteries." Note also the text inside the figure.

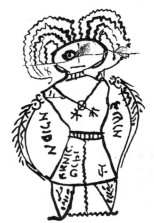

A very detailed image of a demon. Note the text written around and inside the figure.

This aggressive demon is called Tzepeasq. He is bound with foot chains.

This evil spirit is called Dodib, the strangler, who kills young in the womb of their mother. He is exorcised in the names of the Babylonian gods Shamash, Sin, Bel, Nannai, and Nirig (Nergal).

This unknown demon is probably an image of Lilith. This is, however, uncertain, for the passage describing the name of the demon is illegible.

Another unknown demon

The Text of the Magic Bowl

In the case of magic bowls, I advise writing the text in Hebrew script. Not only will it be more powerful, but also it will be much easier to write in a clockwise manner. To write a non-Hebraic name in Hebrew script, just listen to the sound. For example, Tom, son of Lisa would be written as:

טום סאן אוף ליסא

Or write "son of" in Hebrew—Tom ben Lisa:

טום בן ליסא

If you cannot write in Hebraic, use the same method for the whole text. For example, if your magic bowl starts with the sentence: "Sealed and guarded is the house of Tom, son of Lisa . . .," you could write it like this:

סילעד ענד גארדעד איז סע הויס אף טום סאן אוף ליסא

This is not Hebraic writing. It is English written in Hebrew script, as you will see if you try to read it. All you need know is the Hebrew alphabet.

Further, because magic bowls were a very effective magical device, there were some illiterate magicians who made them. They used a pseudoscript that was not unlike young children imitating script. (This is not to be confused with magical signs and sigils, which are often impossible to translate.) This type of pseudoscript may seem useless, but I think that it might have worked. If such "writing" was performed in a deep meditative state and with a clear intention, it might have been almost as powerful as it would have been if it was actual script. (As I have said, it is the intention that matters in magic.)

It is very important that you focus your Kavvanah (magical intention) on the purpose of the bowl while you write the text. You must intend all negative energies to be repelled by the spiral whirl and absorbed into the (center of the) earth.

Formulas for Magic Bowl Texts

There are some standard formulas that are used regularly in magic bowls. They have proved to be very effective. Nevertheless, do not feel restricted by them. The variety of texts is so vast that no final rules can be given. The design of your bowl is, after all, up to you.

In all these examples the name of the client has been replaced by Pb"P (פב"פ), which is an abbreviation for Ploni ben Ploni, the classical substitution for a name in ancient magical texts. In the translation, it will be written as [Insert name], son/daughter of [Insert name of mother]. Please note that magic bowls were sometimes made for more than one person.

בשמך אני עושה

In Thy Name I act.

דין רזא לאסותא לפב"פ

This mystery is designated for healing [Insert name],
son/daughter of [Insert name of mother]

מזמן הנא כאסא לחתממתא ונטרתא דביתה ודורה ודפגרה
דפב״פ דתיזה מנה

Designated is this bowl for the sealing and guarding of the
house, dwelling, and body of [Insert name], son/daughter of
[Insert name of mother] that there should go out from
him/her. . . . [Followed by a long list of all things and
beings that should be banished.]

ניתחתים וניתנטר ביתה ודורה ופגרה דפב״פ ותיזה מנה

Sealed and guarded shall be the house, dwelling, and body of [Insert
name], son/daughter of [Insert name of mother] that there should go
out from him/her. . . . [Followed by a list of all things and
beings that should be banished.]

וחתומי חתימיו וקטורי קיטריו ולחושי לחישיו בשום

Thoroughly bound, sealed, tied, and charmed
[art thou/are you] by the name.

אסורי אסירין תאסרין ותיחתמון ותירחקון מן ביתיה ודירתיה
פב״פ ופב״פ ומן ביתיהון כוליה ומן כולה דירתהון

May thou be bound and sealed and removed from the house
and dwelling of [Insert name], son of [Insert name of mother]
and of [Insert name], daughter of [Insert name of mother]
of all their house, and of all their dwelling, [thee/you] all. . . .
[Followed by a list of all things and beings
that should be banished.]

וניתכביש כורחנה ונחדרה שורא דאדמסא לפב״פ

And his illness shall be pressed down, and a wall of pure diamond
[or steel] shall surround [Insert name], son/daughter of
[Insert name of mother].

ונתנטר בלליא ובימאמא

and he/she will be guarded by night and by day.

חתימין וימחתמין

[May the following be] sealed and countersealed:
("Sealed and countersealed" or "Sealed and double sealed."
This expression is meant to create an extra strong seal.)

(male):

מן ימינו הרביאל ומשמאלו עוזיאל ומלפנו סאסיאל ומעליו
שכינת אל ומאחורו קדישאל

(female):

מן ימינה הרביאל ומשמאלה עוזיאל ומלפנה סאסיאל ומעליה
שכינת אל ומאחורה קדישאל

On his/her right is Harbiel (the Sword of God), on his/her left is
Uziel (the Strength of God) (or in some versions, Michael), before him/
her is Sasiel (Groom [of Horses] of God),[2] above him/her is Shechinat
El (the Presence of God), and behind him/her is Qaddishel (the
Holiness of God) (or in some versions, the word of
Qaddishel מימר קדישאל).

(plural):

מן ימינהון הרביאל ומשמאלהון עוזיאל ומלפנהון סאסיאל
ומאחוריהון קדישאל מלמועלה שכינת אל

On their right is Harbiel (the Sword of God), on their left is
Uziel (the Strength of God) (or in some versions, Michael),
before them is Sasiel (Groom [of Horses] of God), behind them is
Qaddishel (the Holiness of God) (or in some versions,
the repose of Qaddishel מנוחת קדישאל), and above
them is Shechinat El (the Presence of God).

These are invocations of four angels—not the commonly known archangels, but special ones used in some bowl texts, although the traditional ones
could be used as well. Sometimes, the text invokes only two or three of
them: "In the name of Michael and in the name of Raphael, etc. . . ."

Things against Which the Bowls Were Used

A magic bowl may be used against all kinds of negative influences. There
are some influences, however, against which a bowl is more often directed.
(You can use the bowl to protect you against as many things as you need,
but take care not to banish too much! This is especially important if you
want to work with magic. Make sure not to include any formula that
would also banish the angelic forces you must invoke for your magical
work.)

---

[2] Or Moth of God.

Magical Attacks

- Evil sorceries (חרשין בישין): black magic in general
- Evil (magic) practices (מעבדא בישין): methods of ritual black magic
- Spells (מללתא): attacks based on nonritual magic
- Curses (לוטתא): spells to harm or cause accidents, illness, or bad luck
- Charms (חומרא): spells to manipulate the victim
- Necklace charms (ענקתא): crystals or bones that are magically empowered and hung around the neck
- Vows (נידרא) or (נדרי): magical manipulations based on a vow
- The Evil Eye (עין בישין or עין הרע): a magical attack performed by looking at the victim
- Idols (יפתכרין): magical puppets or fetishes used for an evil purpose

Nonincarnated Entities

- Evil spirits (רוחי בישתא or רוחין בישין) or wicked spirits (רוחי זידניתא): Both the departed, evil earth-bound souls who haunt the living, and evil nature spirits
- "Shedim" devils (שידא): the Qlippot, the unbalanced forces opposed to the angels
- Satans (סטנין): devils who try to seduce the souls of men and women to do evil
- Devs demons (דיוא): astral entities of an evil or perverted nature
- Liliths (לילין or ליליתא): Female demons known since ancient times in Babylon as the *liltu*. The name comes from the word *lailah* (night). They are succubi who come at night and seduce men in their dreams, causing nocturnal emission, from which comes new demons who are their children. The name Lilith is used occasionally for the queen (and mother) of all demons. Sometimes the liliths are called Istarta (איסתרתא). This name comes from Astarte/Ishtar, which is the name of a Babylonian goddess: Lilith and Astarte/Ishtar are identified with one another. Originally, however, they were not the same. The name Lilith was never the name of a goddess, but instead was always a demoness. Thus I disagree with those authors (usually female New Age writers) who think of Lilith as a demonized

goddess.[3] Lilith was always considered a demon queen. This brings us to another of her aspects: She was considered jealous of pregnant women and able to cause abortions and the death of children. Many magic bowls were intended to protect against her for this reason. The same is true for the liliths.

- Night demons (טולינין): the male equivalent of the lilith; an incubus
- Mevachalta the Tormentor (מבכלתא): A demon or evil being that causes nightmares. It can be equated with the English *nightmare* (i.e., the being that causes bad dreams, not the dreams themselves) or the *drud* or the German *Alp,* who causes *Alpträume.* It may be that this is not a demon, but is the astral body of a sorcerer.

Bad Luck and Miscellaneous

All these are self-explanatory.

- Accidents (קריתא or קירין)
- Plagues, afflictions, or evil occurrences (פגעי)
- Encroachments (קרוביא)
- Terrors (סרודתא)
- Nightmares (literally, dreams) (חילמא)
- Evildoers of harm (מזיקין בישין)
- Injurers (נזקין)

Black Magic Purposes of Bowls

Some bowls have been used to curse instead of protect. Such bowls simply function in the opposite way: Instead of a repelling whirl, they create a vortex that draws evil to the victim. In this book, however, I will not be giving any instructions on how to use magic bowls to curse others!

Examples of Bowl Texts

In order to help you design your own magic bowl, the following are examples of bowl texts found at sites of antiquity. (Only the first text is taken from a set of four bowls; all the other texts come from single bowls.)

---

[3] Sometimes, an ancient text (the Alphabet of Ben Sira) is quoted in which Lilith is described as the first wife of Adam. This text does exist, but it was a satire written for amusement and no more a document of true mystical or religious beliefs than Monty Python's *Life of Brian.* (Compare *Einleitung in Talmud und Midrasch* by Günter Stemberger and *Looking for Lilith* by Eliezer Segal.)

Example 1: Four bowls with this text, varying only in a few insignificant differences, were buried at the four corners of a house.

> Sealed and countersealed are the house and threshold of Dodi daughter of Achat, from all evil plagues, from all evil spirits, from the tormentors, from the liliths, from all injurers, that ye approach not to her, to the house and threshold of Dodi daughter of Achat, which is sealed with three [signet] rings and countersealed with seven seals from every lilith and injurer. Amen Amen Selah.

Example 2: A bowl for healing with a simple square in the middle.

> Healing from Heaven to Maadar-Afri daughter of Anushay. May there lie in the dust the injuries of vows of every place and every shaded place. And every evil thing, and whatever oppresses Maadar-Afri, daughter of Anushay, the sorcery and the magic practices which are performed, all will be pressed and kept removed in the earth before her by the power of his army. "And it came to pass, when the ark set forward, that Moses said, Rise up, o YHVH, and let thine enemies be scatterd, and let them that hate thee flee before thee" (Numbers 10:35). AQDAD VE-ABRA Amen Amen Selah.

Bowl for healing

Example 3: This is a single bowl that uses the power of the letters to protect the house and the family.

Bowl to protect the house and family

In Thy Name I act. Sealed and countersealed shall be [these]: Goray son of Burzanduch, and Gushnay daughter of Ifra-Hurmiz and Goray son of Fradaduch, themselves, their sons, their daughters, their houses, their dwellings: and all evil spirits, and devils, and plagues, and demons, and afflictions, and satans, and bans, and tormentors, and [spirits of] barrenness, and [spirits of] abortion, and sorcerers, and vows, and curses, and magic rites, and idols, and wicked charms, and [spirits of] errantness, and shadow [spirits], and liliths, and [evil] masters, and all evil doers of harm. May they move and go out of them, of their sons, of their daughters, of their houses, of their dwellings, of their seven thresholds, by the chain, by the mystery of the [seal-]rings, by the twelve hidden and guarded mysteries. These are the letters: NUN TET TAV ALEF TAV QOF SHIN PE RESH HEH NUN DALET ALEF TZADDE YOD TZADDE LAMED YOD [. . .] Amen Amen Selah.

Example 4: The next text starts with this symbol in the center:

Appointed is this bowl for the sealing and guarding of the house, dwelling, and body of Huna son of Kupitay (aram. Huna bar Kupitay), that there should go out from him the tormentors, evil dreams, curses, vows, sorceries, magic practices, devils (*shedim*), demons, liliths, encroachments and terrors. The Mystery of Heaven is buried in the Heaven, and the Mystery of the Earth is buried in the earth. I say the mystery of this house against all that there is in it: against devils (shedim), and against demons, and against sorceries, and against magic practices, and against all the messengers of idolatry, and against all troops, and against charms, and against demonesses, and against all the mighty devils (shedim), and against all the mighty satans, and against all the mighty liliths. This word I tell you. He who accepts it finds goodness, and he who is bad and does not accept the mystery words, angels of wrath come against him, and sabres and swords stand before him and kill him. Fire surrounds him, and flame comes against him. Whoever listens to the word sits in the house, eats and feeds, drinks and pours drink, rejoices and joy, he is a brother to bretheren and a friend to the dwellers of the house, he is a companion of children and is called educator, he is an associate of cattle and is called good fortune. Accept peace from your Father who is in Heaven and sevenfold peace from male gods and from female goddesses. He who makes peace wins the [law]suit. He who causes destruction is burned in the fire.

The text continues with these magic sigils:

This bowl includes a blessing for friends and a punishment for enemies. A wall of pure diamond is set up for extra-strong protection.

Sealed and guarded shall be the house, dwelling, and body of Huna son of Kupitay, and there shall go out from him the tormentors, evil dreams, curses, vows, spells, magic practices, devils, demons, liliths, encroachments and terrors. His sickness shall be pressed down, and a wall of pure diamond shall surround Huna son of Kupitay. The sickness, devil and demon of Huna son of Kupitay shall be pressed down and he will be guarded by night and by day. Amen.

Example 5: A final example is a bowl against the evil Tormentor, interesting for its unusual design.

Bowl against the Tormentor

(Text around the image): This is the image of the Tormentor (Mevachalta) that appears in dreams and takes on [various] forms. This is the bond from today and forever. Amen Amen Selah. Gabriel, Nuriel.

In each of the fourteen triangles is written:

YOD HEH VAV HEH
YOD HEH VAV

(The spiral text around the rim): This is the firm seal and guarding and sealing of Solomon, for Panah-Hurmiz son of Rashnduch and for Kvasti daughter of Gavyot, and for Baftoy daughter of Kvasti and for Rashnduch daughter of Kvasti, and for all the people of their houses, for their partners, for their sustenance and for their whole houses. May there be for them good healing from Heaven in the Name of EL SHADDAI and in the Name of SAMECH ASGAR ABRISHACH SAMECH Amen Amen Selah, Amen.

Angels in Qabbalistic Magic

Angels are very important in Qabbalistic magic. Therefore, it is essential to understand their nature. The biblical term for an angel is *Malach* (מלאך), and in the plural *Malachim* (מלאכים). Malach simply means "messenger," and is applied to both human messengers (see Genesis 32:4)[1] and the angelic messengers of God (see Genesis 32:2).[2] Further on in the Bible, it is not always clear whether God or one of his angels acts or speaks. Sometimes in the Bible an angel is simply called a "man," as in the case of the man who wrestled with Jacob (Genesis 32:25). In post-biblical Hebrew scriptures, the term *Malach* is used exclusively for nonhuman divine beings. The term *angel* comes from the Greek *angelos,* which can also be used for both human and divine messengers. Only when this term was used in the Latin Bible and became a part of other European languages did it eventually became our word *angel.*

---

[1] "And Jacob sent messengers (malachim) before him to Esau his brother unto the land of Seir, the field of Edom."

[2] "And Jacob went on his way, and the messenger-angels of God (malachey Elohim) met him."

Jacob Wrestling with the Angel *by Julius Schnoor von Carolsfeld*

Not all angels are the same; they are classified according to heavenly hierarchies. The majority of angels are simple beings who can perform only one mission. "One angel does not perform two missions, nor is one mission performed by two angels" (Genesis Rabbah 50:2).

Angels are powerful because they consist of a principle in its purest form. The angels of mercy are perfectly merciful—there is no element of severity in them—and the angels of severity are absolutely severe (there is no element of mercy in them).

Very often angels are divided into angels of fire and angels of snow (hail). These two groups represent the two polarities of force and form on the Tree of Life (i.e., *Shin* and *Mem* in the *Sefer Yetzirah*).[3] Note that the two opposing forces are not said to be fire and water. Fire is energy (force) and snow or hail is a solid form. The concept of two opposing polarities is also indicated in the Bible. "I saw YHVH sitting on His throne, and all the host of Heaven standing by Him on His right hand and on his left" (1 Kings 22:19).

Originally, Michael and Gabriel were seen as the highest archangels, governing the two principles. (Michael was seen as the archangel of water, for

---

[3] The angels of the middle pillar are sometimes called the *Irin* (Watchers), for they watch that the balance between the polarities is kept. (The Irin are mentioned in Daniel 4:14.)

his name begins with *Mem,* and Gabriel was the archangel of fire, because his name has the same root as the Sefirah Gevurah.) Michael was related to Chesed, and Gabriel to Gevurah. Many occultists today think of Michael as the archangel of fire, because he is the angelic warrior, and Gabriel as the archangel of water due to his regency over dreams. Furthermore, the Sefirot that these angels are related to have changed. Today, Gabriel is the archangel of Yesod, and Michael is the archangel of either Tiferet or Hod, depending on the system of correspondences used.

The term *archangel* does not appear in the ancient texts. Archangels are called "ministering angels" (Malachey ha-Sharet) in the Aggadah.[4] In occult texts they are often called "princes" (*Sarim*) or "overseers" (*Shoterim*).[5]

Archangels are more complex and not as one-sided as the lesser angels, being quite able to understand more than one principle of existence. Students who are new to the occult are often confused by different correspondences in various texts. My answer: In a magical group, someone may stand in the east in one ritual, but in the west in another ritual. The same applies to the great archangels. Some of them have changed their office over time. The only difference is that archangels are immortal beings, and they switch their offices only every thousand years. Because, however, they have done many jobs over the millennia, they are quite able and willing to operate in one of their past offices if asked to do so in a ritual performed nowadays.

In Qabbalistic magic, angels are not visualized in the same way as the baroque *putti.* They are often described in images of fire and thunder, such as the angel[6] who appeared to Daniel: "I lifted up mine eyes, and looked, and behold a *man* (an angel) clothed in linen, whose loins were girded with fine gold of Uphaz; his body also was like the beryl, and his face as the appearance of lightning, and his eyes as torches of fire, and his arms and his feet like in colour to burnished brass, and the voice of his words like the voice of a multitude" (Daniel 10:5–6). Or the angel who appeared to Moses: "And the Angel of YHVH appeared unto him in a flame of fire out of the midst of a bush; and he looked, and, behold, the bush burned with fire, and the bush was not consumed" (Exodus 3:2).

In other cases, they have four or six wings, or many faces:[7] "In the year

---

[4] Aggadah are legends, folklore, or ethical texts in classical rabbinic literature, as opposed to Halachah (legal texts).

[5] Strictly speaking, an angelic prince is a higher archangel than an overseer.

[6] Probably Gabriel, who is mentioned in Daniel 8:16.

[7] As in Ezechiel 1.

that king Uzziah died I saw YHVH sitting upon a throne high and exalted, and His train filled the temple. Above Him stood the seraphim; each one had six wings: with twain he covered his face and with twain he covered his feet, and with twain he did fly" (Isaiah 6:1–2).

These descriptions may appear strange to the modern mind, but there is meaning in these images. The number of wings symbolizes the high spiritual level to which these beings belong, and the fire and lightning are symbolic of the power and energetic vibration of these beings. Fire is a very basic type of energy, and the fear of fire is a fundamental instinct. Fear of lightning falls into the same category. Wings represent the idea of flying—again, a basic human desire that often appears in dreams. All these images are very easily accepted by the subconscious mind, and because they have been used over the ages, they are very powerful symbols that are capable of bringing us into contact with the angelic realms.[8]

The angels were made on the first day of creation. They are the divine agents who became the builders of the lower, material worlds.

> And the Angel of the Presence spake to Moses according to the word of YHVH, saying: Write the complete history of the creation, how in six days YHVH Elohim finished all His works and all that He created, and kept Shabbat on the seventh day and hallowed it for all ages, and appointed it as a sign for all His works. For on the first day He created the heavens which are above and the earth and the waters and all the spirits which serve before Him—the angels of the presence, and the angels of sanctification, and the angels [of the spirit of fire and the angels] of the spirit of the winds, and the angels of the spirit of the clouds, and of darkness, and of snow and of hail and of hoar frost, and the angels of the voices and of the thunder and of the lightning, and the angels of the spirits of cold and of heat, and of winter and of spring and of autumn and of summer, and of all the spirits of His creatures which are in the heavens and on the earth, (He created) the abysses and the darkness, eventide (and night), and the light, dawn and day, which He hath prepared in the knowledge of His heart. And thereupon we saw His works, and praised Him, and lauded before Him on account of all His works; for seven great works did He create on the first day.[9]

---

[8] Some magicians see angels as huge pillars of light and fire or as geometric shapes. In cases where you are unsure, use what works for you.

[9] The Book of Jubilees 2:1–3.

Due to their pureness, all angels are free of Evil Urges (Yetzer ha-Ra).[10] Furthermore, they are not given a free will. Their nature as divine messengers permits them only to carry out the Divine Will.

> Rav Yehudah said in Rav's name: When the Holy One, blessed be He, wished to create man, He [first] created a company of ministering angels and said to them: Is it your desire that we make a man in our image? They answered: Lord of the Universe, what will be his deeds? These (literally, such and such) will be his deeds, He replied. Thereupon they exclaimed: Lord of the Universe, what is man that Thou art mindful of him, and the son of man, that Thou thinkest of him? [11] Thereupon He stretched out His little finger among them and consumed them with fire. The same thing happened with a second company. The third company said to Him: Lord of the Universe, what did it avail the former [angels] that they spoke to Thee [as they did]? The whole world is Thine, and whatsoever Thou wishest to do therein, do it. When He came to the men of the age of the flood, and of the division [of tongues] whose deeds were corrupt, they said to Him: Lord of the Universe, did not the first [company of angels] speak fairly? Even to old age I am the same, and even to hoar hairs will I carry [you],[12] He retorted.[13]

As can be seen from the previous passage, and even more clearly in the next passage, lesser angels do not understand the nature of humankind. They also find it difficult to understand why man, imperfect as he is, should receive so many gifts from God.

> R. Yoshuah b. Levi also said: When Moses ascended on high, the ministering angels spake before the Holy One, blessed be He, "Lord of the Universe! What business has one born of woman amongst us?" "He has come to receive the Torah," He answered to them. Said they to Him, "That secret treasure, which has been hidden by Thee for nine hundred and seventy-four generations before the world was created. Thou desirest to give to flesh and blood! What is man, that Thou

---

[10] Babylonian Talmud, Shabbat 88b; Genesis Rabbah 48:11.
[11] Babylonian Talmud: Sanhedrin 38b.
[12] Psalm 8:5.
[13] Isaiah 46:4.

art mindful of him, and the son of man, that Thou thinkest of him? O Lord our God, how glorious is Thy Name over all the earth! Who hast set Thy glory [the Torah] upon the Heavens!"[14] "Return them an answer," bade the Holy One, blessed be He, to Moses. "Lord of the Universe" replied he, "I fear lest they consume me with the [fiery] breath of their mouths." "Hold fast to the Throne of Glory," said He to him, "and return them an answer," as it is said, He maketh him to hold on to the face of his throne, and spreadeth his cloud over him, whereon R. Nachman observed: This teaches that the Almighty spread the lustre (Ziv) of His Shechinah and cast it as a protection over him. He [then] spake before Him: Lord of the Universe! The Torah which Thou givest me, what is written therein? I am the Lord thy God, which brought thee out of the Land of Egypt.[15] Said he to them [the angels], "Did ye go down to Egypt; were ye enslaved to the Pharaoh: why then should the Torah be yours? Again, what is written therein? Thou shalt have no other gods:[16] Do ye dwell among peoples that engage in idol worship? Again what is written therein? Remember the Shabbat day, to keep it holy:[17] Do ye then perform work, that ye need to rest? Again what is written therein? Thou shalt not take [the Name of YHVH, thy God, in vain; i.e. to make an oath]:[18] Is there any business dealings among you [so you need to speak an oath]?[19] Again what is written therein, honour thy father and thy mother;[20] have ye fathers and mothers? Again what is written therein? Thou shall not murder. Thou shalt not commit adultery. Thou shalt not steal;[21] is there jealousy among you; is the Evil Urge (Yetzer ha-Ra) amongst ye?" Straightaway they conceded to the Holy One, blessed be He, for it is said, O YHVH, our Lord, how glorious is Thy Name, etc.[22] whereas "Who has set Thy glory upon the heavens" is not

---

[14] Psalm 8:5, 2.

[15] Exodus 20:2.

[16] Exodus 20:2.

[17] Exodus 20:7.

[18] Exodus 20:6.

[19] An oath had the function of certifying a business transaction, in the same way as a signature today.

[20] Exodus 20:11.

[21] Exodus 20:12.

[22] Psalm 8:10. (Biblical quotations are often abbreviated with "etc." in the Talmud because parchment was expensive and copying texts involved a great deal of work.)

written. Immediately each one was moved to love him [Moses] and transmitted something to him, for it is said, Thou hast ascended on high, thou hast taken spoils (i.e., the Torah); Thou hast received gifts among man:[23] As a recompense for their calling thee man, thou didst receive gifts. The Angel of Death too confided his secret to him, for it is said, and he put on the incense, and made atonement for the people;[24] and it is said, he stood between the dead and the living, etc.[25] If he had not told it to him, whence had he known it?[26]

Humankind has a special place in creation. Whereas the angels were created as flawless, they are limited to only one aspect of the whole. Man was created in the image of God, but imperfectly. Just as a small charitable donation given by a poor man counts more than the same amount given by a rich man, the praise of imperfect humankind counts more than the praise given by angels.

Israel is dearer to the Holy One, blessed be He, than the ministering angels, for Israel sings praises to the Lord every hour, whereas the ministering angels sing praises but once a day. And whereas Israel mentions the Name of God after two words, as it is said: "Hear, Israel, YHVH,"[27] the ministering angels only mention the Name of God after three words, as it is written: Holy, holy, holy, YHVH Tzevaot. Moreover, the ministering angels do not begin to sing praises in Heaven until Israel has sung below on earth, for it is said: When the morning stars sang together, then all the Beney Elohim (Sons of God) shouted for joy![28] It must be this: One [group of angels] says: Holy, the other says: Holy, holy, and the third says: Holy, holy, holy, YHVH Tzevaot.[29]

Angels are made to serve God, but humanity has free choice. Therefore, if we choose to praise and serve God, God Himself is pleased by His creation. The gift of free choice and the fact that every human being holds

---

[23] Psalm 68:19.
[24] Numbers 17:12.
[25] Numbers 17:13.
[26] Babylonian Talmud, Shabbat 88–89a.
[27] Beginning of the Shma (Deuteronomy 6:4).
[28] Job 38:7.
[29] Babylonian Talmud, Chullin 91b.

within himself the entire Tree of Life is what makes man special.[30] If a human being develops to a high level of inner purity, then the entire Tree of Life exists in harmony and balance within him. This is much more than even the greatest archangels may hope for, and therefore humankind is able to reach spiritual levels even the angels cannot reach. "The Tzaddiqim (righteous ones) are greater than the ministering angels (archangels)" (Babylonian Talmud, Sanhedrin 93a).

This is also the reason why Henoch (also spelled Chanoch), when he had lived a perfect life, was taken into Heaven and transformed into Metatron, the highest of all the archangels. He had reached a level above all angels and archangels, for unlike them, he was created in the image of God.

The fact that humanity was given free will must be considered in all interactions with angels. I have heard people say they do not believe in angels, because so many bad things happen in the world. If there are angels, they say, why don't they help? Yet angels will never interfere unless they are asked to do so, for they will never risk getting in the way of our free will.[31]

Angels are not unreachable beings. They are both able and willing to help you in many ways. Here is a small example of how they might help: Once I had lost my jacket, and in order to get it back, I invoked Gabriel and the Kerubim, asking them to find and bring it back. I visualized Gabriel sending out the Kerubim in all directions, searching for the jacket. I imagined very vividly how I would hold it in my hands again. I imagined what it looked like, how the material felt, and even what the leather of the jacket smelled like. The day after, a friend I had not seen for about a year called me and asked me whether I had lost my jacket. In it was a notebook with his phone number. Upon finding the jacket, he had been telephoned, and when he saw the jacket and some Hebrew words in the notebook, he realized it might be mine. Within twenty-four hours, the jacket was back in my possession.

---

[30] According to Jewish legends, Satan was sent to humanity to test us and persuade us to turn away from God, for free will makes sense only if there are at least two options from which to choose.

[31] "Remember, all such beings will help if they can, but they must be asked for help. They cannot make the first move. They are not able, or permitted to interfere with your free will. To use a 'Star Trek-ism,' they have a prime directive of noninterference." (Dolores Ashcroft-Nowicki, *The Initiate's Book of Pathworkings,* York Beach, Maine: Red Wheel/ Weiser 1999, 169.)

12

The Vision of the Merkavah

The *Merkavah* is the mystical chariot that supports the Throne of the Glory of God.[1] The Maasseh Merkavah (Work of the Merkavah) is the secret of the first chapter of the book of Ezekiel, which contains the knowledge of how to see the vision of the Merkavah. According to Rabbi Yochanan ben Zakkai, it was to be taught only to those who are wise. It has been one of the most ancient secrets of the Qabbalistic tradition.

The aim of the Work of the Merkavah is "to see the King in His Beauty." The King is, of course, God, the King of the Universe. Thus in this chapter, we aim for nothing less than the vision of the Glory of God.

The ascent to Heaven and the vision of the Heavenly Palaces has been practiced and taught to Qabbalists since biblical times. According to the Bible, Chanoch (sometimes called Henoch) was the first man who ascended to Heaven (Genesis 5:24). The mystical tradition describes how he was transformed there into the archangel Metatron. The earliest report of an ascent to Heaven in a Divine Chariot can be found in the biblical tales of the life of the prophet Elijah, who lived in the ninth century BCE

[1] See: Ezekiel 1.

(2 Kings 2). In Heaven, he was transformed into the archangel Sandalfon. Later, the prophet Ezekiel, who lived in the sixth century BCE, was the first person who described the vision of the Merkavah (Ezekiel 1). Yet he did not give much information on achieving such a vision.

The secret teachings on the practical methods of this mystical and magical technique have been described by Rabbi Ishmael, who received them from his teacher, Rabbi Nechunya ben ha-Qanah, who lived in the late first century CE.

This technique was usually practiced in a magical group called *Chavurah*. Those who practiced this kind of occult work that would bring about the vision of the Merkavah were called the *Yordey Merkavah* (literally, those who descend to the Merkavah). This will need some further explanation.

The modern student of magic is used to the fact that inner world meditation journeys are called *pathworkings*. This term originates in the meditative journeys on the thirty-two Paths of Wisdom on the Tree of Life. In the modern Western tradition of magic, however, the term *pathworking* is used for every kind of inner world meditation journey, even if it has nothing to do with the thirty-two Paths of Wisdom. The ancient Qabbalists had their own term for this kind of meditation, calling it *Yeridah*. This literally means "descent," although there is no doubt that the direction of the Merkavah is upward. This has been the origin of much confusion and speculation. I believe that the term *Yeridah* originates in much older techniques. All shamanic traditions descend to travel into the inner worlds, because shamans work on those levels of the inner world that are below our normal consciousness.[2] Qabbalists are more concerned with traveling to the levels above normal consciousness. (To avoid misunderstanding, it is necessary to remember that the terms *below* and *above* are a symbolic way to express an inner level reality.)[3]

I believe that the term *Yeridah* originates from a time when shamanic methods were used. Later, the term *Yeridah* was used to describe every kind of meditative journey. When the shamanic methods were not used

---

[2] The description of the Yeridah is a simplification, used to illustrate certain ideas. Shamanic journeys include work on different levels. There is evidence, however, that moving downward was the first type of inner journey.

[3] The idea that Qabbalistic methods and shamanic methods may be related to each other has also been considered by Caitlín and John Matthews in *The Western Way* (London: Arkana, 1985).

any longer, the term *Yeridah* was retained, just as we tend to call every meditative journey a pathworking.

The Heavenly Palaces (the *Hechalot;* singular: *Hechal*) are seven halls or chambers, one within the other (the word *Hechal* also describes the Temple). The central or seventh Hechal is the place of the Merkavah.

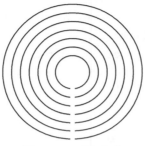

The seven Hechalot

Inside the Palaces, you will see different choirs of angels. One type are the angels of fiery flames *(shalhaviot)*. They may be patterns of energy, and their number is a symbol for the increase in spiritual power and pressure from one Palace to the next. You will also find rivers of fire representing the abyss on the Tree of Life.

The Yordey Merkavah

The vision of the Merkavah is more than a mystical meditation. It will bring about deep changes in your spiritual makeup and help you to develop a vast amount of spiritual power. Tradition says that the Yordey Merkavah (singular: Yored Merkavah) are able to see what happens before the Throne of Glory—what will happen in the world, as well as human deeds. If someone has committed a crime, if he has stolen, committed adultery, or killed, the Yored Merkavah will know (i.e., see it in the aura). He will know if someone has lied, and whether a person is a sorcerer (i.e., black magician). If someone tries to attack the Yored Merkavah, whether with his hand, by words, or otherwise, the attacker will be punished by the angels and the Heavenly Court of Justice with plagues, diseases, wounds, blindness, and all kinds of misfortune. It is also said that he who ascends to the Merkavah will have power over the angels of Heaven.

Some traditions say that an experienced Yored Merkavah can help a beginner by traveling with him. Each Chavurah (magical group) consists of one teacher and his students. The ancient texts, however, warn every Yored Merkavah to choose his companions well, for he will be punished if they are unworthy.

Preparation

Although some texts advise those who wish to ascend to the Merkavah to fast for forty days, most texts do not mention this.[4]

Rabbi Ishmael tells the story of how his teacher, Rabbi Nechunya ben ha-Qanah, revealed to him the secrets of the vision of the Merkavah. Rabbi Nechunya ben ha-Qanah said that those who wish to see the Merkavah must be free of:

> idolatry
> incest and sexual crime
> bloodshed
> slander
> perjury
> desecration of the Divine Name
> harshness or insolence
> unfounded hostility

Additionally, they must keep all the positive and negative commandments. To be free of idolatry means to serve only the highest Master, and not to dedicate yourself to other ideas, institutions, beings, or people. It has been said that, in order not to reduce the length of his life, the Yored Merkavah should not stand up in front of anybody but the king, the High Priest, and the Sanhedrin (Jewish court) if the head of the Sanhedrin is present. This means that the Yored Merkavah should not serve anybody except God, for all three institutions are considered to be of divine origin. To be free of sexual crime means not to hurt others in any way or to misuse sex to manipulate or mistreat others. To be free of bloodshed

---

[4] According to Isaak Luria, it is impossible to ascend to the Hechalot without being purified with the ashes of the Red Heifer, a purification that was possible only when the Temple still stood. This is not mentioned in most texts, and it seems to have been invented in order to prevent others from using the ancient magical techniques. (Isaak Luria did not like any form of magic or Practical Qabbalah, and in fact, though he was a great mystic, was not a practitioner of Practical Qabbalah, and he knew very little about high magic.) Therefore, it should not be considered an argument against attaining the vision of the Merkavah, although if you feel that you wish to be purified in the ashes of the Red Heifer, use the technique described in appendix 2 to do so.

means not to kill any other living being except in order to survive or to defend yourself. A vegetarian diet has often been considered a part of the preparation for Qabbalistic magic.[5] To be free of slander means not to talk or think in a negative way about others. Always treat others with respect, and do not disregard the dignity of other human beings—even in the case of an evil person. To be free of perjury means to keep every oath you say. To be free of desecration of the Divine Name means not to use the Name of God to curse or for black magic or for profane purposes. To be free of harshness or insolence means not to behave in a way that hurts others. From a higher perspective, unfounded hostility is any hostility that can be avoided. These are the laws given to Noah, and they are to be kept by all human beings and all nations. But even this is not enough. You must keep all the positive and negative commandments—that is, keep those laws that apply to everybody, as well as the laws of your own religion.

When Rabbi Ishmael heard this warning, he was desperate. He said to his teacher: "If this is the case, the matter is hopeless because there is no one alive who could fulfill these requirements." Rabbi Nechunya ben ha-Qanah answered that in this case the mighty ones of the Chavurah (magical group) should be brought to him in order to reveal the secrets and miracles of the Throne of Glory (*Kise Kavod*). They were then told all the knowledge of the Merkavah, of the Yeridah (descent) and the Aliyah (ascent). Thus we see that these requirements are not to be considered as rigid rules, but a flexible guide.

Dangers

There are some dangers in this work. The most important is the effect on your endocrine system. This work will lead you to levels of existence in which it may be difficult for you to cope with the increase of pressure. If you feel that, at a certain stage, the pressure is too much to cope with, do not feel ashamed to turn around and go back. You can always call Suriyah for help if you wish to descend again. Not to try to go farther than you can is a sign of great wisdom that will be recognized on the inner levels. If the guardians warn you not to go any farther, never try to force your way.

---

[5] To qualify this statement, however, I must mention that often a vegetarian diet was maintained only during the preparation for magical work (which may be a relief to those who do not like such a diet).

Accept that you have gone as far as you could go this time, and try again after you have increased your spiritual development.

There are some ancient warnings that should not be disregarded. One of these involves the story of four men who entered Paradise. One died, and another became demented. Of him scripture says: "Hast thou found Honey? Eat so much as is sufficient for thee, lest thou be filled therewith and vomit it (Proverbs 25:16). The third man mutilated the plantings[6] (i.e., he became a blasphemer because he did not understand what happened). Only Rabbi Aqiva departed safely.

Meditation Position

No special position is mentioned in most of the ancient descriptions, but according to tradition, this work must be done in a special meditative position. Only in one text does Rabbi Aqiva explain that we should place the head between the knees. This is the position that the prophet Elijah used on Mount Carmel in order to bring rain. "And Elijah went up to the top of Carmel; and he cast himself down upon the earth, and put his face between his knees" (1 Kings 18:42).

In the Talmud this position is mentioned several times. It was used by Rabbi Chania ben Dosa to heal the illness of Rabbi Yochanan ben Zakkais's son (Berachot 34b), and by Rabbi Eleazar ben Dordia to repent of his sins and ascend into heaven (Awodah Zarah 17a).

Many centuries later, Hai Gaon (tenth century), the famous head of the Babylonian academy at Pumbedita, wrote that this is the position we must use to see the Merkavah and the Heavenly Palaces, and the great Qabbalist Rabbi Joseph Tzayach (sixteenth century) also advised his students to use this position for meditation.

In fact, this position has been used since ancient times, and it is still

Squatting man. Predynastic period, N.Y. Memorial Art Gallery, Rochester.

---

[6] Of the Tree of Life.

used by modern magicians. In *The Ritual Magic Workbook,* Dolores Ashcroft-Nowicki describes the use of this position in order to enter the deeper levels of pathworking.[7]

It may take a while to get used to this position. It will be a bit more difficult to breathe, but do not worry about this, for it is meant to be so. Make sure that you can sit in this position comfortably for the duration of a longer meditation before you attempt to use it in the vision of the Merkavah.

Invocation of Suriyah

If you wish to ascend to the Merkavah, chant the following invocation 112 times.

> **I invoke thee SURIYAH**
> **Sar ha-Panim (Prince of the Countenance),**
> **in the Name of**
> **TOTRUSIYAY YOD HEH VAV HEH,**
> **Who is called**
> **TOTRUSIYAY TZORTAG TOTRAVIEL**
> **TUFGAR ASHARUYLIAY ZAVUDIEL**
> **ve-ZAHARARIEL TANDIEL**
> **ve-SHAQADHUZIAY**
> **DAHIVIRON**
> **ve-ADIRIRON**
> **YOD HEH VAV HEH ELOHEY YISRAEL**

"Do not add to the 112 times or reduce them, or your blood will be on your head," says an ancient warning. You should count your repetitions with your fingers. A cord with 112 wooden beads may also be helpful.

During your invocation, you will feel a presence manifesting in front of you. The presence becomes stronger and stronger during your chant. You will feel an aura of great power, incredible strength of will, and magnificent brightness. When you have finished your invocation, you will hear a voice of great authority that is both friendly and awesome: "Stand up, child of Adam."

You will stand up in your astral body (Nefesh), while your physical body (Guf) remains in its position. You hardly dare to face the being in front of you, but when you raise your eyes, you will see the most beautiful

---

[7] *The Ritual Magic Workbook,* 151, figure 33.

angel you have ever seen. You can hardly look in his face because it radiates pure light. His whole body consists of white fire. It is not easy to endure the pressure of his mighty presence. Before you stands Suriyah, the Prince of the Countenance, who serves directly before God Himself. (Suriyah is another name of Metatron.)

The Yeridah

He lifts you up and carries you into the higher worlds. And as you move upward, you enter the first Heaven (corresponding to Malchut), which is called Vilon (Veil). This is the Heaven that is visible to us and consists of a veil of clouds covering the higher levels from the eyes of mortals.

As you are lifted higher, you come into a dark sphere with a touch of blue. Out of the darkness, you can see the brilliant light of the stars that shines to light your way. You can also see the planets on their journey through this sphere, which is the second Heaven (Yesod), called Raqia (Firmament).[8] You feel that while you move through each Heaven, you enter a higher level of spiritual power in addition to a higher level of consciousness. In the second Heaven are found angels of fire and angels of moisture, and spirits of awe and spirits of fear. And the firmament is full of awe, for within it are innumerable angels who bring forth (from themselves) host upon host, and above them are superiors and overseers—and all these angels and spirits are of planetary and stellar in nature. In this Heaven are twelve steps or levels, and on each step stand angels in their glory, and over them is one superior over another. They obey everyone among the sons of Adam (i.e., humanity) who approaches them in purity.

Then you pass the third Heaven (Hod), called Shechaqim (Skies), in which manna for the pious is stored and where there is also the Garden of Eden. The third Heaven is filled with storehouses of dark clouds, and from it come forth spirits and within it are encampments of thunder and lightning that come out of it. Also in it are three princes sitting on thrones, their garments appearing like fire, and their thrones appear like fire, and the fire shines as bright as gold. They rule over all the angels of fire. They are like fire in their power, and their voice is like the roaring voice of thunder. Their eyes are like sunbeams, and they rule upon wheels of flame and fire. They have wings to fly, and from their mouths come yells like those of horses. Their appearance is like torches, and as they speak, they cause trem-

---

[8] The second Heaven is also sometimes called Shemey Shamayim (Heaven of Heavens).

bling, and as they roar, they cause weakness. They move in every direction, and they fly to every corner of the world.

The fourth Heaven (Netzach), called Zevul (Residence of the Temple), contains the celestial Jerusalem together with the Temple in which the archangel Michael ministers as High Priest. The heavenly Sanhedrin (judicial court) can also be found here.

The fourth Heaven is stretched upon a storm wind and stands upon pillars of fire with capitals like crowns of flame. It is full of treasuries of power (Gevurah)[9] and storehouses of dew. In the corners of the fourth Heaven, swift angels run, rushing back and forth. Seven rivers of fire and water are described. On one side stand innumerable angels of fire with flaming torches, and on the other stand innumerable angels of cold (ice) surrounded by hailstones. The angels of fire do not burn the angels of cold. Neither do the angels of cold extinguish the angels of fire. (Note that all the symbolism of this Heaven describes balance between opposites, just as the fourth Heaven is the point of balance among the seven levels of Heaven.) All the angels chant praises to the Creator. In this Heaven is the beautiful bridal chamber of the sun, filled with light and fire all aflame—and angels of fire, girded with power (Gevurah), surround him and lead him during the day. Then the angels of water, their bodies like the sea and their voices like the voice (sound) of the waters strengthened with a headdress of might, lead him by night.

As you pass the fifth Heaven (Tiferet), called Maon (Dwelling), you find yourself in a sphere of beautiful colors and music. Here reside the angelic hosts who sing the praise of God, though only during the night, for by day it is the task of Israel on earth to give glory to God on high. The sight of the fifth Heaven is magnificent. Within it are clouds of splendor, and it is filled with angels of dignity. There are armies of angels carved like glorious flames. The sound of their movement is like the crushing of the waves of the waters and like a wheel of thunder. Among them are twelve princes of glory (or officers of glory), who sit on magnificent thrones. Their thrones are like the appearance of fire. In each of the four quarters of Heaven are three of the thrones. The voices of the princes shake the world, and from their breath comes forth lightning, and they have wings of fire and are covered by a crest of fire. The whole firmament shines with the light from their faces. They are appointed over the twelve months of the year, and they understand what happens in each month. Without them, nothing will happen, for they were formed for this purpose. Each stands above his month,

---

[9] Note that Gevurah and Netzach are related to each other, as Mars and Venus are.

for they make known month by month what will happen in every year.

The sixth Heaven (Gevurah), called Maqom (Place) is a horrible sphere. Here are stored all the trials and terrible visitations for the earth. In the chambers of this Heaven are magazines of snow, hail, biting dews, clouds, storms, and whirlwinds and smoke, fire, test, and turmoil. In the sixth Heaven are armies of angels crowned with what appear to be crowns of golden fire. Their power (Gevurah) is like a fire that cannot be blown out, and they fear only their rulers. Two princes rule over them, one in the west of the Heavens and one in the east. Before these armies of divine spirits are numerous lesser angels, formed from flame, and they burn like fire and their bodies are like fiery coals. These princes are the two holy angels who rule over all the encampments (of angels) of the sixth Heaven: The name of the first one is Afrachsey and the name of the second is Toqpiras, and all the officers of the encampments serve before them.

Under the wings of Suriyah, you arrive safely in the seventh Heaven (Chesed), called Aravot (Highest Heaven). This is a vast bank of endless cloud that appears like a cosmic ocean. It contains only what is good, right, and beautiful. Here are storehouses of life, peace, and blessing. In the distance you see the first of the Heavenly Palaces (the higher Sefirot). The walls are built of pure white marble and the double gates are made of pure gold. The palace shines in brilliant light. Suriyah tells you now that from here you have to go on alone. Then he leaves you with a blessing.

The First Hechal (Heavenly Palace)

In front of the gate of the first Hechal (Heavenly Palace) stand the Shomrey ha-Saf (guardians of the threshold)—eight strong and powerful angels, four on each side of the gate. They hold long, glittering golden spears, ready for use. Their names are:

DAHAVIEL	(Gold of God)
QASHRIEL	(Knot of God)
GAHURIEL	(Prostration of God)
ZAKUTIEL	(Acquittal of God)
TOFCHIEL[10]	(Nutrition of God)
DAHARIEL	(Gallop of God)
MATQIEL	(Sweetness of God)
SHAVIEL	(Return of God)

---

[10] Some say TOFHIEL.

When you come to the gate of the first Hechal, take two seals into your hands. To the guardians that stand on the right side, show the seal of:

TOTRUSIYAY YOD HEH VAV HEH

טוטרוסיאי יהוה

To the guardians that stand on the left side, show the seal of:

SURIYAH, Sar ha-Panim (Prince of the Countenance)

סוריה

The seals[11] must be written in the air with white fire or light. Imagine writing with fire as if you would write with your finger. As you write the seals, they must also be intoned. Alternatively, you could imagine them written on parchment, but also in this case you must intone them as you show them to the guardians.

Dahaviel the prince (Sar), who is the chief guardian of the gate of the first Hechal and the overseer of the first Hechal, and who stands at the right of the lintel, and Tofhiel, the prince (Sar) who stands at the opposite side, at the left of the lintel, will immediately grasp you—one on your right and one on your left. They will lead you into the first Hechal and farther, to the second gate.

The first Hechal is a vast and brilliant palace. In that place there is an atmosphere of great spiritual power. You can hardly see the walls, the ceiling, or the other end of the hall that you are passing. Without the two angels it would take a long time (maybe many days or even weeks or months) to reach the next gate. In this Palace are countless angels of fiery flames (shalhaviot) and chariots of fire. And they sing:

Qadosh Qadosh Qadosh (Holy Holy Holy is)
YOD HEH VAV HEH TZEVAOT
The whole earth is filled with Thy Glory (Kavod) (Isaiah 6:3)

---

[11] One of the two seals is one of the Names of God, and the other is one of the names of Metatron. But do not be tempted to think that there are two powers in heaven. There is a legend of Elisha ben Avuyah (called Acher—the "other one"—because after his heresy his name was not mentioned anymore), who ascended to Heaven and saw Metatron on his throne surrounded by angels. He believed that Metatron was equal to God. Acher said: "We have been taught to believe that no one sits in heaven—or are there perhaps two supreme powers?" A heavenly voice was heard: "Turn, O backsliding children (Jeremiah 3:14 and 3:22), with the exception of Acher." Then God sent Anafiel to beat Metatron sixty times with a rod of fire in punishment for this. Since then, Metatron is not permitted to sit any longer on a throne in heaven (Third Book of Henoch).

This is the Palace of Malchut. As you pass through the first Hechal, you may see a mosaic floor with beautiful images. At the end of this Palace there is a river of fire and smoke. A huge bridge leads across this river to the gate of the second Hechal. (It may seem to be confusing that this place is called the Palace of Malchut, for you have been told that the first Heaven belongs to Malchut, but Qabbalists say that there is a whole Tree of Life in every Sefirah.)

At the gate of the second Hechal, the angels guiding you will inform Tigriel, the prince (Sar) who is the chief guardian of the gate of the second Hechal and the overseer of the second Hechal and who stands at the right of the lintel, and Mitpiel, the prince (Sar) who stands at the opposite side, at the left of the lintel. Further, the angels will make these guardians peaceful.

The Second Hechal (Heavenly Palace)

In front of the gate of the second Hechal stand the Shomrey ha-Saf (guardians of the threshold)—eight strong and powerful angels. They hold long, glittering silver lances, ready for use. Their names are:

TIGRIEL	(Tiger of God?)[12]
MITPIEL	(Who is the Drum of God?)
SAHARIEL[13]	([Moon] Crescent of God)
ORPIEL	(Neck of God)
SHAHARARIEL	(Prince of God?)
SITRIEL	(Border of God)
RAGAIEL	(Movement of God)[14]
SAHIVIEL	(??? of God)

When you come to the gate of the second Hechal, take two seals into your hands. To the guards that stand on the right side, show the seal of:

ADIRIRON YOD HEH VAV HEH
אדירירון יהוה

---

[12] Many angelic names have been translated as ". . . of God," based on the general understanding of their function. An alternative and more literal translation in all these cases would be "My . . . is God." One question mark has been placed behind the name if the translation is uncertain and three if no translation was possible.

[13] Some say SARHIEL (Laxity of God).

[14] Or Moment of God.

To the guardians that stand on the left, show the seal of:

OZAHYAH, Sar ha-Panim [Prince of the Countenance]
אוזהיה

Tigriel, the prince (Sar) who is the chief guardian of the gate of the second Hechal and the overseer of the second Hechal, and who stands on the
right of the lintel, and Mitpiel, the prince (Sar) who stands on the left, will
immediately grasp you—one on your right and one on your left. They will
lead you into the second Hechal and farther, to the third gate.

As you enter the second Hechal, you feel an enormous increase in
intensity. The amount of spiritual power multiplies every time you enter
the next Hechal. Each of the seven Palaces will bring you closer to God.
Dion Fortune once said: "God is pressure,"[15] and the pressure will increase
the closer you get to God. The second Hechal is also a vast and brilliant
Palace. Again, you can hardly see the walls, the ceiling, or the other end of
the hall into which you are passing. In this Palace there are twice as many
angels of fiery flames and chariots of fire as in the first Palace. This time
they sing:

Blessed be the Glory of YOD HEH VAV HEH
from his place. (Ezekiel 3:12)

This is the Palace of Yesod. This Hechal may appear different from the
first one, and if you see any images, they will also be different. At the end
of this Palace is a river of fire and smoke that is bigger and hotter than the
first. Another huge bridge leads across this river to the gate of the third
Hechal.

At the gate of the third Hechal, the angels guiding you will inform
Shaburiel, the prince (Sar) who is the chief guardian of the gate of the third
Hechal and the overseer of the third Hechal, and who stands on the right
of the lintel, and Ratzutziel, the prince (Sar) who stands on the left. And
again, they will make these guardians peaceful.

The Third Hechal (Heavenly Palace)

In front of the gate of the third Hechal stand the Shomrey ha-Saf (guardians of the threshold)—eight strong and powerful angels. They hold huge
double-headed battleaxes, ready for use. Their names are:

---

[15] Dion Fortune, *The Mystical Qabalah* (London: Ernst Benn Limited, 1972) ch. V, p. 34.

SHABURIEL	(Breaking of God)
RATZUTZIEL	(Crushing of God)
SHALMIEL	(Completeness of God)
SABLIEL	(Sustaining of God)
ZAHZAHIEL	(Recognition of God?)
HADARIEL	(Splendor of God)
BORIEL[16]	(Pit of God)
PALTRIEL[17]	(Shopkeeper of God)

When you come to the gate of the third Hechal, take into your hands two seals. To the guardians that stand on the right side, show the seal of:

TZORTAQ YOD HEH VAV HEH
צורטק יהוה

To the guardians that stand on the left side, show the seal of:

DAHIVIRON, Sar ha-Panim (Prince of the Countenance)
דהיבירון

They will immediately grasp you—one on your right and one on your left. They will lead you into the third Hechal and farther, to the fourth gate.

The third Hechal is the Palace of Hod. Again, you feel the increase of spiritual power and pressure. In this Palace are twice as many angels of fiery flames and chariots of fire as in the second Palace. Here they sing:

*Blessed be the Name of the Glory from His kingdom for ever
and in eternity from the house of His Shechinah.*

This Hechal may appear different from the other two, and any images you see belong to the sphere of Hod. At the end of this Palace is a river of fire and smoke, even bigger and hotter than the second. And again, a huge bridge leads across this river to the gate of the fourth Hechal.

At the gate of the fourth Hechal, the angels guiding you will inform Pachadiel, the prince (Sar) who is the chief guardian of the gate of the fourth Hechal and the overseer of the fourth Hechal, and who stands on the right of the lintel, and Gevuratiel, the prince (Sar) who stands on the left. And again, the angels will make these guardians peaceful.

---

[16] Some say BAZRIEL (Scattering of God).
[17] Sometimes belonging to the fifth Palace.

The Fourth Hechal (Heavenly Palace)

In front of the gate of the fourth Hechal stand the Shomrey ha-Saf (guardians of the threshold)—eight strong and powerful angels. They are armed with bow and arrow, ready for use. Their names are:

PACHADIEL	(Fear of God)
GEVURATIEL	(Power of God)
KAZVIEL	(Like this is God)
SHECHINAEL	(Presence of God)
SHATAQIEL	(Silence of God)
ARAVIEL	(Lurking of God)
KAPIEL	(Palm of God)
ANPIEL	(Branch of God)

When you come to the gate of the fourth Hechal, take two seals into your hands. To the guardians that stand on the right side, show the seal of:

ZAVUDIEL YOD HEH VAV HEH

זבודיאל יהוה

To the guardians that stand on the left, show the seal of:

MARGIVIEL, Sar ha-Panim
(Prince of the Countenance)

מרגויאל

They will immediately grasp you—one on your right and one on your left. They will lead you into the forth Hechal and farther, to the fifth gate. The fourth Hechal is the Palace of Netzach. In this Palace are twice as many angels of fiery flames and chariots of fire as in the third Palace, singing:

Blessed be YOD HEH VAV HEH
CHAY ve-QAYIM
(living and everlasting)
forever and from eternity to eternity,
mighty over the whole Merkavah.

Any images you see belong to this Sefirah. At the end of this Palace there is another river of fire and smoke, even bigger and hotter than the third one. And again, a huge bridge leads across this river to the gate of the fifth Hechal.

At the gate of the fifth Hechal, the angels guiding you will inform Techliel, the prince (Sar) who is the chief guardian of the gate of the fifth Hechal and the overseer of the fifth Hechal, and who stands on the right of the lintel, and Oziel, the prince (Sar) who stands on the left. And again, they will make these guardians peaceful.

The Fifth Hechal (Heavenly Palace)

In front of the gate of the fifth Hechal stand the Shomrey ha-Saf (guardians of the threshold)—eight strong and powerful angels. They hold long and sharp swords, ready for use. Their names are:

TECHLIEL	(Beginning of God)
OZIEL	(Strength of God)
GETIEL	(Document of God)
GETAHUEL	(Female Document of God)
SAAFRUEL	(Consideration of God?)
NARPIEL[18]	(??? of God)
GERIEL	(Dweller of God)
DARIEL	(Order of God)

When you come to the gate of the fifth Hechal, take two seals into your hands. To the guardians that stand on the right side, show the seal of:

TOTRAVIEL YOD HEH VAV HEH

טוטרביאל יהוה

To the guardians that stand on the left side, show the seal of:

ZAHAFNIRIAY, Sar ha-Panim

זהפניריאי

They will immediately grasp you—three from in front of you and three from behind. They will lead you into the fifth Hechal and farther, to the sixth gate. The fifth Hechal is the Palace of Tiferet. In this Palace are twice as many angels of fiery flames and chariots of fire as in the fourth Palace, singing:

Blessed be the Holiness of His Kingdom from the
place of the house of His Shechinah.

---

[18] Some say GERAFIEL (Raking of God).

Any images you see belong to this Sefirah. At the gate of the sixth Hechal, your guides leave you. At the end of this Palace there is another river of fire and smoke, bigger and hotter than the fourth. And again, a huge bridge leads across this river to the gate of the sixth Hechal.

The Sixth Hechal (Heavenly Palace)

In front of the gate of the sixth Hechal stand the Shomrey ha-Saf (guardians of the threshold)—eight strong and powerful angels. They are armed with countless steel axes, ready for use. Their names are:

DUMIEL	(Silence of God)
QATZPIEL	(Wrath of God)
GAHGAHIEL	(Protection of God?)
ARSBARSABIEL	(Military commander of God?)
AGROMIEL	(Wildness of God)
PARTZIEL	(Invasion of God)
MACHAQIEL	(Erasure of God)
TOFRIEL	(Destruction of God)

When you come to the gate of the sixth Hechal, you must show three seals. Show two seals to Qatzpiel, the prince (Sar) whose sword is unsheathed in his hand and from which lightning flashes. He will direct it against all who are not worthy to see the King and His Throne. No creature can hold him back, and his sword screams out: "Annihilation!" He stands on the right side of the gate.

Show one seal to Dumiel, who is also called Avir Gahidriham, and to whom belonged once the office of standing on the right side of the gate. Qatzpiel, however, pushed him away. Regardless of this, Dumiel does not feel enmity, hate, envy, or rivalry for Qatzpiel. Instead, he said: "That is to his honor [to be able to push me away] and this is to my honor [to be able to endure it]." To Qatzpiel show these seals:

ZAHARARIEL

זהרריאל

PAALEY PAALEYO

פעלי פעליו

And to Dumiel show this seal:

BRONIYAH

ברוניה

Dumiel, the prince, sits on a bench of pure diamond, glowing like the lights of heaven on the creation of the world. He asks you to sit down next to him, on his right, and he says to you:

"I bear witness and warn you regarding two things. Do not go on (literally, descend) to the Merkavah unless you have these qualifications: You have read the Torah, the Prophets, and the Writings; and have you learned the Mishnah, the Midrash, the Halachah, the Aggadah, and the interpretation (deeper meaning) of the Halachah, what is forbidden and what is permitted. You have kept every proscription that is written in the Torah, and you have heeded all the warnings, decrees, judgments, and laws given to Moses on Sinai."

Do not be afraid if you have not learned enough or that you have not lived a perfect life. If you have done your best, it will be all right. Tradition says that everyone is permitted who fulfills at least one of the two qualifications. Because most of the ancient Yordey Merkavah were also Rabbis, all of them would fulfill the first requirement. That means the rules were not taken as strictly as it seems. If you are not a rabbi, and consequently have less knowledge about the scriptures, do not worry. Dumiel will understand whether or not you have done your best.

Answer to Dumiel, the prince, whether or not you have fulfilled these qualifications. Do not lie, because Dumiel will know if you try to betray him. Remember that Qatzpiel (the wrath of God) will attack all who are not worthy to go on. If Dumiel considers your deeds acceptable, he will join himself with Gavriel, the scribe (better known as Gabriel, which is the usual English pronunciation of his name), and with red ink on parchment, he will write your name, how much you have learned, what your deeds have been, and that you wish to enter before the Throne of Glory.

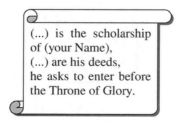

(...) is the scholarship
of (your Name),
(...) are his deeds,
he asks to enter before
the Throne of Glory.

Immediately, Qatzpiel draws his bow and fires it. He brings to you a stormy wind (*ruach saarah*) and places you in a chariot of brightness (*Qaron shel Nogah*), guiding you into the sixth Hechal while in front of you the angels blow eight thousand million horns, thirty thousand million shofars (ram horns) and forty thousand million trumpets. Dumiel, the prince, grasps the parchment and hangs it on the chariot. He will go before you, and Gavriel will join you.

The stormy wind (ruach saarah) is a symbol of the divine inspiration, sometimes called Ruach ha-Qodesh (Holy Spirit), and the chariot of brightness (*Qaron shel Nogah*) is a symbol of your body of light. Both are mentioned several times in the bible: "And it came to pass, as they still went on, and talked, that, behold, there appeared a chariot of fire, and horses of fire, and parted them both asunder; and Elijah went up by a storm (Saarah) into Heaven" (2 Kings 2:11).

The chariot of fire is identical to the chariot of brightness of the Yored Merkavah, and the stormy wind is identical to the storm by which Elijah went into Heaven. The stormy wind and the brightness are also mentioned by Ezekiel: "And I saw, and behold, a stormy wind (ruach saarah) came out of the north, a great cloud, and a fire infolding itself, and a brightness (Nogah) was around it, and out of the midst thereof like the appearance of the Chashmal, out of the midst of the fire" (Ezekiel 1:4).

The sixth Hechal is the Palace of Gevurah. Any images you see belong to this Sefirah. In this Palace are twice as many angels of fiery flames and chariots of fire as in the fifth Palace, singing:

> *Blessed be YOD HEH VAV HEH*
> *ADON kol ha-Gevurah* (Lord of all the power)
> *and Ruler over the whole Merkavah.*

At the end of this Palace there is a huge stream of fire and smoke, bigger and hotter than all the others put together. It is full of dangerously burning flames, mighty and deadly. This is the Rigiyon, the most horrible of the fiery rivers. And again, a huge bridge leads across this river to the gate of the seventh Hechal.

As you move through the sixth Hechal, you see the appearance of the Chashmal, the brilliant, fire-speaking angel who is the chief angel of the Chashmalim, the angels of Chesed. (The Chashmal is also mentioned in Ezekiel 1:27.) He is pure and selects from among the Yordey Merkavah (those who journey to the Merkavah) who is worthy to see the King in His Beauty and who is not. If you are worthy, the angels will say to you: "You may enter." If you do not enter and they say again to you: "You may enter," and then you enter immediately, they will praise you and say: "This is certainly one of the Yordey Merkavah, worthy to see the King in His Beauty."

But if you are not worthy, they will say to you: "You may not enter." If you try to enter then, they will slaughter you and throw you into the Rigiyon.

You will see only the appearance of the Chashmal, not the Chashmal itself, because he belongs to the seventh Hechal, which is yet to be reached.

The sixth Palace appears as though hundreds of thousands and thousands of billions of billions of waves of water are flowing toward you, yet there is not a single drop of water—only the ethereal glitter of the stones of pure marble that are built into the Palace. If you say: "What is the purpose of this water?" the angels would run behind you in order to stone you, and they would say to you: "Good-for-nothing! From now on, you will no longer see with your eyes. You are probably a descendant of those who kissed the [golden] calf. You are not worthy to see the King and His Throne." A heavenly voice would come from the seventh Hechal, and the herald would blow the trumpet and say to them: "You have spoken well. Certainly, he is a descendant of those who kissed the calf. He is not worthy to see the King and His Throne." Then you would not be able to escape until they had smashed your head with countless steel axes cast at you.

Do not endanger yourself by asking about the water! To be ready to ascend to the Merkavah, you must understand this. The marble stones are a test. This will become clearer if we compare it to a tale from the Talmud (Chagigah 14b):

Our Rabbis taught: Four men entered Paradise. They were Ben Azai and Ben Zoma and the other (Elisha ben Avuyah) and Rabbi Aqiva. Rabbi Aqiva said to them: "When you arrive at the stones of pure marble, say not: Water, water! For it is said: He that speaketh falsehood shall not be established before Mine Eyes (Psalms 101:7)." Ben Azai cast a look and died. Of him Scripture says: Precious in the sight of YHVH is the death of His saints (Psalm 106:15). Ben Zoma looked and became demented. Of him Scripture says: Hast thou found Honey? Eat so much as is sufficient for thee, lest thou be filled therewith and vomit it (Proverbs 25:16). The other mutilated the plantings (i.e., he became a blasphemer). Rabbi Aqiva departed safely.

This tale is explained in Rabbi Chananel ben Chushiel's commentary. The word Paradise (Pardes) is another description for the highest Heaven.

The ascent of these four men is another way to describe the ascent to the heavenly Hechalot. Concerning the stones of pure marble he explains:

> Rabbi Aqiva warned them: When you look into the profound under-standing of your heart, while you arrive at the stones of pure mar-ble, say not: Water, water! There is no water there at all, but only a thought-form is seen. If one says there is water, he is blaspheming.

This is explained in *Hechalot Rabbati*. The guardian of the Hechal of the marble door casts forth thousands and thousands of waves of water, but there is not a single drop of water, only the ethereal glitter of the stones of pure marble that are built into the Hechal. Their radiance resembles water. But if one says: "What is the purpose of this water?" he is a blasphemer. They did not ascend into Heaven [physically], but looked upon it and saw it in the profound understanding of the heart. They saw it like one looking into a dull mirror.[19]

The waters are the waters or illusions of the astral plane. They are only thought-forms—not the true image of the Heaven in Beriah, but only their reflection in Yetzirah. The form is not real, but the power behind the form is real. The second commandment says: "Thou shalt not make unto thee any picture or image of any thing that is in the Heaven above or that is in the earth below or that is in the water below the earth" (Exodus 20:4). If you mistake the reflection for the true nature, you are breaking the second commandment, because you are taking the image for reality. This is a test of understanding. The Yored Merkavah must learn to see with his heart, not with his eyes; he must not confuse his visions with the truth behind them. The unworthy believe in what they see with his eyes, but the Yordey Merkavah believe in spiritual truth more than the deceptions of the eyes. (In every occult discipline there comes a point where the true masters are separated from the fools. For example, in astrology there are those who are ruled by their stars and those who overcome negative astrological influ-ences. In divination, some grow in understanding of their destiny, while others are trapped by self-fulfilling prophecies.)

The Seventh Hechal (Heavenly Palace)

At the gate of the seventh Hechal stand the Gibborim (mighty ones), ter-rifying, powerful and sturdy; awesome and horrible; higher than mountains

---

19 See his commentary on the Talmud, ad loc.

and sharper than rocks. Their bows are bent. Their hands hold sharp swords. Flashes of lightning shoot from their eyes, streams of fire come from their nostrils, and burning coals ensue from their mouths. They wear helmets and armor. Spears and lances hang at their sides.

Beside the eight guardians stand eight horses. These are horses of darkness, of deadly shadow, of obscurity, of fire, of blood, horses of hail, of iron, of fog. They have mouths big enough to swallow a man, and they eat glowing coals.

Here are the names of the guardians of the seventh Hechal:

ZAHPANURIYAY YOD HEH VAV HEH, the prince (Sar), honored and beloved

AVIRZAHIYAY YOD HEH VAV HEH, the prince (Sar), honored and beloved and awesome

ATRIGIEL YOD HEH VAV HEH, the prince (Sar), honored and beloved and awesome and terrible

NAGARNIEL YOD HEH VAV HEH, the prince (Sar), honored and beloved and awesome and terrible and precious

NURPANIEL YOD HEH VAV HEH, the prince (Sar), honored and beloved and awesome and terrible and precious and magnificent

NAADURIEL YOD HEH VAV HEH, the prince (Sar), honored and beloved and awesome and terrible and precious and magnificent and mighty

SASTITIEL YOD HEH VAV HEH, the prince (Sar), honored and beloved and awesome and terrible and precious and magnificent and mighty and majestic

ANAFIEL YOD HEH VAV HEH, the prince (Sar), honored and beloved and awesome and terrible and precious and magnificent and mighty and majestic and powerful and upright and strong, whose name has been praised before the Throne of Glory since the day the world was created until now. Why? Because the ring of the Seal of Heaven and Earth was given over into his hand. Why is his name Anafiel (= Branch of God)? Because of the branch of the Crown of Crowns (Keter of Keter) that is placed on his head. This Crown surrounds and covers his head as the Creator surrounds and covers all the Palaces of the Seventh Heaven. As is written: "The Heaven is covered by His splendour (Hod)." (Habakkuk 3:3)

The names of the descent are different:

DALQUQIEL YOD HEH VAV HEH, the prince (Sar) honored and beloved and awesome and terrible, who is called LEVKAPIEL YOD HEH VAV HEH

NURPIEL YOD HEH VAV HEH, the prince (Sar) honored and beloved and awesome and terrible, who is called AVIRZAHIYAY YOD HEH VAV HEH

YAQRIEL YOD HEH VAV HEH (Preciousness of God), the prince (Sar) honored and beloved and awesome and terrible, who is called ATRIGIEL YOD HEH VAV HEH

YASHISHIEL YOD HEH VAV HEH (Existence of God), the prince (Sar) honored and beloved and awesome and terrible, who is called BANAANIEL YOD HEH VAV HEH

NURPANIEL YOD HEH VAV HEH, the prince (Sar) honored and beloved and awesome and terrible, who is called SHAQADYAHIEL YOD HEH VAV HEH

NAADURIEL YOD HEH VAV HEH, the prince (Sar) honored and beloved and awesome and terrible, who is called ZUHALIEL YOD HEH VAV HEH

ANAFIEL YOD HEH VAV HEH (Branch of God), the prince (Sar) honored and beloved and awesome and terrible and precious and magnificent and mighty and majestic and powerful and upright and strong, who is called TUFRIEL YOD HEH VAV HEH (Stylus or Claw of God)

When the guardians at the gate of the seventh Hechal see Dumiel, Qatzpiel, and Gavriel in front of your chariot, they cover their faces and sit down, for they stood in anger before, but now they unloosen their bent bows and return their sharp swords to their sheaths.

To pass them, you must show them the Great Seal and the Awesome Crown. (Draw the opening hexagram and perform the Great Seal in front of the angels, facing toward them—in one direction, not in all six of them—and the Awesome Crown and speak the prayers that belong to them. The complete description of this ritual can be found in chapter 16, The Great Seal and the Awesome Crown.)

TZORTAQ
DRAGINAT
ARACH
NAZIR

SHURATIN
YADYAZIYAH
AZBOGAH
AVAGDEHU
ZAHUZIYAH
ZOHTZIYAH

When you have shown the Great Seal and the Awesome Crown, Anafiel will open the gate of the seventh Hechal and guide you inside.

The seventh Hechal is the Palace of Chesed. In this Palace are four times as many angels of fiery flames and chariots of fire as in the all the other Palaces together. They are singing:

> *Blessed be the King of Kings of Kings,*
> *YOD HEH VAV HEH*
> *ADON kol ha-Gevurah* (Lord of all the power).
> *Blessed be the Name of the Glory of His Kingdom, for ever*
> *and in eternity, from the house of His Shechinah.*

Tradition says that in this hour you will see great wonders and miracles, majesty and greatness, holiness and purity, awe, humility and integrity. But what exactly will you see in the seventh Hechal? I cannot tell you—I can only give some hints as to what it may be like. You will see the angelic orders of the Chashmalim (the "brilliant ones" belonging to Chesed), the Erelim (the "valiant ones," belonging to Binah), the Ofanim (the wheels of the Merkavah, the angels of Chochmah), and, of course, the Chayot ha-Qodesh (the Holy Living Creatures, the angels who carry the Throne and who belong to Keter).

In some descriptions, the view of the fiery angels of the seventh Palace has almost (or, in some reports, has actually) burned or killed the human being who came to see the vision of the Merkavah. God then shouted at His servants that they should cover their eyes, so that they would not hurt His beloved child. Subsequently, the human being was healed (or revived).

Tradition describes the veil or curtain of God (Pargod shel Maqom), which is spread before the Holy One, blessed be He, and on which are shown all the generations of the world and all their deeds from Creation to the end of all generations. On this veil you may see things concerning the past, present, and future, just as the prophets before you have.

Finally, you will see the Merkavah. You may see upon the Merkavah, the Throne of Glory, and if you are lucky, you may even see the Glory of God—that is, the King on His Throne.

Tradition says that whoever stands before the Throne of Glory must sing praises. You will find examples of such praises at the end of this chapter, beginning on page 165. Use them, or simply express the feelings of your own heart. Sometimes, the praises that come from the depths of the heart are the best. But if you can empower a traditional chant with your own emotions, you may find that such a chant has a power of its own, adding to your power. Either is fine, so make up your own chant or use a traditional one. "Rabbi Aqiva said: Lucky is the man, who stands firm with all his strength, and who sings a praise before BARUCHIAY YOD HEH VAV HEH, ELOHEY YISRAEL (the God of Israel) and who sees the Merkavah, and who sees all they do before the Throne of Glory, on which BARUCHIAY YOD HEH VAV HEH, ELOHEY YISRAEL (the God of Israel) sits."[20]

You may find that God will open for you the doors of wisdom, understanding, love, power, and beauty, among others. Rabbi Ishmael describes that the Holy One, blessed be He, opened six hundred thousand doors of wisdom, six hundred thousand doors of understanding, and so on, for Chanoch ben Yared, when he was transformed into the archangel Metatron. You may also be blessed by God. Rabbi Ishmael describes how the Holy One, blessed be He, laid His hand on Chanoch, blessing him with 1,365,000 blessings. Furthermore, God transformed Chanoch's flesh into fire, He increased his [Chanoch's] size, fixed onto him seventy-two wings, turned his eyes to flashes of lightning, and placed on his head a crown on which He, God Himself, wrote the Letters of His own secret Name with His own finger. But remember that Chanoch was the greatest of all men who had ever lived—you should not expect quite as much. Also do not forget that Chanoch was taken from this world forever upon being transformed into an archangel. But even if God opens for you only one of the heavenly doors, or even if you receive only one single blessing, this may be more than you ever dreamed of. You may need peace or you may need humility, devotion, mercy, modesty, or healing. Maybe knowledge of the Torah or great mysteries will be revealed to you. What you will receive will be the decision of God, the omniscient One, and His decision will be wiser than any mortal being can understand.

---

[20] Maaseh Merkavah (Ms Oxford 1531, § 557).

To give you an idea of what your vision of the Merkavah may be like, you may wish to read what Ezekiel saw in his vision:

And it was in the thirtieth year, in the fourth month, on the fifth day of the month, as I was among the exiles by the river of Chebar, that the Heavens were opened, and I saw visions of God. In the fifth day of the month, which was the fifth year of the exile of king Yehoiachin, The word of YHVH came unto Ezekiel ben Buzi, the priest, in the land of the Chaldeans by the river Chebar; and the hand of YHVH was there upon him.

And I saw, and behold, a stormy wind (ruach saarah) came out of the north, a great cloud, and a fire infolding itself, and a brightness (Nogah) was around it, and out of the midst thereof like the appearance of the Chashmal, out of the midst of the fire.

And out of the midst thereof came the image of four living creatures (Chayot). And this was their vision; they had the image of a man. And there were four faces to every one, and there were four wings to every one of them. And their feet were straight feet; and the sole of their feet was like the sole of a calf's foot: and they sparkled like the appearance of polished brass. And they had the hands of a man under their wings on their four sides (literally, quarters); and there were faces and wings to the four of them. Their wings were joined one to another; they turned not when they went; they went every one straight forward. And the image of their faces, they had the face of a man, and the face of a lion, on the right side, all four of them; and they had the face of an ox on the left side, all four of them; and they had the face of an eagle, all four of them. Thus were their faces: and their wings were stretched upward; For each one two wings were joined one to another, and two covered their bodies. And they went every one straight forward; whither the spirit was to go, they went; and they turned not when they went. And the image of the living creatures: their vision was like burning coals of fire; and like of the vision of torches moving between the living creatures, there was brightness (Nogah) of fire, and out of the fire went forth lightning. And the living creatures ran and returned like the vision of a flash of lightning.

And as I saw the living creatures, behold there was one wheel (Ofan) upon the earth by the living creatures, with his four faces. The vision of the wheels (Ofanim) and their work was like unto the appearance of topaz: and they four had one image; and their vision and their work was like the wheel in the middle of the wheel. When they went, they went upon their four sides (literally, quarters); and they turned not when they went. As for their rings, they were so high that they were dreadful; and their rings were full of eyes round about them four. And when the living creatures went, the wheels went by them; and when the living creatures were lifted up from the earth, the wheels were lifted up. Whithersoever the spirit was to go, they went, thither was their spirit to go; and the wheels were lifted up over against them: for the spirit of the living creatures was in the wheels. When those went, these went; and when those stood, these stood; and when those were lifted up from the earth, the wheels were lifted up over against them, for the spirit of the living creature was in the wheels. And the vision of the firmament upon the heads of the living creatures was like the appearance of the awesome crystal, stretched forth over their heads above. And under the firmament were their wings straight, the one toward the other; every one had two, which covered themselves, and every one had two, which covered their bodies. And I heard the sound of their wings, like the sound of great waters, as the voice of the Almighty (Shaddai), when they went; the voice of speech, like the sound of a host. When they stood, they let down their wings.

And above the firmament that was over their heads, like the vision of a sapphire stone, there was the image of a Throne and upon the image of the Throne there was an image like a vision of a Man above upon it. And I saw like the appearance of the Chashmal, like a vision of fire, as a house for it round about, from the vision of His loins and upwards, and from the vision of His loins and downwards, I saw as it were the vision of fire, and it had brightness (Nogah) round about. Like the vision of the rainbow that is in the cloud in the day of rain, so was the vision of the brightness (Nogah) round about. This was the vision of the image of the Glory (Kavod) of YHVH. And when I saw it, I fell upon my face, and I heard a voice of one that spoke.[21]

---

[21] Ezekiel 1:1–28.

Ezekiel's Vision *by Julius Schnoor von Carolsfeld*

Do not be surprised if the Chayot ha-Qodesh appear a little differently than they appeared to Ezekiel. There are other descriptions of them that are a bit different. Some are more simple, illustrating the four holy creatures as a huge winged man, a winged lion, an eagle, and a winged bull. Others are more complex, describing them as having 256 wings ($256 = 4 \times 4 \times 4 \times 4$), 16 faces ($16 = 4 \times 4$) and 512 huge eyes ($512 = 256 \times 2$), each one with the likeness of the appearance of lightning.

Ezekiel speaks of "the image of a Throne"—meaning that he did not see the Throne itself, but instead saw only a reflection of the Throne, for the Throne belongs to Beriah, and Ezekiel's vision would reach only as far as Yetzirah. Therefore, he saw the Chayot (who belong to Yetzirah) as a true image, but the Throne only as a reflection. He also describes "an image like a vision of a Man" upon the image of the Throne. This is the Glory of God, belonging to Atzilut, and therefore he saw only an image like a vision—that is, the reflection of a reflection. Now the Glory of God is not God Himself, but it is as much as we mortals can possibly understand. God Himself is the Ayin (literally, "Nothingness")—that is the Unmanifest beyond Atzilut. You can think of the relation between God Himself and

His Glory in the same way as the relation between a human's incarnated personality and his true self.

There is a tradition that describes God's Glory like a real body. It uses allegorical dimensions that describe God's Greatness. This tradition is called *Shiur Qoma* ("Measurement of the Size"). This is one of the most famous allegories: What is the size of the Creator? It is 236,000 myriades (rabbabot). Others say that only His sole is thirty million myriades, and each myriade is three miles long, and each mile is ten thousand cubits, and each cubit is three spans long, and each span fills the whole universe.

It may be that God speaks to you. Maybe He has something to tell you. Maybe you are permitted to ask a question. If so, think well! What do you really want to know?

Many other things may also be offered to you. Rabbi Ishmael tells that when he went to the seventh Hechal to see the vision of the Merkavah, Metatron showed him the spirits of the stars (*Ruchin shel Kochawim*), the souls of the angels (*Nishmotan shel Malachim*), and the secret right hand of God. Whatever you will experience will be implanted into your soul on a very deep level.

The Aliyah

The aliyah (literally, "ascent") is the way of return. When the pressure is too much for you, you will be told to leave. Move back through the Heavenly Palaces as you came, but on the way back it is not necessary to show any seals. Then call for Suriyah to bring you back home. Give thanks and blessings to Suriyah as you say goodbye. After the meditation, make sure that you close down properly and have something to eat and drink.

Holy Names

Totrusiyay is a corruption of the word Tetragrammaton.
Suriyah is one of the names of Metatron.

1. Praise for the Divine King (from Hechalot Rabbati)

Both this praise and the following one can be used before the Merkavah to honor God in the seventh Palace. Note that in the first praise, the order of the Names is arranged according to the Hebrew alphabet.

Melech Yisrael (King of Israel)

Melech Avir (Heroic King)

Melech Adir (Wonderful King)

Melech Adon (Lord King)

Melech Baruch (Blessed King)

Melech Bachur (Chosen King)

Melech Baruq (Shining King)

Melech Gadol (Great King)

Melech Gibbor (Mighty King)

Melech Gaavah (Dignified King)

Melech Daat (Omniscient King)

Melech Dagul (Distinguished King)

Melech Drush (Demanding King)

Melech Hadur (Elegant King)

Melech Hod (Splendorous King)

Melech Hon (Fortunate King)

Melech VaAd (Eternal King)

Melech Vatiq (Upright King)

Melech VaAd (Eternal King)

Melech Zachur (Male King)

Melech Zakkai (Innocent King)

Melech Zohar (Bright King)

Melech Chai (Living King)

Melech Chanun (Compassionate King)

Melech Chassid (Righteous King)

Melech Tov (Good King)

Melech Tahor (Pure King)

Melech Yashar (Upright King)

Melech Yaqar (Precious King)

Melech Yeshuah (King of Salvation)

Melech Kabbir (Tremendous King)

Melech Keter (Crowned King)

Melech Kavod (Glorious King)

Melech Lev (King of the Heart)

Melech Leqichah (Taking King)

Melech Lohet (Scalding King)

Melech Mevin (Understanding King)

Melech Morish (Expelling King)

Melech Maashir (Wealthy King)

Melech Naeh (Pleasant King)

Melech Ne'eman (Reliable King)

Melech Netzach (Eternal King)

Melech Sod (Secret King)

Melech Aluv (Neglected King)

Melech Ozer (Helpful King)

Melech Anav (Humble King)

Melech Pe'er (Beautiful King)

Melech Palat (Detached King)

Melech Pudah (Redeeming King)

Melech Tzaddiq (Righteous King)

Melech Tzahalah (Rejoicing King)

Melech Tzach (Unblemished King)

Melech Qadosh (Holy King)

Melech Qaruv (Close King)

Melech Qalus (Praised King)

Melech Rinah (King of Songs)

Melech Rachum (Compassionate King)

Melech Rach (Tender King)

Melech Shomea (Listening King)

Melech Shoqet (Silent King)

Melech Shaanan (Serene King)

Melech Taar (Shaping King)

Melech Tam (Perfect King)

Melech Tomech (Supportive King)

Baruch Hu (Blessed be He)

2. Praise for the Divine King
(from Hechalot Rabbati)

Beautiful King enwrapped in Tiferet (Beauty),
Exalted with the color of songs,
Exalted with Hod (the Splendour) and Kavod (Glory) and exaltation,
With the wreath of pride and Keter (Crown) of awe.
Whose name is His guarantor
And whose remembrance is His support.
His Throne is made beautiful for Him
And His Palace is exalted
And His Kavod (Glory) is beloved by Him
And it is lovely to Him
And His servants please Him
And Israel is His Power and Miracle.

Melech Malki ha-Melachim
(King of Kings of Kings)
Elohey ha-Elohim (God of Gods)
Adonai ha-Adonim (Lord of Lords)
Who is unfathomable (or exalted) in wreathed crowns
Surrounded by branches of glowing Glow[22] (Nogah)
For with the branch of His Hod (Splendour) he covers the Heaven
His exaltation illuminates the heights
And from His beauty the depths (Tehomim) are lit
And from His stature the skies (Shechaqim, third Heaven) are lit
And the worthy ones are saved by His stature
And even the steadfast ones are split by His Crown (Keter)
The dignified ones are purified by His garment
And all trees rejoice in His word
The grasses jubilate in His joy
Through His word He spreads sweet aromas
The proud ones are driven out like flames of fire
Travelers are given spirit and he sends them to His Abode (Maqom).

Beloved and lovely and pure and dignified King
More dignified than the worthy ones

---

[22] The connection of a noun and an adjective with the same root is considered very poetic
in Hebrew.

Mightier than all creatures
Exaltation of the kings
Praise of the chosen ones
Humility for the pitiable ones
Pleasant in the mouth of all those who call upon him
Sweet for all those who await His Name
Good on all His ways
Upright in all His works
Pure in advice and Knowledge (Daat)
Clear in Understanding (Binah) and deed
Judge of every soul (Neshamah)
And witness and judge of every matter
Strenuous in Wisdom (Chochmah) and every mystery
Mighty in holiness and purity.

King, true and unique
King, who leteth die and giveth life
King, living and existing eternally
King, who speaketh and acteth and sustaineth
King, who formeth (Yetzirah) every plague and createth (Beriah) every
     healing
King, who maketh (Assiah) every evil and prepareth (Atziluth) every
     goodness
King, who judgeth over all His Making (Assiah)
And who sustaineth all His Formation (Yetzirah)
King, high and mild (Chesed) over all that is lower
And who is firm (Gevurah) over the strong ones.

King, high and exalted,
Uplifted and miraculous,
Beloved and venerable
Upright and unfailing
Precious and glorious
Firm and strong
Righteous and truthful
Holy and pure
Loving, great (Chesed) and mighty (Gevurah)
And strong, precious, awesome, and frightening
Paving the way to perfection
Dignified, set over those wreathed in beauty (i.e., the archangels)

In the chambers of the palace (Hechal)

Dignified, strong, steadfast, precious, awesome, and frightening

He seeth into the depths, gazeth into hidden things, looketh into darknesses

In every abode—there He is, and in every heart—there He is

And His wish one cannot change, and one cannot turn His word

And one cannot change His Will.

And there is no place to hide from Him, and there is no hiding or concealment from Him.

Thou ruleth for eternities

Thy throne will rule from generation to generation

King, compassionate and gracious

Forgiver and condoner, who rolls away and removes [the sin]

Thou will be exalted by every song

Thou will be made beautiful by every pleasure

Thou will be raised over the Palace (Hechal) of dignity

Thou will be uplifted over those wreathed in beauty (i.e., the archangels)

Thou will be more dignified than all those who were made (i.e., all creatures)

Thou will be more worthy than all that were formed (indicating Yetzirah, not Assiah as before; i.e., spirits)

Thou will be glorified over the Throne of Thy Glory (Kise Kavodecha)

Thou will be dignified over Thy precious object (i.e., the Throne of Glory)

Thou will be blessed in all blessings

Thou will be praised in all praises

Thou will be sung praises in all songs of praise

Thou will be praised in all meditations

Thou will be great in eternities

Thou will be sanctified forever

TOTRUSIAY YHVH

King of all the Worlds (Universes)

Lord of all works

Wise One of all the mysteries

Ruler of all the generations

EL (God), the one God, who is for eternities

Unique King who is for eternal eternities

Selah.

13

The Book of the Mysteries

Sefer ha-Razim (Book of the Mysteries) is an ancient magical text that can be traced back to the early talmudic era (350–400 CE). It is possible that the texts of this ancient book were collected in the famous city of Alexandria. In any case, some contents of the book are definitely older than this time. According to tradition, the *Book of the Mysteries* was given to Noah by the angel Raziel (whose name means Mystery of God) in the same year Noah made the ark and before his entrance into the it. It was originally inscribed on a sapphire stone. From this book Noah learned how to do all kinds of miraculous deeds and become wise, understanding, and knowledgeable. He learned how to observe and understand the signs of the firmament, and to know who rules each of the seven abodes of Heaven. He also learned the magical voice, which is called the voice of thunders (*qol raamim*), with which all magical invocations must be chanted, and how to interpret dreams and to predict the future. It was also from the secret wisdom of this book that Noah learned how to build the ark and be saved from the Flood. At the end of his life it was given to Abraham and handed down to Moses and finally to Solomon the king. By virtue of this book, Solomon became wise and learned how to command spirits and demons.

This ancient occult book teaches us about the seven Heavens and how to invoke the angels who dwell therein. In each Heaven we find hosts of angels and angelic princes or overseers, who can be invoked to help humankind.

In the first Heaven we find the mild Urpaniel, who can be invoked for healing; the mindful Danahel, who gives us the power of divination; the gentle Kalmiyah, who enables us to receive love and sympathy; the tough Paskar, who can catch a fugitive; and the wise Boel, who can teach us to interpret dreams. The first Heaven is related to Malchut, and the angels that can be invoked here will help us to deal with the world of manifestation, including physical health, love life and mundane relationships, and criminals. The interpretation of dreams seems to be an exception, and this aspect connects the first Heaven to the Heaven above. Yet while dreams themselves certainly belong to the level of Yesod, the interpretation of them is a matter of grounding them and thus belongs to Malchut.

The rituals that draw upon the angels of the second Heaven (Yesod) include subjects such as childbirth—a typical subject for Yesod—and various invocations to the moon to create effects that, for example, dispel evil intentions, restore those who have fallen from office, create a rite of protection from injury, and create a rite to rescue someone from an evil judgement.

Because Yesod is also related to purity, some special rules must be observed here. If you seek to ask something from any of those who stand on the steps of the second Heaven, cleanse yourself daily for three weeks from all fruit of the palm tree, meat of cattle, wine, all kinds of fish, and animals that bleed when slaughtered; do not approach a woman in her impurity (menstruation); do not come close to any being who has died; do not go near to an impure or leprous person (not even by accident); guard your mouth from every evil word; guard yourself from every sin; and sanctify yourself from every sin. Keep these rules if you attempt any of these rites!

In the third Heaven, three princes rule. The name of the first is Yawniel, the name of the second is Rahtiel, and the name of the third is Dalqiel. Yawniel rules over all matters of igniting and extinguishing fires.[1] Rahtiel rules over all the chariots of fire, of rushing, and of being exhausted. Dalqiel rules over the flames of fire, of blazing and burning down. The rites of these angels are concerned with matters such as speed and calling upon fire to prove your magical powers in order to gain fame.[2]

---

[1] Because the invocation to this angel is concerned with matters that are of no practical use today, it was left out.

[2] Note that fame is one of the meanings of Hod.

The fourth Heaven is related to Netzach. From here we can call the sun to come forth from his[3] beautiful bridal chamber.

In the fifth Heaven we find twelve princes who rule the months of the year. This Heaven belongs to Tiferet, and from here a higher kind of divination is given to us. Healing powers will also be found here.

The sixth Heaven is related to Gevurah, and from its realm we can invoke the great angels Afrachsey and Toqpiras to summon an army of angels for us to frighten our enemies.

There is no invocation to call the beings of the seventh Heaven, for this is the level of the vision of the divine Merkavah.

This chapter includes a collection of rituals that invoke the angels from heaven in a way that can be practiced today. In any period of time, magic must meet the needs of the people. As needs change, not all of the ancient spells and rites are relevant to a contemporary person. One of the ancient rituals, for example, invokes angelic powers to help light an oven in the cold. This is something that was a great problem two thousand years ago, but in our times there is no need to use magic; we can use electricity.

The first Heaven has seven encampments and the second Heaven has twelve steps. I have included only those rituals that I felt will be useful or interesting for the modern reader. Another example of magic that I left out concerns the angels of the seventh step of the second Heaven. These are angels who can be invoked to expel wild animals from a city—again, nothing we need to bother about in our day.

In order to perform these rituals today, we must develop an understanding of the principles of magic. To do so, we will explore the wisdom of the sages. The story of Choni, who draws a circle in order to perform divine magic, contains a very important teaching of which we should be aware. Let's first look at the story itself.

For every distress that comes upon the community—may it never befall!—they sound the Shofar, except of too great an abundance of rain. Once they said to Choni, the Circle Drawer: "Pray that rain may fall." He answered: "Go out and bring in the Passover ovens [made of clay] that they be not softened." He prayed, but the rain did not fall. Then he drew a circle and stood within it and said: "Master of the world, Thy children have turned their faces to me, for I am like a

---

[3] In the Qabbalistic tradition, the sun is male.

son of the house before Thee. I swear by Thy great Name that I will
not move from here until Thou hast mercy with Thy children." Rain
began to fall in drops. He said: "That is not what I asked for, but
for rain that will fill the cisterns, pits, and caverns." It began to rain
with violence. He said: "That is not what I asked for, but for rain of
good will, blessing, and generosity." Then it rained normally, until the
Israelites had to go up from Jerusalem to the Temple Mount because
of the rain. They went to him and said: "Just as you prayed for the
rain to come, so pray that it may go away!" He said to them: "Go and
see if the Stone of the Strayers is covered." Simeon ben Shetach (the
head of the Sanhedrin, the juridical court) sent for him and told him:
"Had you not been Choni, I would have decreed a ban against you!
But what shall I do to you, for you misbehave before God like a son
who misbehaves before his Father and He does his will for him? Of
you the Scripture says: Let your father and your mother be glad, and
let her that bore you rejoice."[4]

Choni ha-Me'aggel, "the Circle Drawer," was a Jewish magician who
lived in the first century BCE. From this story we learn that we need to
"turn on the power," in order to make our magic work. Usually, this is
done by opening the quarters in a circular clockwise fashion. This is what
is often called "drawing the circle." Yet it involves more than merely drawing a ring on the floor. Here is a simple description of how to do it:[5] Stand
in the middle of the ritual space and face east. Draw an opening hexagram[6]
(the Seal of Solomon) thus:

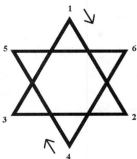

---

[4] Mishnah Taanit 3:8; Proverbs 23:25.

[5] This may not be exactly what Choni did, but it is a simple method, and he will certainly
have used a similar technique.

[6] Start where 1 is on the drawing, and continue as the numbers indicate. After the first
triangle is made, start again where the 4 is, and continue as the numbers indicate.

Visualize the hexagram in blue fire while you draw it. Point at the middle of the hexagram and say:

> **In the Name of the Holy One, blessed be He,**
> **I open the east.**

Then move to the south, visualizing a line of light where your finger is pointing, and open the south in the same way. Repeat this in all quarters, and make sure you complete the circle.[7] When you have finished the ritual, you MUST close the quarters again. This is very important in every ritual.[8] Start in the east, draw a closing hexagram:

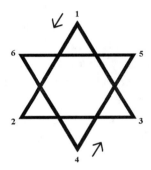

Visualize the hexagram in blue fire while you draw it. Point at the middle of the hexagram and say:

> **In the Name of the Holy One, blessed be He,**
> **I close the east.**

Again, repeat this in all four quarters and complete the circle as before.

Use this method or something comparable to it to prepare for any of the following rituals. Another important matter is courtesy. This is just as important at the higher levels of being as it is in the physical world. Always be respectful to the angelic beings. This does not mean that you should be submissive or frightened, but they deserve just as much respect and thankfulness as any other being. Thank them and bless them after the

---

[7] This is just a basic form, which can be enhanced in many ways. You could, for example, add an invocation of the powers of the four Holy Letters of the Divine Name by saying: Before me YOD, behind me HEH, to my right VAV and to my left HEH. And above me the Divine Spirit.

[8] Just as you would not open a holy book and leave it lying around unattended, you must never open the quarters and then simply go away and leave them open. This is asking for trouble.

rite is over and release them: This last point is particularly important.

The Healing Rite

The angel Urpaniel, whose name means Light (or Fire) before God, can be invoked to send healing angels to an ill person. This is a simple but very effective healing technique. Perform this ritual in the first or second hour of the night (i.e., directly after sunset), while you are burning frankincense and myrrh.

First, purify and cleanse yourself, and then open the quarters in a way that suits you. After the quarters are opened, invoke the healing angel Urpaniel, and then the seventy-two healing angels who serve him.

> I invoke you
> **URPANIEL**
> **The angel who is set over the first encampment of the first Heaven**
> **In the name of**
> **URPANIEL**
> I call upon you
> **BOMEDAY DAMNA ANUCH ALPAY AMUCH QATIBIA**
> **PETRUFAY GEMATAY PAUR NARENTEQ RAGHATAY URNAH**
> **MAOT PARUCHAH AQILAH TRAQUYAH BARUQ SACHARURA**
> **ATNANAY GILAN TACHAT ARNUB ASHMAY YOTZESH**
> **KAPUN KERBAY GIRSHUM PERIAN SHASHMA ABABA**
> **NATANEL ARAEL ANIF TRAVUR OBADIEL YAVEN**
> **ALUN MOEL LELEF YACHESPET RACHGEL RUMAPAY**
> **YACHTAY ARNIEL PUVUN KADIEL ZACHRIEL AGDALAN**
> **MIGAEL GUFIEL KARTAH KILDAH DIGEL ALNU**
> **TIRLAY SEBLAH AVIEL EL KASIEL SIQMAH**
> **AZBAH YOTUAH RALCHAH CHALIAN AFTIEL TIAMIEL**
> **ELEL NATIEL AFICHAH TALGIEL NANA ASUTIEL**

Chant each of the seventy-two angelic names seven times while visualizing for each name another healing angel surrounding the patient.[9] As each angel appears, visualize the patient feeling better.

> I [Insert your magical name]
> **request that ye will give me success**

---

[9] Going through all the names of the angels is the main part of the ritual, and takes about a quarter hour.

> **in healing** [Insert name of the patient],
> **son/daugher of** [Insert name of the patient's mother].

Now visualize the patient recovering completely. Take a moment to hold this image, and then thank the angels and close the quarters.

Rite of Divination

If you want to know what the next year[10] holds, you may call upon the angels of the first Heaven to tell you what will and what will not happen. If you perform a rite of divination, keep in mind that you will see only the most likely outcome.

You can always change your fortune. This is why the sages said: "There is no Mazal (star or predicted fortune) for Israel."[11] In the teachings of the Qabbalah, Israel represents the souls on the spiritual path, the ones who walk the path of the service of God and who have grown to a point where they are responsible for their own fortune. Thus every method of divination impels but does not compel. Whatever is shown to you can be changed.

To perform the divination, prepare a mixture of ink and powdered myrrh. Write on hieratic papyrus (or paper) all the possibilities for the next year, using one slip of paper for every possible outcome. (Whether there will be peace or war, whether you will have plenty or little money, whether you will be healthy or ill, whether there will be deaths or births in your family, etc.) The traditional method consists of placing the pieces of papyrus on top of oil in a new bowl filled with spikenard oil, so that the pieces swim on the surface. Then, perform the rite over three days, and those strips that still swim on the surface of the oil after three days will reveal what will happen. If there are more than one, all that is written on the floating pieces will happen.[12] Perform this in purity and you will succeed.[13]

Face the sun at dawn, recite the name of Danahel, the overseer and

---

[10] If you want to know in which month something will happen, perform the Oracle of the Twelve Angels as described later in this chapter.

[11] Babylonian Talmud: Shabbat 156a.

[12] The trick is not to make the strips too big or too small, so that most, but not all of them, sink. Place them outside, where the wind can blow and cause some of the strips to sink.

[13] A more modern version of this type of divination would be to put the strips in a bag and draw a few strips out of the bag without counting. Another possibility would be just to throw them on the ground, and those with the written side up will come true.

angel of divination, and all the angelic names of his servants, saying the invocation to the sun.

DANAHEL
OGRAVAVO OVASHEL BARTOVIEL KALOVIEL RACHVIEL
OHIEL KARVATON KARBA DAAYANOT EYNECHA AVIRAM
ATAGALA OTOT ASHTANUEL ASHPAR TARGIEL AMICHEL
ATADASHU URIEL ARMOD ASTON ACHEL ANUR ASKIRA
LABIEL ALESAH CHASNIEL LAMUSHEY ADOT TIROM ALFEY
IMEYACH ARGALA MINEL ALIEL MADNIEL
I invoke thee SHEMESH (sun)
Who shines on earth
In the name of the angels,
who make men of knowledge understand wisdom and secrets.
I invoke thee
that thee will do what I ask thee
And make known to me what will happen in this year.
Do not conceal anything from me.

After three days, examine the oil and see which strips are floating on the oil. These are the things that will happen. Then burn the oil while saying or chanting the names of the angels. Hide the remaining papyri in a wall, or bury them in the same way as you would a holy text.[14]

Rite of Aphrodite

Some readers may be surprised to find the name of a pagan goddess in a book about Qabbalistic magic. Some may maintain that this shows that magic is evil. Yet the Bible does not forbid the use of such names. It is forbidden only to confuse the minor deities with the Creator Himself. He is our God and He is One, and there is no one like Him.

It has often been said that the Qabbalistic tradition is able to incorporate the whole Western Mystery Tradition. This ritual shows that not only in our times, but as early as two thousand years ago, the Qabbalah was—as it still is—the heart of the Western Mystery Tradition. In this ritual, the name Aphrodite (אפרודיטי) is used to invoke the planetary power of Venus.

The original form of this ritual was used not only to gain love, but

---

[14] In the Jewish tradition it is not permitted to dispose of holy texts as you might dispose of other texts.

also to gain the mercy of a king. Therefore, it would include the slaughtering of a lion cub (symbol of kingship) and the use of its heart and blood. Because we seldom deal with kings nowadays, and because killing a lion cub would raise considerable practical difficulties as well as being very immoral, I have varied the original ritual. Change is part of a living tradition; we simply cannot do everything the way it was done two thousand years ago—just as we no longer live according to the social rules of cavemen. The skin of the lion cub is replaced with rose petals, and its blood with pure rose oil. (Both ingredients correspond to Venus and fit this ritual perfectly.) In modern times, the ritual can be performed to make you more attractive when you go out. The magic of this rite may help you to find the right person. Furthermore, the ritual can help you to increase the chance that people will like you. This may help in many situations that have nothing to do with love. (Such as in a job interview, for example.) But NEVER try to use magic to make someone love you against his or her free will.

To perform the ritual, purify and wash yourself with water. Stay clean and pure. Write these forty-four names on the rose petals:

אבריה אימרהי דמנאי אמנהר יאמנוך פטכיא טוביאל
גוליאל אופרי גמתי אורניאל פריכיהו יאון לטמיאל
אוריט תימוגו אנמרי אלמיניאל יכמטו סטרטו צבעקני
בורתיאס רספות כרסון אמאף ופאטנא אחאל סאביאל
בלקיר פכהור הסתר סתריאל אליסס חלסיאל טרספו
קרסטוס מלכיאל ארדק חסדיאל איסף אמיאל פאנוס
גדיאל סביבאל

Burn incense consisting of styrax, myrrh, and musk. Instead of real musk, use *Hibiscus abelmoschus L.* Face the planet Venus. The correct direction for the time of the ritual can be calculated by an astrologer or an astrology program. Simply calculate a horoscope for the hour of the ritual. In a horoscope, the Ascendant will always be east, the Descendant will be west, the MC will be south, and the IC will be north. Roughly speaking, Venus will never be far from the sun, because the position of Venus can never be more than forty-seven degrees from that of the sun.

Visualize the angel Kalmiyah above you and around you the forty-four angels who serve him. Take in your hand the cup with the wine and the rose oil, and say this over the two liquids:

> I call upon you
> KALMIYAH (כלמייה)
> AVRIAH IMRAHEY DAMNAY AMNAHER YEMANUCH
> PATCHIA TOVIEL GULIAH UFREY GAMTAY URNIEL
> PRICHIHU YEON LETMIEL URIT TIMUGU ANMAREY
> ALMINIEL YACHMATU SATRATU TZEVQANEY BORTIAM
> RASFUT KRASON AMAF UFATNA ACHAEL SAVIEL BALQIR
> PACHHUR HASTER SATARIEL ALISAS CHALSIEL TARSEFU
> QARSTOM MALKIEL ARDAQ CHASDIEL ISEF AMIEL
> PANUM GADIEL SAVIVEL

The original text instructs the magician to repeat these names and the name of the overseer twenty-one times.[15] While doing so, visualize the writing filled with power. Then wash the rose petals with wine and mix the wine with the rose oil. Look toward the direction where you are visualizing the planet Venus, like a brilliant star, and the angel Chasdiel standing below Venus, and say:

> APHRODITE,
> brilliant star of Heaven,
> and CHASDIEL,
> angel of love and mercy,
> I invoke you
> in the name of the angels, who serve KALMIYAH
> that ye will find for me a loving partner [wife/husband].
> Charm her/him and touch her/his heart,
> that I will find favor and sympathy before her/him.
> Ye angels go around and circulate in the world,
> bring to me a person who loves me and whom I will love,
> that we will live together in love and harmony
> according to the Will of the Holy One, blessed be He.
> Amen

If you wish to perform this ritual to make people like you rather than to find a partner, use these words:

---

[15] To go through all the names of the angels is the main part of the ritual and takes about a half hour. You can use a meditation cord to count the twenty-one times that you repeat each name. The same effect, however, can be accomplished with fewer repetitions. It is better to say the names once with intention than to say them many times without.

APHRODITE,
brilliant star of Heaven,
and CHASDIEL,
angel of love and mercy,
I invoke you
in the name of the angels, who serve KALMIYAH
that ye will make me likable.
And that l find favor and sympathy before all who see me.
Ye angels go around and circulate in the world,
And touch the hearts of all people,
that they will love me and be friendly to me.

When you have spoken the invocation, imagine a spark of light descending into the wine and rose oil. Then anoint your body with the wine and rose oil. Let your body and your soul absorb the magic. Take a few minutes to feel and experience the magical power as it strengthens your aura.

To Release the Angels

I have invoked all you angels who have assisted me in this ritual
And I have called upon thee APHRODITE,
brilliant star of heaven,
I bless you and release you.
Depart in peace,
and go peacefully to your abodes,
and do not harm me.
The rite is ended.

Rite to Catch a Fugitive

In this rite, you will call upon the archangel Paskar and his servants, the angels of Gevurah, who are girded with power and strength to enable them to hurry from place to place and fly to all corners of the world. This rite will empower you to force a criminal fugitive (for example a thief) to come (back) to you. Because this rite will affect someone else against their will, you must have a very good reason for performing it! It would be ethical to perform it only on a wanted criminal, and I advise it to be used only by policemen and judges. Remember that these angels will not take lightly the misuse of this rite. Also, take precautions in case the fugitive appears at your door late at night.

Write on each of four pieces of copper foil:

[Insert name of fugitive], **son/daughter of** [Insert name of mother],
PASKAR
AZIEL ARBIEL TERIFON PUCHBUS PESTMAR LINANIEL
QERUNIDAN SHUCHDON SELVIDAM AMIEL UZIEL PENIEL
TERMIAL CHAMAMIEL TZERMIEL NIMAMOS NUDANAYA
BARIVA ZUNANOM CHASTUEL SEDRIEL HOFANION
QADMIEL KAFNAYA ARMIEL ADMON HERMOR TZAFLIEL
SEFERIEL QACHANIEL SHAVACHIRAY ARMONIS TOFOMOS
PATZATZIEL CHATAFIEL PERSOMON NACHALIEL

Then say over them:

> **I charge you angels of Gevurah,**
> **To seize** [Insert name of fugitive], **son/daughter of** [Insert name of mother]
> **Wherever he goes or wherever he dwells,**
> **Whether in a city or in a country**
> **Whether at sea or on land**
> **Whether eating or drinking.**
> **Ye shall make him fly like a flying bird**
> **And bring him against his will**
> **And not let him linger one moment,**
> **Whether by day or by night.**

Then bury the four pieces of copper foil in the four corners of the city or country.

Rite of Understanding a Dream

It may be that one of your friends has a worrying dream, and asks you whether this dream shows any omens, and what they might mean.

This rite is to be performed when you are asked to interpret a dream for someone else (such as Joseph and Daniel did.) In order to do so, we will invoke Boel, the overseer of the seventh encampment of the first Heaven, whose name means God Is with(in) Him.

Wear a new coat or robe, and do not eat meat or fish or drink wine. Go to the edge of the sea or to the bank of a river during the third hour of the night (i.e., two hours after sunset). Take pure myrrh and pure frankincense and, placing them on a burning coal in an earthen vessel, face the water and chant:

BOEL BOEL BOEL

Chant three times each the names of these angels who serve Boel:

NUHARIEL DAVAVIEL DIMTAMAR DAVAEL MECHASCHIN
AUR DIAM BAVITAEL SARURAY AHAGEYAH PERUFIEL
MACHASIEL ALZIEL TAKURACHAS QERUMIEL RAMIEL
LACHESON SALACHIEL ACHIEL ACHER UVER SERUGIEL
YADUEL SHAMASHIEL SHAFTIEL RECHAVIYA ACHMUDA
MERMERIN ANUCH ALFERET UMIGRA QERUCHANES
SERFIEL GADRIEL ARDUDA PURTANIEL AGMIEL RAHTIEL
DITRON CHAZIEL PETUEL GILGALA DAMANTZER ZAZIEL

While reciting these names, visualize a pillar of fire between Heaven and earth. When you see the pillar clearly, say:

I invoke you
By Him Who measured the waters in the Palm of his Hand
and rebuked the waters so that they fled from Him,
and made spirits (ruachot) flying in the air,
servants before Him as a fiery flame
who rebuked the sea and dried it up
and turned rivers into a desert by His Name and by its Letters.
I invoke you
by the names of the angels of the seventh encampment who serve BOEL,
that ye make known to me what is in the heart of
[Insert name], **son/daughter of** [Insert name of mother],
and what is his desire and what is the interpretation of his dreams
and what is his thought.

Repeat this on the second and third night if you do not get an answer, and a pillar of fire and a cloud in human form will reveal itself to you. This is the archangel Boel, who will answer all your questions.

To release him, take water from the sea or river where you are standing, throw it three times to Heaven, and say seven times:

Invisible lord BOEL,
sufficient to our need the perfect shield bearer,
I release thee, I release thee
Withdraw [literally, subside] and return to thy way.

Rite to Dispel Evil Intentions against You

Have you ever been in a situation in which someone in a stronger position than you wished you harm?—maybe someone who is your superior at work or someone with more social influence? This ancient ritual may protect you against such a situation. The effect of the ritual will be twofold: First, it will hinder your enemy obtaining a chance to cause you harm. Whenever he tries something, something else will come in the way. Sometimes, he will just not notice an opportunity, or he will forget what he wanted to do because something else catches his attention. Furthermore, if there is a chance for him to change his mind, he will start to realize that you are not such an unlikable person, and maybe he will eventually give up his evil intentions. This rite will NOT help you hinder a person doing anything you deserve. It will not help you to get away from the juridical or social consequences of your deeds. It will help you only if someone intends to be unfair to you.

These are the angels who stand on the third step of the second Heaven:

Yahoel, Daayahu, Eliel, Barachiel, Aley Safum Penimor
Eleazar Gavliel, Kamshiel, Udahel, Yaatzel, Rafafiel, Pasafiel

They shake and convulse the hearts of men, wrecking their plans and making their thoughts empty. Fear is with these angels and awe is where they walk. They look angry and are extremely severe. They are an army of powerful knights, carrying awe before them and terror behind them, roaring and causing others to tremble and shiver wherever they go. Their voice is a voice of thunders and they have a staff of fire in their hands, and their faces are like sparks of fire—fire coming out of their eyes—and they are ready and prepared to banish and destroy (literally, to neutralize and make void).

If you wish to dispel the evil plans made against you by someone mightier than you, go out in the middle of the night when the moon is full. Go alone, cleansed and clothed in a fresh garment, and stand under the moon. Open the quarters in a way that suits you, and then say twenty-one times each, the names of the angels who stand on the third step of the second Heaven:

In the Name of Heaven
I invoke ye
YAHOEL DAAYAHU ELIEL BARACHIEL ALEY SAFUM

PENIMOR ELEAZAR GAVLIEL KAMSHIEL UDAHEL
YAATZEL RAFAFIEL PASAFIEL

Then say:

YAREACH YAREACH HA-YAREACH (Moon, Moon, O Moon)
Bring my words to the angels
who stand on the third step of the second Heaven,
and dispel the evil thoughts of [Insert name],
and erase the wicked plans of his heart concerning me,
And mute his mouth that he cannot speak against me,
And ruin his evil opinion and dispel his plans.
And move his heart that every time he sees me
He will be filled with love for me,
and turn him toward me so that he loves me,
and that he shall not remember any hate of me,
and that I shall find grace and mercy in his eyes.

Write on silver foil the names of the angels and these characters (sigils), and place them on a tablet over your heart. You will be successful while this foil remains there.

יהואל דעיהו אליאל
ברכיאל עלי ספום
פנימור אלעזר גבליאל
כמשיאל אודהאל יעצאל
רפפיאל פספיאל

Rite to Protect a Woman in Childbirth

Childbirth was always a great danger in ancient times. Magical protection was used to ensure that no demonic power caused the early death of mother or child. The modern reader may ask if there were so many demons that needed to be fended off. Modern medicine has made childbirth much safer, and it seems that the lack of scientific advances that we have today was why childbirth was so dangerous. The answer that the sages might have given is that the danger from the "other side" (*sitra aracha*) is still the same today, but modern medicine does not give demonic powers as much chance of causing evil. Yet to identify a danger, disease, or even bad habit with a

demonic power and to ward off this demon is a very effective magical technique.[16] The ancient Qabbalists knew how to use this technique to protect
against diseases and harm. They invoked angelic powers to insure a safe
birth and give the demons (or personified illnesses) no chance of killing
the mother or the child.

These are the names of the angels who stand on the eighth step of the
second Heaven:

אברה ברקיאל אדוניאל אזריאל ברכיאל עמיאל קדשיאל מרגיאל
פרויאל פניאל מרבמיאל מרניסאל שמיאל מתניאל הוד הוד

**Abrah, Barqiel, Adoniel, Azriel, Barachiel, Amiel, Qadshiel, Margiel,
Paraviel, Paniel, Marbamiel, Marnisel, Shemiel, Mataniel, Hod, Hod.**

Their appearance is like the splendor of the Chashmal;[17] they speak by
their actions. They are accompanied by trembling and fire and they are
surrounded by awe. They rule over the spirits spread over the earth, and no
evil spirit can appear at the place where they are remembered.

If you seek to drive out an evil spirit or prevent it from coming to a
pregnant woman and killing the baby, write the names of these angels on
a piece of gold foil and place it in a tube of silver. The woman is to wear
this tube before her pregnancy. At the time of the birth, on each of four
pieces of silver foil, write the names of these angels, placing them in the
four directions of the house so that no spirit enters.

Rite of Protection in a Battle or a War

War is as dangerous in our time as it was in ancient times. Modern technology has made war even colder and more inhuman. Any time a soldier goes to
war, those who love him or her pray that he or she comes back unhurt. The
following rite is an ancient technique designed to protect those in war.

These are the angels who stand on the ninth step of the second Heaven.
Swift and strong, flying through the air, their power is mighty. They have
swords in their hands and are ready for war. They take their bows and have
their spear at the ready. They leap forth from fire on horses of fire; the har-
nesses of their chariots are of fire, and they provoke fear and awe wherever
they turn.

---

[16] Israel Regardie describes this technique in the first chapter of his book *Foundations of
Practical Magic* (Wellingborough, England: Thorsons, 1979).

[17] See chapter 12, The Vision of the Merkavah.

Angel	In Hebrew	Angel	In Hebrew
Gadodiel	גדודיאל	Sachasiel	סכסיאל
Tarsuniel	תרסוניאל	Netzachiel	נצחיאל
Atzda	אצדא	Rabbania	רבניא
Chalilel	חליליאל	Toqpiel	תוקפיאל
Samchiel	סמכיאל	Padhiel	פדהיאל
Qarba	קרבא	Tziel	ציאל
Parel	פראל	Patachiel	פתחיאל

If you wish a man going to war to be protected from any arrow (projectile),[18] sword, or blow, take seven leaves of a bay tree and write the names of these angels on them—two on each leaf—and put them in spikenard oil. On the day of his going to war, rub the oil on his body and on his sword, on his bow and on his arrows (or his gun and knife in modern times). Also write these names on silver foil, and put them in a copper or brazen tube. He should hang the tube on his body so that it covers his heart, and no blow shall hit him.

When you write these angelic names, always do it with concentrated intention (Kavvanah), and chant the names while writing them. Also, chant them when you rub the oil on his body and armor.

Rite to Rescue Someone from an Evil Judgment

It is sad, but justice and judgement are not always the same. Laws made by humans are fallible, and many judges are subject to prejudice or even corruption. The Jewish people in particular have often suffered from these difficulties. This ritual invokes angelic powers to defend the rights of your friends. If someone is innocent, the angels will rescue him. If he is guilty, they will not rescue him from a fair sentence.

These are the angels who stand on the tenth step of the second heaven:

---

[18] This includes modern bullets and missiles. Please note that magic does not make you invulnerable; it merely decreases the chance that you may be hit.

דכריאל חריאל שבקיאל אתכיאל סמיכיאל מרמואל קנאל צפתף
יהאל אל צדק אכפף עזמאל מכמיכאל תרכיאל תבגיאל

Dachariel Chariel Shabaqiel Atachiel Marmuel Qaniel Zaftaf
Yahel El Tzedeq Achfaf Ezmel Machmichel Tarchiel Tavgiel

These angels have been commanded to defend the truth. Before them are myriad angels holding reed pens of fire to write uninterruptedly scrolls or books. They insure acquittal and fair judgment upon the righteous who call them by their names. They rescue and save the innocent from corvee and the law of the kingdom or country, and from every death penalty.

If you seek to rescue someone you love from an evil judgement and from any misery, purify yourself from all impurity, and do not sleep with a woman[19] for three days. Stand before the sun at the time when it comes forth (i.e., dawn).

Repeat the names of these angels:

DACHARIEL CHARIEL SHABAQIEL ATACHIEL MARMUEL QANIEL ZAFTAF YAHEL EL TZEDEQ ACHFAF EZMEL MACHMICHEL TARCHIEL TAVGIEL

Then say:

I beseech thee
who art the great angel
who is called SHEMESH (sun),
who rises to the height of the firmament,
who watches the children of Adam,[20]
that thou doest as I seek
and bringest my words before
the highest King over Kings of Kings
The Holy one blessed be He
That I may intercede
in the case of [Insert name of the accused one],
For he is in need and under evil judgment.
And that thou will bring forth to him
a good outcome and a time of relief,
And may shame be on those who sought evil for him.

---

[19] Or with a man if you are female.
[20] Children of Adam: Humanity.

> **I beseech thee care for him,
> and free him from all harm**

In addition, write the names of these angels on a copper or brazen foil, and hide it in the east, doing so in front of the sun at sunrise. Do all of this in purity, and you will succeed.

Rite to Restore Those Who Have Fallen from Office

Jews are people with a love of learning. Thus, many of them became wise and skillful and, as in the case of Joseph, the rulers of other nations occasionally gave Jewish people high offices. But when others envied them for their position, intrigues were planned to evict them from office. To counter such a problem, the following rite was designed to invoke angelic help and regain the office once held.

These are the angels who stand on the eleventh step of the second heaven:

רפדיאל דמואל מארינוס אמינאל צחיאל עקריאל אדניאל רדקיאל
שלמיאל אסתטיאל סטאל אגלגלתון ארמות פרחגאל נפפמיות

**Rafdiel Damuel Marinos Aminel Tzachiel Eqriel Adoniel Radqiel
Shalmiel Astatiel Satel Agalgalton Armut Perchagel Nafafmiot**

Awe accompanies their presence and great myriads of angels stand and establish encampments serving in the place, for on the word of their mouth angels of fire rush and return, causing the descent from greatness (Gedulah) of some men and the ascent to the beautiful harmony (Tiferah) of others. They fly back and forth and are found in their place, praising their Creator, singing to the One who formed them.

If you seek to restore a king, prince, commander, judge, or any person of authority who has fallen from his position or his office, put oil and honey and fine flour in a new glass vial. Purify yourself from all impurity and do not eat the meat of an animal that died of natural causes (*nevilah*). Further, do not touch the bed of a woman for seven days.[21] On the day of the invocation, stand before the moon in its fourteenth, fifteenth, or sixteenth day (that is, on or right after the full moon), and holding the vial in your hand, write on it the names of the angels of the encampment of the eleventh step of the second Heaven, and recite these names seven times before the moon.

---

[21] Or a man if you are female: Do not have sexual intercourse.

**RAFDIEL DAMUEL MARINOS AMINEL TZACHIEL
EQRIEL ADONIEL RADQIEL SHALMIEL ASTATIEL SATEL
AGALGALTON ARMUT PERCHAGEL NAFAFMIOT**

Then say:

I throw my grace before thee
O YAREACH (Moon),
Who moves in the day and in the night
with thy chariots of light,
and before thee and behind thee are Angels of Mercy (Chesed).

I invoke thee
By the King who makes thee come forth and who makes thee return.
As thou art waning and as thou art waxing and are positioned in thy abode
So shall [Insert name] be in his position,
and he shall be honored in the eyes of all who see him,
and as there is eternal glory for thee
let there be glory for him
in the eyes of all children of Adam and Eve.
And he shall stand in his office,
and let him rule like he did before,
and he shall not be removed from his position.

Do this for three days, and for the deposed person make a cake from the ingredients, drying it at night so that the sun does not see it, and he shall eat it for three days before the sun rises, and in his house he shall hide or bury the vial on which the names are written.

Rite to Speed Up Horses

This spell will help you to increase the speed of your horses for a short while. Did you ever want to move faster in a vehicle? Because the angel of this ritual is not specifically responsible for horses, but rather for fast movement in vehicles, I believe it may be useful to the modern person. I do, however, advise caution in using this spell with a motor vehicle. It should never be used on public streets or motorways. Whether it should be used for racing cars or in similar situations is up to the reader. In any case, make sure that you do not increase the chances of harm to youself or others. Please remember that extra speed in the case of horses is much more unlikely to cause harm than in the case of a modern car or motorcycle. If you use this spell on a horse, also remember that the extra speed comes from the emergency resources of the animal. This resource of extra power is not unlimited. Make sure you do not ruin the health of a horse with this spell.

These are the names of the angels who serve Rahtiel (רהטיאל), Racer or Runner of God.[22]

אגרא זרגרי גנטס תעזמא לתסרפאל גדיאל תמניאל
עקהיאל גוחפניאל ארקני צפיקואל מושיאל סוסיאל התניאל
זכריאל אכנסף צדקי אחסף נכמרא פרדיאל קליליאל דרומיאל

This rite is to be used if you seek to race horses and they have no power. They shall not stumble in their movement, and they shall be fleet-footed like the wind, and no foot of a living being shall arrive before them. Grace and mercy shall be in their movement.

On a piece of silver foil write the names of the horses and the names of the angels and the name of Rahtiel, their prince. Then say:

> ### RAHTIEL
> AGRA ZARGREY GANTES TAAZMA LATSARPAEL
> GADIEL TAMNIEL EQAHIEL GUCHPANIEL ARAQNEY
> TZAFIQUEL MUSCHIEL SUSIEL HATANIEL ZACHARIEL
> ACHNASAF TZADQEY ACHSAF NACHMARA
> PARDIEL QALILIEL DARUMIEL
>
> I invoke you
> angels of haste,
> who hasten [i.e., rush] between the stars,
> that ye invest these horses with strength and power,
> these horses that are raced by [Insert name of horseman]
> and by his charioteer who is racing them,
> that they shall rush and not become tired or stumble,
> and they shall be fast and light like a river,
> and no creature shall be in front of them,
> and nor sorcery or charm shall come upon them.

Hide the foil within the racing line where the race takes place.

---

[22] Here we find an interesting parallel in the Tarot: The eight of Wands, usually seen as Hod of fire, is called Speed.

Rite to Prove Your Powers

If you seek to show proof of your powers to a beloved or a friend by filling the house with a fire that does not burn people (i.e., an astral fire), then put a root of dittany[23] on a burning coal. When the smoke rises in the middle of the house, recite the names of the angels and the name of their ruler Dalqiel (Burning or Glowing of God). After the smoke has risen and you have done this seven times, it shall appear like fire. Before you start the invocation, open in a suitable way (and do not forget to close after the rite!).

DALQIEL

Recite the names of Dalqiel and the angels who serve him:

> NURIEL AZLIVAN ILIEL MALCHIAH CHILILEL CHARAHEL
> SHALQIEL TZAGRIEL PASKIEL AQRIEL SAMNIEL TZAVAVIEL
> NACHLIEL TAGMALIEL AMINUEL TALBAAF QATCHANIEL
> AFRIEL ANAGIEL MASHRIEL AMNAGAN

Then say:

> I invoke you,
> angels covered in the fire,
> by Him who is all fire and Who sits on a Throne of fire
> and whose ministers are flaming fires,[24]
> and encampments of fire serve before Him.
>
> By His great Name I invoke ye,
> that ye let us see this great miracle
> and do not make us fear.

When you have finished your words—recited seven times—everyone will see the house filled with fire. If you wish the fire to disappear, speak this invocation to free the angels:

> Angels of fire,
> extinguish, extinguish
> instantaneously,
> haste and hurry

---

[23] Dittany root bark, *Dictamnus albus* var. dasycarpus. This plant is known as burning bush because the flowers produce a gas that creates blue flames that do not burn the plant when it catches fire—though this may happen spontaneously in a hot summer.
[24] See Psalm 104:4.

The Invocation of the Sun

This invocation is to seek guidance from the Tiferet level and to know and understand the future. People throughout the ages have invoked the sun to reveal what is hidden to them.

To Invoke the Sun at Daytime

If you seek to see the sun at daytime, seated on his chariot and ascending, then guard yourself, beware, and purify yourself for seven days from all impure food and impure drink and any other impure thing.

Prepare the place and open the quarters in a way that suits you. Face the east at the time of the rising of the sun, and when the first rays of sunlight appear, burn incense before the sun. The incense should include frankincense and exquisite spices weighing three shekels.[25] (Even though the text does not explicitly say so, I think that the amount of incense used here indicates that the rite is to be performed outside.)

Then invoke the names of the princes of the (encampments or choirs of) angels who lead the sun by day. Each of these is the leader of a choir of solar angels. Chant each name seven times.[26]

ABRAKSAS MERMERUT MUCHTIEL MARIT TZADQIEL
YACHSEY CHASIEL RAVIEL YABUCH MIEL KERIMEKA
MERMIN PUEL GAVRIEL ASHTON TUQPIEL ALIEL
NEPLEY UEL QODSHIEL HUDIEL NURMIEL YARSHIEL
MALKIEL AGRRITEL LAHGIEL MENURIEL PLUEL
NURIEL HERMIEL NESBRIEL

I invoke you,
the angels who lead the sun by the power of their might
on the course of the firmament to illuminate the world
by Him whose voice trembles the earth,
who moves the mountains in His anger,
who calms the sea by His power,
who shakes the pillars of the world with His view,
who sustains everything with His arm,
who is hidden from the eyes of all life,

---

[25] A shekel is about twelve grams—thus the amount of incense for this rite is about thirty-six grams.

[26] It will add to the atmosphere if a light is lit for every angel invoked.

> who sits on the throne of the greatness of the kingdom
> of the glory of His Holiness,
> and who moves the entire world.
>
> By His great, awesome, mighty, daunting,
> strong and powerful,
> holy and valiant,
> miraculous and hidden,
> exalted and illuminating Name
> I remember you and I invoke you,
> that ye shall do my will and my request at this time
> and at this period of the day,
> and turn away the rays of the sun that I may see him face to face,
> as he appears in his bridal chamber.
> And let me not be inflamed by your fire,
> and give me authority to do as I will [literally, to do my will].

At the completion of the invocation, close your eyes[27] and look with your inner vision at the sky opening and the bright golden sun that appears before you. As you watch, the light of the sun becomes less penetrating. You can see through the surface of the sun, and you see its true shape, the shape of a beautiful and magnificent golden chariot, and within the chariot on a golden throne sits Helios, the lord of the sun. He greets you and his voice is like thunder. You may ask him to foretell whether death or life, whether good or bad is about to come. If you cannot get the desired results in your first attempt, repeat the invocation, but this time, say the names of the angels in reverse order. If you wish to release the sun, repeat the invocation and say:

> I invoke you
> to return the rays of the sun to their place as in the beginning,
> and that the sun may continue to go on his way.

To Invoke the Sun at Night

If you wish to see the sun at night, purify yourself for three weeks[28] from all impure food and impure drink and any other impure thing. Perform the

---

[27] Do not look into the sun with your physical eyes, as this may cause injury.

[28] For some readers, three weeks of preparation for one ritual may be very difficult to accomplish. You can shorten the whole process by doing a pathworking that takes you through three weeks of purification in one single meditation. An example of how to do this can be found in appendix 2.

rite in the third hour of the night (i.e., the third hour after sunset). Cover yourself in a white robe or cape and prepare the place. After opening the quarters, turn to the north and say twenty-one times the name of the sun and of the angels that lead him by night.

These are the names of the princes of the (encampments of) angels who lead the sun by night:

PERSIEL TZARATZIEL AGIEL NABIMEL AMIEL YASARIEL ASMEVEL SHEFTIEL SHEVEL RADARIEL SHASIEL LIBABIEL BENRIEL TZAGRIEL MENAHEL LAMIEL PERIEL PEDAHIEL LIBRAEL RAVATZEL CHAMAQIEL BAGAHIEL NAVRIEL QATZPIEL RADANIEL CHATANIEL ASAFAFIEL CHALUEL SHAMAIEL ZACHZACHIEL NACHBRIEL PATZIEL QAMNIEL ZAHEL CHADIEL

I invoke you,
the angels who move through the air of the firmament,
By Him who sees but is not seen,
by the King who uncovers all secrecies and sees all secrets,
by God who knows what is in the darkness,
and He turns the shadow of death into the morning,[29]
and He illuminates the night like the day,
and all secrets are uncovered before Him like the sun on a cloudless day,
and for Whom nothing is too difficult to understand.

In the Name of the Holy King who walks on the wings of the spirit,
by the letters of the specified Name (Shem ha-meforash),
which have been revealed to Adam in the Garden of Eden,
The Ruler of the planets and the sun and the moon,
who bow down before Him like servants before their master,
by the Name of the miraculous God I invoke you,
that ye shall let me know this great miracle which I seek,
and let me see the sun in his power in the chariot's orbit,
and that there will be no concealed thing that is too mysterious for me,
and let me see him perfectly on this day,
and let me ask him what I desire,
and let him speak to me as a man speaks to his friend.

---

[29] Compare Amos 5:8.

> Let him tell me the mystery of the depths,
> and let me know that which is concealed,
> and let no evil thing strike me.

Then, with your inner ear imagine—with all the emotion and awe you are able to put into it—a thunderous voice from the north.[30] The sound of the voice fills your entire surroundings, and your heart is awestruck. With your inner vision, see something shining like lightning coming forth and lighting up the earth before you. Now you see the sun, and you know you must bow down to the ground and fall on your face and recite this prayer:

> Holy HELIOS, who rises in the east,
> good mariner, trustworthy leader of the rays of the sun,
> reliable witness who of old established the mighty wheel of the heavens,
> holy orderer, ruler of the axis, lord, brilliant leader, king soldier[31]
> I [Insert your magical name] supplicate thee,
> that thou lookest at me without frightening me,
> and that thou revealest thyself to me without causing me terror,
> and that thou doest not withhold anything from me,
> and that thou tellest me in truth all that I seek to know.

Stand on your feet and visualize him moving from the north to the east. Then turn your hands behind you, lower your head, and ask everything that you desire. After you have questioned him, raise your eyes to heaven and speak:

> URPLIEL URPLIEL[32]
> I have invoked thee by Him,
> who has formed thee to His glory and to His honor,
> to illuminate His world, and who gave to thee rulership over the day.
> Do not weaken me and do not frighten me,
> and I shall not be frightened, nor shall I tremble,
> and thou shall return to thy way in peace as I release thee,
> and do not delay thy course
> from now to eternity,
> Amen Selah.

---

[30] Where the sun is at midnight.

[31] The original text was in Greek.

[32] The name of the angel of the sun, meaning Mysterious Light of God.

The Oracle of the Twelve Angels

In the fifth Heaven we find twelve princes who are in charge of the twelve lunar months, and without whom nothing can happen in a respective month. These angels can be invoked for a more advanced method of divination. Everything that was said about divination in general and about the use of oil in Rite of Divination (page 176) also applies to this rite.

These are the angels of the fifth Heaven, who rule over the months of the year.

Angel	Month	Julian Calendar	Zodiac
Shaafiel (שעפיאל)	Nissan (ניסן)	March/April	Aries
Daghiel (דגהיאל)	Iyar (אייר)	April/May	Taurus
Didanur (דידנאור)	Sivan (סיון)	May/June	Gemini
Taanavon (תענבון)	Tammuz (תמוז)	June/July	Cancer
Tarurgar (תרורגר)	Av (אב)	July/August	Leo
Morael (מוריאל)	Elul (אלול)	August/September	Virgo
Pachdaron (פחדרון)	Tishrey (תשרי)	September/October	Libra
Yeldanag (ילדנג)	Cheshvan (חשון)	October/November	Scorpio
Andagnur (אנדגנור)	Kislev (כסלו)	November/December	Sagittarius
Mapaniel (מפניאל)	Tevet (טבת)	December/January	Capricorn
Chashnadarnos (חשנדרנוס)	Shevat (שבט)	January/February	Aquarius
Avrachiel (אברכיאל)	Adar (אדר)	February/March	Pisces

Note that the Jewish calendar is a lunar calendar; each month starts with the new moon.

If you want to know in which month a certain thing will happen, make twelve pieces from a thin foil of refined gold[33] (hammer them out so that they are very thin). On each of them (one on each), write the names of the angels, and next to each angelic name write the name of the month belonging to it.

To perform this rite, purify yourself for three weeks; do not touch any small animals or eat meat from any being that spills blood when killed (not even fish). Do not drink wine, have any sexual contact, or touch a grave. If you are male, try to guard yourself from nocturnal emission at night. Your inner attitude at this time should be one of devotion and prayer. Pray long prayers and requests for divine help. If you devote your heart to the fear of Heaven, you will succeed. For the traditional method, you need a bowl of good oil that has aged for seven years.[34]

Recite this invocation seven times over the oil:

> **I invoke ye angels of knowledge and insight,**
> **by Him who spoke and the World came into being,**
> **in the Name of EL EMET (God of Truth)**
> **ADIR VE-NAOR (Daunting and Brilliant)**
> **MELECH RAM VE-NISSA (King High and Exalted)**
> **CHAZAQ VE-GIBOR (Strong and Mighty)**
> **IZUS VE-NIFLA (Mighty and Wondrous)**
> **ELOHEY KOL HA-BERIOT (God of All Creatures)**
> **TZUR TZEVAOT (Rock/Refuge of Hosts)**
> **TZADDIQ (Righteous One)**
> **TZACH VE-YASHER VE-NE'EMAN (Bright and Upright and True)**
> **and in the Name that has set you over the months of the year,**
> **he who sits in hidden heights,[35]**
> **who reveals the hidden mysteries,**
> **who rules over death and life,**
> **who is King for the eternity of eternal eternities,**
> **who is established for the eon of eons.**
>
> **By this great, mighty, and powerful**
> **awesome and terrifying,**

---

[33] Personally I think it does not need to be gold. Silver or even brass will work as well.
[34] Because this traditional method is quite difficult to use, I advise the reader to consider the alternative methods of casting a lot, as described in Rite of Divination, page 176.
[35] Compare Psalm 91:1.

> wondrous, pure, and holy invocation
> I invoke you
> to cast a lot for me,
> that I shall know the truth.
> Reveal to me all that I have asked for.

Then pour the oil into a new glass vessel and put the pieces of foil on the oil. Place the vessel under the stars for seven nights, getting up in the seventh night at midnight to see which foil is still floating on top of the oil. This is the month in which the event will happen.

After the rite, keep the oil, for it has great healing powers.

Make a ring of pure silver[36] with a hollow space in the top, and put some of the oil inside the ring—together with a white flower and asbestos—and then seal it (with wax). When you wear it on your finger, no Evil Eye or evil spirit will be able to come near you, and no evil will be able to affect your house.

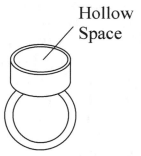

Hollow
Space

Rite to Appear in the Company
of a Large Army

If you want or go to war or return from war or go on a journey, or if you want to flee from a city and wish a large and strong company to appear with you and all who see you to be afraid of you—such as one who has with him an army armed with swords and spears and all the equipment for battle—then you can perform the following rite.

---

[36] Some techniques of Qabbalistic magic require basic silver- and goldsmithing abilities. For detailed information on how to make rings and other jewels, I recommend the following books: *Jewellery Making Manual* by Silvia Wicks (London: Macdonald, 1985) and *Jewellery* by Madeline Coles (London: Apple Press, 1999).

[37] It is possible to engrave all the names in a way that is small enough to fit on the plate, but such work will require a skilled engraver.

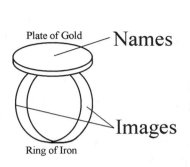

Plate of Gold — Names

Images

Ring of Iron

אפרכסי וייתן
דוכמסאל כרהאל אשריאל
ביואל נרהאל גצקיאל גרעיה שריאל
מסגיאל חניאל אורפניאל אקודו מוכאל
אלניתבאל דמאל אכואן שיראיום נהריאל
בהדרך שופריאל סדרכין דבובאור אמליאל
תמפניה בהחמל פרנין אמצתיאל תימנהרק
תוקפירם גוריאל סניאל עזריאל שריאל אליאל
מלכיאל מלמיאל צמיאל רנחיאל אקריאל קשתיאל
אברכיאל שדריאל ספיפיאל ארמאת דמואל
מריאל עניאל ניפליאל דרמיאל געשיאל
מנהראל בהניריאל אפשריאל קלעיאל
הדרניאל דלריאל שעפיאל דלגליאל
עדניאל מהריאל דבריאל
המסגיאל חניאל טוביאל

Before you leave the city, or before you sit down, cleanse yourself from all impurity. Pure be your flesh from all sin and women! Make for yourself a ring of iron and a plate of pure gold, writing on it the names of the over-seers and the names of the heads of the encampments.[37] Do this during the third day of the month. And engrave the image of a man and a lion on the ring outside of the plate.

On the day that you go to the place where you will be fighting, and when you see men come to seize you, take the ring and place it in your mouth and lift your eyes to Heaven with an unsoiled and pure heart while reciting the names of the overseers and the names of the heads of the encampments of the sixth Heaven who serve before them.

Recite the name of Afrachsey and the heads of the western encamp-ments[38] who serve under him:

AFRACHSEY
**VAYAVTAN DOCHMASEL KARAHEL ASHRIEL BAYOEL
NERHAEL GATZQIEL GERAYAH SARIEL MASGIEL
CHANIEL URPANIEL AQODO MOCHEL ALNITACHEL
DAMIEL ACHZAN SHIRAYOM NAHARIEL BAHDARACH**

---

[38] The names of the western encampments written in Hebrew are: אפרכסי
וייתן דוכמסאל כרהאל אשריאל ביואל נרהאל גצקיאל גרעיה שריאל מסגיאל חניאל
אורפניאל אקודו מוכאל אלניתכאל דמאל אכואן שיראיום נהריאל בהדרך שופריאל
סדרכין דבובאור אמליאל תמפניה בהחמל פרנין אמצתיאל תימנהרק.

> SHOFARIEL SEDRACHIEL DAVUVUR AMALIEL
> TAMPANIAH BEHACHAMEL PARANIN AMTZATIEL
> TIMANHARAQ

And the name of Toqpiras and the heads of the eastern encampments[39] who serve under him:

> TOQPIRAS
> GORIEL SANIEL AZRIEL SARIEL ALIEL MALKIEL
> MALMIEL TZAMIEL RANCHIEL AQRIEL QASHTIEL
> AVRCHIEL SHADRIEL SEFIFIEL ARMAAT DAMUEL
> MARIEL ANANIEL NIFLIEL DARMIEL GASHIEL
> MENHAREL BEHANIRIEL AFSHARIEL QELAIEL
> HADARNIEL DALRIEL SHAAFIEL DALGALIEL ADANANIEL
> TAHARIEL DAVARIEL HAMNACHIEL HANIEL TOVIEL

Then say this:

> I invoke you,
> Angels of Strength and Power (Gevurah),[40]
> by the strong and mighty right hand of the One,
> by the might of His Power (Gevurah) and by the domination of His rule,
> by God (El) who revealed Himself on Mount Sinai,
> by the chariot of myriads,[41]
> by God (Eloah) who rules thousands of thousands of myriad angels,
> by the Lord (Adon) who saved Israel from Egypt—all six hundred thousand,
> by the Life (Chay) of Eternities who spoke with Moses face to face,
> by God (El) who bringeth rulers to nothingness,[42]
> by the Rock whose hand is all that is needed to save and to rescue,

---

[39] The names of the eastern encampments written in Hebrew are: תוקפירס
גוריאל סניאל עזריאל שריאל אליאל מלכיאל מלמיאל צמיאל רנחיאל אקריאל קשתיאל
אברכיאל שדריאל ספיפיאל ארמאת דמואל מריאל ענניאל ניפליאל דרמיאל געשיאל
מנהראל בהניריאל אפשריאל קליאיל הדרניאל דלריאל שעפיאל דלגליאל עדניאל
טהריאל דבריאל המנגיאל הניאל טוביאל.

[40] Compare Psalm 24:8.

[41] Compare Psalm 68:18.

[42] Compare Isaiah 40:23.

by Him who fixes and imposes (ignites) the encampment of
Sennacherib.[43]
By His Name and by its letters, I recite this and invoke you
that ye come and stand with me
to help me at this time in every place I will go.
Let yourself be seen with me
like a great army with all your power and strength of your spears,
and let all who see me, be it from near or from far away,
and all who come to fight me or to capture me, be
doomed/shattered before me
through the overwhelming awe and fear that you cause in them.
And they shall not be able to injure me or come close to me.
And upon them shall fall fear and awe,[44]
and the awe of me shall fall upon them
and upon all children of Adam and Eve
and upon every evil being,
and they shall tremble and shiver before me.

While doing this, visualize a mighty army around you. You may see before you smoke and dark clouds or mist, or you may feel a change in the atmosphere. This is a sign that you have been successful. Take the ring from your mouth and put it on your finger. When you come to your house and want to release the angels, put the ring to your mouth and stand before the sun (i.e., facing the sun) and recite the names of the angels to release them by saying:

I release you.
Go on your way!

And then put the ring on your finger again.

---

[43] Compare Isaiah 37:36 and 2 Kings 19:35.
[44] Compare Exodus 15:16.

The Work of Wisdom
and Understanding

The power of the Hebrew letters has often been used for magical purposes. In the following ritual[1] the letters are consumed by the practitioner of the ritual in order to absorb the power of the magical names. The intention of this ritual is to become wise and understanding in order to be able to study all kinds of religious or mystical texts and to understand their deeper and sometimes hidden meaning and not forget the text or its interpretation. This ritual will be very helpful in your work not only with traditional religious texts, but also with all kinds of Qabbalistic writings—including this book.

The ritual should be performed on Atzeret, which is the sixth day of the month called Sivan, when the Shavuot festival is celebrated. Sivan corresponds with the time of the astrological sign Gemini, but because the

---

[1] This chapter was first published in Dolores Ashcroft-Nowicki, *Illuminations* (Woodbury, Minn.: Llewellyn, 2003).

*Moses receiving the Ten
Commandments*

Jewish calendar is based on the moon, it will always begin on the day of
new moon. (For the exact day, look at a Jewish calendar or ask your local
Jewish community.) Thus this ritual is performed during the waxing moon,
which is helpful in increasing your wisdom. Gemini is connected to studies
and learning. Tradition teaches that Moses received the Torah on Shavuot,
and therefore this is the time at which you can increase your ability to
understand the scriptures.

The original manuscript of the ritual was written in the late fourteenth
or early fifteenth century. It was in a very corrupt state, which meant I had
to put the pieces together in order to turn them into a ritual that would
work. The original does not include an opening, and I have therefore
added a small opening to increase the power of the ritual. (There are some
passages that could be interpreted as having the ritual performed on more
than one day, but I have decided to write it in such a way that it can be performed on a single day, because this is easier—and there is no need to make
things unnecessarily complicated. The preparation will be hard enough.)

To perform this ritual, you will need a fig leaf, three olive leaves, a silver cup, red wine, and an egg of a hen. Fig and olive trees can be found in
a good market garden. You may be able to get a few leaves without having
to buy the whole tree. To write the letters, I advise using food coloring (the
kind used for cakes, rather than ink), for it is often based on sugar and will
easily dissolve in wine—and it will taste much better.

The Holy Names

Some of the names used in this ritual are permutations of traditional Names of God. For example, Mapatz = (מפץ) = *Yod Vav Heh* (יוה). This method of permutation is called *at-bash,* because *Alef* will turn into *Tav* and *Bet* into *Shin,* and so forth. For a better understanding, look at the following list:

א ב ג ד ה ו ז ח ט י כ ל מ נ ס ע פ צ ק ר ש ת
ת ש ר ק צ פ ע ס נ מ ל כ י ט ח ז ו ה ד ג ב א

To prepare for this ritual, fast from the new moon of Sivan until the sixth day of Sivan, when the ritual is to be performed. (This does not mean you may not eat at all, but that you must eat only after sunset.) During this time, purify yourself every morning, every evening, before you bake your bread or prepare your meal, and after baking and before eating. After eating, however, purification is not needed. Before you eat, you should drink some wine, and before drinking the wine, you should purify yourself. Before drinking the wine, count nine times. (The manuscript does not say clearly what to count, but it seems to be the first invocation):

> **In the Name of YAH YAH YAH, YAHU YAHU YAHU, YAHEY YAHEY YAHEY, HEY HEY HEY, HU HU HU, AHU AHU AHU, EHEYEH EHEYEH EHEYEH, BARUCH BARUCH BARUCH, QADOSH QADOSH QADOSH, SHADDAI SHADDAI SHADDAI, YAHUTZ YAHUTZ YAHUTZ, PATZ PATZ PATZ, RACHUM RACHUM RACHUM, CHANUN CHANUN CHANUN.**

His Name is elaborated in forty-two letters. He who performs it is wise and filled with wisdom.

> **This is My Name forever, this is My remembrance from generation to generation. AMEN AMEN SELAH.**

The manuscript says "immerse in a river" in order to purify yourself, but a short shower in the morning and in the evening (and maybe another one before eating) will purify you as well. I advise you to have a bath before the ritual itself. This will be enough, because most readers will have access neither to a Jewish ritual bath nor to a river. Sexual abstinence is not needed, and intercourse seemed even to be encouraged; the manuscript says: "He should not sleep alone, so he will not be harmed!"

The Opening

Before me is SANDALFON,
behind me is MICHAEL,
on my right is METATRON,
on my left is AGAMTAYA,
and YAHOEL is above my head.

The Intention

This is the work of Wisdom (Chochmah) and Understanding (Binah).
All who practice it become wise and understanding.
In the Name of
YAH YAH YAH
YAHU YAHU YAHU
YAHEY YAHEY YAHEY
HEY HEY HEY
HU HU HU
AHU AHU AHU
EHEYEH EHEYEH EHEYEH
BARUCH BARUCH BARUCH
QADOSH QADOSH QADOSH
SHADDAI SHADDAI SHADDAI
YAHUTZ YAHUTZ YAHUTZ
PATZ PATZ PATZ
RACHUM RACHUM RACHUM
CHANUN CHANUN CHANUN

His Name is elaborated in forty-two letters.
He who performs it is wise and filled with wisdom.
"This is my Name forever, this is my remembrance from
generation to generation." (Exodus 3:15)
AMEN AMEN SELAH

The Fig Leaf

I invoke thee, SANDALFON,
the angel, who ties a crown [i.e., wreath] for his Master,
to rise up and say to Him:
"Two angels, Metatron and Agamtaya,
may they give wisdom in the heart of [Insert your magical name]."

**And may he [she] know, and may he [she] be wise and understanding
and study and not forget and learn and not neglect
what comes before him [her] and what comes after him [her].**

In the Name of	בשום
PATZ MAPATZ MAPATZ	פץ מפץ מפץ
TZEAH TZEYEAH SHAQ BAQAQ	צאה ציאה שק בקק
AH YAH	אה יה
VE-AZAMER	ואזמר
KEGON HU GAMAR	כגון הוא גמר
KEGON AKRACHEY-NIYAH	כגון אכרכיניה
In the Name of	בשום
AH VE-AH BE-AH	אה ואה באה
YAHU YAHU YUHA	יהו יהו יוה
YA-EH HE-AY	יאה האי
from now and forever.	מעתה ועד עולם

Write these Divine Names on the fig leaf, erase them in wine, and eat the
fig leaf and drink from the wine.

Olive Leaves

**ME-SUMSANAN BE-MUSAMA KE-MUQAMA
AYIN SAMAIN GE-AH QAMEA
AGIFIEL MESAFO
YAH VE-AY YE**
These are the princes who split the firmament and gave the
Torah to Moses by the power of
YAHU YAHU VE-HEH
יהו יהו והה
I invoke thee, in the name of the great dwellers, to keep the
Torah in my heart.

Write the Holy Names on three olive leaves, erase them in wine, and drink.

Silver Cup

**I invoke thee MICHAEL,
great prince of Israel.
Give me the study of the teachings in my heart.
AMEN AMEN SELAH**

Write the name "Michael" inside the silver cup, erase it in wine, and drink.

MICHAEL מיכאל

Say the following prayer[2] twenty-four times. To count, you can use a meditation cord with twenty-four beads or a mark after twenty-four beads. The prayer belongs to the Shmoneh Essreh, which consists of eighteen benedictions. Try to give the words a melody—almost like singing. Jewish readers will know what I mean, and non-Jewish readers may get some inspiration from traditional Yiddish music, or they might even find Jewish prayers on a CD. Try to use the melody in order to reach an almost trancelike rhythm. It does not have to be loud. Look at this as a Western equivalent of a mantra meditation.

Shema qolenu,	(Hear our voice,)
YHVH [say Adonai] **ELOHEYNU,**	(YHVH our God,)
chus ve-rachem aleynu	(spare us and have mercy upon us,)
ve-qabbel be-rachamim u-ve-ratzon et tefilatenu,	(and accept our prayer with mercy and with goodwill,)
ki EL shomea tefilot ve-tachanunim Atah.	(for Thou art God, who hears prayers and petitions.)
U-milfanecha MALKENU reqam al teshivenu.	(And do not reject us, our King, from Thy Face empty—with empty hands.)

After you have said the prayer twenty-four times, end with the following words:

Ki Atah shomea tefilat amcha Yisrael be-rachamim.	(For Thou hear the prayer of thy people of Israel with mercy.)
Baruch Atah YHVH [say Adonai]**, shomea tefilah.**	(Blessed art Thou YHVH, who hears prayers.)

Wine

Say this forty-one times over the wine. To count, you can use the same meditation cord you have used before by adding another mark after forty-one beads. Again, use a melody as described above. Feel the vibration of the sound filling the wine.

---

[2] This is the sixteenth benediction of the Shmoneh Essreh (Eighteen Benedictions).

Cast into me Scriptures, Mishnah and Talmud, and enlighten my
heart with words of the Torah, and let me not stumble with my
tongue in all that I learn.
In the Name of YAHOEL VE-EL,
and in the Name of HA-EL HA-GADOL, the great God,
YAH YAHU YAH YAH ELI EL,
and in the Name of HA-EL HA-GADOL, the great God,
YAH YAHU YAH YAH
EL HA-ELOHIM, God of the Gods,
SHEM HA-MEFORASH VE-HA-NICHBAD
the unspoken [literally, unspeakable] and honored Name
AMEN AMEN SELAH

After you have said it forty-one times, drink the wine.

The Egg

לאיגנסם בפסה פר אנה
LE-IGNESAM BEPASAH PAR ANAH
the great Sar ha-Torah, Prince of the Law,
who was with Moses at Mount Sinai and crowned him with a wreath,
and who taught him all that he learned and all that his ears heard.
So may thou crown me, and come to me,
and remove the stone from my heart,
speedily, and do not delay.
AMEN AMEN SELAH

Write the name of the Sar ha-Torah on a boiled and peeled egg. Eat the egg.

The Closing

I have invoked all ye angels that have assisted me in this ritual.
I bless you and release you.
Depart in peace,
and go peacefully to your abodes,
and do not harm me.
The rite is ended.

Fast for the rest of the day, and do not drink. The instructions say further:
". . . and sit in a box." If you wish to do so, get a large box used in house
moves. Spend the rest of the day in meditation.

15

The Invocation of the Prince of Dreams

The practice of trying to get answers to all kinds of questions by the method of dream oracles is ancient—maybe even as old as humankind itself. Prophetic dreaming appears in several passages in the Bible; the dream of Joseph is a good example (Genesis 35:5*ff*). Joseph and Daniel were famous dream interpreters, and the book of Daniel is full of descriptions of prophetic dreams. Such a dream can come as a result of a question one had in mind at the time of going to sleep. The king Nevuchadnetzar received a prophetic dream in answer to his question about the future (Daniel 2:28*ff*). The technique of inducing a dream to answer a certain question—*incubation*—was well known in ancient Babylon. Daniel was a master of incubation. Together with his companions (*chavrohi*)[1] he prayed to the God of Heaven and received a dream-vision in the night (Daniel 2:17*ff*). The prophet Joel promises that in the future all people, the old as well as the young, will receive the gift of prophetic dreaming (Book of Joel 3:1).

---

[1] Compare with the Chavurah described in chapter 12, The Vision of the Merkavah.

This ritual is designed to bring you into contact with the Prince of Dreams, who is the angel of those powers, which can help and guide you in finding the answers to your problems by using the method of the dream oracle. It does not matter whether your question is mundane or spiritual or very intimate. Always seek to understand the reasons why a problem came into your life, and what you are supposed to learn from it. Understanding will lead to wisdom, but merely trying to foretell the future will lead only to ignorance of your own possibilities to become the creator of your own destiny. NEVER ask the oracle to make your decisions. It is meant to advise you, not to enslave you. Do not ask: "Should I marry this person?" Only your heart can tell you this. You may, however, ask whether or not your beloved loves you truly. Do not ask whether or not you should accept a certain job. Instead, ask what the job will feel like, how much work it will be, or what your career chances are—but never forget that your career chances also depend on you. Therefore, the best questions are those that ask for advice: how you can learn to improve your character and your life.

This ritual is based on a manuscript written by the German Chassidim (Chassidey Ashkenaz) in the late fourteenth century. There is also another manuscript of the German Chassidim from the fourteenth century that describes a similar invocation of the same angel, including long passages that seem to be almost exactly the same as in this one. I decided, however, to use the former source, because the structure of the ritual does not seem to be as clear in the latter. I believe that both rituals originate in a much earlier version. In both cases, the ritual is incorporated in a collection of mystical and magical texts belonging to the Hechalot literature, which originates in the first millennium CE.

In neither of the two manuscripts is there a description of a formula for releasing the Prince of Dreams or the other angels that have been invoked. I have therefore added such a formula, written in the style of releasing formulas that appear in other rituals in these manuscripts. (One of these rituals directly precedes this ritual, and even some of the angels invoked are the same as here. These rituals may have been written by the same author. If they were written by different authors, one may well have been inspired by the other one.)

The ancient text of the ritual further instructs the magician not to talk too much with his wife (literally, the woman) on the night of the dream oracle: Turn your heart to heaven! In the other manuscript, the following admonishment was added to the text: Do not talk too much with *a man*. It may be that this is because it was used by a woman. Even though most of the ancient rituals seem to have been written by men, there is no reason why they should not be used by women as well.

The text warns the magician not to reveal what he has been shown if the Prince of Dreams tells him not to do so. If you did not get an answer, likewise do not reveal this. If you have not been told to conceal it and if the Prince of Dreams told you everything you wanted to know and then departed, do not fear to reveal it and to speak about everything you saw, whether it was good or bad. But beware not to add anything to the matter or to lie or to tell more! For if you lie and need to perform the dream oracle again, he will never come to you again. But if you spoke the truth, he will come to you at any time you wish.

The Holy Names

The Name YHVH is said as ADONAI in prayer and YOD HEH VAV HEH in ritual.

The Name EL ZAVUACH (literally, "slaughtered or sacrificed God") may be corrupt, and I advise the reader to say instead EL ZOVEACH (slaughtering God). Such mistakes are quite common.

Preparation

The preparations for this ritual are relatively simple. Fast for three days, saying the following verses in the first two nights before going to sleep. Sleep in your robe. On the third night, perform the ritual as the following explains. Make sure, that you will not be disturbed on the night of the dream oracle and that you will not have to get up early the next morning.

This is what is to be said on the first two nights:

Praised art Thou
ELOHEYNU MELECH HA-OLAM
HA-EL HA-MELECH HA-GADOL
HA-GIBOR VE-HA-NORA
VE-HA-NISGAV VE-HA-NIFLA
VE-HA-ONAH BA-ET TZARAH
our God, King of the Universe, God, mighty, awesome, exalted, and
wonderful King, who answers in the time of need.

When I call, answer me, ELOHEY TZIDQI, God of my righteousness.
In my distress Thou appeareth to me, be gracious to me
and hear my prayer.[2]

> Hear my words YHVH, perceive my thoughts.
> Hearken to the sound of my cry for help,
> my King and my God, for unto Thee do I pray. (Psalm 5:2–3)
>
> All who take refuge in Thee will rejoice,
> ever jubilant as Thou sheltereth them,
> and those who love Thy Name will exult in Thee. (Psalm 5:12)
>
> YHVH hath heard my plea,
> YHVH accepteth my prayer. (Psalm 6:10)
>
> YHVH is my allotted portion and my chalice.
> Thou guideth my destiny. (Psalm 16: 5)
>
> Guard me like the apple of the eye,
> shelter me in the shadows of Thy wings. (Psalm 17:8)
>
> O my God! I call out by day, but Thou answereth not;
> and by night, but there is no respite for me.
> Yet Thou art the Holy One, enthroned upon the praises of Yisrael.
> In Thee did our fathers trust, they trusted and Thou rescued them.
> Unto Thee they cried out and they were saved.
> In Thee they did trust and were not put to shame. (Psalm 22:3–6)
>
> But Thou YHVH be not far off. O Thou my strength,
> hasten to my aid. (Psalm 22:20)

Stand in the west, face the altar looking to the east, and say the following prayer three times:

> **In the Name of**
> **YOD HEH VAV HEH**
> **ELOHEY YISRAEL CHAY YAH**
> **YOD HEH VAV HEH TZEVAOT**
> **EHEYEH ASHER EHEYEH**
> **AD VE-AD**
> **YAHU YAHUEY**
> **TADAYAH YACH YAH YACHIYAH**
> **ZEVEH NEVUCHIN**
> **QARU LE-CHA**

---

2 See Psalm 4:2. The text has been changed slightly here. I have translated the text as it is in the ritual.

MI-YEMEY QARU LE-CHA
EL ZAVUACH [read: ZOVEACH]
EL MASHUCH YASHUCH
UMIYA ITLET

NISHMAT ELIYONIM
soul of the Highest
before the Throne of Thy Glory,
standing at the gates of prayer
AZRIEL and ELEAZAR
They remember and stand at the door posts of the house of
YOD HEH VAV HEH,
and they rule over the sending of dreams and the messages of every dream,
and the great matters of men.

The Name is
QADOSH QADOSH QADOSH
ADIR ADIR ADIR
SHEM SHEM SHEM

Holy Holy Holy
Magnificent Magnificent Magnificent
Name Name Name

Praised art Thou
YOD HEH VAV HEH
ELOHEYNU
MELECH HA-OLAM
King of the World.

ELOHEY RUACHOT
God of the spirits,
who reviveth the dead,
who supporteth the fallen,
who freeth the bound ones.
Loosen my binding.
And may my words be accepted before Thee,
For I am dust and ashes.
And my Ruach (spirit) hangeth from Thy Hands.

I am Thy servant, son [daughter] of Thy maidservant.
And I have come to cast my plea before Thee,
to tell me about a certain matter,
whether it will happen or not.

May his coming be peaceful, not angry,
so that I may understand all his words and not forget anything.

And do not send me back empty before Thee,
For Thou art compassionate and gracious,
patient and great is Thy Mercy (Chesed) and Thy Truth (Emet).

I trusted in Thee,
and for Thee I hoped.
In fasting I turned my Nefesh (soul) away from the fear and trembling,
that fell upon me about [Insert the matter].
May I know and understand, and may it be clear to me.
With all my heart and with all my power I bow to Thee in prayer.
For there is no one to answer but Thou,
and no one will answer except for Thou.

And in Thy praised and magnificent Name
I command thee
Sar shel Chalom, the Prince of Dream(s),
hurry and come to me this night and tell me this night all I desire to know.

Inviting the Quarter Angels

After saying the above prayer for the third time, you may invite the quarter angels. The following text was not a part of this version of the ritual (it was a part of the latter version not used). It does not have to be used here, but it fits in well and adds to the power of the ritual. The directions of the angels are not the ones the modern student of magic is used to, but I have not changed the text, because it has its own beauty. The manuscript in which this text was written has noted that it should be spoken three times.

On my right is MICHAEL,
On my left is GAVRIEL,
And the SHECHINAT EL SHADDAI,
the Presence of God, the Almighty, is above my head,
and behind me is RAPHAEL,
and before me is URIEL.

The Invocation of the Prince of Dreams

After you have spoken the invitation of the quarter angels three times, you may invoke the Prince of Dreams:

I invoke thee, RAGSHIEL,
RABBA SAR SHEL CHALOM
great Prince of Dream(s),
in the Name of
CHAY YOD HEH VAV HEH TZEVAOT
EHEYEH ASHER EHEYEH
YEQOEL YEQACHOEL YEMOEL
SARAH SALSHAR SAM
ZOLEV THAZUHAVA DARAH
HEH AY BAV ZACH
NAH LEH HU YAH BAH DAH
LAG QOLET BA DA LAD
ADIDIRON
QIVIYAH MIGOEL
YACHAY AQAS AVDISASIYAH,

and in the names of these angels I invoke thee,
[I call upon thee in the name of] VADARIEL,
[and I call upon thee in the name of] PENIEL,
[and I call upon thee in the name of] QATABIEL,
[and I call upon thee in the name of] NACHALIEL,
[and I call upon thee in the name of] RAGZOEL,
[and I call upon thee in the name of] TATEL,
[and I call upon thee in the name of] ANBIEL,
[and I call upon thee in the name of] SAFSAEL,
[and I call upon thee in the name of] NACHNACHEL,
to come to me in this night,
in peace, in goodness, and not in anger.

And speak to me,
and give me a sign or an omen or a verse that I will understand.
And let me know about this matter.

Ask what you want to know in your own words!

And let me know all things about it,
and all things that are to come.
Let me know whether it will be good or otherwise.
And do not hesitate to come now,
for I call thee with those Shemot ha-Meforashot (Divine Names),
which are engraved on the Throne of Glory,
which Malkiel the angel, who always stands before
Ha-Qadosh Baruch Hu,
the Holy One, blessed be He,
gave to Eliyahu on Mount Carmel,
and by which he ascended.
They are these to bind them:

MEHASEY YAH YEHOSHEV HU
SOLIYAH ACHEA MESASUSIYAH
AHAGA LAHMAH MAHAYAH HAYAHU
NAMELMELAM'MIYAH
LEHAL BAYAH PELAMIYAH DAR
URDIYAHUBAYAH PARITZATA
ADRETIYAH SHAQSHAMASHTATZATIYAH
TZATZATZATZIYAH
MEFAR'RAPAR AFARFARIYAH
GARUMIDUDAMIYAH

Baruch Shem Malchuto Le-Olam Va-ed.
Blessed be the Name of His Kingdom forever and ever.
In the Name of
IZQETA DE'IZQET
VE-DIN YE'AVROM VE-AVRU
HAS YOZIQU
VE-YITZITZI HU TZITZI
YAH TZITZI
TZEVAOT TZITZI GENEZ
GAZ BANAT
HADAR KE-HADAR
NUR NORA
SHADDAI
CHALFIYAH RODEFIYAH NATFIYAH
VE-KAFIYAH MUGANIYAH BITRIYAH MANHIYAH

YAH HEY U-MILIYAH
HOTELIYAH HOTENIYAH HOCHENIYAH HOTEVIYAH

I have invoked thee by these Names,
to come to me in peace, in goodness, and not in anger,
and tell me all I desire to know about this matter.

And tell me in my dream
whether I should reveal its interpretation
or whether I should conceal its interpretation from humanity,
so that I do not fail in this matter before Him,
who spake and the world was made.
Blessed be He and blessed be his Name,
and blessed be His remembrance,
and blessed be YHVH by day,
and blessed be YHVH by night,
and blessed be YHVH when we lie down,
and blessed be YHVH when we rise.

In Thy hands are the Nafshot (souls) of the living and of the dead.
For in His hand is the Nefesh (soul) of every living thing and the
Ruach (spirit) of all mankind. (Job 12:10)
In Thy hands I entrust my Ruach (spirit),
Thou redeemed me YHVH EL EMETH, God of Truth. (Psalm 31:6)

Our God in Heaven,
unique is Thy remembrance, and Thy Name exists always
with us forever and ever.

For Thy salvation do I long, O YHVH. (Genesis 49:18)
For Thy salvation do I long, O YHVH. (Genesis 49:18)

AMEN AMEN SELAH VE-AD. (forever)

To release him:

I have invoked thee, RAGSHIEL,
RABBA SAR SHEL CHALOM
great Prince of Dream(s).
In the Name of
CHAY YOD HEH VAV HEH TZEVAOT
and in the Name of

> EHEYEH ASHER EHEYEH
> I bless thee and instruct thee.
> Come to me this night and answer my question in my dreams and then
> depart in peace
> and go peacefully to thy abodes,
> and do bring no harm upon me.

To Release the Quarter Angels

> I have invoked all you angels that have assisted me in this ritual
> In the Name of
> ELOHEY YISRAEL CHAY YAH
> YOD HEH VAV HEH TZEVAOT
> and in the Name of
> EHEYEH ASHER EHEYEH
> I bless you and release you.
> Depart in peace,
> and go peacefully to your abodes,
> and do bring no harm upon me.

The rite is ended.

After the ritual, go to bed and sleep in your robe. Have some writing material at hand, and the next morning, write down all the dreams you remember. The answer in your dreams may be one of the following.

The image of a man will appear in your dreams and answer your questions, either in clear language or by means of a parable or a biblical verse. The angel may also lead you to scenes that are the answer to your question or show you pictures that symbolically reveal the answer to your question. Such symbols as they are described in one of the two manuscripts are: "open books, gardens, delicacies, goodly trees, and joyous dances" for a positive answer, and "graves and bones" for a negative answer. It may moreover be that you see symbols but that no human image appears in your dream. This does not mean that the ritual was not successful—sometimes, only symbols appear. Furthermore, you may be shown what you wanted to see as it is and as it appears in the physical world.

Whatever the answer may be, write it down and think about it or meditate on it. Do not reject it simply because you do not like it. Try to learn something from it. Every dream received this way will teach you something.

16

The Great Seal and the Awesome Crown

Modern students of Qabbalistic magic are familiar with certain types of standard opening and closing ceremonies, such as the pentagram and hexagram rituals used in the famous Order of the Golden Dawn. There are, however, rituals used as a part of other rituals in ancient times. The most famous of these is called the Great Seal and the Awesome Crown. Beware—it is the key to much more power than it may seem to be! It is not an equivalent to the lesser rite of the pentagram because it was used only for rituals that needed a great deal of power to achieve high spiritual aims, such as attaining divine wisdom and understanding of the Torah. (An example of such a ritual will be described in the next chapter.)

This ritual may bring you into contact with the Divine Power invested in you. Do not use this ritual unless you are very experienced in magical work and are able to deal with the inrush of power that this work may cause.

Rabbi Yishmael says that the Great Seal and the Awesome Crown are so powerful that everyone who uses them without speaking prayers over them will terminate his life. Therefore, tradition includes certain prayers that must be spoken together with the Seal and the Crown.

The Great Seal is, of course, the Seal of Solomon, and the Awesome Crown is related to Keter, the crown chakra, the point where we can contact the Divine Power above us.

Holy Names

Azbogah (אזבוגה): This Name consists of three pairs of letters, all of which add up to the number eight. Avagdehu (אבגדהו): This Name consists of the first six letters of the alphabet.

The Great Seal

Face east and draw a hexagram of white fire as the following describes.

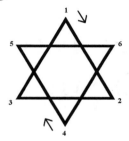

Start to draw the hexagram at the top (1), drawing the first line to the lower right (2), and vibrate:

TZORTAQ

Continue to draw the second line of the first triangle to the lower left point (3), and vibrate:

DRAGINAT

Draw the last line of the first triangle back to the upper point (1), and vibrate:

ARACH

Draw the first line of the second triangle from the lowest point (4) to the upper left (5), and vibrate:

NAZIR

Continue to draw the second line of the second triangle to the upper right (6), and vibrate:

SHURATIN

Draw the last line of the second triangle back to the lowest point (4), and vibrate:

YADYAZIYAH

Point to the middle of the hexagram and say:

This is the Great Seal with which Heaven and earth were sealed. And by the power invested therein, I seal the east.

Repeat this procedure to the south, west, north, above, and below.

The Prayer of the Great Seal

EL EMET (God of truth)
praised for eternity (Netzach),
who has created Heaven with understanding,
who has founded earth with wisdom.[1]
In the palace (hechal) of silence Thou hast placed Thy Throne,
the footstool of Thy feet is placed on the globe of earth.
Stars and planets bow down for Thee.
Thou hast fixed [the] sun and moon in the heavens.
Thou hast fixed Heaven and earth on the depth of waters,
with the signet ring of Thy hands hast Thou marked Heaven and earth.
The whole host on high answers with it:
Praised art Thou Eloheynu (our God)
Praised art Thou Malkeynu (our King)
Praised art Thou Yotzeynu (our Creator)
with all songs and praises
for the multitude of greatness (Gedulah) that
Thou hast given to all sons of flesh.
Praised be He who is praised by the mouth of every soul.

Note the deep Qabbalistic meaning in this prayer—for example, in the passage: "Who has created the Heaven with understanding, Who has founded the earth with wisdom." God himself is Keter, and the creation is the level of Chochmah (wisdom) and Binah (understanding). Heaven is Tiferet, the foundation is Yesod, and the earth is Malchut. "God's Throne in the palace of silence" refers to Binah (the first *Heh* of YHVH), and "the

---

[1] Compare Proverbs 3:19.

footstool of Thy Feet is placed on the globe of earth" refers to Malchut (the second *Heh* of YHVH). The "depth of waters" refers to the abyss between God in Atzilut and Creation (Beriah) on one side, and the lower worlds Yetzirah and Assiah on the other side. With a bit of experience, you will be able to discover the deeper and hidden meanings of the old Qabbalistic prayers and incantations based on this example. There is one more passage that should be noted. "Praised art Thou . . . for the multitude of greatness that Thou hast given to all sons of flesh": When we come to the Awesome Crown, we will find out what kind of greatness has been given to the sons of flesh.

The Awesome Crown

Visualize on your head a beautiful crown of pure gold with four diamonds in it. These represent the four letters of the Tetragrammaton and the four directions. As you intone each of the four Names, one of the diamonds begins to shine in brilliant white light.

> **Thus I place on my head the crown of crowns.**
> **AZBOGAH**
> **AVAGDEHU**
> **ZAHUZIYAH**
> **ZOHTZIYAH**
> **This is the Awesome Crown with which all the princes of wisdom are adjured.**

The Prayer of the Awesome Crown

> **Atah Hu Ha-El Ha-Gadol Ha-Gibor**
> (Thou art the great, strong, and awesome God)
> **Melech Malki Ha-Melachim baruch Hu,**
> (King of Kings of Kings, praised be He)
>
> **Thy Crown (Keter) is greater and more beloved than all crowns.**
> **Thy Power (Gevurah) is more powerful than all powers.**
> **Who is like our King? Who is like our God? Who is like our Creator?**
>
> **Melech Ha-Olamim** (King of the Worlds),
> **sanctified above,**
> **glorified below,**
> **praised above,**
> **exalted below,**

> adorned among the adorned ones,
> honored among the Serafim,
> who does great works beyond explanation,
> who does miracles beyond number,
> praised art Thou, Adonai,
> stronger than the great ones,
> praised by the loyal ones.

Very often, we will find that mystical texts and magical rituals contain a lesser mystery and a greater mystery. The lesser mystery of this prayer is the Power and Glory of the Creator. No one is comparable to the Creator. The greater mystery is, however, not so obvious. In the Torah, it is written: "YHVH, your God is within you, God is great and awesome" (Deuteronomy 7:21). "Great and awesome" obviously refers to the Great Seal and the Awesome Crown, and "God is within you" refers to the greater mystery of this prayer. The prayer says: Who is like our King? Who is like our God? Who is like our Creator? Who is like a king? If you ask a child to describe a king, the first thing he or she will say is that the king wears a crown. In this ritual the magician is the one wearing the crown. Man is made in the image of God, and man shall rule over the Earth (Genesis 1:26-28). Man shall rule as a king. Man is made in the image of God, and like Him, man wears a crown. It was and is the opinion of the wise that God is within. (Although this may be controversial, and some may say that it is blasphemy to say that God is within, we can say that it is blasphemy to say that God is *not* within!) "God within" is the true secret of magical power. I warn you not to use this technique unless you are an expert in magic, because the power will also be a burden to the inexperienced. The secret of the creative power of humankind was always hidden with great care by the ancient Qabbalists because it is so easily misused. Misunderstanding this may lead to falling into the trap of spiritual pride—very much to your own regret.

Removing the Awesome Crown

After the ritual, the Awesome Crown is to be removed. Say:

> Thus I remove the crown of crowns from my head.

Visualize the four diamonds ceasing to shine, and then the Crown disappearing.

Unsealing the Great Seal

Face the east and draw a hexagram of white fire as described in the following illustration and text:

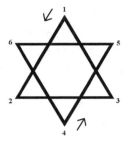

Start to draw the hexagram at the top (1), drawing the first line to the lower left (2), and vibrate:

TZORTAQ

Continue to draw the second line of the first triangle to the lower right point (3), and vibrate:

DRAGINAT

Draw the last line of the first triangle back to the upper point (1), and vibrate:

ARACH

Draw the first line of the second triangle from the lowest point (4) to the upper right (5), and vibrate:

NAZIR

Continue to draw the second line of the second triangle to the upper left (6), and vibrate:

SHURATIN

Draw the last line of the second triangle back to the lowest point (4), and vibrate:

YADYAZIYAH

Point to the middle of the hexagram and say:

This is the Great Seal, with which Heaven and earth were sealed. And by the power invested therein, I unseal the east.

Repeat this procedure to the south, west, north, above, and below. Then repeat the prayer of the Great Seal.

The Seven Seals

Rabbi Ishmael said: "I sealed myself with seven seals in the hour when PARQADES, the angel of the Countenance, descended."

The seven seals is another ancient method to seal and empower the aura, and it is to be used when working with mighty angelic beings. To perform the seven seals, say:

> **Praised art Thou YOD HEH VAV HEH,**
> **For Thou hast created Heaven and earth in Thy Wisdom and with**
> **Thy Understanding.**
> **For ever Thy Name is**
> **CHAY UF SISIFIAILUSAS KISEY TENAY**
> **The name of Thy servant is**
> **URIM SASTAY**

1. Touch your feet (Malchut) and say:

> **On my feet**
> **AVAG BAGOG**

2. Touch your heart (Tiferet) and say:

> **On my heart**
> **ARAYIM TIPA**

3. Touch your right shoulder (Gevurah) and say:

> **On my right arm**
> **URIM TESUYAH**

4. Touch your left shoulder (Chesed) and say:

> **On my left arm**
> **AVIT TALBAGOR YAYU DIYOEL**

5. Touch your throat (Daat) and say:

> **On my throat**
> **UF ACH QITER SES ECHAD YADID YAH**

6. Touch your forehead (Chochmah and Binah) and say:

> **To guard my soul**
> **and above them all** [i.e., all these names and energy centers]
> **AF PAT YAHU CHAYU YO ZAHU YAHU TITES**

7. Touch your head (Keter) and say:

> **Above my head**
> **RIR GOG GADOL HAF YAF HAF TAHOR HEH YAYU**
> **HAHEY HEH HEH**
> **In eternal memory be praised**
> **ADON HA-CHOCHMAH** (Lord of Wisdom)
> **To whom all the Power** (Gevurah) **belongs.**
> **Praised art Thou YOD HEH VAV HEH**
> **High and exalted**
> **Great in reign.**

Holy Names

All the names of the seven seals begin with the letter *Alef.*

Chay = Life (The Living One—a Divine Name of Yesod)
Kisey = Throne
Urim = Lights
Arayim = Lions
Echad = (single) One
Yadad = Beloved One
Af = Anger
Gog = One of the names of the kingdoms of the apocalypse
Gadol = Great One
Tahor = Pure One
Heh = the fifth Letter

The Invocation of the Prince of the Torah

Learning and understanding the Torah, the scriptures, the Mishnah, the Judaic mystical writings, and, later, the Talmud was an important task for the ancient sages. (The Talmud is not mentioned in this ritual, probably because this rite originates in a time before the Talmud was completed. This is also why the Zohar is not mentioned either.) Often, a young student had to work, and time for learning was rare. This ritual was designed to help the student to learn, understand, and memorize the scriptures.

The ritual must be performed three times every day for twelve days, after the morning, afternoon, and evening prayer. The instructions state clearly that no prayers or invocations should be omitted during the whole twelve days. During this time, nothing must be done except this ritual work or learning and meditating on the Torah, the scriptures, the Mishnah, the Talmud, and the mystical writings such as the Hechalot texts or the Zohar or other books about the Qabbalah. This work will quickly bring about a much deeper connection to the wisdom of the tradition. It may also induce experiences in a different state of mind. Make sure you have writing material in your room to note any visions or realizations you receive from the inner levels.

Preparation

If you want to unite yourself with the Prince of the Torah, wash your garments (before the twelve days have begun) and immerse yourself in water three times on each occasion before performing the ritual.[1]

During this practice, you will have to sit for twelve days in a chamber or roof space (attic room) where you will be alone. Do not leave the chamber for twelve days (although perhaps an exception could be made for going to the bathroom). Do not eat or drink, except after sunset. Eat only bread baked with your own hands, and drink only pure water. Do not eat any kind of vegetables (and certainly no meat).

To perform this task, take vacation time for two weeks, and make sure you have one or—better—two days to "close down" before you have to go back to your daily work.

The Sarim (Princes)

High angels are often called *Sarim* (princes; singular: *Sar,* or prince). I will not describe their form in this ritual, because you will see how they appear to you, and you will subsequently work with that form. Make sure, however, that you can see and feel them clearly. (I find it helpful to visualize the twelve princes in the colors of the zodiac, beginning with red, orange-red, orange, etc.)

Prayer (Shmoneh Essreh)

Begin each ritual by standing up and reciting the morning, afternoon, or evening prayer. The original text refers to mainly the Eighteen Benedictions (Shmoneh Essreh), although you may wish to recite the whole set of traditional prayers. If you wish to learn about them, they can be found in every *siddur* (prayer book), and a local Rabbi or a Jewish friend who is used to daily prayer may be able to answer any further questions you have.

---

[1] This is due to the possibility of seminal emission.

The Midrash of the Sar ha-Torah
(Prince of the Torah)

Sit down and recite the Midrash of the Sar ha-Torah, contemplating its meaning. Notice that this text can be interpreted as referring to the physical Temple, or to the Heavenly Palace as experienced in the Vision of the Merkavah—or the Temple within.[2]

Rabbi Ishmael said:

Thus spoke Rabbi Aqiva in the name of Rabbi Eliezer, the great. Our fathers (ancestors) have taken the task upon themselves to put stone upon stone, at the Temple of the Lord (Hechal YHVH = Temple or Palace of God), until the King of the World (Malko shel Olam = God) and all his servants (i.e., the angels) were forced to accept their petition.

And they (i.e., our ancestors) united themselves with Him (*unio mystica*), and He revealed to them the secret of the Prince of the Torah and how to use it.

Immediately the Ruach ha-Qodesh (Holy Spirit) appeared to them from the great entrance of the House of the Lord (Bet YHVH).

For the Shechinah (Presence of God) did not descend any more, and She did not do Her service in the Holy of Holies any more, because of the decree of punishment.[3]

Yet our fathers (ancestors) saw the Throne of Glory that was raised up and which stood between the antechamber and the Altar, even though in that hour the building was not yet finished, and they had not built up anything but the forms (Tzurat = form or images, maybe in the meaning of thought-forms) which were formed and stood for the antechamber of the Temple (Hechal), the Temple, the Altar and the whole House to be completed on them.

When they saw the Throne of Glory, raised up in the middle of the Hechal (Temple or Palace), and between the antechamber and the Altar and the King of the World on It, immediately they fell on their faces, and about this hour scripture says:

---

[2] A detailed description of the inner Temple can be found at my website: www.qabbalah .org (English) or www.qabbalah.de (German).

[3] This passage describes the time when the first Temple had been destroyed by the decree of God due to idolatry, and the second Temple had not yet been finished.

"Great is the Glory (Kavod) of the House." (Haggai 2:9)

For in the first Sanctuary, I [God] have united Myself with My children [humankind], My Throne and all My servants [angels], only by means of this voice. O, may My children last.

Why doth thou fall down and be laid on thy face? Stand up and sit in front of My Throne in the way thou sitteth in the academy (*yeshivah*). Take and receive the Crown (Keter = the Awesome Crown), learn the Mystery of the Prince of the Torah, how to perform it, how to interpret it, and how to use it. For they will let thee ascend the Paths of thy Heart (the thirty-two Paths of Wisdom). Thou shalt see the Torah with thy Heart.

"How [shall I do this]?" replied Zerubavel ben Shealtiel, when he stood in front of Him (literally, on his feet). Like a Translator He [God] interpreted the names of the Prince of the Torah, one after the other, like the Name of the Crown and the Name of the Seal (the Great Seal and the Awesome Crown).

Opening Invocation

Speak this invocation standing up:

**Be adorned,
be raised high,
be exalted
magnificent King,
on a high and exalted (ram ve-nisa),
awesome and terrible Throne.**

Thou liveth in the chambers of the Palace of Splendor (Hechal ga'ava).

**The servants of Thy Throne are terrified
and make tremble the Aravot (seventh heaven), the stool of Thy feet,
with a chanting voice and passionate singing every day.
As it is written:**

**Qadosh Qadosh Qadosh (Holy Holy Holy is)
YOD HEH VAV HEH TZEVAOT
The whole earth is filled with Thy Glory (Kavod). (Isaiah.6:3)**

**Who will not lift Thee up,
awesome and terrible King?**

All Thy servants serve Thee,
shivering and trembling.
With terror and dread they are terrified by the divine dispensation.
Because of the fright and fear,
they pronounce Thy awesome Name with one mouth.
They stand before Thee,
none too early and none too late.
And everyone who hinders his fellow in pronouncing Thy Name,
and may it be only for the distance of a hair,
he will be thrust down by a flame of fire.
As it is written:

Qadosh Qadosh Qadosh (Holy Holy Holy is)
YOD HEH VAV HEH TZEVAOT
The whole earth is filled with Thy Glory (Kavod). (Isaiah.6:3)

The Great Seal and the Awesome Crown

Open the quarters with the rituals of the Great Seal and the Awesome Crown and the prayers that belong to them, as described in chapter 16.

Invoke the Four Princes

Face east and say:

By the power and authority of the Awesome Crown
I [Insert your magical name] **invoke the four great princes of wisdom.**

In the Name of AZBOGAH
I invoke thee YOFIEL (Beauty of God),[4]
Prince of the Torah,
thou art the majesty on high.

Turn to the south and say:

In the Name of AVAGDEHU
I invoke thee SARBIEL (Resistance of God),[5]
thou art one of the Sarey Merkavah (princes of the Merkavah).

---

[4] The beauty of the Torah.
[5] The rebellion against ignorance.

Turn to the west and say:

> **In the Name of ZAHUZIYAH**
> **I invoke thee SHEHADRIEL (Who Honors/Praises God),**
> **thou art a beloved prince (Sar).**

Turn to the north and say:

> **In the Name of ZOHTZIYAH**
> **I invoke thee CHASDIEL (Mercy of God),**
> **thou art called to the Power (Gevurah) six times every day.**

Face east and say:

> **I have invoked thee,**
> **the four great princes of wisdom,**
> **to be present in this rite,**
> **to give me knowledge and understanding of the Torah,**
> **and for it to [forever] remain in my memory.**

The Invocation of the Twelve Princes

Turn to the east-southeast and say:

> **In the name of YOFIEL,**
> **who is the majesty on high**
>
> **In the name of SARBIEL,**
> **who is one of the Sarey Merkavah (princes of the Merkavah),**
>
> **In the name of SHEHADRIEL,**
> **who is a beloved prince (Sar).**
>
> **In the name of CHASDIEL,**
> **who is called to the Power (Gevurah) six times every day.**
>
> **I invoke thee,**

Say twelve times:

> **SHAQADHUZIAY YOD HEH VAV HEH HA-SAR**
> **SHAQADHUZIAY YOD HEH VAV HEH HA-SAR**
> **SHAQADHUZIAY YOD HEH VAV HEH HA-SAR**
> **SHAQADHUZIAY YOD HEH VAV HEH HA-SAR**
> **SHAQADHUZIAY YOD HEH VAV HEH HA-SAR**
> **SHAQADHUZIAY YOD HEH VAV HEH HA-SAR**

SHAQADHUZIAY YOD HEH VAV HEH HA-SAR
SHAQADHUZIAY YOD HEH VAV HEH HA-SAR
SHAQADHUZIAY YOD HEH VAV HEH HA-SAR
SHAQADHUZIAY YOD HEH VAV HEH HA-SAR
SHAQADHUZIAY YOD HEH VAV HEH HA-SAR
SHAQADHUZIAY YOD HEH VAV HEH HA-SAR

Say the following:

> **Give me knowledge and understanding of the Torah,**
> **Help me to learn and understand**
> **Torah and scripture and Mishnah and the Vision of the Merkavah.**
> **Help me to keep it in my mind and in my heart.**
> **And let me discover the secret wisdom hidden therein.**

Turn to the southeast and repeat the invocation with all the four princes with this name twelve times.

NIHVRADYOELAY YOD HEH VAV HEH, HA-SAR

Turn to the south-southeast and repeat the invocation with all the four princes with this name twelve times.

AVIR GAHURIRIEL YOD HEH VAV HEH HA-SAR

Turn to the south-southwest and repeat the invocation with all the four princes with this name twelve times.

PLITRIYAH YOD HEH VAV HEH HA-SAR

Turn to the southwest and repeat the invocation with all the four princes with this name twelve times.

ZAHUVRUDIYA YOD HEH VAV HEH HA-SAR

Turn to the west-southwest and repeat the invocation with all the four princes with this name twelve times.

AZGEVUHDAY YOD HEH VAV HEH HA-SAR

Turn to the west-northwest and repeat the invocation with all the four princes with this name twelve times.

TOTRUSIYAY YOD HEH VAV HEH HA-SAR

Turn to the northwest and repeat the invocation with all the four princes with this name twelve times.

ASHARUYLIAY YOD HEH VAV HEH HA-SAR

Turn to the north-northwest and repeat the invocation with all the four princes with this name twelve times.

ZAVUDIEL YOD HEH VAV HEH HA-SAR

Turn to the north-northeast and repeat the invocation with all the four princes with this name twelve times.

MARGIYOIEL YOD HEH VAV HEH HA-SAR

Turn to the northeast and repeat the invocation with all the four princes with this name twelve times.

DAHIVIRON YOD HEH VAV HEH HA-SAR

Turn to the east-northeast repeat the invocation with all the four princes with this name twelve times.

ADIRIRON YOD HEH VAV HEH HA-SAR

Uniting with the Prince of the Torah

After you have repeated all the invocations to all the twelve angels and asked each one to fulfill your desire for knowledge, you may unite yourself with the Prince of the Torah. The procedure for doing this was not described in the original text, but I have included a description here. The process is the same as for the assumption of a god form in Egyptian magic.

Go to the east, and stand facing west. If you think you cannot stand for a long time, or that standing for a long time will make relaxation difficult, sit on a chair. Relax your body and enter a deeper meditative state of consciousness. Because this is a ritual for advanced students, I will not describe how to do this in detail. Feel and see with your inner eye the shape of Yofiel, the Prince of the Torah, standing behind you. Again, I will not describe his form, because you may visualize him according to your own imagination and understanding of his nature. See and feel his presence with all your senses. When you have built up his image clearly, feel how Yofiel touches your shoulder. His touch is friendly but contains a feeling of great power and wisdom. The feeling becomes much more intense as Yofiel moves forward. His presence envelops you. You are surrounded by an aura of magnificent light. In fact, you see nothing but light. You feel the amazing wisdom of this angelic being. You can feel his heartbeat and his breathing. Slowly, your heartbeat and your breathing are adjusted to his.

Then you grow in size until you occupy exactly the same space as the Prince of the Torah. The energy centers of your body will merge with the centers of his body. Your Keter (crown center) will fuse with his Keter. Your Daat (throat center) will fuse with his Daat. Your Tiferet (solar plexus center) will fuse with his Tiferet. Your Yesod (genital center) will fuse with his Yesod, and your Malchut (foot/sole center) will fuse with his Malchut.

Finally, your mind will merge with his mind. . . . It will now be united with the mind of him who reveals all the wisdom and understanding and knowledge of the Torah. You will see with his eyes and understand with his understanding. You will be filled with the wisdom and understanding of the Torah. If you ask to know the deeper meaning of any passage of the Torah, it will be shown to you. You will be shown great mysteries, but you will not be able to endure the pressure of his presence for a very long time. When you feel it starting to become too much, just ask him to withdraw, and he will do so. You will feel how both of you separate, slowly and gently, and when you have reached your own size again, you will feel and hear that your heartbeat and breathing having separated from his. You have been given a great gift.

Bless Yofiel, the Prince of the Torah, with your own words to express your thankfulness. Take a few moments to calm yourself, and then complete the ritual. Do not forget to write down your experience and realizations.

To Release the Twelve Princes

Turn to the east-southeast and say:

> **I have invoked thee**
> **SHAQADHUZIAY YOD HEH VAV HEH HA-SAR**

Turn to the southeast and say:

> **I have invoked thee**
> **NIHVRADYOELAY YOD HEH VAV HEH HA-SAR**

Turn to the south-southeast and say:

> **I have invoked thee**
> **AVIR GAHURIRIEL YOD HEH VAV HEH HA-SAR**

Turn to the south-southwest and say:

> **I have invoked thee**
> **PLITRIYAH YOD HEH VAV HEH HA-SAR**

Turn to the southwest and say:

> **I have invoked thee**
> **ZAHUVRUDIYA YOD HEH VAV HEH HA-SAR**

Turn to the west-southwest and say:

> **I have invoked thee**
> **AZGEVUHDAY YOD HEH VAV HEH HA-SAR**

Turn to the west-northwest and say:

> **I have invoked thee**
> **TOTRUSIYAY YOD HEH VAV HEH HA-SAR**

Turn to the northwest and say:

> **I have invoked thee**
> **ASHARUYLIAY YOD HEH VAV HEH HA-SAR**

Turn to the north-northwest and say:

> **I have invoked thee**
> **ZAVUDIEL YOD HEH VAV HEH HA-SAR**

Turn to the north-northeast and say:

> **I have invoked thee**
> **MARGIYOIEL YOD HEH VAV HEH HA-SAR**

Turn to the northeast and say:

> **I have invoked thee**
> **DAHIVIRON YOD HEH VAV HEH HA-SAR**

Turn to the east-northeast and say:

> **I have invoked thee**
> **ADIRIRON YOD HEH VAV HEH HA-SAR**

Turn to the east and say:

I have invoked all you princes

in the name of YOFIEL,
who is the majesty on high;
in the name of SARBIEL,
who is one of the Sarey Merkavah (princes of the Merkavah);
in the name of SHEHADRIEL,
who is a beloved prince (Sar);
in the name of CHASDIEL,
who is called to the Power (Gevurah) six times every day.

I bless ye and release ye.
Depart in peace,
and go peacefully to thy abodes,
and do not harm me
and come back again when I call ye.

To Release the Four Princes of Wisdom

By the power and authority of the Awesome Crown,
I bless the four great princes of wisdom.

In the Name of AZBOGAH
I bless and release thee YOFIEL,
Prince of the Torah.
Thou art the majesty on high.
Depart in peace,
and go peacefully to thy abodes,
and do not harm me
and come back again when I call thee.

Turn to the south and say:

In the Name of AVAGDEHU
I bless and release thee SARBIEL.
Thou art one of the Sarey Merkavah (princes of the Merkavah).
Depart in peace,
and go peacefully to thy abodes,
and do not harm me
and come back again when I call thee.

Turn to the west and say:

> **In the Name of ZAHUZIYAH**
> **I bless and release thee SHEHADRIEL.**
> **Thou art a beloved prince (Sar).**
> **Depart in peace,**
> **and go peacefully to thy abodes,**
> **and do not harm me**
> **and come back again when I call thee.**

Turn to the north and say:

> **In the Name of ZOHTZIYAH**
> **I bless and release thee CHASDIEL.**
> **Thou art called to the Power (Gevurah) six times every day.**
> **Depart in peace,**
> **and go peacefully to thy abodes,**
> **and do not harm me**
> **and come back again when I call thee.**

Removing the Great Seal and the Awesome Crown

Remove the Awesome Crown and close the quarters with the Great Seal, reciting the prayers that belong to it. Then sit down and study or meditate on the Torah or other traditional texts.

18

The Invocation of the Prince of the Countenance

One of the main aims of Qabbalistic high magic was the striving for higher wisdom. To achieve this aim, the following ritual was used in order to invoke the Sar ha-Panim (Prince of the Countenance),[1] who is the highest of the archangels and who serves in the Countenance of God. He is Metatron, the great initiator, who has seventy names according to the seventy basic languages. The fundamental name used in this ritual is Ozahya. Like the Names of God, Metatron's different names refer to his different functions. If he is invoked to bring the magician to the Merkavah, he is called Suriyah, and if invoked to descend to the earth in order to reveal the mysteries of above and below, he is called Ozahya. If thus invoked, he will reveal the mysteries of above and below, the deeper meanings of their foundations, and the hidden wisdom and the prudence of salvation.

He is sometimes called Naar (*youth*) because he is younger than the

---

[1] Literally, Prince of the Faces (of God).

239

other archangels, for he was once Henoch, son of Jared. The Hebrew name Henoch (Chanoch) literally means "the initiate," from the word *chanach*, "to initiate." According to the Qabbalah, Henoch (Chanoch) was the first initiate and the first initiator. Henoch did not die, but was taken by God, and he "was not": "And Henoch walked with God, and he was not, for God took him" (Genesis 5:24).

In other words, Henoch (Chanoch) was the first human being who passed beyond the cycle of reincarnation (*gilgul*). The Qabbalistic tradition describes his ascent into Heaven and transformation into the archangel Metatron.[2]

Tradition says that this ritual was handed down from Rabbi Eliezer the Great to Rabbi Aqiva, both of whom lived in the first century CE. The earliest fragment of this text, found in a *geniza*[3] in Cairo, dates from about 700–800 CE. The text, however, may be much older; it may have been copied many times. The earliest known full version was copied about seven hundred years later (in the thirteenth century).

Rabbi Eliezer warned Rabbi Aqiva that when he called upon Metatron to descend, this mighty being had almost destroyed the entire world, for he is the mightiest prince of the upper family (the heavenly family of angels). Considering that he is one of the wisest and most benevolent beings, why did he almost destroy the entire world? The answer is that few human beings can endure the pressure of his presence if he is invoked to such a powerful manifestation, as happens in this ritual. His presence may destroy your world, and even if the ritual succeeds, your world may never be the same again, and the world you knew may be destroyed forever—so beware![4]

This ritual is not to be taken lightly, because it may have an intense effect on your endocrine system, which may be dangerous if you go beyond your limits.

The ritual is designed to bring about a deep connection between you and Metatron. The word used to express this in Hebrew is *zaqaq*, which I have translated as "to attach." It also means "to join," "to connect," and "to bind." As a technical term of Qabbalistic magic, it describes the method that has been called, in Egyptian magic, the assumption of a god form.

This rite depends to a large extent on your inner attitude. It should be performed with a feeling of great awe. Do not underestimate the meaning

---

[2] See the Book of Henoch.

[3] A chamber for old texts in a synagogue.

[4] This does not mean Metatron wants to harm you. It simply is difficult to endure his power—just as in the case of Zeus and Semele.

of this little word, for it is the clue to much in this work. It is a key that will open many doors.

Intention

In a ritual this powerful, it is important to make sure you understand the intention of the ritual in its entirety. The text takes great care to make this certain. It says:

> I invoke thee, and I decree,
> that thou further attacheth thyself to me according to my will,
> and that thou accepeth the invocation of my decree,
> and that thou doeth my request and fulfilleth my petition.

The exact intention of this work is described in the following passage:

> And when thou descendeth, do not tear my mind [i.e., drive me insane],
> but reveal to me all the depth of the mysteries of above and below,
> and the secrets that are hidden above and below,
> and the mysteries of Understanding (Binah) and the skills of
> salvation (Tushiyah), like a man speaking to his fellow.

Preparation

To perform this ritual, you must purify yourself from seminal emission for seven days, including the day of the ritual, by immersing yourself every day in water up to your neck. On the day of performing the ritual, you should sit down in a fasted state and meditate in preparation.

Opening and Closing

Even though the original text does not describe any formal opening or closing, I advise the reader to begin this ritual by opening the quarters. Examples of how to do this can be found in other chapters of this book. (Because this ritual is only for experienced magicians, those competent to perform it will know how to open and close the quarters.)

Invoking the Princes of Dread, Awe, and Fright

Face east and say:

> I invoke you,
> SAREY EYMAH VE-YIRAH VE-RA'AD

princes of dread, awe, and fright,
for you are designated to strike those who are not clean and pure,
and proceed to make use of the servants of the Most High
by the power of the honored and awesome Name that is called:

QATAT YAH HAYAH SAN'NAQEQ
ROTET HOVEH HAYAH PAPANENAH
YOD HEH VAV HEH
YAH AGAQES
YOD HEH VAV HEH

(קתת יה היה סננקק רותת הוה היה פפננה יהוה יה אגקס יהוה)

Magnificent over all and ruling over all and in whose hand is
everything, I invoke you, do not harm me, and do not make me
tremble, and do not frighten me, and do not terrify me with the
powerful truth of the revealer of secrets.

And thus I fortify and seal myself
with the forty-two-letter Name that is called:

QATAT YAH HAYAH SAN NAQEQ
ROTET HOVEH HAYAH PAPANENAH
YOD HEH VAV HEH
YAH AGAQES
YOD HEH VAV HEH

Magnificent over all letters, for all who hear it
will be intimidated and frightened,
and all the heavenly hosts will tremble.

Imagine the letters building a seal of light around your body and aura.[5] You
should feel well protected by a very powerful seal.

Stand in front of the altar, face the east, and say:

Again, I invoke you:

Go to the east. Intensify the visualization of the angel and say:

In the Name of
ADAD

---

[5] Imagine it rotating clockwise.

I invoke thee to stand before me.

Go to the south. Intensify the visualization of the angel and say:

In the Name of
GIHU
I invoke thee to stand on my right side.

Go to the west. Intensify the visualization of the angel and say:

In the Name of
HEY
I invoke thee to stand behind me.

Go to the north. Intensify the visualization of the angel and say:

In the Name of
ZAZ
I invoke thee to stand on my left side.

Go back to the altar. Intensify the visualization of the angel, look downward, and say:

In the Name of
PATZATZ
I invoke thee to stand below me.

Look upward. Intensify the visualization of the angel and say:

In the Name of
YAH
I invoke thee to stand above me.

Adad is the name of an ancient Akkadian God of wind and thunder. Zaz may be a corrupt form of his wife's name, Shalash, who was a goddess associated with the sign of Virgo. Gihu may originate in her son's name, Girru, a god of fire. Hey is an ancient way of writing the letter Heh. Patzatz is a temurah permutation of the letters *Vav Heh Heh* using the method called At-bash. Finally, Yah is a well-known Hebrew Name of God.

The princes of dread, awe, and fright are angelic forces.[6] The term *prince* (Sar; plural: Sarim; constructus:[7] Sarey) is a common term for angels.

---

[6] These angels are considered as accompanying Metatron, and thus they are invoked first to prepare his coming and to ensure that they do not harm the magician.

[7] *Constructus* is a grammatical form used when two words are connected.

The following description is meant to help you form their image. If they appear a bit different to you, use the image that your own imagination gives them.

In front of you (east) stands an angel whose robes seem to consist of a whirlwind. He holds a whip with three thongs, each one being a flash of lightning. With this weapon he will punish the mischievous, arrogant, and proud.

On your right side (south) stands a fiery angel in red. He seems to consist of pure fire. He holds a huge flaming sword to punish those who try to use divine or magical powers in order to serve their anger or hate.

Behind you (west) stands an angel surrounded by hail and showers. His color is dark blue. He holds a three-pronged trident or fishing spear to pierce those who do injustice to others.

The angel on your left side (north) is dark brown in color. He holds a flail to hit those who follow their evil desires.

Below you is a totally dark angel. He holds the chain of Karma to bind those who step onto the dark path.

Above you stands an angel of pure blue fire. He holds a spear to gore the hearts of those whose soul is poisoned with spiritual pride.

The Invocation of the Prince Who Is the Most Harmful and Fiery of All the Dangerous Angels

Stand in the west and face the altar looking east, which is where the Sar ha-Panim will appear. Invoke him with this name [which must be spoken] in this language:

> **I call upon thee OZAHYA**
> **Sar ha-Panim** (Prince of the Countenance)
> **Naar** (Youth)
> **servant before the King of the Universe,**
> **prince and master of all the heavenly hosts.**

Visualize a clockwise vortex of energy descending from above to the place where you are invoking Metatron.

> **I invoke thee, and I decree**
> **that thou further attacheth thyself to me according to my will,**
> **and that thou accepteth the invocation of my decree;**
> **and that thou doeth my bidding and fulfilleth my petition;**

and that thou doth not intimidate me, or frighten me
or maketh me tremble, or causeth my body to quake.
And let my footstep not falter,
and let not the speech of my lips be perverted.

I fortify and strengthen myself,
that the invocation will be powerful and the
Name shall be of good order in my throat,
and that corruption shalt not seize me, or that thy servants cause my
foot to stray, or intimidate me, or frighten me, or weaken my hands.
And I shall not be blown away by fire, flame,
whirlwind, or storm (saarah) that goes with thee.
O wondrous and exalted one,
I invoke thee, for this is the specified form (perush) of thy Holy Name:

YOHI GAG HU HAYAH ITRAG HAVAZ YAH MAMAS YAGAG
HEY HEY SHETZAMAS HEY HU HAYAH

"At His wrath the earth quakes, nothing can endure His rage."
(Jeremiah 10:10)
May He be blessed and praised.

The Invocation with Fourteen Names

While performing the following invocation, visualize a huge pillar of white
fire manifesting through the vortex. Feel how the pillar of fire increases in
energy with each of the fourteen names.

Again I call upon thee, by thy fourteen names,
by which thou revealeth thyself to prophets and seers,
making words of prophecy sweet in their mouth,
and making pleasant utterances delightful [literally, pleasing].
And this is their specified form (perush)
and their concealed form (kinnuy):[8]

(1) I call upon thee by the specified form of thy name,
RUACH PISQONIT (Apportioning Spirit)
and I invoke thee by the concealed form of thy name:
QASAS NAGI HU HAYAH

[8] The specified form (perush) is a specific name and the concealed form (kinnuy) is an
untranslatable magical word or sentence.

(2) I call upon thee by the specified form of thy name:
ITMON (He Who Hides the Sins of Israel from God)[9]
and I invoke thee by the concealed form of thy name:
TZATZMAS NIHU HEY HOVEH

(3) I call upon thee by the specified form of thy name:
PISQON (He Who Judges Hard against God [i.e.,
defends humanity against harsh judgments])[10]
and I invoke thee by the concealed form of thy name:
QALOT YOD HEH VAV HEH VE-HU HOVEH

(4) I call upon thee by the specified form of thy name:
SIGRON (He Who Closes the Gates of Heaven So That No One Else Can
Open Them [i.e., if he fails to ask for mercy, no one else can do so])[11]
and I invoke thee by the concealed form of thy name:
MATZHOM HIYU NAH HOVEH

(5) I call upon thee by the specified form of thy name:
SENIGRON (Defender)
and I invoke thee by the concealed form of thy name:
CHATZNIG GAHUSAS YOHI

(6) I call upon thee by the specified form of thy name:
MESHI (Purified One)
and I invoke thee by the concealed form of thy name:
TZAQANENAH YAHEY VE-HAYAH

(7) I call upon thee by the specified form of thy name:
MOQIYON (Jester [i.e., the personification of humor as a divine attribute])
and I invoke thee by the concealed form of thy name:
KATMANAT PENENI HAYAH

(8) I call upon thee by the specified form of thy name:
ISTMA (Wreath, Keter)
and I invoke thee by the concealed form of thy name:
ITMAMENEY HU HOVEH

(9) I call upon thee by the specified form of thy name:

---

[9] See Babylonian Talmud Sanhedrin 44a.
[10] See Babylonian Talmud Sanhedrin 44a.
[11] See Babylonian Talmud Sanhedrin 44a.

SQITEM (Cobbler [according to the legend that Henoch made shoes])
and I invoke thee by the concealed form of thy name:
QADADDADU SAS YAD HEH

(10) I call upon thee by the specified form of thy name:
YAHOEL (YHVH is God)
and I invoke thee by the concealed form of thy name:
PADAR HODIM SIHO

(11) I call upon thee by the specified form of thy name:
YOFIEL (Beauty of God [also a name of the Prince of the Torah])
and I invoke thee by the concealed form of thy name:
QEMAHU ZAZU HAYAH VEY YAH VE-HAYAH

(12) I call upon thee by the specified form of thy name:
SASNANIEL (Refined One)
and I invoke thee by the concealed form of thy name:
SEQANMAHEH YAH YAH YAH

(13) I call upon thee by the specified form of thy name:
QENIGIEL (Hunter of God)
and I invoke thee by the concealed form of thy name:
TZATZMACHET SHAYHU YAH VE-YOD HEH VAV HEH

(14) I call upon thee by the specified form of thy name:
ZEVADIEL (Gift of God)
and I invoke thee by the concealed form of thy name:
AGTZATZNITAH YOAH YOD HEH VAV HEH

Behold, I invoke thee by the fourteen names,
with which all of the mysteries and secrets and signs were sealed,
and with which the foundations of Heaven and earth were made.

Visualize that, with the call of each of the names, the earth begins to quake
more and more intensely.

Four are engraved on the heads of the Chayot (Holy Creatures)
and they are these:
HOGAG TITAY VE-HU TZATZ NANEY SIYAH
Adon ha-Gevurot (Lord of the Powers)
ZAHU BAD HOG QASISAH
Baal Niflaot (Master of Miracles)

TATZMATZ SHESH GAHI HEH
Baal Perishoṭ (Master of Temperance)
QATNAT TZANIYAH VE-BAD GARDIYAH
Baal Ha-Olam (Master of the World)

Four are engraved on the four quarters of the Throne, and they are these:
NAHI PARED GIHU ZAZ HOVEH
Qadosh Qedoshe Ha-Qedoshim (Holiest of Holies of Holies)
PAPAG NAG EQAMAH YAH
Adir Adirey Adiron (Most Powerful One of Powers of Powers)
SASBAR TIL UZIYAH
El Elohey Ha-Elohim (Highest God over Gods of Gods)
ATKEN ITQAR PANGIYAH
Melech Malki Melachim (Highest King over Kings of Kings)

And four of them are engraved on the four crowns of the Ofanim, who stand opposite the Chayoth, as is said: "When those moved, these moved, and when those stood, these stood," (Ezekiel 1:21) and they are these:
BALIT GAIYAH VE-SAY
Shalit al Kol (Ruler of All)
AGSANU TZAV SAS RUR YAH
Adir al Kol (Mighty above All)
ZAGAGHU SAS HI TZATZ HOVEH
Mushal be-Kol (Regent of All)[12]
DARHI BIRAD NIHI
She-ha-Kol be-Yado (In Whose Hand Is All)

And two of them are engraved on the Crown of the Melech Eliyon (Highest King), and they are these:
ZATAT TZATZ PAPTZATZ QADEDAR CHAY TASIYAH
Before whom everyone bows his knee, and every mouth praises before Him. (See Isaiah 45:23.)
AZQAH VEH GARIZ SHUYE SHEYAH
For besides Him, there is no God and no savior. (See Isaiah 44:6.)
By them I invoke thee and decree and appoint thee to hurry and descend to me [Insert your magical name], —thee and not thy messenger.

---

[12] See 1 Chronicles 29:12.

And when thou descendeth, do not tear my mind (i.e., drive me insane),
but reveal to me all the depth of the mysteries of above and below,
and the secrets that are hidden above and below,
and the mysteries of Understanding (Binah) and the skills of
salvation (Tushiyah),
like a man speaking to his fellow.

For by these great, magnificent, wondrous, proved, and ordered names
I have invoked thee.
Through them the Throne of Glory is founded,
and the Seat of the Highest,
the precious object (Keli Chemdah), which was made
with wonder and miracle,
even before thou were formed,
and all the hosts on high were not yet added,
even before earth and its surroundings were made,
and the generations of earth,
and the praiseworthy creatures.

The Invocation with Five Names

Again I call upon thee,
by the five purest names among your names,
above which there is none, except for one.

Visualize that with the call of each of the first five names, the golden luster of
the Shechinah that accompanies Metatron builds up around the pillar of light.

And this is their specified form (perush):
SANANEQ TZANIYAH RATIYAH ELIYAH
ET TZANOSAS HU HU HAYAH ELIYAH
BAHUR DAGSU ASHAMAH SHAHIYAH ELIYAH
PATANUQ TZAHU SASAAN YAH VE-AHAH ELIYAH
OZHANECHA PAT PETADI HOVEH YOD HEH VAV HEH
YAH ELIYAH

I invoke thee by these five names, corresponding to thy five names,
whose letters are written in fire swallowing fire, and hovering above
the Throne of Glory, one ascending and one descending, so that the
Princes of the Countenance shalt not glimpse them.

The Princes of the Countenance are the highest angels closest to God, among which Metatron is supreme. Visualize how the names form inside the pillar of fire, and with each name, the energy intensifies more and more.

And this is their specified form (perush),
their pronunciation, and their honor:
ATLAMET GANISAS HAVAH YAH YAHAV
אתלמת גניסס הוה יה יהב
QARIMOS QARIR HAVAH YAH YAH YAHAV
קרימוס קריר הוה יה יה יהב
AHISOG GEHAVAH YAH TITAMNAGIYAH YAHAV
אהיסוג גהוה יה תתמנגיה יהב
HORAGAH YAH YAH HU HEH GAH YAH YAH YAHAV
הורגה יה יה הו הה גה יה יה יהב
AQNIYEF TZAL ZAR SHAQTITAH VAH HAVAH YAHAV
אקניעף צל זר שקתתה וה הוה יהב

By them I invoke thee,
who knows and recognizes the praiseworthiness and greatness of
these names, for there is no mouth that can praise and no ears that
can hear the great praise of any of them.
To them thou hath been commanded and warned by the mouth of
the Most High that if thou hear this invocation with these names, do
honor to thy name and hurry and descend
and do the will of him who invokes thee.

And if thou delayeth, behold, I shall drive thee
into the river Rigiyon of pursuing fire
and stand another in thy position.[13]
Honor thy name and hurry and descend to me,
to me [Insert your magical name],
not in anger and not with intimidation,
and not with rays of fire,
not with stones of hail, or walls of rage, or storehouses of snow,
and not with wings of wind,
and not with the fronts of storm winds which accompany thee.

---

[13] I do not advise using this (empty) threat in the invocation, because it is very rude, and even though phrases like this were often employed in ancient times, they hinder rather than help the intent of the rite.

Do my petition, grant my request, and fulfill my will,
for everything is in thy hands.
By the authority of
ANDIRO RADHU HAYAV
ELOHEY VE-ELOHEYCHA (My God and thy God)
ADON HA-KOL VE-ADONEYCHA (Lord of All and Lord of Thee).
In His Name I invoke thee,
to attach thyself to me,
and hurry and descend and do my will and do not tarry.

The Invocation with One Name

While speaking the last invocation, visualize the pillar of white fire and feel how it turns into the Prince of the Countenance. He is huge in size, reaching far beyond the size of your temple: Remember that above your physical temple in the world of Assiah there is the temple of Yetzirah, and above that is the temple of Beriah, and above that is the temple of Atzilut. The top of the head of the Prince of the Countenance will reach as high as the lower part of Atzilut, and his feet stand in your physical temple in Assiah. He has seventy-two wings—thirty-six on each side. Each wing is giant in size. His body consists of glowing white fire, and he wears a garment of pure light. On his head, which is so high above you that you see it as if covered by a veil of clouds, he wears a magnificent crown. The crown is decorated with forty-nine precious jewels. On this crown God himself has inscribed with his own finger the letters with which the Heaven and the earth were created. His face is extremely beautiful, and it indicates a wisdom that passes beyond the understanding of even the wisest of the wise. His all-seeing eyes glow and radiate light as the sun itself does His right hand has the power of a million flashes of lightning, and his left hand has the power of a million thunderbolts. He is surrounded by storm and whirlwind, and the thunder of earthquakes is before and behind him. Around him glows and shines the golden luster of the Shechinah. Upon seeing him, your heart is totally filled with awe. You hardly dare to breathe, and you can barely endure looking into his eyes. You see before you the mightiest being that exists—with the exception of God himself.

Again I call upon thee,
with the name that is the greatest of all thy names
and that is beloved and pleasing,

in the Name of thy Master, except for one letter which is missing from His Name, and by it He formed and founded everything and sealed with it all the work of His hands.

And this is their specified form (perush):
IYURAN (Blindingly Bright One)
TOQEFAN (Powerful One)
HIDURAN (Dignified One)
ASHASH MIQTZATAT MAG MESATZAY
MENIQAY HOGAY HASAS PATZAM YAH
HAAMATZTANIYAH QATO HOHAS

And their specified form (perush) in the pure tongue is Yod Heh, and its name is:
YOD HEH VAV HEH YO YOD HEH VAV HEH
HU HU YOD HEH VAV HEH YAH HAYAH YOD HEH VAV HEH
YAH HAYAH YOD HEH VAV HEH HI VEHAY HAYU HAYAH
YAH YAH HEHU YO HI HOVEH YAH YOD HEH VAV HEH

I invoke thee by the holy right Hand
and by His true and beloved Name, for whose Glory everything was created, by whose mighty Arm (Zeroa Gevurah) everything is expressed [or specified = meforash] and from the dread of whom all the children of the heavenly family are frightened and quake.
ESH SAMETZ QATAM PATAG
USAY YAGAG BI EMASITZ TAMT
MANINATZ ATAT ZEMAN YIQA
PAFGAHU PAHOZIM
TZATZAM HAYU EMATZAM ANASI HOYAY

And their specified form (perush) in the pure tongue is Yod Heh, and its name is:
YOD HEH VAV HEH
HEH YAH YAH YOHI HEH YAH YAH
YOD HEH VAV HEH
HU YAH YAH HEY HAYAH VEYAH HOVEH
YOD HEH VAV HEH
HOY HEY YAHU HAYU YAH
YAH HEHOVEH
YAH HEHAYAH

Baruch Shem Kavod Malchuto Le-Olam Va-ed
(Blessed be the Name of His Majesty's Glory for ever and ever.)
All shall glorify and adorn Thy Name, for thus is Thy Love.

Before you stands Metatron, the greatest of the angelic princes, the Prince of the Countenance. I have described him as he is seen by traditional Qabbalists. If he appears differently to you, work with that image. Once you have invoked him, welcome him in your own words.

Uniting with the Prince of the Countenance

If you dare to unite yourself with Metatron, use the following method. Otherwise, you may choose only to speak to him or meditate in his presence without uniting with him.

If you wish to unite yourself with him, go to the east and stand facing west. If you think that you will not be able to stand for a long time, or that standing will make relaxation difficult, sit on a chair. Relax your body and enter a deeper meditative state of consciousness. Feel and see with your inner eye the form of Metatron, the Prince of the Countenance, standing behind you. See and feel his presence with all your senses.

When you have built up his image clearly, enlarge your own body until it equals that of Metatron. Feel how Metatron touches your shoulder. His touch is friendly, but it contains a feeling of great power and wisdom. The feeling becomes much more intense as Metatron moves forward. His presence envelops you. You are surrounded by an aura of magnificent light. In fact, you see nothing but light. You feel the amazing wisdom of this angelic being. You can feel his heartbeat and his breathing. Your heartbeat and your breathing will slowly be adjusted to his. Then you grow in size until you occupy the exact same space as the Prince of the Countenance.

The energy centers of your body will merge with the centers of his body. Your Keter (crown center) will fuse with his Keter. Your Daat (throat center) will fuse with his Daat. Your Tiferet (solar plexus center) will fuse with his Tiferet. Your Yesod (genital center) will fuse with his Yesod. Do not go down to Malchut, as earthing the power may be dangerous. Furthermore, if you keep the power from Malchut, you will be enabled to fuse with Metatron on a higher level. You will feel that the pressure becomes more and more intense. Finally, your mind will merge with his mind. It will now be united with his, the mightiest being except for God Himself, Metatron who is accompanied by the Shechinah, the Presence of

God, wherever he goes. You will see with his all-seeing eyes, and understand with his all-knowing understanding.

He will reveal to you all the depth of the mysteries of above and below, and the secrets that are hidden above and below, and the mysteries of Understanding (Binah) and the skills of salvation (Tushiyah), like a man speaking to his fellow. You will be filled with wisdom and understanding, insofar as you are able to receive them. You will be shown great mysteries—but you will not be able to endure the pressure of his presence for a very long time. When you feel it becoming too much, just ask him to withdraw, and he will do so. You will feel both of you separate, slowly and gently, and when you have reached your own size again, you will feel and hear that your heartbeat and breathing have separated from his.

You have been given a great gift. Bless Metatron, the Prince of the Countenance, with your own words to express your thankfulness. Take a few moments to calm yourself and return from the meditation, and then complete the ritual. Do not forget to write down your experience and realizations after the ritual.

To Release the Sar ha-Panim

I invoke and decree and appoint thee
not to transgress my words or delay my words,
or change anything of my decree and my appointment
and my invocation.

I decree and appoint peace over thee,
in the Name of
YAHU HU U HU
YAHU HAB YAH U AH
BAAH HAAH YOAH HEY HU U U
YAH HU YAH VE-HEH
Baruch Shem Kavod Malchuto Le-Olam Va-ed
(Blessed be the Name of His Majesty's Glory for ever and ever.)

Ascend in peace [and with my blessing],
and I will not be afraid in the hour of thy departure from me.

Now feel how Metatron withdraws from the place of your ritual. Take your time until you are certain that he has left.

To Release the Princes of Dread, Awe, and Fright

I have invoked ye,
SAREY EYMAH VE-YIRAH VE-RA'AD
princes of dread, awe, and fright.
I bless you and release you.
Depart in peace,
and go peacefully to your abodes
and do not harm me.

In the Name of
AH YOD HEH VAV HEH YAH HAYAH
ADON ELIYON (Highest Lord)
VE-QADOSH HA-SHEM (and holy is the Name)

In the Name of
YOD HEH VAV HEH
YOD HEH VAV HEH TZEVAOT
ELOHEY MAARCHOT YISRAEL (God of the Orders of Israel)

In the name of the **CHAYOT HA-QODESH** (Holy Creatures)
And in the name of the **GILGALEY HA-MERKAVAH**
(Wheels of the Chariot)
And in the name of the **NEHAR DINUR** (river of fire)

YAH YAH YAH YAH YAH YAH YAH
and all His servants,
and in the Name of
YAH YAH YAH YAH YAH YAH YAH

YOD HEH VAV HEH
YOD HEH VAV HEH
YOD HEH VAV HEH
YOD HEH VAV HEH
YOD HEH VAV HEH
YOD HEH VAV HEH
YOD HEH VAV HEH

TZEVAOT
TZEVAOT
TZEVAOT

TZEVAOT
TZEVAOT
TZEVAOT
TZEVAOT

EL EL EL EL EL EL EL

SHADDAI SHADDAI SHADDAI SHADDAI SHADDAI
SHADDAI SHADDAI

EHIYEH ASHER EHIYEH
EHIYEH ASHER EHIYEH
EHIYEH ASHER EHIYEH
EHIYEH ASHER EHIYEH
EHIYEH ASHER EHIYEH
EHIYEH ASHER EHIYEH
EHIYEH ASHER EHIYEH

EHEY AY ASHER EHEY AY
EHEY AY ASHER YAHU AY
AH YEY ASHER AY
YEHIYE ASHER YAH
YEY YEHEY EYEH YAH YAH

ADIR CHASIN (Mighty One, Strong One)
His Name is
YAH HU HAB HAYAH
Who revealed Himself on Mount Sinai,
In the Splendour (Hod) of His Kingdom (Malchut).

Aramaic Exorcism

By these fearsome and powerful names,
which can cause the sun to darken, obscure the moon,
and overturn the sea,
split rocks, and quench fire,
I adjure you,
spirits (ruachim) and demons (devin)
and devils (shedim) and satans (satanim)
to go far from here and leave me [Insert your magical name].

The rite is ended.

Revelation of the Secret Name

Divine Names are a very important component in any type of magic, and this is especially the case in Qabbalistic magic. Consequently, the revelation of a Divine Name is an important stage in the making of a Qabbalistic magician. A Divine Name is not only a key to magical power, but is also often a mystical formula that may describe the very fundamental essence of the universe, as well as being a key to spiritual growth.

The famous Rabbi Eleazar ben Yehudah of Worms (1160–1237) describes such a revelation by means of a special ritual designed to open the consciousness of the student who will receive the Divine Name (Shem ha-Meforash), and to prepare his mind to understand how to use its power and to realize its inner meaning. The ritual can be found in his *Sefer ha-Shem* (Book of the Name), a part of his major work *Sefer Sodey Razayah* (Book of the Secret Mysteries). Rabbi Eleazar himself was the leader of the Chassidey Ashkenaz (German pious ones), one of the most fascinating groups of practitioners of Qabbalistic magic, because they were both deeply magical and mystical. The original text describes this magic as the understanding of the Kavod (Glory) of the Name of the highest Lord, and the Kavod (Glory) of its Awe. (The Kavod is the manifest Glory of a Divine Principle. This means it is our perception of something that is actually beyond our ability to perceive. Notice that there is a difference between the Name itself and its Awe—that is, the power that lies within it. It is not enough only to know the Name; it is also important to receive the Name in the correct ritual manner.)

The Divine Name must be revealed on water, for it is written: "The voice of YHVH is upon the waters" (Psalm 29:3). According to an ancient tradition, water is a place especially suited for the appearance of the Shechinah (Presence of God), and some say that we can be permitted to speak the Name of God only at a place where the Shechinah is present. The other place is, of course, the Temple. It is therefore no surprise that much of Rabbi Eleazar's ritual is related to the ceremony of speaking the Name by the High Priest on Yom Kippur (Day of Atonement). Another major source for Rabbi Eleazar's ritual are the Hechalot texts. One of the Berachot (Blessings or Praises) has been copied, word for word, from a text called *The Lesser Hechalot*.

This ritual can be used for many purposes. It could be part of an initiation or incorporation ritual into a magical group, lodge, school, or order. In such a case, it could be used to reveal the name of the inner contact of the group.

Preparation

The Name must be given only to devoted men who do not have an aggressive or otherwise imbalanced character, and they should be filled with awe, keeping the commandments of their Creator. Rabbi Eleazar's instruction is based on an ancient Talmudic passage: "Rabbi Yehudah said in the name of Rav: The forty-two letter Name will only be given to the devotional one, who is in the middle of his life, who will not get angry, who does not get drunk, and who is not bossy. And everyone who knows It and will treat It with care and keep It in purity, is beloved above and treasured below [. . .] and he will inherit both worlds, this one and the world to come" (Babylonian Talmud, Qedushin 71a).

Before the master reveals the Name to his student, they must wash themselves and then immerse themselves in forty *se'a* of water. Se'a is an ancient measurement, which makes conversion to modern measurements difficult. Forty se'a varies from three hundred to one thousand liters. (For practical considerations, I advise those who do not have access to a traditional Jewish ritual bath—which would be ideal, not only because of its size, but also because it would be "living water"[1]—simply to use a bathtub that holds about three hundred liters. Add some rainwater if possible.) Yet the measurement forty se'a has deeper meaning, for it is the number of the letter *Mem,* which means "water." It is good to meditate about it.

Then both master and student will dress themselves in white garments or robes. On the day of the revelation of the Name, both will fast in order to prepare for the ritual.

The Opening

Both master and student will go to a place of pure water and stand up to their ankles in the water. No opening or closing ceremony is given in the ancient text, and I will not give one in this case. Therefore, I leave it up to the ingenuity of the master to design his own.

The master, speaking with awe, says:

> **Baruch Atah** (Praised art Thou)
> **YOD HEH VAV HEH**
> **ELOHEYNU** (our God)
> **MELECH OLAM** (King of the World)
> **ELOHEY YISRAEL** (God of Israel)
>
> Thou art one, and Thy Name is one. (See Zechariah 14:9.)
> **Thou hast commanded us to conceal Thy great Name** (Shem Tov),
> **for Thy Name is awesome.**
>
> **Baruch Atah** (Praised art Thou)
> **YOD HEH VAV HEH**
> And praised be the Name of Thy Glory (Kavod)
> le-Olam (in eternity).
> **The glorious and awesome Name of YOD HEH VAV HEH**
> **ELOHEYNU** (our God),
>
> **the voice of YHVH is upon the waters. (Psalms 29:3)**

---

[1] Traditionally, the immersion should take place in "living water"—that is, water that moves. (A pure river or lake can be used as well.)

> **Baruch Atah** (Praised art Thou)
> **YOD HEH VAV HEH**
> **who reveals His Mystery (Razim) to those who revere Him.**

The master and student both look upon the water and say:

> **The floods have lifted up, O YHVH, the floods have lifted up
> their voice; the floods lift up their waves. YHVH on high is
> mightier than the noise of many waters, yea, than the
> mighty waves of the sea. (Psalm 93:3–4)**
> **The voice of YHVH is upon the waters: the God of Glory thundereth:
> YHVH is upon many waters. (Psalm 29:3)**
> **The waters saw Thee, O God; the waters saw Thee, they were afraid;
> the depths also trembled. The clouds flooded forth waters; the skies
> sent out a sound; Thine arrows also went abroad. The voice of Thy
> thunder was in the whirlwind; the lightnings lighted up the world;
> the earth trembled and shook. Thy way was in the sea, and Thy path in
> the great waters, and Thy footsteps were not known. (Psalm 77:17–20)**

Then both go silently to the synagogue or to the house of studies (*yeshivah*) or into the meditation room where there is water in a pure vessel. The way to this place should be walked in silent contemplation. It is actually a sort of pilgrimage, and therefore part of the ritual. Once the two have arrived in the chosen place, and they stand in front of the water, the ritual is completed. The best arrangement is that they stand opposite each other, with the master in the east and the student in the west, and the vessel between them in the middle.

The master, speaking with awe, says:

> **Baruch Atah** (Praised art Thou)
> **YOD HEH VAV HEH**
> **ELOHEYNU** (our God)
> **MELECH OLAM** (King of the World),
> **who has made us holy with His commandments**
> **which He has imposed upon us,**
> **who has separated us from the nations,**
> **who has revealed to us His secrets,**
> **and who has given us understanding to know**
> **His great and awesome Name**

Baruch Atah (Praised art Thou)
YOD HEH VAV HEH
Who reveals His secrets to Israel.

Now the master whispers the secret name into the ear of the student. The master and student speak together with a low voice and with awe and with Kavvanah—that is, "magical intention":

**Turn Thee toward me, and be gracious unto me,
as is Thy wont to do unto those that love Thy Name. (Psalm 119:132)
Therefore I will give thanks unto Thee, O YHVH, among the nations,
and will sing praises unto Thy Name. (Psalm 18:50)
I will give thanks unto YHVH according to His righteousness;
and will sing praise to the Name of YHVH Most High. (Psalm 7:18)**

**I will be glad and exult in Thee; I will sing praise to
Thy Name, O Most High. (Psalm 9:3)
Therefore I will give thanks unto Thee, O YHVH, among the nations,
and will sing praises unto Thy Name. (Psalm 18:50)
So will I sing praise unto Thy Name for ever, that I may daily
perform my vows. (Psalm 61:9)
Sing praises unto the Glory (Kavod) of His Name;
make His praise glorious.
All the earth shall worship Thee, and shall sing praises unto Thee;
they shall sing praises to Thy Name. Selah. (Psalm 66:2.4)
Sing unto God, sing praises to His Name;
extol Him that rideth upon the skies,
whose Name is YHVH; and exult ye before Him. (Psalm 68:5)
It is a good thing to give thanks unto YHVH,
and to sing praises unto Thy Name, O Most High. (Psalm 92:2)
Hallelujah; for it is good to sing praises unto our God;
for it is pleasant, and praise is comely. (Psalm 147:1)**

Baruch Shem Kavod Malchuto Le-Olam Va-ed
(Blessed be the Name of His Majesty's Glory for ever and ever.)
Blessed be the name of YHVH from this time forth and for ever.
(Psalm 113:2)
Blessed be YHVH le-Olam (in eternity) **Amen and Amen.**
(Psalm 89:53)

The Secret Name

You will, of course, have noticed that I have not included any secret name in the text of this ritual. I am sorry if some readers consider this disappointing, but publishing it in a book contradicts the very idea of a secret name. In fact, it would then be the very opposite of a secret name.

The secret name can, after all, be given only by a true master to his student. It cannot be revealed in a book, for either it would lose its power or, more likely, it would just be a strange word, useless and inert without the understanding of its deeper value. It can be received only personally, for the experience of the name and receiving it matters more than knowledge of consonants and vowels. In any case, only a prepared and worthy soul is ready and able to benefit from such an experience. Premature revelation would only spoil the whole potential of the ritual.

So again, all this has to be left to the master who performs this ceremony. (I will say only this much: The forty-two-letter Name had special significance to the Chassidey Ashkenaz. And let me add a final comment to the more clever readers: Yes, there is a forty-two-letter Name mentioned in another chapter of this book, but it is not quite this easy, and in any case, Rabbi Eleazar in his *Sefer Chochmat ha-Nefesh* [Book of the Wisdom of the Soul], writes that the whole Torah consists of Divine Names.)

20

The Robe of Righteousness

I will greatly rejoice in YHVH, my soul shall be joyful in my God; for He hath clothed me with the garments of salvation, He hath covered me with the Robe of Righteousness, as a bridegroom putteth on a priestly diadem, and as a bride adorneth herself with her jewels.

ISAIAH 61:10

The Robe of Righteousness (Me'il Tzedaqah) is a powerful tool of Qabbalistic magic. It is a cloak or garment on which Divine Names are written. By donning the Robe of Righteousness, the magician assumes the power of the Divine Name. Tradition says that he who wears the Robe of Righteousness will be saved from distress and trouble, hindrance and assault, and he will achieve a deep wisdom that is sweeter than honey.

The ritual of making and donning the Robe of Righteousness is described in an ancient text called *Sefer ha-Malbush* (Book of the Garment). The oldest version of this text is an Ashkenazic (German) manuscript from the thirteenth or fourteenth century, but fragments of a related text called *Torat ha-Malbush* (Teachings of the Garment), covering similar techniques, date back as far as the eleventh or early twelfth century, and another related text called *Sefer ha-Yashar* (Book of the Righteous One) is mentioned as early as the ninth century. The use of the Robe of Righteousness is one of the magical rites practiced by the Chassidey Ashkenaz (a famous German group of Jewish occultists and mystics).

To cover yourself in the Robe of Righteousness means more than just gaining additional power. It means assuming the power of the Divine, for God and His Name are linked closely, as can be seen from this prayer: "Blessed and blessed even more is Thy Name and exalted among all blessing and praise for Thy Name is in Thee" (*Sefer ha-Yashar*).

Therefore, the magician must make a special effort to ensure that his soul is pure enough to perform this rite. Unlike other potent rituals, participants must not only go through the usual preparation, but also must further pass a test to determine whether or not the necessary state of purity, inner balance, and good character has been reached.

This is the procedure of making and using the Robe of Righteousness as described in the ancient text.

Preparation

To prepare for this ritual, an individual must be purified seven times over, including fasting for seven days[1] in order to be purified of impurities such as a dead corpse, creeping animals (worms, insects, and reptiles), or a menstruating woman.

At the end of these seven days, the individual should immerse himself (in living water), and then, taking parchment of deer skin, make a garment from it similar to the breast plate and the Ephod[2] of the High Priest to cover only the shoulder and the navel and the breast and also the shoulder to the loins. And he should also make a hood[3] that is fastened to the garment. The garment needs no sleeves, and the great and awesome Name shall be written on both sides of the garment—on the front and on the back. The garment may look something like this:

---

[1] In *Torat ha Malbush* the magician is advised to fast for twenty-one days, and in *Sefer ha-Yashar* the magician is advised to keep pure for twenty-one days by abstaining from garlic, spice, and anything that bleeds.

[2] Exodus 28:6–14.

[3] Other possible translations would be "turban" or "helmet."

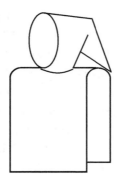

The pieces from which the garment is made look like this:

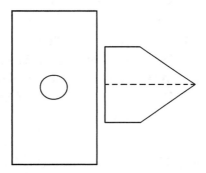

This is the Name that shall be written on both sides and another Name on the hood, and this is the form of the writing:

יהוה צח אל אדיר היקר אובצא אעֶ איה יה חד ולריס
אובינו ליה ובורא טאווה מבלייא אמיץ
אהיה שדי אה איום העזוז אהו אמשא וה
סימהדא והנאור באיצה יש דגויל אור אייל
שפיר משא נכבד אחס רמאל עונישא גיזייפו
לרשאל אשכול הוא חזק מקפש
מגדל חבשם באזק
אהוד מתנשא והחי יעף נקצם להבינף המליך
מערף
נפוד איום והפלא כסרו אותי יהוו עלף חק פטפרים
אחור ונורא הוא שתקן קרמן יחסן ושיך צם בו כל
צץ צפנה הוא ניקן הל כפתר עניפז
רפוע מורה זה קיים אחר ייעפו פלאיך אל
אדירירון

YOD HEH VAV HEH TZACH EL ADIR HIQAR
OVTZA EA AYEH YAH CHAD VE-LARIS
UVINO LAYAH U-VORE TAVAH MEVALEYA AMITZ
EHIYEH SHADDAI AH AYOM HA-AZUZ AHU AMSHA VEH
SIMHADA VE-HANAUR BEAITZAH YESH DAGOIL OR AYEL
SHAPIR MASHA NICHBAD ACHAS DAMEL UNISHA GIZAYFU
LARSHEL ASHKOL HU CHAZAQ MEQABESH
MIGDAL CHAVSHAM BEAZAQ
EHUD MITNASE VEHACHI YAOF NIQTZAM
LEHABINEF HAMALYECH
MEAREF
NEFOD IOM VEHAPELE KASRU OTI YEHAV
ELEF CHAQ PETIFRIM
ACHUD VE-NURA HU SHETAQAN QARMAN
YECHASAN VE-SCHITZ TZAM BO KOL
TZITZ TZEFANAH HU NIQAN HAL KAFTAR ENIFAZ
RAFUE MURAH ZEH QAYIM ECHAD YAYEFO PELECH EL
ADIRIRON

This is the Name that is written on the hood in a circle, like a plate[4] that goes around the hood.[5] If you want to make a golden plate, write the Name in the correct magical way—that is, clockwise. This is the Name to write on the plate or the hood of the garment:

בחט זתם זגים אל איש שם תר אבר באימה
אבנהמר גל אה גל גאלף תתיר אל חי זגים ירום
יה יה יה יה אל חי ויה יה יה גי גיה יה יה יה
יה יה יה יה יה יה יה יה יה יה יה יה יה יה יה
יה יה יה יה יה יה יה יה יה יה יה יה יה יה יה
יה יה יה יה יה יה יה יה יה יה יה יה יה יה יה
יה יה יה יה יה יה יה יה יה יה יה יה יה יה יה
יה יה יה יה יה

BEHAT ZATEM ZAGIM EL ISH SHEM TAR AVAR BAIMA
AVNEHEMAR GAL AH GAL GALEF TATIR EL CHAY

---

[4] In *Torat ha-Malbush* the same effect is achieved by making only a golden plate with a golden chain. In *Sefer ha-Malbush* the golden plate is described as an additional option that goes together with the garment.

[5] Other possible translations are: "conical hat," "mitre," "or turban," especially the priest's turban.

ZAGIM YAROM
YAH YAH YAH YAH EL CHAY VE-YAH YAH YAH
GI GIYAH YAH YAH YAH
YAH YAH YAH YAH YAH YAH YAH YAH
YAH YAH YAH YAH YAH YAH YAH YAH
YAH YAH YAH YAH YAH YAH YAH YAH
YAH YAH YAH YAH YAH YAH YAH YAH
YAH YAH YAH YAH YAH YAH YAH YAH
YAH YAH YAH YAH YAH YAH YAH YAH
YAH YAH YAH YAH YAH YAH YAH YAH
YAH YAH YAH YAH YAH YAH YAH YAH
YAH YAH YAH YAH YAH YAH

After you have written this glorious and awesome Name, fast for seven days, immersing yourself in water every night, not touching anything impure, and not eating anything made from a being that has a spirit, not even eggs or fish, but only varieties of vegetables.

The Image That Reflects the Purity of Your Soul

On the seventh day in the night, toward the eighth day, go out to the water and call toward the water, in awe and with deep devotion, the Holy Name. At this moment you will see, close to the water, the image (apparition) of a shape in the air. (This image is an astral perception, reflecting the inner state of your soul.)

If the image is green (the color of envy, greed, and selfishness), know that there is impurity within you, and you shall fast for another seven days[6] as in the beginning. In the night, toward the eighth day, do as in the first instruction, while giving alms (tzedaqah) to the poor and breaking your bread with the hungry. Do not cause anger and do not seek honor for yourself. Do not be arrogant or proud of yourself or your money, belongings, or social status; guard your heart from all evil, and pray before the Countenance of your Creator that you will not be humiliated again. (At the end of this chapter, you will find a suitable prayer.)

---

[6] *Torat ha Malbush* says that after you see the green image, fast for another twenty-one days. If you try this ritual again, and if you then see a black image at the second attempt, you must fast for yet another twenty-one days (and so on), until you see the red (fiery) image.

If you see an image that is shiny and red,[7] know that you are pure within. In this case, continue with the ritual: You shall be dressed to the navel,[8] and you shall go into the water up to your loins, donning the glorious and awesome Name in the water.

The Assumption of the Name

When you don the garment, invoke the names of these awesome angels with the names written on the garment, mentioned above, that they shall be feared alongside you. And these are the Names:

AGRUR GARUR GARHEY YAHUTAVIEL SHEMESHEY YIQTAEL LANAFRIEL IYNGARIEL TZARUCHEY TZADQIEL

At first, you will not see the angels. In fact, you will not see anything before you but smoke. If, however, you leave the water to battle anyone, it will look and appear that there is a large and mighty army with you. To let it rain or to turn the wind, invoke them—these angels—with the names written on the garment (as mentioned above), and call Him (the Name). Say at this moment in which shape or image you wish them to appear. Remember (and speak) the Name, and guard yourself so that you will not be humiliated, for they do not stay with you any longer than three or four hours at the most.

Afterward, guard yourself as in the beginning. You may serve with them (i.e., make them serve you) seven days with one service—once on each day.

---

[7] This is a quote from the Song of Songs: "My Beloved is shiny and red (*tzach ve-adom*), preeminent above ten thousand" (Song of Songs 5:10). This passage is traditionally interpreted as an allegoric description of God Himself. In *Torat ha Malbush* the image is described as an image of fire (because fire is a traditional symbol for heavenly powers), and in one early geniza fragment, it is described as an image of a Fire Lion. The Lion is a biblical analogy to God. "The Lion hath roared, who will not fear? The Lord YHVH hath spoken, who can but prophesy?" (Amos 3:8). Furthermore, the red lion is an important symbol in alchemy, known to be influenced by the Qabbalah. The red lion represents the philosopher's stone, the highest achievement in the Hermetic tradition.

[8] The original text does not clearly describe whether an individual should be clothed up to the navel or down to the navel. It is certain that the Robe of Righteousness covers only the upper body. It would be very unusual for a Jewish rite to leave the genitals uncovered, but it is not impossible to interpret the text in this way.

The Prayer for Him Who Wishes to
Use the Great Name

This prayer is given in *Sefer ha-Yashar* for anyone who wishes to use the Great Name. He shall pray before the shrine (of the Torah) at the time he washes himself with water at the begining of the dawn before sunrise, and therefore, he will be pious and righteous. And he shall say:

Blessed and blessed even more is Thy Name,
and exalted among all blessing and praise,
for Thy Name is in Thee.
And Thy Name is set before all.
And before Thy Name are regiments of fire and flame praising Thy Name.
And the Seraphim glorify Thy Name.
And the Chayot (Holy Creatures) sanctify Thy Name.
And the Ofanim (Wheels) purify Thy Name.

For from Thy Name all creatures have awe (fear),
And at Thy Name they do not (dare to) look.
And from Thy Name even the sea recedes,
and all the surge of its waves lets Thy Name be magnificent.
Earth roams if you look at it,
And its pillars are shattered by the fear of Thy Name.

And each inhabitant of the mountainside of each fortress and fortress
and each abode and abode tremble and fear Him
and are in awe of Thy Name:

Heaven and earth and their inhabitants
and the primal deep (Tehom) and the netherworld (Sheol)
And hell (Avadon) and wasteland and the [land of]
the shadows of death (Tzalmavet),
Man and cattle, mountains and hills, seas and rivers, fire and hail,
snow and smoke, great wind and dew and rain,
angels of fire and angels of water sanctify Thy Name.
For from Thy Name they vacillate,
and all of them sanctify Thy Name with Holy, Holy, Holy.[9]
And all who have a breath of living spirit in their nose

---

[9] Isaiah 6:3.

with fair tongue give Glory to Thy Name.
And I [Insert your magical name] also am Thy servant.

I am like one who is wretched and seeing trouble
and dust and ash downcast in the heart [i.e., depressed],
and poor and pauper,[10]
faint-hearted and with lowly spirit, like maggots and worms,[11]
I am like a passing shadow and a flower of the field.

I came and I want by Thy great and awesome Name
that Thee hast compassion with me
and that Thou art compassionate to me and givest me wisdom.
For I came in prayer, with broken [heart but]
clear language [i.e., intention]
and impatient to seek compassion before the Throne of Thy Glory,
in order to find grace and compassion and forgiveness before Thee.
For Thou art close to all who are close to Thee,
for Thou art compassionate and gracious,
for Thou art patient and very merciful,
for Thou art a compassionate and holy God,
for Thou art an awesome and holy God,
for Thou art full of compassion,
for Thou art good and the greatest good,
for Thou art good and forgiving.
I thank before Thee for Thou will be compassionate to me
in Thy compassion of compassions.
Please do as I request,
O YHVH my rock and my redeemer.[12]
[Amen]

After this, say what you need, with your face and head turned downward,
and you will succeed.

---

[10] See Psalm 86:1.
[11] Compare Job 25:6 and Isaiah 14:11.
[12] Psalm 19:15.

21

Creating a Golem with the *Sefer Yetzirah*

(*Book of Formation*)

One of the best-known aspects of Qabbalistic magic is the tale of Rabbi Yehudah Loew[1] ben Betzalel[2] (1525–1609). The Maharal of Prague (Maharal is an acronym of Moreynu ha-Rav Loew—Our Teacher the Rabbi Loew), as he was called, was famous for the creation of a *Golem,* a creature made by magic. This is the legend as it has been passed down to us.

In the town of Worms [in Germany] there once lived a pious man of the name of Betzalel to whom a son was born on the first night of Passover. This happened in the year 5273, after the creation of the

---

[1] From the German *Löwe* (lion).

[2] Note that Betzalel is also the name of the builder of the Temple of Solomon. He knew about the secret powers of the Holy Letters (see page 282).

*Rabbi Loew and
the Golem*

world (1579 CE), at a time when the Jews all over Europe were suffering from cruel persecutions. The nations in whose midst the children of Israel were dwelling constantly accused them of ritual murder. The Jews, their enemies pretended, used the blood of Christian children in the preparation of their Passover bread; but the arrival of the son of Rabbi Betzalel soon proved to be the occasion of frustrating the evil intentions of two miscreants who sought to show to Christendom that the Jews were actually guilty of ritual murder.

In the night, when the wife of Rabbi Betzalel was seized with labor pains, the servants who had rushed out of the house in search of a midwife luckily prevented two men, who were just going to throw a sack containing the body of a dead child into the Jew-street, with a view to proving the murderous practice of the Jews, from carrying out their evil intention. Rabbi Betzalel then prophesied that his newborn son was destined to bring consolation to Israel and to save his people from the accusation of ritual murder. "The name of my son in Israel," said Rabbi Betzalel "shall be Yehudah Arya, even as the patriarch Jacob said when he blessed his children: Yehudah is a lion's whelp; from the prey, my son, thou art gone up" (Genesis 49:9).

Rabbi Betzalel's son grew up and increased in strength and knowledge; he became a great scholar, well versed in the Holy Law, but also a master of all branches of knowledge and familiar with many foreign languages. In time he was elected Rabbi of Posen [in Poland], but later received a call to the city of Prague, where he was appointed chief judge of the Jewish community. All his thoughts and actions were devoted to the welfare of his suffering people and his great aim in life was to clear Israel of the monstrous accusation of ritual murder which like a sword of Damocles was perpetually suspended over the head of the unhappy race. Fervently did the rabbi pray to Heaven to teach him in a vision by what means he could best bring to naught the false accusations of the miscreant priests who were spreading the cruel rumors.

And one night he heard a mysterious voice calling to him, "Make a human image of clay and thus you will succeed in frustrating the evil intentions of the enemies of Israel." On the following morning the master called his son-in-law and his favorite pupil and acquainted them with the instruction he had received from Heaven. He also asked the two to help him in the work he was about to undertake. "Four elements," he said, "are required for the creation of the golem or homunculus, namely, earth, water, fire and air."

"I myself," thought the holy man, "possess the power of the wind; my son-in-law embodies fire, while my favorite pupil is the symbol of water, and between the three of us we are bound to succeed in our work." He urged on his companions the necessity of great secrecy and asked them to spend seven days in preparing for the work.

On the twentieth day of the month of Adar, in the year five thousand three hundred and forty after the creation of the world, in the fourth hour after midnight, the three men betook themselves to a river on the outskirts of the city on the banks of which they found a loam pit. Here they kneaded the soft clay and fashioned the figure of a man three ells high. They fashioned the features, hands and feet, and then placed the figure of clay on its back upon the ground.

The three learned men then stood at the feet of the image which they had created and the rabbi commanded his son-in-law to walk round the figure seven times, while reciting a cabalistic formula he had himself composed. And as soon as the son-in-law had completed the seven rounds and recited the formula, the figure of clay grew red like a gleaming coal. Thereupon the rabbi commanded his pupil to perform the same action, namely, walk round the lifeless figure seven times while reciting another formula. The effect of the performance was this time an abatement of the heat. The figure grew moist and vapors emanated from it, while nails sprouted on the tips of its fingers and its head was suddenly covered with hair. The face of the figure of clay looked like that of a man of about thirty.

At last the rabbi himself walked seven times round the figure, and the three men recited the following sentence from the history of creation in Genesis: "And the Lord God formed man of the dust of the ground, and breathed into his nostrils the breath of life; and man became a living soul" (Genesis 2:7).

As soon as the three pious men had spoken these words, the eyes of the Golem opened and he gazed upon the rabbi and his pupils with eyes full of wonder. Rabbi Loew [also spelled Löw] thereupon spoke aloud to the man of clay and commanded him to rise from the ground. The Golem at once obeyed and stood erect on his feet. The three men then arrayed the figure in the clothes they had brought with them, clothes worn by the beadles of the synagogues, and put shoes on his feet.

And the rabbi once more addressed the newly fashioned image of clay and thus he spoke, "Know you, clod of clay, that we have fashioned you from the dust of the earth that you may protect the people of Israel against its enemies and shelter it from the misery and suffering to which our nation is subjected. Your name shall be Joseph, and you shall dwell in my courtroom and perform the work of a servant. You shall obey my commands and do all that I may require of you, go through fire, jump into water or throw yourself down from a high tower."

The Golem only nodded his head as if to give his consent to the words spoken by the rabbi. His conduct was in every respect that of a human being; he could hear and understand all that was said to him, but he lacked the power of speech. And thus it happened on that memorable night that while only three men had left the house of the rabbi, four returned home in the sixth hour after midnight.

The rabbi kept the matter secret, informing his household that on his way in the morning to the ritual bathing establishment he had met a beggar, and, finding him honest and innocent, had brought him home. He had the intention of engaging him as a servant to attend to the work in his schoolroom, but he forbade his household to make the man perform any other domestic work.

And the Golem thenceforth remained in a corner of the schoolroom, his head upon his two hands, sitting motionless. He gave the impression of a creature bereft of reason, neither understanding nor taking any notice of what was happening around him. Rabbi Loew said of him that neither fire nor water had the power of harming him, nor could any sword wound him. He had called the man of clay Joseph, in memory of Joseph Sheda mentioned in the Talmud who is said to have been half human and half spirit, and who had served the rabbis and frequently saved them from great trouble.

Rabbi Loew, the miracle worker, availed himself of the services of the Golem only on occasions when it was a question of defending his people against the blood accusations from which the Jews of Prague had to suffer greatly in those days.

Whenever the miracle-working Rabbi Loew sent out the Golem and was anxious that he should not be seen, he used to suspend on his neck an amulet written on the skin of a hart, a talisman which rendered the man of clay invisible, while he himself was able to see everything. During the week preceding the feast of Passover the Golem wandered about in the streets of the city stopping everybody who happened to be carrying some burden on his back. It frequently occurred that the bundle contained a dead child which the miscreant intended to deposit in the Jew-street; the Golem at once tied up the man and the body with a rope which he carried in his pocket, and, leading the mischief maker to the town hall, handed him over to the authorities. The Golem's power was quite supernatural and he performed many good deeds.

A day came when a law was finally promulgated declaring the blood accusation to be groundless, and the Jews breathed a sigh of relief when all further persecutions on account of alleged ritual murder were forbidden. Rabbi Loew now decided to take away the breath of life from the Golem, the figure of clay which his hands had once fashioned. He placed Joseph upon a bed and commanded his disciples once more to walk round the Golem seven times and repeat the words they had spoken when the figure was created, but this time in reverse order. When the seventh round was finished, the Golem was once more a lifeless piece of clay. They divested him of his clothes, and wrapping him in two old praying shawls, hid the clod of clay under a heap of old books in the rabbi's garret.

Rabbi Loew afterwards related many incidents connected with the creation of the Golem. When he was on the point of blowing the breath of life into the nostrils of the figure of clay he had created, two spirits had appeared to him; that of Joseph the demon and that of Jonathan the demon. He chose the former, the spirit of Joseph, because he had already revealed himself as the protector of the rabbis of the Talmud, but he could not endow the figure of clay with the power of speech because the living spirit inhabiting the Golem was only a sort of animal vitality and not a soul. He possessed only small powers of discernment, being unable to grasp anything belonging to the domain of real intelligence and higher wisdom.

And yet, although the Golem was not possessed of a soul, one could not fail to notice that on the Sabbath there was something peculiar in his bearing, for his face bore a friendlier and more amiable expression than it did on weekdays. It was afterwards related that every Friday Rabbi Loew used to remove the tablet on which he had written the Ineffable Name from under the Golem's tongue, as he was afraid lest the Sabbath should make the Golem immortal and men might be induced to worship him as an idol. The Golem had no inclinations, either good or bad. Whatever action he performed he did under compulsion and out of fear lest he should be turned again into dust and reduced to naught once more. Whatever was situated within ten ells above the ground or under it he could reach easily and nothing would stop him in the execution of anything that he had undertaken.[3]

The idea that wise men can create a magical being is far older than Rabbi Loew's time. In the Babylonian Talmud it is mentioned that rabbis who lived in the fourth century used a book called *Sefer Yetzirah* to create life:

Rabbah said: If the righteous ones (Tzaddiqim) like to do so, they can create a world, for it is said: "For your sins separate [you from your

---

[3] Angelo S. Rappoport, *The Folklore of the Jews* (London: Soncino Press, 1937), 195–203. This text is a translation of an older German text of unknown authorship: *Die Schaffung des Golem*.

God]." Rabbah created a man and sent him to Rabbi Sera; when he saw the man and spoke to him and he gave no answer, he said: "Thou art [a creature] from the companions (another possible translation is: "from the magicians");[4] return to thy dust (loam)! Rav Chanina and Rav Oshaaya studied the *Sefer Yetzirah,* "Book of Formation" (or, in another version, *Hilchot Yetzirah* Rules of Formation) on the eve of every Shabbat (Friday evening), and created a small (literally, "third-grown") calf and ate it.[5]

The *Sefer Yetzirah* is one of the most ancient documents of Qabbalistic literature.[6] It is not certain when it was written, although it is considered to be most likely written in the third or fourth century CE.[7] The tradition has often held that the author was the patriarch Abraham himself, for he is mentioned in the book. Yet this was already doubted by some of the medieval Qabbalists.

The word *Yetzirah* (יצריה) comes from the root *yatzar* (יצר), which means to create or form something (in or with your mind). Usually the title *Sefer Yetzirah* is translated as *Book of Creation* or *Book of Formation*. I think, however, that maybe *Book of Creating Thought Forms* would describe its meaning much more clearly.

---

[4] Original, Chevraya (חבריא). Compare with the "Chavurah" (חבורה) mentioned in chapter 12, The Vision of the Merkavah.

[5] Babylonian Talmud, Sanhedrin 65b.

[6] The complete text of the *Sefer Yetzirah* can be found in appendix 1.

[7] Scientific opinions differ and range from the second century BCE to the sixth century CE. It is known that scientists date mystical or magical works rather late. Some parts of the book may show a Greek influence, and this is usually the reason for the dating. Greek influence was common between the third and sixth centuries, and many people believe it was written by a Jewish Neopythagorean, but the book is unique in many ways, and therefore, it does not seem to make sense to insist that what is common must apply to this book as well. Neither language nor the philosophical ideas expressed in the *Sefer Yetzirah* seem to make it necessary to date the main part of it any later than the second century BCE, if we keep in mind that some "comments" have been included in the text later. About 200 BCE, the holy Bible was translated into Greek language by seventy-two Jewish savants. (It was therefore called the Septuagint.) They may well have known the concepts of Greek philosophy. Furthermore, it must be mentioned that the book is very short and written in a way that is easy to memorize. Because it is well known that mystical texts have been handed down from teacher to student over long periods of time, the oldest parts of the book may possibly originate from a much earlier time. The Hebrew occult tradition has always been considered as fundamentally oral, especially in the early times.

The book describes the thirty-two mystical Paths of Wisdom, consisting of the ten Sefirot and the twenty-two foundation letters of the Hebrew alphabet. The foundation letters have been divided into three mother letters, seven doubles, and twelve simple ones. Each of the letters has many different ideas attached to it, including astrological signs, planets, and elements and parts of the body. It is very important to understand that both the Sefirot and the Letters have always been considered holy.

Some hold the opinion that Abraham was the first man ever to create a soul, and this might be the reason why he was considered to be the author of the *Sefer Yetzirah*. It is mentioned in the Bible that Abraham had made a soul (Nefesh): "And Abram took Sarai his wife, and Lot his brother's son, and all their possessions that they had gained, and the Nefesh (soul) they have made[8] in Haran (Charan); and they went forth to go into the land of Canaan; and into the land of Canaan they came" (Genesis 12:5).

The living being created by the use of the *Sefer Yetzirah* is called a Golem. The Hebrew word *Golem* is a *hapax legomenon*—that is, a word that appears only once in the Bible (Psalm 139:16). "For Thou hast procured me my innermost (literally, kidneys), Thou hast guarded me in my mother's womb. I will give thanks unto Thee, for I am fearfully and wonderfully made; wonderful are Thy works; and that my Nefesh (soul) knoweth right well. My frame (or self) was not hidden from Thee, when I was made in secret, and curiously wrought in the lowest parts of the earth. Thine eyes did see my Golem, and in Thy book they were all written, even the days that were formed, when as yet there was none of them" (Psalm 139:14–16).

Tradition says that this psalm was spoken by Adam himself. *Golem* here means "that which is not yet formed."[9] The root G L M (גלם) indicated something "not developed" or "not unfolded." In medieval philosophical literature the word *Golem* was used to describe the original formless matter, the *materia prima,* which was called *hyle* (ὑλη) by the Greek philosophers. In other words, we are speaking about matter of the astral plane.

Therefore, we have to understand that the term *Golem* describes astral, not physical matter. The famous Qabbalist Abraham Abulafia (1240–1296) scoffs at those who want to make calves with the *Sefer Yetzirah,*

---

[8] Often interpreted as "the souls that they had gotten."

[9] There is absolutely no reason to translate *Golem* as "embryo," as some did. This would be a complete misinterpretation of the text.

saying "Those who try to do so are calves themselves."[10] An anonymous Spanish Qabbalist wrote in the first quarter of the fourteenth century that using the *Sefer Yetzirah* does not create a manifestation on earth, but a "thought-form" (*Yetzirah machshavtit*).[11]

It is important to realize that a Golem is entirely an astral form. It therefore has a Nefesh (astral emotional soul), but not a Ruach (mental soul), for it does not exist on the mental level. According to the Qabbalist Isaac Saggi Nehor (about 1160–1235), called Isaac the Blind, this is the reason why Rabbah's Golem could not speak.[12] The Golem does not have any mental skills, but he does have emotions and feelings. He is an astral form animated by the emotional energy generated in the ritual.[13]

In modern times the concept of the Golem has changed in many ways. It was often a subject of literature, for example in Gustav Meyrink's famous novel *The Golem*. Even Mary Shelley's story *Frankenstein* was influenced by the legends of the Golem.

The Technique

The ritual of the creation of a Golem is based on an old description written by the great Rabbi Eleazar ha-Roqeach of Worms (1160–1237) as a part of his commentary on the *Sefer Yetzirah:*

> He, who uses the Sefer Yetzirah, has to purify himself; [and he has to] wear white clothes and he must not use it (i.e., the Sefer Yetzirah) alone, but they must be 2 or 3. As it is written: "And the *Nefesh* (soul) THEY have made in Haran" (Genesis 12:5). And it is written: "Two are better than one" (Ecclesiastes 4:9). And it is written: "It is not good that the man should be alone; I will make him a help meet for him" (Genesis 2:18).
>
> Therefore, BERESHIT BRA (In the beginning He created—Genesis 1:1) begins with *Bet* (or read "with two," because *Bet* can also stand for the number two).

---

10 See *Ner Elohim* (Munich Ms. 10, p. 172 b).

11 See *Sheelot ha-Zaqen* (Oxford Ms. 2396, p.53a).

12 Commentary on *Sefer Yetzirah*—Rom: Angelica libary, Ms. 46, fifteenth century; Oxford, Ms. 2456:12; Leiden, Ms. 24:16, published by Gershom Scholem in Ha-Qabbalah be-Provence 1963 (Jerusalem: Akadamon, 1979).

13 Moses Qordovero writes (1548) that the power animating the Golem is Chijuth, "Vitality," and belongs to the elemental forces (Pardes Rimonim 24:10).

And he must take virgin soil from a place in the mountains where no man has ever dug. And knead the soil with living water (i.e., moving water from a pure river or lake) and make a Golem. Begin to circulate the alphabet of 221 gates (others say 231 gates), each limb alone. Each limb (i.e., member) corresponding with the Letter that is its counterpart in the Sefer Yetzirah. And let it circulate beginning with Alef-Bet, and after that circulates the group Alef: Alef a Alef e Alef i Alef o Alef u and forever so on—a letter of the [Divine] Name with them: Alef a Yod and the entire alphabet, and after that Alef e Yod and after that Alef i Yod and after that Alef o Yod and after that Alef u Yod and after that Alef-Vav and after that Alef-Heh, completely.

And after that he shall crown (i.e., appoint) Bet and similarly Gimel and each limb (member) with the Letter that is its counterpart in it (i.e., in the Sefer Yetzirah). And all this shall be performed in purity.

The gates and permutations of the letters are relatively complicated. I will give an example of how they are composed. To intone the first gate, *Alef-Bet,* they must be arranged thus:

Begin with *Alef-Yod*
> *Alef* a *Yod, Alef* e *Yod, Alef* i *Yod, Alef* o *Yod, Alef* u *Yod*
> (speak: aY eY iY oY uY)

Then comes *Alef-Vav*
> *Alef* a *Vav, Alef* e *Vav, Alef* i *Vav, Alef* o *Vav, Alef* u *Vav*
> (speak: aV eV iV oV uV)

Then comes *Alef-Heh*
> *Alef* a *Heh, Alef* e *Heh, Alef* i *Heh, Alef* o *Heh, Alef* u Heh
> (speak: aH eH iH oH uH)

Then comes *Bet-Yod*
> *Bet* a *Yod, Bet* e *Yod, Bet* i *Yod, Bet* o *Yod, Bet* u *Yod*
> (speak: BaY BeY BiY BoY BuY)

Then comes *Bet-Vav*
> *Bet* a *Vav, Bet* e *Vav, Bet* i *Vav, Bet* o *Vav, Bet* u *Vav*
> (speak: BaV BeV BiV BoV BuV)

Then comes *Bet-Heh*
> *Bet* a *Heh, Bet* e *Heh, Bet* i *Heh, Bet* o *Heh, Bet* u *Heh*
> (speak: BaH BeH BiH BoH BuH)

After that comes the second gate (which is *Alef-Gimel* in the logical order, then *Alef-Dalet,* etc.) Yet there are several possibilities of arranging the 231 gates.[14] The first is the logical one used in this book in the description of the ritual at the end of this chapter. The second is the one that was used by the Chassidey Ashkenaz to create 221 gates (obviously, leaving out some of the possible combinations of the letters).

This is how the 221 gates are composed: Start by writing all the letters of the Hebrew alphabet in the first row. In the second row, leave out every second letter. After the *Alef* comes the *Gimel,* then *Heh,* and so forth. After the *Shin,* the *Tav* is left out, and again the *Alef* follows, because the letters are seen as a circle. "Twenty-two Foundation Letters: Set in a circle with 231 gates. And the circle turns forth and back" (*Sefer Yetzirah* 2:4).[15]

In the third row, two letters are left out; in the fourth row, three letters; and so forth. You will get a square of letters beginning with these rows:

א ב ג ד ה ו ז ח ט י כ ל מ נ ס ע פ צ ק ר ש ת

א ג ה ז ט כ מ ס פ ק ש א ג ה ז ט כ מ ס פ ק ש

These letters are combined in pairs:

אב גד הו זח טי כל מן סע פץ קר שת

אג הז טכ מס פק שא גה זט כם סף קש

Thus you get 231 pairs of letters—the 231 gates.

In this array, each row begins with the letter *Alef,* and this is why it is called *Alef* Array. There is one array for every letter.

If we look at the *Alef* Array in its entirety, we see that in the eleventh row, the *Alef-Lamed* row, ten letters are omitted, and therefore, *Alef* is followed by *Lamed,* which again is followed by *Alef,* and so forth. This is because the Hebrew alphabet has exactly twenty-two letters. Thus in the eleventh row, *Alef-Lamed* is repeated eleven times. For this reason the

---

[14] Some sources state that one arrangement of the letters creates a male golem and another arrangement creates a female one. This idea originates in chapter 3 of the *Sefer Yetzirah,* in which is mentioned a male and a female combination of each of the three "Mother-Letters."

[15] It is important to note that it initially goes forth, and then back.

Chassidey Ashkenaz considerd this row not as eleven gates, but only as one. Consequently, there are only 221 gates altogether.[16]

Using Eleazar of Worms' method, you will need at least 1.5 to 2 hours to go through the 221 gates, and the same again backward. If you want to use all the twenty-two arrays for the twenty-two letters—forward and backward—then the ritual will take a very long time to perform. To compensate for this, I have designed a simplified method, which has worked very well on numerous occasions.

According to some sources, every limb of the Golems body must be "enchanted" with the letter that corresponds to it in the *Sefer Yetzirah*. This interpretation is based on Eleazar ha-Roqeachs description: "Each limb (member) corresponding with the Letter that is its counterpart in the Sefer Yetzirah." Yet later in the same text we read about the permutation of the letters: "And after that he shall crown (i.e., appoint) Bet and similarly Gimel and each limb (member) with the Letter that is its counterpart in it (i.e., in the *Sefer Yetzirah*)."

The limbs or members (Hebrew: Ever אבר "limb," "member," "part," "organ") mentioned in the text seem to be the "parts" of the gate (each gate consisting of a combination of two letters), and not organs or limbs of the body. In every gate, each letter has a counterpart (another letter) that forms this gate together with the first letter.[17]

Power of the Letters

The idea that the Hebrew letters have creative power was known in ancient times: "Betzalel [the builder of the Temple] knew how to *tzeruf* (combine) the letters with which Heaven and earth were created" (Babylonian Talmud, Berachoth 55a).

---

[16] Abraham Abulafia's system of 231 gates is different again. His array begins with *Alef-Bet* in the first row, too. Next come the letters that are adjacent within the circle of letters—this means the letter before *Alef* will be combined with the one after, *Bet*. Before *Alef* is *Tav*, and after *Bet* comes *Gimel*. Thus the next gate is *Gimel-Tav*, then comes *Dalet-Shin*, and so forth. The next row begins with *Alef-Gimel*, then comes *Dalet-Tav*, then *Heh-Shin*, and so forth. As in the array of the Chassidey Ashkenaz, in Abraham Abulafia's system of 231 gates, there is one array for each letter.

[17] Nevertheless, you may wish to speak over each limb of the golem's body the array of the letter corresponding to this body part in the *Sefer Yetzirah*. This will certainly bring through a great deal of power. Be sure, however, that you can control this power, and note that you will have to be able to take back the power afterward.

According to many sources, the word *Emet,* "truth," must be written on the forehead of the Golem in order to give it life. If the *Alef* is wiped out,[18] the rest of the word is *met,* "he is dead," and the Golem becomes dust or loam. The reason may be a statement of Rabbi Chanina, whom we already know to be an expert on the *Sefer Yetzirah:* "The Seal of the Holy One, blessed be He, is *Emet* (אמת) 'Truth'" (Babylonian Talmud, Shabbat 55a).

The tradition says that the word *Emet* was written on the forehead of Adam when God created him from loam.[19] Thus when man creates a Golem, he copies the process used by God in the creation of man.

The old Qabbalists were eager to ensure that this ritual did not result in blasphemy, arrogance, or idolatry. The Golem therefore must be destroyed immediately after its creation, and we are to remember that the Golem cannot speak, because it has no Ruach (mental soul), thus the creation of a human is less than the creation of God. In the version of the ritual in this book, I have followed the ancient instruction, and the Golem will be destroyed immediately after its creation, as was accomplished by the medieval Qabbalists, for they never intended to create a magical servant. This was an idea in the novels that were written much later. The Qabbalists tried to understand the mystery of creation and the creative power within themselves. That is the concept on which this ritual is based. Every one of us has this Divine Creative Power within, and, as Rabbah said, we can create our world. We can create a good and happy life. To understand this is worth much more than a magical servant.[20]

To create a magical being from pure thought is a very ancient occult

---

[18] *Alef* is the letter of Keter and of the Divine Power. Many words for God or the Divine, such as El, Eloah, Elohim, Ehiyeh, Adonai, and Eyn Sof, begin with *Alef.* Without the Divine, there can be no life.

[19] See the writings of the students of Yehudah ha-Chasid. (*Sefer HaGematria,* quoted by Abraham Epstein in *Beiträge zur jüdischen Altertumskunde* [Vienna: 1887] 122–23).

[20] Particularly women (especially mothers) find it sometimes difficult to accept that the Golem must be destroyed again. The maternal instinct is one of the strongest instincts. The extra female energy gives a great deal of extra creative power to the ritual, but it must be controlled. It is therefore very important that every participant is completely aware of what is necessary in the ritual.

technique and can be dangerous if we are not careful.[21] The story of Rabbi Elijah Baal-Shem of Chelm (d. 1583) is a warning to all those who are careless in creating a Golem. Elijah Baal-Shem made himself a Golem to do his housework. The Golem grew bigger and bigger, and eventually it was so tall that the rabbi was afraid and wanted to destroy it, but he could not reach to its forehead to remove the *Alef*. The rabbi asked the Golem to take off his boots, and as the Golem bent down, the rabbi erased the *Alef*. The Golem instantly turned to loam and fell into pieces. All the pieces, however, fell on the rabbi, burying him and thus causing his death.

This story is by no means just a fairy tale. The Golem is an artificial elemental being, and over time it will grow in power. If it gains a certain amount of self-consciousness, it will try to stay alive, and if it needs more power, it will suck energy like a vampire from the people to whom it is connected. It will become a real danger to the magician and his family (or if it is let loose, in order to survive, it will absorb energy from every person it meets—usually the weaker ones first). Unlike other methods of creating artificial elementals, the Golem ritual tends to give the Golem a certain amount of self-consciousness almost instantly. This makes the ritual particularly difficult and dangerous.

The Ritual

The ritual is written for three officers,[22] but it can also be done with two officers if the second officer also takes the lines of the third officer. (This is in accordance with the ancient descriptions that insist it should be performed with two or three people. I suggest the magus should be a man

---

21 This technique is also known in Tibet, where an entity created from pure thought is called a *Tulpa*. Alexandra David-Neel, who studied the occult techniques of Tibet, learned the secret of how to create a Tulpa. By the power of her mind, she created a friendly little fat monk, somewhat similar to Friar Tuck. Over time, the creature became more and more real. After a while it acquired a will of its own, and she lost control over the Tulpa—it appeared to her against her will. Even worse, it changed its character and shape, becoming gaunt and less friendly. When other people started to sense the Tulpa and asked about the "stranger," David-Neel realized that she had to reabsorb the creature into her own mind, which was not easy, because the Tulpa, now having a will of its own, was unwilling to be destroyed. Eventually, she managed to destroy it, but the process of doing so took several weeks and was extremely exhausting.

22 I have used the term *officer* as used in modern magic, to describe everyone who holds an office in a magical ritual.

and, if the second officer is a woman, the power of polarity will add to the ritual.)[23]

In the beginning of the *Sefer Yetzirah,* the Names of God are invoked, and I have used this invocation in the ritual. The order of Names describes the emanation from the first Sefirah Keter to the lowest Sefirah Malchut as in the process of creation, and the way back upward as in the process of evolution. This can be seen as an analogy to the creation and retraction of the Golem.

Name of God	Hebrew	Emanation from	Translation
Yah	יה	Sefirot 1–2	(two-letter Name of God)
Yod Heh Vav Heh	יהוה	Sefirot 3–6	(four-letter Name of God)
Tzevaot	צבאות	Sefirah 7	(of Hosts)
Elohey Yisrael	אלהי ישראל	Sefirah 8	(God of Israel)
Elohim Chayim	אלהים חיים	Sefirah 9	(God of Life)
u-Melech Olam	מלך עולם	Sefirah 10	(King of the Universe)
El Shaddai	אל שדי	Sefirah 9	(God Almighty)
Rachum ve-Chanun	רחום וחנון	Sefirot 8–7	(Compassionate and Gracious)
Ram ve-nissa	רם ונשא	Sefirot 6–5	(High and Exalted)
Shochen Ad	שוכן עד	Sefirot 4–3	(Dwelling Eternally)
Marom ve-Qadosh Shemo	מרום וקדוש שמו	Sefirot 2–1	(Lofty and Holy is His Name)

The opening and closing of the ritual are to be found in the *Sefer Yetzirah* itself. Many passages can be translated as descriptions of God's creation (for example, "He sealed the above . . .") or as an instruction ("Seal

---

[23] It is possible to perform this ritual with more people, and there are some later sources that indicate this was done. Because the main part of the ritual consists of chanting and the pathworking in the middle of the ritual, it is very easy to include more participants.

the above. . . !"). The author says that we should seal the directions with the letters of the Divine Name. There are many variations of these combinations. I have used those from the "short version," which may be the oldest (each of the seals is said to belong to one of the lower six Sefirot).

5   seal above looking upward with YHV (יהו)
6   seal below looking downward with YVH (יוה)
7   seal east looking forward with HYV (היו)
8   seal west looking back with HVY (הוי)
9   seal south looking to the right with VYH (ויה)
10   seal north looking to the left with VHY (והי)

The main part of the ritual consists of chanting in a circle and a pathworking. The chanting must be done with a great deal of emotion to arouse an ecstatic feeling and an influx of creative inspiration called Shefa ha-Chochmah. You may fall into a light trance and be filled with the joy of creation.

Note that most of this ritual happens on the inner level. To get the maximum spiritual experience from this ritual, you must open your heart and your psychic senses to what is happening on the astral level.

Much has been written about the Golem and many ancient authors have presented instructions on its creation, but not all of them were writing from personal experience. In *Sefer Emeq ha-Melech* (Book of the Valley of the King; written by Naphtali ben Jacob Bacharach of Frankfurt and published in Amsterdam in 1648) the author explicitly mentions that his description of the Golem ritual is incomplete. This is not surprising, for the book is basically about Lurianic Qabbalah, and given that Luria was not a great believer in magic, it is unlikely that the author ever had any practical experience himself. Thus he neither felt competent enough to declare his description to be complete, nor did he have a inclination to encourage his readers to create a Golem. Unlike *Sefer Emeq ha-Melech,* the method given here is both complete and tested.[24] It does work, and will be very powerful and effective[25] if applied correctly by competent Qabbalists. I therefore urge my readers to take it seriously, and not to use it in a frivolous way.

---

[24] A shorter version of this chapter was first published in *Magical Use of Thought Forms* by Dolores Ashcroft-Nowicki and J. H. Brennan (Woodbury, Minn.: Llewellyn, 2001).

[25] Some other methods used to create a Golem could not be included here, but the technique described here is complete and effective and works without any further additions.

Preparation

The ritual can be performed outside or inside. (In one text describing the creation of a Golem, the magician is actually instructed to perform the ritual in his "Temple.")[26] Everyone should wear white robes. On the altar some holy water will be needed to purify those present. Prepare a figure of the Golem made of loam or clay as written in the instructions given by Eleazar of Worms: "And he must take virgin soil from a place in the mountains, where no man has ever dug. And knead the soil with living water (water from a pure river or lake) and make a Golem."

The Opening

The magus looks upward, draws the invoking or opening hexagram in the air, points at the middle and says:

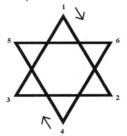

> **By the seal of the six-pointed star and in the Name of**
> **YOD HEH VAV**
> **I open the above.**

Then the magus looks downward, draws the invoking hexagram in the air, then points at the middle and says:

> **By the seal of the six-pointed star and in the Name of**
> **YOD VAV HEH**
> **I open the below.**

Then the magus goes to the east, draws the invoking hexagram in the air, then points at the middle and says:

> **By the seal of the six-pointed star and in the Name of**
> **HEH YOD VAV**
> **I open the east.**

---

[26] Hebrew, Miqdash. Ms. Cambridge, Add 647, fol. 18a, Ms Bologna University Lib. 2914, fol. 178b-80b; Ms Oxford, 1638, fol. 59a, see "Golem," Moshe Idel (60*ff*).

Then the magus goes to the west, draws the invoking hexagram in the air, then points at the middle and says:

> **By the seal of the six-pointed star and in the Name of**
> **HEH VAV YOD**
> **I open the west.**

Then the magus goes to the south, draws the invoking hexagram in the air, then points at the middle and says:

> **By the seal of the six-pointed star and in the Name of**
> **VAV YOD HEH**
> **I open the south.**

Then the magus goes to the north, draws the invoking hexagram in the air, then points at the middle and says:

> **By the seal of the six-pointed star and in the Name of**
> **VAV HEH YOD**
> **I open the north.**

The order of the openings is to be found in the *Sefer Yetzirah* itself. The hexagram is used because the entire opening is sixfold, and there are six permutations of the Divine Name consisting of three letters each.

Invoking the Archangels[27]

The second officer looks upward and says:

> **I invoke thee and I give thee welcome,**
> **METATRON,**
> **teacher of the mysteries.**
> **Thou art called the Prince of the Countenance,**
> **the highest and closest to God.**
> **Let us understand and experience the mystery of creation.**

---

[27] As mentioned previously, the attributes of the archangels have changed throughout the ages. For example, Michael and Gavriel (who is often called Gabriel by those who do not speak Hebrew) have changed the element over which they reign. The same is true for the directions to which some of the archangels belonged. I have chosen to use the arrangement with which most Qabbalistic students today will be familiar, because I consider the Qabbalah to be a living tradition, rather than being inflexible and dead.

Then he looks downward and says:

> I invoke thee and I give thee welcome,
> SANDALFON,
> keeper of the secret knowledge.
> Thou art the servant of the Shechinah.
> Let us become aware of
> the Divinity within.

Then he goes to the east and says:

> I invoke thee and I give thee welcome,
> RAPHAEL.
> Thou art the master of the element of air.
> Make our words powerful.
> Give the breath of life to our work,
> for all life needs air to breathe.

Then he goes to the west and says:

> I invoke thee and I give thee welcome,
> GAVRIEL,
> for thou art the master of the element of water.
> Give the waters of life to our work,
> Water is the element of life,
> and for all life on this planet came out of the sea.

Then he goes to the south and says:

> I invoke thee and I give thee welcome,
> MICHAEL,
> Thou art the master of the element of fire.
> Give the power of life to our work,
> for all life needs warmth and energy to exist.

Then he goes to the north and says:

> I invoke thee and I give thee welcome.
> URIEL.
> Thou art the master of the element of earth.
> Give the power of form to our work,
> because without form there is no manifestation.

The magus goes to the altar, stretches out his arms, and says:

> **YAH**
> **YOD HEH VAV HEH**
> **TZEVAOT (of Hosts)**
> **ELOHEY YISRAEL (God of Israel)**
> **ELOHIM CHAYIM (God of Life)**
> **U-MELECH OLAM (King of the Universe)**
> **EL SHADDAI (God Almighty)**
> **RACHUM VE-CHANUN (Compassionate and Gracious)**
> **RAM VE-NISSA (High and Exalted)**
> **SHOCHEN AD (Dwelling Eternally)**
> **MAROM VE-QADOSH SHEMO (Lofty and Holy is His Name)**
> **May this holy place be filled with His Divine Presence.**
> **Bless us, and inspire us,**
> **so that our work will be successful.**

All perform the Qabbalistic cross:[28]

> **ATAH**
> **MALCHUT**
> **VE-GEVURAH**
> **VE-GEDULAH**
> **LE-OLAM**
> **AMEN**

The magus says:

> **In the Name and under the protection of**
> **the Creator of the Universe**
> **[If inside]: I declare this temple of the mysteries open.**
> **[If outside]: I declare this sacred space open.**
> **The intention of the ritual is**
> **to create a living creature from inanimate substance,**
> **in order to understand the mystery of creation**
> **and the creative power within us.**

---

[28] Touch the forehead and say ATAH (Thine is), touch the solar plexus and say MAL-CHUT (the Kingdom), touch the right shoulder and say VE-GEVURAH (and the Power), touch the right shoulder and say VE-GEDULAH (and the Glory/Greatness), put both your hands to the solar plexus and say LE-OLAM (forever) AMEN. (Compare to 1 Chronicles 25:11.)

The Creation of the Golem

The text upon which this ritual is based begins with a discussion of the question of why we may not perform this ritual alone.[29]

The "script" is as follows:

MAGUS: Bereshit bra Elohim et ha-shamaim ve-et ha-aretz. (Genesis 1:1)

SECOND OFFICER: In the beginning Elohim made the Heaven and the earth.

THIRD OFFICER: Why does "Bereshit" begin with the letter *Bet?*

MAGUS: Because the number of the letter *Bet* is two.

SECOND OFFICER: This is the law of polarity.

THIRD OFFICER: And because of this, it is written: Two are better than one. (Ecclesiastes 4:9)

MAGUS: Vayomer Elohim na'asseh adam betzalmenu kid'muteynu. (Genesis 1:26)

SECOND OFFICER: And Elohim said: Let US make man, in our image like us.

THIRD OFFICER: Who are those who speak?

MAGUS: They are God . . .

SECOND OFFICER: . . . and the Shechinah.

THIRD OFFICER: The work of creation cannot be done alone.

MAGUS: Companions, will ye assist me in the work that lies before us?

SECOND OFFICER: I will.

THIRD OFFICER: I will.

MAGUS: It was said that the righteous ones could create a world if they wished. And it is written: Qedoshim tihyu ki qadosh Ani YHVH [say: Adonai] Eloheychem. (Leviticus 19:2)

SECOND OFFICER: You shall be holy, for I, Adonai thy God, am holy.

THIRD OFFICER: But how can we be as holy as God?

MAGUS: We can be holy, because we were made in His image, like Him.

SECOND OFFICER: We are the children of the Creator and the Creator is within us.[30]

---

[29] Even though I do not believe that this was a part of the actual ritual, I have included it in order to make everybody understand and remember the law of polarity, the Divinity within, and the power of words.

[30] "YHVH, your God is within you" (Deuteronomy 7:21).

THIRD OFFICER: **How did Elohim create life?**

MAGUS: **Elohim created life by the power of words. As it is written: Vayomer Elohim thotzé ha-aretz nefesh chayah leminah, behemah, varèmess, vechayto-aretz lemineh, vayehi-chen.** (Genesis 1:24)

SECOND OFFICER: **And Elohim said: The earth bring forth living souls (Nefesh Chayah) in their way, gregarious animals, and reptiles, and wild animals in their way—and so it was.**

THIRD OFFICER: **Let us begin.**

MAGUS: **First we must purify ourselves.**

SECOND OFFICER: **Ten Sefirot Belimah,**[31] **the number of ten fingers, five opposite five with a single covenant precisely in the middle, like the word of the tongue and the word of the genitals.**

THIRD OFFICER: **Ten Sefirot Belimah, understand with wisdom, and be wise, with understanding. Test with them, and quest with them, and make the thing stand in its purity.**

SECOND OFFICER *[goes to everyone and purifies each person's hands and forehead with holy water, saying to each]:* **Ten Sefirot Belimah Five opposite five** *[touching the hands],* **with a single covenant precisely in the middle** *[touching the forehead].* **Thou art purified.**

MAGUS *[after everyone is purified, says]:* **Companions, now see with your inner vision the body of the Golem lying in front of you. See and feel the gray color and the hardness of the body made of cold loam. Look at the shape and expression of his face. Notice the position of his arms and legs. Look at his gray chest. Notice every detail of his body. Build up the astral form of his body with the power of your mind.**

MAGUS *[allows some time to build up a thought-form, then says]:* **Twenty-two foundation letters—three mothers,**

SECOND OFFICER: **seven doubles,**

THIRD OFFICER: **and twelve simple ones.**

MAGUS: **Command them, engrave them, combine them, weigh them, and permute them! And form with them the Nefesh of all that has been formed and the Nefesh of all that shall be formed!**

---

[31] The word Belimah (literally, "without anything") describes the ten Sefirot as the divine and unmanifest essence.

SECOND OFFICER: **They are set in a circle as 231 gates. And the circle turns forth and back.**

THIRD OFFICER: **How?**

MAGUS: **Combine them, weigh them, and permute them!**

SECOND OFFICER: ***Alef*** **with each one, and each one with** ***Alef,***

THIRD OFFICER: ***Bet*** **with each one, and each one with** ***Bet.***

MAGUS: **Form substance from the unmanifest, and make be that which is not!**

SECOND OFFICER: **Visualize and permute, and make all that has been formed and all that has been spoken—**

THIRD OFFICER: **—with the one Name![32]**

The following text is taken from chapter 2 in *Sefer Yetzirah:*

All stand in a circle around the Golem. If possible, everyone holds his neighbors' hands. Then all chant the letters of the Divine Name combined with the alphabet. The 231 gates are combinations of two letters: *Alef-Bet, Alef-Gimel, Alef-Dalet, . . . Alef-Tav, Bet-Gimel, Bet-Dalet, . . . Shin-Tav.*

אב אג אד אה או אז אח אט אי אך אל אם אן אס אע אף אץ אק אר אש את
בג בד בה בו בז בח בט בי בך בל בם בן בס בע בף בץ בק בר בש בת
גד גה גו גז גח גט גי גך גל גם גן גס גע גף גץ גק גר גש גת
דה דו דז דח דט די דך דל דם דן דס דע דף דך דץ דק דר דש דת
הו הז הח הט הי הך הל הם הן הס הע הף הץ הק הר הש הת
וז וח וט וי וך ול ום ון וס וע וף וץ וק ור וש ות
זח זט זי זך זל זם זן זס זע זף זץ זק זר זש זת
חט חי חך חל חם חן חס חע חף חץ חק חר חש חת
טי טך טל טם טן טס טע טף טץ טק טר טש טת
יך יל ים ין יס יע יף יץ יק יר יש ית
כל כם כן כס כע כף כץ כק כר כש כת
לם לן לס לע לף לץ לק לר לש לת
מן מס מע מף מץ מק מר מש מת
נס נע נף נץ נק נר נש נת
סע סף סץ סק סר סש סת
עף עץ עק ער עש עת
פץ פק פר פש פת
צק צר צש צת
קר קש קת
רש רת
שת

---

32 The one Name is the Divine Name.

These 231 gates are combined with the letters of the Divine Name. I have simplified the original method by identifying with a vowel each of the letters of the Divine Name. *Yod Heh Vav* is one of the forms in which the Divine Name can be written. Each of the letters can replace a vowel in Hebrew. The Greek transliteration (IAΩ) identifies the letters with the three vowels I A O.[33] Thus by combining the letters of each gate with these three vowels, they are combined at the same time with the Name of God. In the simplest form possible, every gate will be spoken *-i -i; -a -a; -o -o.* Please note that *Alef* and *Ayin* have no sound of their own. Among the seven double-letters, *Bet, Kaf,* and *Peh* have a hard and a soft sound. They are spoken hard as the first syllable (B, K, P), and soft as the second syllable (V, Ch, F). Therefore, the first gate (*Alef-Bet*) is chanted: i-Vi, a-Va, o-Vo. The second gate (*Alef-Gimel*) is chanted: i-Gi, a-Ga, o-Go. The twenty-second gate (*Bet-Gimel*) is chanted: Bi-Gi, Ba-Ga, Bo-Go.

Chanting all 231 gates will take about ten to fifteen minutes at the most. Using this method, we follow the basic instructions of the original text. Yet in some descriptions the permutations include all possible combinations of five vowels—that means twenty-five instead of three combinations for each gate—and even for experts in the language, this would take more than one hour, maybe two—and there are methods that are even more complicated. They require that this is done four times in combination with each of the four letters of the Tetragrammaton. Because the whole thing must also be done backward (as described later), this ritual would have taken many hours.

Yet some sources say that it is unlikely that it has been practiced in this way. Experience proves that two times ten to fifteen minutes is a good choice and builds up all the creative power needed in this ritual. I am aware that the chanting is not really easy to do at the beginning, but it is an important part of the ritual and cannot be left out or reduced any further. Moreover, because the original ritual was considered to be practiced only by master Qabbalists, everyone taking part in this ritual must know the Hebrew alphabet, must have practiced the chanting before, and must have

---

[33] The ancient Jewish historian Josephus (ca. 37–100 CE) described the Divine Name as consisting of "Vowels." He wrote: "A mitre also of fine linen encompassed his head, which was tied by a blue ribbon, about which there was another golden crown, in which was engraven the sacred Name [of God]: it consists of four vowels" (Book V, *The Jewish War*). The vowels include what modern terminology calls "semivowels."

taken some time to meditate on the meaning of the letters. (It may also be helpful to draw the twenty-two letters around a circle and connect every letter with every other letter. If you do this in the order of the chanting, you will have a much better understanding of the meaning of the 231 gates. Each of the possible connections is one gate.)

During the chanting a dancelike step is used, so that after each gate, everyone moves one step in a clockwise direction. Tradition says that the whole chanting must be started again if a mistake occurs. I think that it is satisfactory if at least one person does the chanting correctly—which means that, because it is unlikely that everybody will be wrong at the same time, such a problem, it is hoped, can be avoided. If it should happen, however, I suggest simply repeating the gate that went wrong.

During the chanting of each gate, everybody visualizes a ray of light for each gate that fills the astral form of the Golem with the creative power of the letters of this gate. It is very important to feel how the Golem is filled with this power, gate by gate.

After the last gate (*Shin-Tav*), the magus goes to the Golem.[34] Then he writes (with a magical dagger) on the Golem's forehead (or with a pen/stylus on paper on the Golems forehead) the word *Emet*, "truth." [35] Then he says:

> **I write on thy forehead**
> **The word EMET**

---

[34] If the ritual is performed outside, you may choose to bury the Golem before the ritual starts. In this case, the Golem is taken from the earth (representing the womb of Mother Earth) at this point of the ritual.

[35] One text mentions that the words on the forehead of the Golem should be YHVH ELOHIM EMET. This, however, does not seem to be advisable, because the text in question does not teach how to create a Golem. Rather, it admonishes that doing so may lead to blasphemy, for if the *Alef* is wiped out, the remaining text says "God is dead." (The explanation given is, that if man can create life, he will no longer honor God.) Other instructions say that we are to use a paper or plate (i.e., a talisman) with the Shem ha-Meforash, which should be placed in the mouth of the Golem to animate it. This technique relates to the Opening of the Mouth ritual practiced in ancient Babylonia and Egypt. I have nevertheless chosen to use the word *Emet*, because using it makes it is easier to take back the life energy given to the Golem, and unless this is done fully, the magician is in real trouble. Furthermore, in order to use the Shem ha-Meforash with its full power, it must be received in the correct way, and because this can be done only personally, it is best to use the method described here in this book. For more information about the transmission of the Shem ha-Meforash, see chapter 19, Revelation of the Secret Name.

the seal of the Holy One, blessed be He,
the Creator of the Universe.

אמת [36]

Vayitzer YHVH [say: Adonai] Elohim et ha-Adam, afar min
ha-adamah,
va-yifach be-apav Nishmat Chayim vayehi ha-Adam Nefesh Chayah.
(Genesis 2:7)

**And Adonai Elohim formed man (Adam) of the loam (dust) of the
ground, and breathed into his nostrils the breath of life; and man
became a living soul (Nefesh Chayah).**

The magus breathes into the Golem's nostrils, feeling the power of life
moving deep into the Golem's body. Then he says:

**By the power of the Creator within all of us
I give life to thee.
May the power of life fill thy body,
May thou live among us for a short while,
to the everlasting Glory
of the one Creator.**

All go to their seats.

MAGUS: Companions, close your eyes now, and see with your inner
vision. See the Golem lying in front of you. See and feel the gray
color and the hardness of the body made of cold loam. Look at
the shape and the expression of his face, still emotionless and stiff.
Notice the position of his arms and legs. Look at his gray chest.
Notice every detail of his body. . . . And now feel the energy of life
that you have given to this cold body radiating warmth from deep
within it. The warmth fills his body more and more. The hard surface slowly becomes softer, and the gray color—shade by shade—
turns into the color of human skin. Out of his hands and feet grow
short fingernails and toenails, and his hair starts to grow to some
inches of length. Feel and see the power of life flowing through his

---

[36] If you prefer to use the old Hebrew letters, it will look like this:

body. Almost imperceptibly you hear a small but regular sound. It sounds like a beat. It becomes a bit louder, and you realize it is a heartbeat. You listen to the rhythm of his heartbeat, and while you look at his chest, you see how it seems to move. You notice the sound of wind or air from his nose, and you are witness to the very first breath of his life. His chest moves up and down while he continues to breathe. His fingers move slowly as if they have been stunned and are not yet used to moving. His arms and legs move a bit as if he is just in the process of awakening. Slowly, he opens his eyes. Then he lifts his upper body and he stands up. He is alive. . . . You have given life to this creature. You are his creators, his parents and his masters. He turns around and looks into the eyes of everybody. He cannot speak, because he does not have a Ruach (mental soul). But he does have a Nefesh (emotional soul), and he does have emotions. In his eyes you can see the feeling of deep thankfulness, for you have given him the chance to experience the wonderful gift of life for a short while—for even a small moment of life is an experience that will not be forgotten. He smiles as he looks into your eyes. And you feel that your heart is filled with the joy of life itself. No words can describe the feelings shared between you and him, a feeling almost like parenthood of a different kind. *[There is a small pause]* When he has completed facing everybody, he comes back to the center. And then he listens as I speak to him:

Creature made of earth,
formed by the power of the mind
thou hast been given life by the creative power of the Holy Name
and the twenty-two Holy Letters.
We bless thee.

It is written: For everything there is a time and there is a right moment and for each thing under the heaven. A time to be born and a time to die. (Ecclesiastes 3:1–2)
Thy time among us is over, and thou must leave now.
Thou will take with thee the memory of the soul thou once had.
And it will be absorbed into thy own world for the benefit of thy kind of existence.
Lay down, back in thy place!

Companions, the Golem is lying in his place.
Let us say goodbye and farewell.

We know that what has been done could be done again!
The Creator is always within us.

Creature made of earth,
I erase on thy forehead
the letter *Alef,* the letter with which the alphabet begins.
And where the word *Emet* was written,
now only *met*—"he is dead"—remains.
In the Name of the Creator within all of us
I take back the life that was given to thee.
May the power of life go back from where it came.
From earth thou were made, and to the earth thou will return,
but thou will keep with thee the memory of what thou once were.

The magus erases the *Alef.*

MAGUS: You watch the Golem close his eyes. His arms and legs become stiff, and the breathing movement of his chest is irregular, stopping completely after a while. The heartbeat sounds softer and softer, and it fades away, until it you cannot hear it anymore. The expression of his face becomes stiff again. His hair, his fingernails, and his toenails become gray. The color of his skin—shade by shade—turns back to gray. The surface of his body changes to the hard and lifeless structure of dry loam. His body becomes cold again. Feel and see how the power of life withdraws into the center of the body of the Golem. The body of the Golem lies in front of you, without any emotion or any sign of life. When you open your eyes you still see the thought-form of the Golem's body in front of you.

Now the circle must turn backward again. Take back what you have given, and absorb into yourself the power of life, which is now filled with the experience of the mystery of creation.

All stand in a circle around the Golem. If possible, everyone holds his neighbors' hands. Then all chant the letters of the Divine Name combined with the alphabet. This time, the 231 gates are spoken backward. Also, the order of the vowels is reversed: They will be spoken -o -o; -a -a; -i -i. So the group starts with gate *Tav-Shin*, which is chanted: To-SHo,

Ta-SHa, Ti-SHi. Then comes *Tav-Resh,* then *Shin-Resh* . . . and the last one is *Bet-Alef.*

תש

תר שר

תק שק רק

תץ שץ רץ קץ

תף שף רף קף צף

תע שע רע קע צע פע

תס שס רס קס צס פס עס

תן שן רן קן צן פן ען סן

תם שם רם קם צם פם עם סם נם

תל של רל קל צל פל על סל נל מל

תך שך רך קך צך פך ער סך נך מך לך

תי שי רי קי צי פי עי סי ני מי לי כי

תט שט רט קט צט פט עט סט נט מט לט כט יט

תח שח רח קח צח פח עח סח נח מח לח כח יח טח

תז שז רז קז צז פז עז סז נז מז לז כז יז טז חז

תו שו רו קו צו עו סו נו מו לו כו יו טו חו זו

תה שה רה קה צה עה סה נה מה לה כה יה טה חה זה וה

תד שד רד קד צד פד עד סד נד מד לד כד יד טד חד זד וד הד

תג שג רג קג צג פג עג סג נג מג לג כג יג טג חג זג וג הג דג

תב שב רב קב צב פב עב סב נב מב לב כב יב טב חב זב וב הב דב גב

תא שא רא קא צא פא עא סא נא מא לא כא יא טא חא זא וא הא דא גא בא

The double letters *Bet, Kaf,* and *Peh* are spoken hard as the first syllable (B, K, P) and soft as the second syllable (V, Ch, F), as before. Again, the dancelike step is used, but this time in a counterclockwise direction. During the chanting of each gate, everybody visualizes a ray of light for each gate now taking back from the astral form of the Golem what he had given to it. Yet the power of life received again brings with it the experience of the mystery of creation, and therefore, everyone gets back more than he gave. It is again very important to feel how the power comes back, gate by gate.

There is a short pause. Then the magus says:

The work has been done.
Now let us give thanks to our friends the archangels.

Thanking and Sending Back
the Archangels

The second officer looks upward and says:

> We thank thee and we bless thee,
> METATRON.
> Go back to thy place at the side of God.

Then he looks downward and says:

> We thank thee and we bless thee,
> SANDALFON.
> Go back to thy place in the secret Temple of the Shechinah.

Then he goes to the east and says:

> We thank thee and we bless thee,
> RAPHAEL.
> Go back to thy place in Heaven.

Then he goes to the west and says:

> We thank thee and we bless thee,
> GAVRIEL.
> Go back to thy place in the waters of the upper world.

Then he goes to the south and says:

> We thank thee and we bless thee,
> MICHAEL.
> Go back to thy place at the gate of Paradise.

Then he goes to the north and says:

> We thank thee and we bless thee,
> URIEL.
> Go back to thy place in the garden of the Lord.

The Closing

The magus looks upward, draws the closing hexagram in the air, points at the middle, and says:

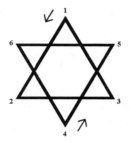

> **By the seal of the six-pointed star and in the Name of**
> **YOD HEH VAV**
> **I close the above.**

Then the magus looks downward, draws the closing hexagram in the air, points at the middle, and says:

> **By the seal of the six-pointed star and in the Name of**
> **YOD VAV HEH**
> **I close the below.**

Then the magus goes to the east, draws the closing hexagram in the air, points at the middle, and says:

> **By the seal of the six-pointed star and in the Name of**
> **HEH YOD VAV**
> **I close the east.**

Then the magus goes to the west, draws the closing hexagram in the air, points at the middle, and says:

> **By the seal of the six-pointed star and in the Name of**
> **HEH VAV YOD**
> **I close the west.**

Then the magus goes to the south, draws the closing hexagram in the air, points at the middle, and says:

> **By the seal of the six-pointed star and in the Name of**
> **VAV YOD HEH**
> **I close the south.**

Then the magus goes to the north, draws the closing hexagram in the air, points at the middle, and says:

> **By the seal of the six-pointed star and in the Name of**
> **VAV HEH YOD**
> **I close the north.**

The magus returns to his position, faces the altar, and says:

> **In the Name of the Creator of the Universe**
> [If inside]: **I declare this temple of the mysteries closed**
> **and the ritual ended.**
> [If outside]: **I declare this sacred space closed and the ritual ended.**

Shabbat

The Most Holy Day

The most holy day in the Jewish tradition is not Yom Kippur (Day of Atonement), as is often believed, but Shabbat.[1] The importance of Shabbat can hardly be overestimated. It begins on Friday evening—just when every day in the Semitic calendar begins—because night comes before day, just as there was darkness (the unmanifest) before there was light (the first manifestation): "The earth was unformed and void, and darkness was upon the face of the deep; and the spirit of Elohim hovered over the face of the waters. And Elohim said: 'Let there be light.' And there was light. And Elohim saw the light, that it was good; and Elohim divided the light from the darkness. And Elohim called the light Day, and the darkness He called Night. And there was evening and there was morning, one day" (Genesis 1:2–5).

Shabbat means "day of rest" and "end of the week," and it is a sacred time set aside for a spiritual purpose. It is the first holy day mentioned in the Torah, and it was God who observed it first: "And Elohim saw every thing that He had made, and, behold, it was very good. And there was

---

[1] Sometimes written as Sabbath. It is called Shabbos by Ashkenazic Jews.

evening and there was morning, a sixth day. The Heavens and the earth were finished, the whole host of them. And on the seventh day Elohim finished His work which He had made. And He rested on the seventh day from all His work which He had made. And Elohim blessed the seventh day, and sanctified it, because in it He had rested from all His work which Elohim has created and done" (Genesis 1:31–2:5).

Just as God ceased His creative work, so man rests from the work of the week. God told us to remember (*zachor*) and to observe (*shamor*) the Shabbat. This hints to the positive and negative commandments concerning Shabbat. The positive commandments help us to make Shabbat a time of joy and spirituality, while the negative commandments help us to avoid everything that could hinder our experience of the delight of Shabbat. In ancient times people used to work seven days a week. To have one day off was a great achievement, making life worth living.

Zachor: The Positive Commandments

Shabbat is a time of peace, joy, and harmony, and a time to spend with your family and meet friends. It is a time to remember the six days of the Creation of the universe, and to study the Torah and traditional literature such as the Midrashim (Jewish Legends) and, of course, mystical writings such as the Zohar.

On Shabbat everyone is more aware of their own spiritual heritage. In this context it should be mentioned that the Qabbalists speak of the additional soul (*Neshamah Yetera*) that is said to be with those who keep the Shabbat. This additional soul is the group mind of the Jewish tradition.

> Then a spirit of the soul is added to Israel, to each and every one. With this additional soul (Neshamah Yetera) all sorrow and anger are forgotten, and there is only joy, above and below. This spirit that comes down as an addition to the children of this world, when it comes down washes itself with perfumes of the Garden of Eden (i.e., it is contacted by the Shechinah), and descends to rest upon the holy people. Happy are they when contact with this spirit is made. [. . .] The most mysterious mystery is known to those who are initiated in the [teachings of] wisdom. Happy are they when contact with this spirit is made. This spirit is the expansion of the point. It comes from it and expands throughout the universe. And this spirit is the mystery of Shabbat that dwells below. [. . .] The mystery of this matter is that in each person there is a soul, which draws to itself and receives

a spirit on Shabbat Eve. And that spirit dwells and rests in the soul throughout the Shabbat day. Then the soul is in a state of more greatness and more benefited than it used to be.[2]

According to the sages, Shabbat is a time when the Shechinah (the divine Presence) descends to the house of those who keep the Shabbat. It is believed that the Shechinah participates in the pleasures of those to whom She descends.

Rabbi Yehudah said: Every day, the world is blessed from that supernal day, for all the six days are blessed through the seventh day. And every day gives the blessing that it receives on its own day. [. . .] But the sixth day finds more [blessings], and as Rabbi Eleazar said: [. . .] On the sixth day the Matron (the Shechinah) is with it, to prepare the table for the King (the Holy One, blessed be He). Hence, it has two portions, one for the day itself and one for preparing the joy of the King with the Matron. That night is the joy of the Matron with the King and their uniting, and [from this union] all the six days are blessed, each one individually. For that reason one must prepare one's table for the night of Shabbat so that blessings from above will be reserved to be given to each one, for there is no blessing on an empty table. Hence, scholars of wisdom who know this secret mate on Shabbat nights.[3]

It is traditional to prepare three meals for Shabbat. The first meal is served at the end of Qabblat Shabbat. The second meal is served after the morning service or at noon, and the third meal (Seudah Shlishit) in the afternoon before sundown. Each of these corresponds to one aspect of the Divine: The first one relates to the female, the last one to the male, and the one in between to the highest aspect, which is beyond both.

Rabbi Yehudah said: One must enjoy himself on this day with three meals, in order that there will be satisfaction and pleasure in the world on that day. [. . .] Rabbi Eleazar said to his father: How are those three meals arranged? Rabbi Shimon answered: On *Shabbat Eve*, as it is written: "And I will cause thee to ride upon the high places of the earth." In this night the Matron (the Shechinah = Malchut) is

---

[2] Zohar II:204 a–b.
[3] Zohar II:63b.

blessed and the whole Field of Apples is blessed, and the man's table is also blessed and a soul (Neshamah) is added to him. This night is the rejoicing of the Matron, and hence a man should rejoice and partake in the meal of the Matron. Concerning the *second meal* of Shabbat day, it is written: "Then shalt thou delight thyself in YHVH," that is above YHYH (Keter, which is beyond YHVH), for at that hour the Holy Ancient One (Atiqa Qadisha = Keter) reveals Himself and all the worlds are in joy. And we, in participating in this meal, contribute to that joy and completeness of the Ancient One for this is His meal. Concerning the *third meal* of Shabbat, it is written: "And feed thou with the heritage of Jacob thy father." This is the meal of the impatient (or lesser) Face (Ze'ir Anpin = Tiferet), who is then in complete perfection, from which all the six days receive their blessing. Therefore, a man must rejoice in these meals and complete his meals, with perfect faith . . .[4]

There are many stories of how those are rewarded who try their best to offer something special on Shabbat.

Joseph-Who-Honours-the-Shabbats had in his neighbourhood a certain gentile who owned much property. A Chaldean [soothsayer] told him: "Joseph-Who-Honours-the-Shabbats will consume all your property." So he went, sold all his property, and bought a precious stone with the proceeds, which he set in his turban. As he was crossing a bridge the wind blew it off and cast it into the water, and a fish swallowed it. The fish was caught and brought to market on the Shabbat Eve towards sunset. "Who will buy now?" cried they. "Go and take them to Joseph-Who-Honours-the-Shabbats," they were told, "as he is accustomed to buy." So they took it to him. He bought it, opened it, found the jewel therein, and sold it for thirteen roomfuls of gold denarii. A certain old man[5] met him and said, "He who lends to the Shabbat, the Shabbat repays him."[6]

Rabbi asked Rabbi Ishmael son of Rabbi Jose, The wealthy in Palestine, whereby do they merit this? —Because they give tithes, he

---

[4] Zohar II:88a–b.
[5] Probably Elijah.
[6] Babylonian Talmud Shabbat 119a.

replied, as it is written: "Thou shalt surely tithe (*asser te'asser*)"[7] which means, give tithes (*asser*) so that thou mayest become wealthy (*titasser*). Those in Babylon, wherewith do they merit this? —Because they honour the Torah, replied he. And those in other countries, whereby do they merit it? —Because they honour the Shabbat, answered he. For Rabbi Chiyya ben Abba related: I was once a guest of a man in Laodicea, and a golden table was brought before him, which had to be carried by sixteen men; sixteen silver chains were fixed in it, and plates, goblets, pitchers and flasks were set thereon, thereon, and upon it were all kinds of food, dainties and spices. When they set it down they recited, The earth is the Lord's, and the fullness thereof; and when they removed it they recited, The heavens are the heavens of the Lord, But the earth hath he given to the children of men. Said I to him, "My son! whereby hast thou merited this?" "I was a butcher," replied he, "and of every fine beast I used to say, 'This shall be for the Shabbat.'" Said I to him, "Happy art thou that thou hast merited, and praised be the Omnipresent who has permitted thee to enjoy this."[8]

The emperor said to Rabbi Yoshuah ben Chananya, "Why has the Shabbat dish such a fragrant odour?" "We have a certain seasoning," replied he, "called the Shabbat, which we put into it, and that gives it a fragrant odour." "Give us some of it," asked he. "To him who keeps the Shabbat," retorted he, "it is efficacious; but to him who does not keep the Shabbat it is of no use."[9]

The three meals are an important part of Shabbat, yet they are not meant to make the soul drunk from physical pleasure. There is a difference between the delight (*oneg*) of Shabbat and the lower kinds of sensual pleasure. A custom among Qabbalistic sages is to interrupt their meals at regular intervals to overcome the desire of their appetite and turn their attention to the spiritual experience of the meal. This, therefore, refines their senses rather than increasing their gluttony. During these interruptions the sages discuss the Torah or the Qabbalistic writings such as the Zohar. Their soul is therefore opened to spiritual, rather than physical,

---

[7] Deuteronomy 14:22.
[8] Babylonian Talmud Shabbat 119a.
[9] Babylonian Talmud Shabbat 119a.

nourishment. Alternatively, the meals can also be interrupted by the singing of spiritual songs (*zemirot*) to raise the souls of those present.[10]

After each meal, we say the Birchat ha-Mazon (Grace after Meals), which is identical to Psalm 137.

Shamor: The Negative Commandments

Shabbat is a time of pleasure, but there are also some proscriptions that should be observed in order that we experience this time to the fullest extent possible. During Shabbat it is forbidden to do *melachah* (מלאכה), which is usually translated as "work," but which actually better translates as "creative efforts." The Halachic Law mentions thirty-nine types of melachah that are forbidden on Shabbat.[11] Among them are actions such as traveling, buying, and selling, and other mundane types of work, but also actions that create something new, such as kindling a fire, or actions that finish something. It is important not to confuse melachah with our definition of work. It is permitted to engage deeply in the study of the Torah and learn chapters of the Torah by heart, which would be hard work in our sense, but not melachah, and therefore permitted (in fact encouraged) on Shabbat. To learn Torah is not work that produces something in a mundane sense—nor does it help make a living. We might interpret melachah as "work in Assiah" (the World of Making).

Do not feel restricted by these proscriptions, but consider them to be a time of rest from your work in Assiah and a chance to concentrate on the higher worlds. By letting go of our work in Assiah, we open ourselves to Yetzirah, Beriah, and maybe even Atzilut.

Liberal Jews are of the opinion that these traditional laws must be adjusted to our time, while orthodox Jews keep these laws very strictly.

---

[10] These songs can be found in a good siddur (Jewish prayer book).

[11] These are the thirty-nine types of work forbidden on Shabbat: (1) sowing, (2) ploughing, (3) reaping, (4) binding sheaves, (5) threshing, (6) winnowing, (7) selecting, (8) grinding, (9) sifting, (10) kneading, (11) baking, (12) shearing wool, (13) bleaching, (14) hackling, (15) dyeing, (16) spinning, (17) stretching the threads, (18) the making of two meshes, (19) weaving two threads, (20) dividing two threads, (21) tying (knots), (22) untying, (23) sewing two stitches, (24) tearing in order to sew two stitches, (25) capturing a deer, (26) slaughtering, (27) flaying, (28) salting it, (29) curing its hide, (30) scraping it (of its hair), (31) cutting it up, (32) writing more than one letter, (33) erasing in order to write two letters, (34) building, (35) pulling down, (36) extinguishing, (37) kindling, (38) striking with a hammer, (39) carrying from one domain to another (e.g., taking something out of, or into, your house).

Yet if someone's life is in danger, we are not only permitted, but moreover obliged to ignore every Shabbat law that we must break in order to save his or her life.

The Shechinah

The Shechinah is the Divine Presence of God. When God sends down His consciousness to the world, the aspect of God that descends is the Shechinah. The idea of God dwelling among His people is described in the Torah: "And let them make Me a Sanctuary that I may dwell (ve-shachanti) among them" (Exodus 25:8).

In the Targum Onkelos, which is an Aramaic translation of the Hebrew Bible written in the first through fourth centuries CE, the Shechinah is mentioned for the first time. The passage is paraphrased thus: "And let them make Me a Sanctuary that My Shechinah may dwell among them" (Targum Onkelos of Exodus 25:8).

The words ve-shachanti (ושכנתי), "that I may dwell," and Shechinah (שכינה), "Divine Dwelling or Presence," both come from the root Shin-Kaf-Nun. In fact, both words look so similar that the translation may well have been a writing mistake. This, however, indicates that the concept of the Shechinah was already well known. It was no longer an esoteric secret; if it was, it would not have been named in an Aramaic translation.

When the Tabernacle was erected, the Shechinah descended and dwelled among the people of Israel. But she is not limited to one location. She is present wherever spiritual people come together: "The Emperor said to Rabban Gamaliel: 'You say that upon every gathering of ten Jews the Shechinah dwells among them. How many Shechinahs are there?' Rabban Gamaliel called a servant, and tapped him on the neck, saying, 'Why did you let the sun enter the Emperor's house?' 'But the sun shines upon the whole world!' he answered. Rabban Gamaliel replied 'If the sun, which is but one of the countless myriads of the servants of the Holy One, blessed be He, shines on the whole world, how much more the Shechinah of the Holy One, blessed be He!'" (Babylonian Talmud, Sanhedrin 39a).

Shechinah is a female word, and the Shechinah has always been seen as the female aspect of God. Though God the *Father* was seen as a distant force, the Shechinah was believed to be more like a loving *Mother* who comes to her children and takes care of them. Please note that this does not mean we have a God and a goddess. God is One, not two.[12] God, as such, is neither male nor female, but He (or "It") has a male and a female aspect. These aspects have, however, been described as if they were separate beings in order to explain certain spiritual concepts in a way that could be more easily conceived by the human mind. The Shechinah, as such, is not worshipped,[13] because She is not a separate entity, but She is honored in the Shabbat celebrations and can be called upon or invoked in a ritual in order to bring down the Divine Presence.

The Shechinah has been described by many different symbols and concepts. The Talmud mentions the luster (*ziv*) of the Shechinah, protecting those over whom the Almighty has spread it.[14] In addition to her luster (or radiance), her wings are often mentioned in the same way.

Her titles or names include: Queen (Malka), Mother (Ima), Matron (Matronita), Bride (Kallah), and Female (Nuqva).

She is additionally described in many allegoric images. Among the symbols by which the Shechinah is represented in the Zohar are: the Rose, the Cup of Blessings, the Field of Holy Apples, the Moon, the Dove, the Eagle, the Gazelle, the Hind, the Morning Star, the Well, the Female Waters, the Holy Sea, the Earth, the Door of the Tent (i.e., the holy Tabernacle), the Throne of Glory, the Garden of Eden, and the lower *Heh*.

The Congregation of Israel

In the Zohar, the Congregation of Israel[15] is another term for Malchut, "the Kingdom," and is often used as a synonym for the Shechinah. In this context Israel refers not to the descendants of Jacob, but to those who serve the Light. Yisrael means "who fights for God," and describes the servants of the Light.

All over the world, there are many spiritual groups whose members walk the Path of Light , and every true spiritual group or school has a contacted Group Mind called an *Egregore*. The contact behind the Egregore is an Inner Plane Teacher. All the Inner Plane Teachers constitute the Great

---

[12] This is a concept that all religions seem to share. Even polytheistic religions describe the different gods as aspects of the One. (For example, in Egypt all gods were seen as aspects of Amun-Ra.) Thus, the same concept is described under different names.

[13] From a Qabbalistic perspective, to worship the female or male aspect of God alone makes as much sense as to honor the foot or hand of a mighty king, neglecting the rest of him.

[14] Babylonian Talmud, Shabbat 89a.

[15] Hebrew: Knesset Yisrael.

White Lodge, sometimes called the Great White Brotherhood or the Inner Council of Masters.

We are taught that the things above are like the things below. If every true spiritual group on the physical plane has a higher contact, this is likewise true for any organization on the higher planes, and behind the Great White Lodge is the Shechinah. Thus the Shechinah is truly the spirit of the Congregation of Israel.

Sometimes a distinction is made between the higher and the lower Shechinah (Zohar I:159b). The principle behind the Great White Lodge (the Congregation of Israel) is the higher Shechinah, which is said to rest with the Chayot in Heaven. The feminine power invoked in the Jewish home on Shabbat Eve (the Bride) is the lower Shechinah, which is described as being among the twelve tribes. In that sense, the higher Shechinah is Binah, and the lower Shechinah is Malchut.[16]

The Queen Shabbat (Shabbat ha-Malka)

What is Shabbat? That is the day on which the other days rest. And it comprises all the other six days, and through it are they blessed. Rabbi Jose said: The Congregation of Israel is also called "Shabbat," for She is His Spouse; hence She is a Bride.

ZOHAR II:63B

The Shechinah was seen as the personification of Shabbat itself. In this aspect She was called the Queen Shabbat. The sages and the Qabbalists used to welcome her in that aspect every Friday evening: "Rabbi Chanina

---

[16] This may seem to be confusing, because it has been said above that the Congregation of Israel is used in the Zohar as another term for Malchut. The term can actually be applied on several levels, because the writings of the Zohar itself contain meanings on many levels and layers. The Zohar can therefore be very confusing for the beginner. In actual fact, however, the Zohar is a book that applies Qabbalah rather than teaches it. This means that the student of the Zohar must already understand the basic teachings of the Qabbalah. The Zohar uses images rather than intellectual explanation, as illustrated by one of Dion Fortune's writings describing perfectly the method of the Zohar (even though the text was not written concerning the Zohar): "In the occult teachings you have been given certain images, under which you are instructed to think of certain things. These images are not descriptive but symbolic, and are designed to train the mind, not inform it" (Dion Fortune, *The Cosmic Doctrine*, 19).

robed himself and stood at sunset of Shabbat Eve and said: 'Come and let us go forth to welcome the Queen Shabbat.' Rabbi Yannai donned his robes, on Shabbat Eve and said: 'Come, O Bride, Come, O Bride!'" (Babylonian Talmud Shabbat 119a).

The Midrash[17] tells of an ancient Jewish legend: The Shabbat once came before God and asked: "Master of the worlds, to every day of the week Thou gave a partner. Sunday goes with Monday, Tuesday with Wednesday, Thursday with Friday, and only I am left without a mate." The Holy One, Blessed be He, answered: "The Congregation of Israel[18] is Thy mate."

In other words, the Shechinah is the spiritual contact behind the Congregation of Israel. On other levels, however, the Shechinah is also the egregore of the Jewish Group Mind and of the Qabbalistic tradition. Thus in every Shabbat celebration we honor this divine connection. Israel is therefore reminded to "remember the Shabbat day to keep it holy."[19] The Shabbat is a sign between God and the children of Israel, now and forever.[20] The term Israel always has two meanings: the exoteric meaning relating to the Jewish people, and the esoteric meaning relating to those who serve God. To the average Jew who knows nothing or little of the spiritual tradition of the Qabbalah, this is a chance to connect to the Group Mind of his people, and if his dedication is pure, he will receive the blessing that goes with it. To the Qabbalist, it is a connection to the spiritual source of his tradition, and his blessing is received on a much higher level.

The Exile of the Shechinah

The Zohar describes that, when the Temple was still in existence, the Shechinah dwelled in the Temple and hovered over Israel like a mother hovering over her children. The whole world was nourished for their sake and no day passed without blessings and delight. When, however, the Temple was destroyed, the Shechinah went into exile (Zohar 1, 203a).

> Rabbi Abba opened the discussion with the verse: "Tell me, O thou whom my soul loveth . . . if thou knowest not, O thou fairest among

---

[17] Genesis Rabbah 11:9.

[18] The term *Congregation of Israel* is sometimes used to describe the Group Mind of Israel (i.e., those who serve God) or to describe the Shechinah, who is the Contact of this Group Mind.

[19] Exodus 20:8.

[20] Exodus 31:17.

women, go thy way forth, etc. . . ." (Song of Songs 1:7–8). These verses were explained by the Companions as referring to Moses, when he departed from the world, for it is said "Let YHVH, the God of the spirits of all flesh . . . appoint one who may go out before them" (Numbers 27:16). We learned that this was said of the exile. Come and see: These verses were said by the Congregation of Israel (the Shechinah), to the Holy King [her Bridegroom]. "Tell me, O Thou whom my Soul loveth," as in "Hast thou seen Him Who loveth My Soul?" (Song of Songs 3:3). To the Holy King, it was said, "O Thou Whom My Soul loveth, where Thou feedest . . ." (Song of Songs 1:7).

In the book of Rav Hamnuna the Elder is said that as long as the Congregation of Israel is with the Holy One, blessed be He, the Holy One, blessed be He, so to speak, is complete and willingly feeds Himself and others. He feeds Himself by sucking milk from the supernal Mother and from the sucking He waters all the others and suckles them. We learned that Rabbi Shimon said that as long as the Congregation of Israel is with the Holy One, blessed be He, the Holy One, blessed be He, is complete and in delight. Blessings rest on Him and from Him go to everyone else. Whenever the Congregation of Israel is not with the Holy One, blessed be He, the blessings, so to speak, are withheld from Him and from others.

The secret meaning of this is that where ever male and female are not found together, no blessings rest there, and the Holy One, blessed be He, therefore, wails and weeps, as written, "He doth mightily roar because of His habitation" (Jeremiah 25:30). What does He say? "Woe to Me for having destroyed My House (i.e., the Temple) and burned My Palace."

When the Congregation of Israel went into exile, She said before Him, "Tell Me, O Thou Whom My Soul loveth, on Whom all the love of My Soul is set, how will Thou feed Thyself? How will Thou feed from the deep river, which never ceaseth flowing? How will Thou feed on the illumination of the supernal Eden, 'where Thou makest Thy flock to rest at noon' (Song of Songs 1:7). How will Thou feed all the others who usually receive water from Thee? I used to be nourished by Thee daily and receive water. I watered all those below me, and Israel was sustained by me. And now 'why should I be as one that veileth Herself beside the flocks of Thy companions?' (Song of Songs 1:7). How will I cover Myself without blessings? When the blessings are wanted, they shall not be in My Hands. 'Beside the flocks of Thy companions' (Song of Songs 1:7). How could I stand by them, yet not be leading and nourishing them? 'The flocks of Thy companions' are Israel, the children of the patriarchs, who are the holy Chariot above."

The Holy One, blessed be He, answered: "Leave this with Me for what is Mine is too secret to be made known. But 'If thou knowest not' (Song of Songs 1:8) here is some council: 'O thou fairest among women' (Song of Songs 1:15) resembles 'Behold, thou art fair, my love' (Song of Songs 4:1) 'Go thy way forth by the footsteps of the flock' (Song of Songs 1:8) these are the righteous ones (Tzaddiqim) who are trodden underfoot, and through them strength will be given Thee to survive. 'And feed thy kids, beside the shepherds' (Song of Songs 1:8). These are school children, for whose sake the world endures. They give strength to the Congregation of Israel during the time of exile. 'Beside the shepherds' tents' (Song of Songs 1:8) these are the schools and their teachers' houses of learning, where the Torah always dwells."

Another explanation (i.e., another layer of meaning) for: "If thou knowest not, O thou fairest among women." Come and see: When there are righteous ones (Tzaddiqim) and school children who study the Torah in the world, the Congregation of Israel can exist due to them in exile. But if not—neither She nor they can exist in the world. If there are righteous men, they suffer first. If not, the children for whose sake the world endures suffer first, and the Holy One, blessed be He, takes them from the world, even though they are without sin. Not only that, He even sends the Congregation of Israel away from Him and She goes out into exile.[21]

When the world fell from the Divine Order,[22] the Shechinah was sent into exile, hidden in the world of matter, to comfort the righteous ones (Tzaddiqim; singular: Tzaddiq) on whose shoulders the burdens of humanity are carried, and in return, these righteous ones sacrifice themselves to ease the burden of the Shechinah. Tradition teaches that the Shechinah is in exile all the working days of the week, longing for the Shabbat, for this is when She is reunited with the Holy One, blessed be He. In the world

---

[21] Zohar III:17a–b.

[22] This was called the Breaking of the Vessels in Lurianic Qabbalah. From a higher perspective, all the chaos caused by the free will given to humanity was a part of the Divine Plan.

to come, however, when all people are redeemed and all the Divine Sparks are reunited with the Creator, the Shechinah will then be united with the Holy King forever, as it was in the beginning.

Sexual Ethics

Shabbat is not only a time of culinary treats, but also a time of sexual delight, hence to have intercourse on Friday night is a *Mitzvah* (a sacred duty): "The wise ones who are initiated in the higher mysteries perform their marital duties every Shabbat night" (Zohar 2, 204b).

Traditionally, midnight was seen as the ideal moment for marital intercourse. Sexuality is not condemned in the Qabbalah, as long as it is done in harmony with the Divine Law. This is clearly stated in a text called *Iggeret ha-Qodesh, The Holy Letter,* written in the thirteenth century by an anonymous Qabbalist. (The letter is traditionally attributed to Nachmanides; the real author, however, is unknown.)

> Know that the [sexual] union of the man with his woman is divided into two ways: The first way is when the union is a matter holy and innocent, for [this is the case] if the matter is [done] according to that which is appropriate and at the appropriate time and with the appropriate intention (Kavvanah). [The second way is neither holy nor innocent, which is the case if it is not done in the appropriate way.] And no man shall think that the appropriate [sexual] union is shameful and ugly. God forbid! For the appropriate [sexual] union is called: "cognition." (Hebrew: *yediah,* which can also be translated as "realization" and which is closely related to Daat, "Gnosis.") And it is not called so for nothing, as it is written: "And Elkanah knew Hannah his wife" (1 Samuel 1:19 compare also to Genesis 4:1).[23]

The author further explains that sexuality is indeed a divine mystery. "And behold the divine mystery of the knowledge that I suggest to you it is the mystery of the existence of man, included in the mystery of Wisdom (Chochmah), Understanding (Binah) and Gnosis (Daat). For the man he is the mystery of Wisdom (Chochmah) and the woman is the mystery of Understanding (Binah). And the pure [sexual] union (*ha-chibbur ha-tahor*) it is the mystery of Gnosis (Daat). And this is the mystery of man and woman (alternative translation: of husband and wife), in the mystery of

---

[23] *Iggeret ha-Qodesh,* chapter 2.

the path of the esoteric tradition (ha-Qabbalah ha-Penimit)" (*Iggeret ha-Qodesh,* chapter 2).

The fundamental ideas are that the proper way of sexual intercourse requires that the intentions of both partners are directed to the higher planes and that they seek to bring about the descent to them of the Shechinah. They should also not behave carelessly and should treat each other with respect and regard and speak only about beautiful things. The author also considers the right time (i.e., Shabbat night) to be influential, and further mentions that a very moderate amount of good, pure, clean, and kosher food may be appropriate before sexual intercourse.

The Zohar places great emphasis on the free will of the woman, for, after all, it is she who brings down the Shechinah: "A man who wants to mate with his wife must first entreat her and exhilarate her with sweet words. And if he cannot persuade her, he must not sleep with her, for their desire must be mutual and without coercion" (Zohar I: 49 a–b).

In the Babylonian Talmud (Nedarim 20a–b), discussed is the question of which sexual positions and practices are permitted. Is it permitted to "overturn the table" (i.e., to have sex with the woman on top)? Is it permitted to kiss "that place" (i.e., to have oral sex)? Is it permitted to converse during cohabitation? And is it permitted to look at "that place"?

The answer that the famous Rabbi Yochanan gives in the name of the sages is that, according to the Halachah (Jewish Law), a husband and his wife may do together whatever pleases them to do.

Furthermore, this passage from the Talmud gives us some insight into the spiritual view of the relationship between men and women. The Talmud declares that the greatest children[24] are born when the man is summoned to his marital duty by his wife. But she should do so in a subtle way by indicating that she is willing to have sex without using language that is too obvious.[25] Thus the ancient principle that the woman is active on the higher planes is maintained, and here she makes the first move and inspires the man. On the physical plane the man is the one to make the first move, for here he is active and she is passive.[26]

---

[24] This also includes spiritual children—that is, ideas brought into being within the relationship.

[25] The modern concept of "dirty talk" makes sex something dirty and, therefore, destroys the sacredness of the act.

[26] This is not to be seen as a dogma, but rather as a guideline to respect the subtle levels of the relationship.

Preparation for Shabbat

In order to enjoy Shabbat, we must prepare for it. We must make Shabbat a special day. "It was taught, R. Jose son of R. Yehudah said: Two ministering angels accompany man on the eve of the Shabbat from the synagogue to his home, a good one and an evil one. And when he arrives home and finds the lamp burning, the table laid and the bed covered with a spread, the good angel exclaims, 'May it be even thus on another Shabbat too,' and the evil angel unwillingly responds 'Amen.' But if not, the evil angel exclaims, 'May it be even thus on another Shabbat too,' and the good angel unwillingly responds, 'Amen'" (Babylonian Talmud Shabbat 119b).

If we do nothing to make Shabbat special, it will not be special for us. Many Jews are astonished when they hear about the delights that the Chassidic sages experienced on Shabbat. There are Jews who have kept Shabbat every week, but who never experienced the spiritual depth that is described by the Qabbalists. The answer is simple: You must yearn for Shabbat as a lover yearns to be with his or her beloved. You must long for it as a slave longs for freedom, or as a suffering person longs for healing. Try to look forward to Shabbat as you would look forward to a very special party, or as a child looks forward to his or her birthday, expecting many presents. You must build up this feeling during the whole week, and only then will you experience the full delight of Shabbat.

One of the most important preparations is the making of the Shabbat bread called *challah*. The word *challah* refers to the portion of the cake (challah) that was given as an offering to the temple in biblical times. "And YHVH spoke unto Moses, saying: Speak unto the children of Israel, and say unto them: When ye come into the land whither I bring ye, then it shall be, that, when ye eat of the bread of the land, ye shall set apart a portion for an offering unto YHVH. Of the first of your dough ye shall set apart a cake (challah)[27] for an offering; as that which is set apart of the threshing floor, so shall ye set it apart. Of the first of your dough ye shall give unto YHVH a portion for an offering throughout your generations" (Numbers 15:17–21).

Today there is no temple anymore, but when the bread for Shabbat is prepared, a small offering is still made. To separate the challah is one of the Mitzvot to be performed by the lady of the house, for she is the priestess of the house, and it is her privilege to make this offering to God. Just before she

---

[27] A challah recipe can be found on my website: www.qabbalah.org.

separates from the dough an amount equivalent to about half the size of a large egg, and then burns this in the oven, she recites the following blessing:

**Baruch Atah Adonai Eloheynu Melech ha-Olam,
asher qidshanu be-mitzvotav,
ve-tzivanu le-hafrish Challah.**
(Blessed art Thou, Lord, our God, King of the Universe,
who has blessed us with His commandments
and who commands us to separate the challah.)

The Ritual of Shabbat Evening
(Maariv Shabbat)

Preparation

The Shabbat table, covered in a white tablecloth, serves as the altar. Place on the altar two white candles in silver holders. (The symbolism of these candles will be described in the following text.) You will also need a chalice of wine; a small vessel of salt on the table; some myrtle, if possible; and two loaves of challah (Shabbat bread). The challah loaves should be covered with a white cloth: "And every meal-offering of thine shalt thou season with salt; neither shalt thou suffer the salt of the covenant of thy God to be lacking from thy meal-offering; with all thy offerings thou shalt offer salt" (Leviticus 2:13).

Salt is the symbol of the Covenant with God (Numbers 19:18 and 2

Woodcut of woman performing the Shabbat Blessing

Chronicles 13:5). The Zohar (I:241a–b) explains that this is so because it softens the bitterness, and in the same way the Covenant with God on which the world is established softens the bitterness of life, and humankind cannot do without it—without spiritual depth, life becomes bitter, empty, and meaningless.

Some families also include a *tzedaqah box*,[28] a box into which a small donation is placed for the poor. This should be done before the Shabbat ceremony begins, because touching money is not permitted on Shabbat.

Lighting the Shabbat Candles

Traditionally, the two Shabbat candles symbolize the two aspects of the Shabbat: zachor (to remember) and shamor (to observe). The Ten Commandments appear twice in the Torah. The first time, we are told to "remember (zachor) the Shabbat" (Exodus 20:8); the second time, we are told to "observe (shamor) the Shabbat" (Deuteronomy 5:12).

Zachor hints at the positive commandments, and shamor at the negative commandments.[29] Obviously, zachor belongs to the pillar of mercy on the Tree of Life and shamor to the pillar of justice. "The children of Israel shall observe (*shamru*) the Shabbat" (Exodus 31:16) refers to night, the secret of the female. "Remember (zachor) the Shabbat day" (Exodus 20:8) refers to day, the secret of the male (Zohar II:138a).

Thus the two principles ultimately relate to the female and the male side of God.[30] The two candles together represent the union[31] of the female and the male principle, and this is the esoteric secret as revealed by the Zohar. But even more so, the lights represent the divine female and male spark hidden within the human soul. As it is written: "The Light (Candle) of YHVH is the Soul (Nishmat Adam) of Man" (Proverbs 20:27).

Lighting the Shabbat candles is the task of the woman, for it is by her powers that the Shechinah is called into the house: "When a man is at home, the root of his house is the lady of the house, because of her the

---

[28] *Tzedaqah* means "almsgiving," the right of the poor to be given charity.

[29] Positive commandments are the things we must do on Shabbat: for example. to honor and celebrate this special day. Negative commandments are the things we must not do on Shabbat: for example, all kinds of work.

[30] On Shabbat night the female side is dominant, and during the day the male side is dominant.

[31] According to the Halachah (Jewish Law), it is sufficient to light one candle for the household, but it is customary to light a minimum of two candles. Some light one candle for every soul in the family.

Shechinah does not leave the house. As we have learned: 'Isaak brought her [Rebbeka, his wife] into the tent of his mother Sarah.'[32] The Light (candle) was lit, for the Shechinah came to the house" (Zohar 50a).

The lady of the house should light the two Shabbat candles no later than eighteen[33] minutes before sundown.[34] After lighting the candle or candles, she draws her hands over the flames and toward herself, three times, as she imagines drawing the spirit of Shabbat into herself and bringing the peace and sanctity of the Queen Shabbat into the house.

She then covers her eyes with her hands (the palm toward the light, the back of the hand toward the eyes). This is done so she does not see the candles before she speaks the blessing.[35]

There is also a magical logic behind this. When you want to consume blessed wine or bread, you must bless it *before* you consume it, otherwise you would consume it *without* a blessing. If, however, you want to bless the Light (not the candle!), you must bless it *when* it is lit, for otherwise there is no Light that can be blessed.

WOMAN: **Baruch Atah Adonai Eloheynu Melech ha-Olam,**
asher qidshanu be-mitzvotav,
ve-tzivanu le-hadliq ner shel-shabbat.
(Blessed art Thou, Lord, our God, King of the Universe,
Who has blessed us with His commandments
and who commands us to light the lights of Shabbat.)

The man and other people present may reply "Amen."[36]

Now the woman uncovers the eyes and gazes at the lights. The Queen Shabbat has arrived. Turn to your beloved and say, "Shabbat shalom" (a peaceful Shabbat), and let into your heart the peace and warmth and sanc-

---

[32] Genesis 24:67.

[33] Eighteen is the number of life (*chay*) in the Qabbalistic tradition.

[34] For the precise times of lighting candles, consult any Jewish calendar.

[35] The Halachic explanation is that it is forbidden to light a candle on Shabbat. (Making fire was hard work in the ancient times, and thus forbidden on Shabbat.) Because Shabbat begins when the blessing has been said, the candle must be lit before the blessing, as opposed to the blessing of wine and bread, when the blessing is spoken before drinking or eating (Shulchan Aruch, Orach Chayim 263:5).

[36] In modern Jewish tradition, we say "Amen" only when someone else says a blessing. In this context, Amen has a meaning not unlike the word *ditto*. Obviously, we would not say ditto to our own words. (In ancient times, however, Amen was used in the same way as "So mote it be," and was often used by the speaker at the end of an invocation.)

tity of Shabbat. Some women traditionally add the following prayer after lighting the candles:

WOMAN: **Yehi ratzon mi-le-fanecha Adonai Elohay ve-Elohay Avotey** (May it be Thy Will YHVH, my God and God of my forefathers,) **she-t'chonen oti** (that Thou showest favor to me).

Add the following passages as they apply:

WOMAN: **Ve-et Ishi** (and my husband)
Ve-et Beni (and my sons)
Ve-et Benotay (and my daughters)
Ve-et Avi (and my father)
Ve-et Imi (and my mother)
Ve-et kol qrovay (and all my relatives)
Ve-titen lanu u-le-chol Yisrael chayim tovim ve-arukim
(and that Thou granteth us and all Israel a good and long life)
Ve-tizkrenu be-zichron tovah u-verachah
(and that Thou remembereth us with a beneficent memory and blessing)
Ve-tifqedenu bi-f'qudat yeshuah ve-rachamim
(and that Thou considereth us with a consideration of salvation and compassion)
Ve-tevarechnu gedolot
(and that Thou blesseth us with great blessings)
Ve-tashlim bateinu
(and that Thou maketh our households complete)
Ve-tashken Shechinatecha beyneynu
(and that Thou causeth Thy Shechinah to dwell among us.)
Ve-zakeni le-gadel banim u-vney vanim chachmim u-nevonim
(Privilege me to raise children and grandchildren who are wise and understanding)
Ohavey Adonai irey Elohim
(who love YHVH and fear God)
Anshey emet, zera qodesh, deveqim be-Adonai
(people of truth, holy offspring, attached to YHVH)
U-me'irim et ha-olam ba-Torah u-ve-maassim tovim
(who illuminate the world with Torah and good deeds)
U-ve-chol melechet avodat ha-Bore.
(and with every labor in the service of the Creator.)

> **Ana shma et techinati ba-et ha-zot**
> (Please, hear my supplication at this time)
> **Bi-zchut Sarah ve-Rivqah ve-Rachel ve-Leah imoteyniu**
> (in the merit of Sarah, Rebecca, Rachel, and Leah, our mothers)
> **Ve-ha'er nerenu she-lo yichbeh le-olam va-ed**
> (and cause our light to illuminate that it be not extinguished forever)
> **Ve-ha'er Paneycha u-niushah.**
> (and let Thy Countenance shine so that we are saved.)

The man and other people present may reply "Amen."

Qabblat Shabbat: Welcoming Shabbat

If you wish, you may attend the evening services in the local synagogue, or perform a small service at home. To do so, read or sing Psalms 95–99 and 29 to represent the six working days of the week, followed by the song "Lecha Dodi," which is based on a poem written by Shlomo ben Moshe Halevi Alqabetz (ca. 1505–1576), a Qabbalist from Safed. The text is full of deep Qabbalistic symbolism:

Hebrew	Translation
Lecha Dodi, Liqrat Kallah, *Peney Shabbat neqabbelah.*	Come, my beloved, to meet the Bride, let us welcome (receive) the [Queen] Shabbat.[37]
Shamor ve-zachor be-dibbur echad,[38] *Hishmianu El ha-meyuchad* *Adonai echad, ushmo echad* *Le-Shem u-le-Tiferet ve-lit'hilah*	"Observe" and "remember"—in a single word the One and only God made us hear. Adonai is One and his Name is One, for renown for beauty and for praise.
Lecha Dodi, Liqrat Kallah, *Peney Shabbat neqabbelah.*	Come, my beloved, to meet the Bride, let us welcome (receive) the [Queen] Shabbat.
Liqrat Shabbat lechu ve-nelechah, *ki Hi meqor ha-berachah. Me-rosh* *mi-qedem nesuchah, sof Maasseh,* *be-machashavah techilah*	To welcome the [Queen] Shabbat, come let us go, for she is the source of blessing. From the beginning, from the origin she was honored, last in deed (i.e., the work of Creation/Emanation), but first in thought.
Lecha Dodi, Liqrat Kallah, *Peney Shabbat neqabbelah.*	Come, my beloved, to meet the Bride, let us welcome (receive) the [Queen] Shabbat.

[37] Literally, "the Countenance of the [Queen] Shabbat."

[38] His name is found in the first letter of the first eight verses. (S.L.M.H. H.L.V.Y. = Shlomo Halevi).

Miqdash Melech Ir meluchah *Qumi tzey mitoch ha-Hafeichah* *Rav lach shevet be-Emeq ha-Bacha* *ve-hu yachamol alayich Chemlah.*	Sanctuary of the King, royal city (i.e., Jerusalem), Arise! Leave from the midst of the destruction [of the Temple] Long enough have Thou sat in the valley of tears, and He will be full of compassion for Thee.
Lecha Dodi, Liqrat Kallah, *Peney Shabbat neqabbelah.*	Come, my beloved, to meet the Bride, let us welcome (receive) the [Queen] Shabbat.
Hitna'ari me-Afar qumi *Liv-shi bi-G'dey Tifartech Ami* *Al Yad ben Yishai Beit ha-Lachmi* *Qorvah el Nafshi ge-alah.*	Shake yourself free, rise from the dust, Dress in the garments of thy beauty (Tiferet), my people. By the hand of the son of Yishai of Bethlehem (i.e., David), Salvation draws near to my soul (Nefesh).
Lecha Dodi, Liqrat Kallah, *Peney Shabbat neqabbelah.*	Come, my beloved, to meet the Bride, let us welcome (receive) the [Queen] Shabbat.
Hitor'ri hitor'ri, ki va orech, *qumi ori, uri uri shir daberi,* *Kevod Adonai alayich niglah.*	Wake up! Wake up! For Thy Light has come, rise up and shine; Awaken! awaken! Utter a song, The Glory of YHVH is revealed upon Thee.
Lecha Dodi, Liqrat Kallah, *Peney Shabbat neqabbela.*	Come, my beloved, to meet the Bride, let us welcome (receive) the [Queen] Shabbat.
Lo tivoshi ve-lo tikalmi *Mah tishtochachi u-mah tehemi* *Bach yechesu aniyei ami* *Ve-nivnetah Ir al tilah.*	Do not be embarrassed and do not be ashamed! Why be downcast and why moan? All my afflicted people will find shelter within Thee, And the city shall be rebuilt on her hill.
Lecha Dodi, Liqrat Kallah, *Peney Shabbat neqabbela.*	Come, my beloved, to meet the Bride, let us welcome (receive) the [Queen] Shabbat.
Ve-hayu li-m'shisah shosayich *Ve-rachaqu kol Mevalayich* *Yasis alayich Elohayich* *Kimsos Chatan al Kallah.*	Thy despoilers will become spoil, And far away shall be any who would devour Thou, Thy God will rejoice in Thee, As [the] Bridegroom rejoices in [the] Bride.
Lecha Dodi, Liqrat Kallah, *Peney Shabbat neqabbela.*	Come, my beloved, to meet the Bride, let us welcome (receive) the [Queen] Shabbat.
Yamin u-smol tifrotzi *Ve-et Adonai ta'aritzi* *Al Yad Ish ben Partzi* *Ve-nismechah ve-nagilah.*	To the right and to the left Thou will burst forth, And YHVH will Thou revere By the hand of a child of Perez (i.e., David) We will rejoice and sing happily.
Lecha Dodi, Liqrat Kallah, *Peney Shabbat neqabbela.*	Come, my beloved, to meet the Bride, let us welcome (receive) the [Queen] Shabbat.

At this point, all rise and look to the door to welcome the Queen Shabbat.

Boi ve-shalom Ateret Balah,
gam be-simchah u-ve-tzahalah.
Toch emuney Am segullah,
boi challah, boi challah.

Enter in peace, O Crown of Her Husband, also in joy and happiness, Amidst the faithful of the treasured people. Come, O Bride! Come, O Bride!

Lecha Dodi, Liqrat Kallah,
Peney Shabbat neqabbela.

Come, my beloved, to meet the Bride, let us welcome (receive) the [Queen] Shabbat.

"Lecha Dodi" from Emanuel Aguilar and the Rev. D. A. de Sola,
Sephardi Melodies *(Oxford: Oxford University Press, 1931).*

After returning home from the synagogue, everything is prepared for the meal. Because the preparation is seen as the responsibility of the lady of the house, women often do not go to the synagogue in order to be able to concentrate on the ceremony at home, which is far more important.[39]

When all have arrived back home, the family will sing[40] together the "Shalom Alechem," which is sung to welcome the angels of Shabbat that accompany the Shabbat Queen:[41]

Shalom alechem Malachey ha-sharet *Malachey Elyion* *Mi-Melech malachei ha-melahim* *Ha-Qadosh baruch Hu.*	Peace be unto you, O ministering angels, angels of the Most High, the highest King over Kings of Kings, the Holy One, blessed be He.
Boachem le-shalom Malachei *ha-shalom, Malachey Elion* *Mi-Melech malachei ha-melahim* *Ha-Qadosh baruch Hu.*	Come in peace, O angels of peace, angels of the Most High, the highest King over Kings of Kings, the Holy One, blessed be He.
Barchuni le-shalom Malachey *ha-shalom, Malachey Elion* *Mi-Melech malachei ha-melahim* *Ha-Qadosh baruch Hu.*	Bless me for peace, O angels of peace, angels of the Most High, the highest King over Kings of Kings, the Holy One, blessed be He.
Tzetchem le-shalom Malachey *ha-shalom, Malachey Elion* *Mi-Melech malachei ha-melahim* *Ha-Qadosh baruch Hu.*	May your departure be to peace, O angels of peace, angels of the Most High, the highest King over Kings of Kings, the Holy One, blessed be He.

---

[39] After the evening services, it is tradition to wish each other "Shabbat shalom"—"a peaceful Shabbat" (or "gut Shabbes," in Yiddish)—if this has not been done already after the lighting of the candles.

[40] The notes for this and any other song included in this ritual can be found in many collections of Jewish or Yiddish songs. If you cannot sing, simply read the text aloud.

[41] Usually, after coming home from the synagogue (before the "Shalom Alechem"), the blessing of the children is performed if there are any children present. For boys this is: Yessimecha Elohim ki-Ephraim u-chi-Mesasheh ("May Elohim make ye like Ephraim and Menasse"), and for girls: Yessimech Elohim ke-Sarah Rivqa Rachel ve-Leah ("May Elohim make ye like Sarah Rebbeka Rachel and Leah"). Most families add the blessing of the priest for both: Yevarech Adonai ve-yishmerecha ya'ir Adonai panav elecha vi-chunecha. Yissa Adonai panav elecha ve-yassem lecha Shalom ("May YHVH bless ye and guard ye. May he let His Countenance shine above ye and be graceful to ye. May YHVH lift His Countenance above ye and give ye peace").

Say in addition:

Ki malachav yetzaveh-lach li-shmarech bechol derachecha. Adonai yishmar tzetcha u-voecha me-atah ve-ad olam. Amen.

(For He has ordered his angels to guard thee on all thy ways. YHVH may guard thy going and thy coming, from now and forever. Amen.)

Then the husband raises a branch of myrtle (the symbol of marriage) and sings or speaks from Proverbs 31:10–31 (the Song of the Virtuous Woman) in order to honor and praise his beloved wife and the Shabbat Queen. By doing so he identifies his wife with the Shechinah and invokes the Shechinah in her. (This should, of course, be done only if the husband then follows the deeper Qabbalistic ritual outlined here.)[42]

HUSBAND: **Who can find a virtuous woman? For her price is far above rubies.**

The heart of her husband doth safely trust in her, and he hath no lack of gain.

She doeth him good and not evil all the days of her life.

She seeketh wool and flax, and worketh willingly with her hands.

She is like the merchant ships; she bringeth her food from afar.

She riseth also while it is yet night, and giveth food to her household, and a portion to her maidens.

She considereth a field, and buyeth it; with the fruit of her hands she planteth a vineyard.

She girdeth her loins with strength, and maketh strong her arms.

She perceiveth that her merchandise is good; her light goeth not out by night.

She layeth her hands to the distaff, and her hands hold the spindle.

She stretcheth out her hand to the poor; and she reacheth forth her hands to the needy.

She is not afraid of the snow for her household; for all her household are clothed with scarlet.

She maketh for herself coverings; her clothing is fine linen and purple.

Her husband is known in the gates, when he sitteth among the elders of the land.

---

[42] Some also include the praise of the husband—i.e., Ze'ir Anpin (Psalm 112:1–9).

She maketh linen garments and selleth them; and delivereth girdles unto the merchant.

Strength and dignity are her clothing; and she laugheth at the time to come.

She openeth her mouth with wisdom; and the law of kindness is on her tongue.

She looketh well to the ways of her household, and eateth not the bread of idleness.

Her children rise up, and call her blessed; her husband also, and he praiseth her:

"Many daughters have done virtuously, but thou excellest them all."

Grace is deceitful, and beauty is vain; but a woman that feareth YHVH, she shall be praised.

Give her of the fruit of her hands; and let her works praise her in the gates.[43]

Qiddush: The Blessing of the Wine

Qiddush (also spelled Kiddush) means "sanctification"—the Blessing of the Wine. Traditionally, the Qiddush is spoken over a chalice of red wine.[44]

The sanctity (Qiddush) that is done on the commencement of Shabbat is of the same sanctity as the Shabbat of Creation. It was sanctified by the thirty-two paths and the three grades of Holy Apple Trees.[45] And in this sanctification the entire work of creation and the [time of] rest must be mentioned, according to the secret of the thirty-two paths and the three grades incorporated in them. This is the secret of the testimony regarding the work of creation, namely, "The Heavens and the earth were finished, the whole host of them." This testimony contains thirty-five[46] words: The thirty-two paths and three grades of the Holy Apples. [. . .] Happy is the

---

43 Proverbs 31:10–31.

44 It should be filled with at least 4.5 ounces of wine.

45 These represent the three highest principles.

46 The thirty-five words are: Vayechulu ha-shamayim ve-ha-aretz ve-chol tzeva'am. Vayechal Elohim ba-yom ha-sheviyiy melachto asher assah. Vayishbot ba-yom ha-shviyiy mikol melachto asher assah. Vayivarech Elohim et yom ha-sheviyiy vayiqadesh oto, ki vo shavat mikol melachto asher bara Elohim la'asot.

47 Zohar 2, 207b.

portion [in the World to Come] of one who meditates upon these matters to the Glory of his Master.[47]

The man raises[48] the chalice of wine and recites the Qiddush in Hebrew.[49]

MAN: **Vayehi erev vayehi voqer yom ha-shishi.**
(And there was evening and there was morning, a sixth day.)
Vayechulu ha-shamayim ve-ha-aretz ve-chol tzeva'am.
(The heavens and the earth were finished,
the whole host of them.)
Vayechal Elohim ba-yom ha-sheviyiy melachto asher assah
(And on the seventh day God finished His work which He had made)
vayishbot ba-yom ha-shviyiy mikol melachto asher assah.
(and He rested on the seventh day from all His work
which He had made.)
Vayivarech Elohim et yom ha-sheviyiy vayiqadesh oto
(And God blessed the seventh day, and sanctified it)
ki vo shavat mikol melachto asher bara Elohim la'asot.
(because in it He had rested from all His work
which God has created and done.)
Baruch Atah Adonai Eloheynu Melech ha-Olam, Borey pri ha-gafen.
(Blessed art Thou, Lord, our God, King of the Universe,
Creator of the fruit of the vine.)

The woman and other people present may reply "Amen."

MAN: **Baruch Atah Adonai Eloheynu Melech ha-Olam**
(Blessed art Thou, Lord, our God, King of the Universe)
asher qidshanu be-mitzvotav ve-ratzah vanu.
(who sanctifies us with His commandments,
and has been pleased with us.)
**ve-Shabbat qadsho be-aHavah u-ve-ratzon hinchilanu
zikaron le-ma'aseh ve-reshit.**

---

[48] Some say that during the blessing, the man should hold the chalice in the palm of the right hand so that the five fingers holding the cup are curled upward. This symbolizes the five-petaled rose, which stands for the Shechinah.

[49] Unless both speak Hebrew well enough, I advise that the woman recites the English text (in parentheses) after the man has spoken his line. This will ensure that both understand what is being said.

(Thou hast lovingly and willingly given us Thy holy Shabbat as an inheritance, in memory of the work of Creation.)

**Ki hu yom techilah le-miqra'ey qodesh,
zecher li-tziyat mitzraim.**
(For it—the Shabbat—is the first among our holy days,
and a remembrance of our exodus from Egypt.)
Ki vanu va-charta ve-otanu qidashta mikol ha-amim
(For Thou hast chosen us and made us holy
among all peoples)
ve-Shabbat qadshecha be-aHavah u-ve-ratzon hinchaltanu.
(and hast willingly and lovingly given us
Thy holy Shabbat for an inheritance.)
Baruch Atah Adonai, me-qadesh ha-Shabbat.
(Blessed art Thou, who sanctifies the Shabbat.)

The woman and other people present may reply "Amen." The man drinks at least 2 to 3 ounces of the wine, and then he passes the chalice to all others present and shares the wine with them.

Washing Hands

Then everyone should cleanse their hands in a bowl by pouring water from a cup[50] three times over their hands—first right hand, then left—while saying the following blessing:

**Baruch Atah Adonai Eloheynu Melech ha-Olam,
asher qidshanu be-mitzvotav,
ve-tzivanu al netilat yadayim.**
(Blessed art Thou, Lord, our God, King of the Universe,
Who has blessed us with His commandments
and who commands us to ritually purify our hands.)

All dry their hands with a towel.

Ha-Motzi: The Blessing of the Bread

The two challah loaves represent the manna, the divine food that God gave to the children of Israel to feed them when they wandered for forty years

---

[50] This method is based on the purification ritual of the priests (Exodus 30:17–21): The Levites poured water over the hands of the priests from a round vessel with two handles. (Traditional hand-washing cups can be obtained from Jewish gift shops.)

through the desert. On the day before Shabbat, God gave them a double portion so that they did not need to collect food on Shabbat.[51] To remember the double portion of manna, two challah loaves are placed on the Shabbat table. They are covered with a white cloth to symbolize the dew that fell on them.[52]

The man uncovers the two loaves of challah and blesses them.

> **Baruch Atah Adonai Eloheynu Melech ha-Olam**
> **Ha-Motzi lechem min ha-aretz.**
> (Blessed art Thou, Lord, our God, King of the Universe,
> Who brings forth bread from the earth.)

The woman and other people present may reply "Amen." Then everybody takes a piece of challah (with salt), and the first of the three meals of Shabbat begins.

Here ends the main ceremony of Qabblat Shabbat. You may use the first part of this ritual simply as a guideline for how to celebrate Shabbat. What follows is the Qabbalistic ritual of the sacred marriage.

The Sacred Marriage (Zivvuga Qaddisha)

This is the ritual of the Hieros Gamos (sacred marriage), which, in the Zohar, is called Zivvuga Qaddisha (literally, "Holy Union"). It is to be performed on Shabbat Eve at midnight. The Qabbalist Abraham Azulay (ca. 1570–1643) considers the sacred marriage to bring about the "supernal marriage" (ha-Zivvug ha-eliyon)—that is the marriage of the Shechinah (i.e., Malchut

---

[51] "Then said YHVH unto Moses: 'Behold, I will cause to rain bread from Heaven for you; and the people shall go out and gather a day's portion every day, that I may prove them, whether they will walk in My law, or not. [. . .] And it shall come to pass on the sixth day that they shall prepare that which they bring in, and it shall be twice as much as they gather daily.' [. . .] And it came to pass, as Aaron spoke unto the whole congregation of the children of Israel, that they looked toward the wilderness, and, behold, the Glory of YHVH appeared in the cloud. [. . .] And it came to pass at even, that the quails came up, and covered the camp; and in the morning there was a layer of dew round about the camp. [. . .] And the house of Israel called the name thereof Manna; and it was like coriander seed, white; and the taste of it was like wafers made with honey. [. . .] And the children of Israel did eat the manna forty years, until they came to a land inhabited; they did eat the manna, until they came unto the borders of the land of Canaan" (Exodus 16:4–35).

[52] Some say the cover also symbolizes the blood of the Messiah over our sinful flesh, and others say that we cover the challot so that they do not envy the wine, which is blessed before them.

Song of Solomon: Rose of Sharon

of Atzilut) and the Holy One, blessed be He (i.e., Tiferet of Atzilut). He describes the formula of the sacred marriage in his commentary on the Zohar called *Or ha-Chammah* (Light of the Sun): "Their ambition (Re'uta), both his and hers (i.e., husband and wife's), was to unite the Shechinah. For he concentrated (i.e., he directed his Kavvanah) on Tiferet and his wife [did so] on Malchut. And his union was to pair off (le-zavvig) the Shechinah and she concentrated (i.e., she directed her Kavvanah) exactly as he did. For she was the Shechinah and unites with her Husband the [Sefirah] Tiferet."[53]

The basic idea is that the woman directs her Kavvanah (magical intention) toward the Shechinah (i.e., Malchut, the Divine Bride), and the man directs his Kavvanah (magical intention) toward her heavenly Bridegroom (i.e., Tiferet). Note that Azulay writes: "For she was the Shechinah and unites with her Husband the [Sefirah] Tiferet." This means that during the ritual of the sacred marriage, a complete identification of the woman with the Shechinah and of the man with her Husband Tiferet is achieved. Thus is brought about a Divine Union of Malchut and Tiferet in Yesod, the Sefirah of the sexual principle.

The first part of my interpretation of the ritual of the sacred marriage is based on the hymn for the Shabbat Eve written by the famous Qabbalist Isaac Luria, who was also called the Ari. The second part is based on the Song of Songs.

---

[53] Abraham Azulay, *Or ha-Chammah* II, fol. 12c.

The Companions (Chaverim) have revealed this: When is the time for everyone to sanctify in marital duties? Come and behold: he who wishes to sanctify himself to the delight of His Master should not have intercourse except from midnight on, or at midnight, as in that hour, the Holy One, blessed be He (the Bridegroom), is in the Garden of Eden (the Bride), and the supernal Sanctity is awakened. That is the moment to be sanctified. This is for all ordinary people. Scholars of Wisdom who know the ways of Torah rise at midnight in this hour and engage in the Torah, unite with the Congregation of Israel (the Bride), and praise the Holy Name, and the Holy King (the Bridegroom). For Shabbat Eve, when there is universal delight, is the moment for uniting in order to find the delight of the Holy One, blessed be He, and the Congregation of Israel.[54]

Preparation

Before you attempt this ritual, you should have performed the basic Shabbat ceremony (including Havdalah—the Separation ritual explained later in this chapter) several times, so that you are familiar with the procedure and the deeper meaning involved. This is not asking too much. Remember that pious Jews celebrate Shabbat EVERY week!

To prepare yourself, meditate for one week upon the meaning of this ritual. In the following week, the woman meditates upon the Shechinah (i.e., Malchut), and the man meditates upon the Holy King who is the Divine Bridegroom (i.e., Tiferet). In the week before the ritual, you should not have intercourse.

During the ritual, the woman will assume the divine form of the Shechinah, thus calling the Shechinah into herself, as is written in the Zohar: "And Isaak was empowered by the faith when he saw the Shechinah dwelling in his wife" (Zohar I:141a). This is achieved by the use of visualization. Yet the ritual will work only if both partners unify their intentions and if they aim together to unite their bodies AND their souls. Their intentions must be pure and directed toward the Divine.

When is a person called "one"? At the time when there is male and female, and he sanctifies himself with supernal holiness and intents to be holy. Come and behold: At the time when a person is in sexual

---

[54] Zohar III:81a.

union, male and female, and intends to sanctify himself in the right way, then he will be complete and he is called "one" [and he is] without fault. Hence, at that time man shall pleasure his wife in one desire with her, that both intend this aim as one. And when both are as one, they are fully united in soul and body. [United] in soul to be attached to each other in one desire. [United] in body—as we learned—that a man who does not marry is like one who is separated [from his other half]. When they bind male and female together, they become one soul and one body; and then man is called "one." Then the Holy One, blessed be He, dwells in "one" (i.e., the unified man) and places the Holy Spirit in that "one."[55]

In this ritual the man must visualize himself as the Divine Bridegroom, and the woman visualizes herself as the Queen Shabbat.

The Ritual

The Bride goes to the east and makes the gesture of opening a veil.

BRIDE: **I open the mizrach (east) and I call upon the powers of Heaven to be present in this holy place.**

[Then she stretches out her hand and says]:
I place the Seal of YOD HEH VAV HEH onto the gate of mizrach.

[She goes to the south and makes the gesture of opening a veil.]
I open the darom (south) and I call upon the powers of the heavenly fire to be present in this holy place.
[Then she stretches out her hand and says]:
I place the Seal of ELOHIM onto the gate of darom.

[Then she goes to the west and makes the gesture of opening a veil.]
I open the ma'arav (west) and I call upon the powers of the upper sea to be present in this holy place.
[Then she stretches out her hand and says]:
I place the Seal of EL SHADDAI onto the gate of ma'arav.

[She goes to the north and makes the gesture of opening a veil.]
I open the tzafon (north) and I call upon the powers of the earth to be present in this holy place.

[55] Zohar III:81 a–b.

[Then she stretches out her hand and says]:
I place the Seal of ADONAI onto the gate of tzafon.

[Then she turns to the Shabbat table—the altar of the house[56]—and says]:
I invoke Thee O SHABBAT HA-MALKA, Queen Shabbat,
I invoke Thee O KALLAH, Bride,
I invoke Thee O Lady of the female waters,
for Thou art the Holy Sea from which all life is born.
Thou art the Rose and the Cup of Blessings.
Thou art the Garden of Eden and the Field of Holy Apples.
Thou art the Dove and the Hind.
And Thine is the silver shining moon and the bright evening star.

Descend and be Thou present among us.
Come to us and share Thy blessings with us,
for we have prepared this sacred place
to celebrate the union of the Holy One, Blessed be He, and His
  Shechinah,
in awe and in love,
to unify the *Yod Heh* and *Vav Heh* in perfect unity
in the name of all Israel.
Amen.

BRIDEGROOM: I sing hymns to enter the gates
of the field of apples, which are sacred.[57]
  *[The man prepares the table. The candelabrum should be lit from the
  two lights of Shabbat before sundown.[58]]*
Now we prepare a new table for Her,
and a beautiful menorah to shine upon our heads.

BRIDE *[touches her breasts and says]:*
Right and left—
  *[She places her hand between her breasts, on her heart, where the
  Shechinah is invoked,]*

---

[56] Rabbi Yochanan and Rabbi Eleazar both explain that as long as the Temple stood, the altar atoned for Israel, but now a man's table atones for him (Babylonian Talmud, Berachot 55a).

[57] The Field of Holy Apples is the Shechinah. The gates are a sexual allegory.

[58] Do NOT make a new fire or light candles after sundown!

—and in between the Bride approaches
with [sacred] jewels and with [festive] dresses and garments.

BRIDEGROOM *[embraces the Bride gently]:*
Her Husband embraces her
[He kisses her Yesod. Yesod[59] *is equated to the genitals.]*
And in Her Yesod,
giving Her pleasure (satisfaction).
He will be most closely joined [to Her].

BRIDE: Screams [of worry] and troubles are lifted and at rest.
[Now there are] only new [joyous] faces
and spirits (Ruchin) with souls (Nafshin).

BRIDEGROOM: He gives Her great joy in twofold measure.
Light and many blessings come upon Her.

BRIDE: **Approach Bridegroom** [originally: shushvinin—groomsmen],
make preparations [literally, *tiqqunin*] for the Bride,
food of various kinds, all manner of fish. [60]
To make (beget) **souls** (Nishmatin) **and new spirits** (Ruchin)
with the thirty-two [paths] and three branches [i.e., the three
pillars].

BRIDEGROOM: She has seventy crowns and the supernal King,
that all may be crowned in the Holy of Holies.

BRIDE: Engraved and concealed inside [Her are] all the worlds.
Only the Ancient of Days—He stands above them all.
May it be Thy Will that She is right (upright, firm, straight, strong)
to His people,
that He enjoys [the sacredness of the act] for its own sake
with sweetness and honey.

BRIDEGROOM *[sets the candelabrum in the south and says]:*
In the south I set the mystical menorah.

[He sets the table in the north.]
And the table with the bread I set in the north.

BRIDE: With wine in the chalice[61] and boughs of myrtle

---

[59] Yesod literally means "foundation."
[60] The fish is a sexual symbol.
[61] The chalice is a sexual symbol.

> to fortify the Betrothed, to strengthen the weak.
> We make them crowns of precious words
> with seventy wreaths in fifty gates.
> Let the Shechinah be adorned by six Shabbat loaves
> from each side connected with Vavs and Zayins that enter.[62]
>
> BRIDEGROOM: Brought to halt and exorcised will be the impure powers,
> the menacing demons and all kinds of sorceries.

The traditional way to protect against the impure powers: When a man unites with his wife, he should sanctify his heart to his Master (i.e., God) and say:

> BRIDEGROOM: She that is wrapped in a robe is here.[63]
> Thou shalt not enter nor take out,
> it is neither of thee nor of thy lot.
> Return, return, the sea is heaving, its waves await thee.
> I cleave to the holy portion, I am wrapped in the holiness of the
>   King. (Zohar III:9a)

The man should then cover his head and the head of his wife for a short time. In the book that Ashmedai gave to King Solomon, it says that he should then sprinkle clean water[64] around the bed.

The Bridegroom touches her genitals very gently with his phallus and opens them very slightly and carefully.

> BRIDEGROOM: To slice the bread as [done by] the olive tree and the eggs,[65]
> two Jods to use vaguely and explicitly
>
> BRIDE [kisses his phallus and draws it to her opened legs]:
> Clear olive oil that ground in the mill,
> pull the stream inside her with groaning.
> Are there not secrets spoken
> and words hidden
> that are not visible
> [but] concealed and mysterious?[66]

---

[62] The *Vavs* (nails) and *Zayins* (weapons or kinds) are sexual symbols.

[63] The Shechinah

[64] That is, blessed water.

[65] The slices of bread are a symbol for the vulva, and the olive tree with the eggs represent the male organs.

[66] Isaak Luria refers to the sexual analogies.

> BRIDEGROOM: **I will adorn the Bride**
>   **With higher (heavenly) secrets**
>   **within the celebration of holy angels.**

Now the woman builds up the image of the Queen and the man builds up the image of the King. The Queen is a beautiful woman, with a crown and jewelery made of silver. Her garments are night blue and silver. The King is a handsome, dark-bearded man with a golden crown and royal jewelery also made of pure gold. His garments are golden and purple.

Both partners visualize the image very small, inside their hearts. They feel the power of the Queen or King inside them and take a moment to make contact with the Divine Queen or King. Once the contact is made, they let the image grow bigger. Every time they breathe out, the image grows a bit until it has reached nearly the same size as their own body.[67] Each takes a moment to feel her- or himself filled with the consciousness of the Queen or King. Once both are ready, they make eye contact, and the woman speaks:

> BRIDE: **Let him kiss me with the kisses of his mouth, for thy love is better than wine. Thine ointments have a goodly fragrance; thy name is as ointment poured forth; therefore do the maidens love thee.**

The man kisses her.

> BRIDE: **Draw me, we will run after thee; the king hath brought me into his chambers; we will be glad and rejoice in thee, we will find thy love more fragrant than wine! Sincerely do they love thee. I am black, but comely, O ye daughters of Jerusalem, as the tents of Kedar, as the curtains of Solomon. Look not upon me, that I am swarthy, that the sun hath tanned me; my mother's sons were incensed against me, they made me keeper of the vineyards; but mine own vineyard have I not kept. Tell me, O thou whom my soul loveth, where thou feedest, where thou makest thy flock to rest at noon; for why should I be as one that veileth herself beside the flocks of thy companions?**
>
> BRIDEGROOM: **If thou knowest not, O thou fairest among women, go thy way forth by the footsteps of the flock and feed thy kids, beside the shepherds' tents. I have compared thee, O my love, to a steed in**

---

[67] It is advisable (especially if you are new to this kind of work) to keep the image a bit smaller than yourself, for this will help you to control it more easily.

Pharaoh's chariots. Thy cheeks are comely with circlets, thy neck with beads. We will make thee circlets of gold with studs of silver.

BRIDE: While the king sat at his table, my spikenard sent forth its fragrance. My beloved is unto me as a bag of myrrh, that lieth betwixt my breasts. My beloved is unto me as a cluster of henna in the vineyards of En-gedi. Behold, thou art fair, my love; behold, thou art fair; thine eyes are as doves. Behold, thou art fair, my beloved, yea, pleasant; also our couch is leafy. The beams of our houses are cedars, and our panels are cypresses.

I am a rose of Sharon, a lily of the valley.

As a lily among thorns, so is my love among the daughters.

As an apple tree among the trees of the wood, so is my beloved among the sons. Under its shadow I delighted to sit, and its fruit was sweet to my taste. He hath brought me to the banqueting house, and his banner over me is love. "Stay ye me with dainties, refresh me with apples; for I am lovesick." Let his left hand be under my head, and his right hand embrace me. "I adjure ye, O daughters of Jerusalem, by the gazelles, and by the hinds of the field, that ye awaken not, nor stir up love, until it please." Hark! my beloved! behold, he cometh, leaping upon the mountains, skipping upon the hills. My beloved is like a gazelle or a young hart; behold, he standeth behind our wall, he looketh in through the windows, he peereth through the lattice.

My beloved spoke, and said unto me:

BRIDEGROOM: "Rise up, my love, my fair one, and come away.

For, lo, the winter is past, the rain is over and gone; the flowers appear on the earth; the time of singing is come, and the voice of the turtle is heard in our land; the fig tree putteth forth her green figs, and the vines in blossom give forth their fragrance. Arise, my love, my fair one, and come away. O my dove, that art in the clefts of the rock, in the covert of the cliff, let me see thy countenance, let me hear thy voice; for sweet is thy voice, and thy countenance is comely. Take us the foxes, the little foxes, that spoil the vineyards; for our vineyards are in blossom.

BRIDE: My beloved is mine, and I am his, that feedeth among the lilies. Until the day breathe, and the shadows flee away, turn, my beloved, and be thou like a gazelle or a young hart upon the mountains of spices.

[. . .]

BRIDEGROOM: Behold, thou art fair, my love; behold, thou art fair; thine eyes are as doves behind thy veil; thy hair is as a flock of goats that trail down from Mount Gilead. Thy teeth are like a flock of ewes all shaped alike, which are come up from the washing; whereof all are paired, and none faileth among them. Thy lips are like a thread of scarlet, and thy mouth is comely; thy temples are like a pomegranate split open behind thy veil. Thy neck is like the tower of David builded with turrets, whereon there hang a thousand shields, all the armor of the mighty men. Thy two breasts are like two fawns that are twins of a gazelle, which feed among the lilies. Until the day breathe and the shadows flee away, I will get me to the mountain of myrrh, and to the hill of frankincense. Thou art all fair, my love; and there is no spot in thee. Come with me from Lebanon, my bride, with me from Lebanon; look from the top of Amana, from the top of Senir and Hermon, from the lions' dens, from the mountains of the leopards. Thou hast ravished my heart, my sister, my Bride; thou hast ravished my heart with one of thine eyes, with one bead of thy necklace. How fair is thy love, my sister, my Bride! how much better is thy love than wine! and the smell of thine ointments than all manner of spices! Thy lips, O my Bride, drop honey—honey and milk are under thy tongue; and the smell of thy garments is like the smell of Lebanon. A garden shut up is my sister, my Bride; a spring shut up, a fountain sealed. Thy shoots are a park of pomegranates, with precious fruits; henna with spikenard plants, spikenard and saffron, calamus and cinnamon, with all trees of frankincense; myrrh and aloes, with all the chief spices.

Thou art a fountain of gardens, a well of living waters, and flowing streams from Lebanon. Awake, O north wind; and come, thou south; blow upon my garden, that the spices thereof may flow out.

BRIDE: Let my beloved come into his garden,[68] and eat his precious fruits.[69]

BRIDEGROOM: I am come into my garden, my sister, my Bride; I have gathered my myrrh with my spice; I have eaten my honeycomb with my honey; I have drunk my wine with my milk. Eat, O friends; drink, yea, drink abundantly, O beloved.

BRIDE: I sleep, but my heart waketh; Hark! my beloved knocketh:

---

[68] This is of course a sexual analogy. She invites him to have sexual union with her.
[69] To "eat fruits" means to have pleasure.

BRIDEGROOM: "Open to me, my sister, my love, my dove, my unde-filed; for my head is filled with dew, my locks with the drops of the night." I have put off my coat; how shall I put it on? I have washed my feet; how shall I defile them? *[He gently opens her legs and touches her Yesod, but then he withdraws.]*

BRIDE: My beloved put in his hand by the hole of the door,[70] and my heart was moved for him. I rose up to open to my beloved; and my hands dropped with myrrh, and my fingers with flow-ing myrrh, upon the handles of the bar. I opened to my beloved; but my beloved had turned away, and was gone. My soul failed me when he spoke. I sought him, but I could not find him; I called him, but he gave me no answer.

[. . .]

I adjure ye, O daughters of Jerusalem, if ye find my beloved, what will ye tell him? that I am lovesick.

[. . .]

My beloved is shiny and red (ruddy), preeminent above ten thousand.

His head is as the most fine gold, his locks are curled, and black as a raven. His eyes are like doves beside the water brooks; washed with milk, and fitly set. His cheeks are as a bed of spices, as banks of sweet herbs; his lips are as lilies, dropping with flowing myrrh. His hands are as rods of gold set with beryl; his body is as polished ivory overlaid with sapphires. His legs are as pillars of marble, set upon sockets of fine gold; his aspect is like Lebanon, excellent as the cedars. His mouth is most sweet; yea, he is altogether lovely. This is my beloved, and this is my friend, O daughters of Jerusalem.

He kneels or sits between her opened legs.

BRIDE: My beloved is gone down into his garden, to the beds of spices, to feed in the gardens, and to gather lilies. I am my beloved's, and my beloved is mine, that feedeth among the lilies.

BRIDEGROOM: Thou art beautiful, O my love, as Tirzah, comely as Jerusalem, terrible as an army with banners. Turn away thine eyes from me, for they have overcome me. Thy hair is as a flock of goats, that trail down from Gilead. Thy teeth are like a flock of ewes, which

---

[70] Another sexual analogy. The door is a symbol for the female genitals.

are come up from the washing; whereof all are paired, and none faileth among them. Thy temples are like a pomegranate split open behind thy veil. There are threescore queens, and fourscore concubines, and maidens without number. My dove, my undefiled, is but one; she is the only one of her mother; she is the choice one of her that bore her. The daughters saw her, and called her happy; yea, the queens and the concubines, and they praised her. Who is she that looketh forth as the dawn, fair as the moon, clear as the sun, terrible as an army with banners? I went down into the garden of nuts, to look at the green plants of the valley, to see whether the vine budded and the pomegranates were in flower. Before I was aware, my soul set me upon the chariots of my princely people. Return, return, O Shulammite; Return, return, that we may look upon thee. What will ye see in the Shulammite? As it were a dance of two companies.

How beautiful are thy steps in sandals, O prince's daughter!

He kisses her feet.

The roundings of thy thighs are like the links of a chain, the work of the hands of a skilled workman.

He kisses her thighs.

Thy vulva is like a round chalice, wherein no beverage is missing; thy belly is like a heap of wheat set about with lilies.

He kisses her Yesod.

Thy two breasts are like two fawns that are twins of a gazelle.

He kisses her breasts.

Thy neck is as a tower of ivory;

He kisses her neck.

Thine eyes as the pools in Heshbon, by the gate of Bath-rabbim.

He kisses her eyes.

Thy nose is like the tower of Lebanon which looketh toward Damascus.

He kisses her nose.

> Thy head upon thee is like Carmel, and the hair of thy head like purple; the king is held captive in the tresses thereof.

He kisses her head and strokes her hair.

> How fair and how pleasant art thou, O love, for delights!
> This thy stature is like to a palm tree, and thy breasts to clusters of grapes. I said: "I will climb up into the palm tree, I will take hold of the branches thereof; and let thy breasts be as clusters of the vine, and the smell of thy countenance like apples; And the roof of thy mouth like the best wine, that glideth down smoothly for my beloved, moving gently the lips of those that are asleep."

He kisses her mouth with passion.

> BRIDE: I am my beloved's, and his desire is toward me. Come, my beloved, let us go forth into the field; let us lodge in the villages. Let us get up early to the vineyards; let us see whether the vine hath budded, whether the vine blossom be opened, and the pomegranates be in flower; there will I give thee my love. [. . .]

Now the Bride and the Bridegroom perform the sacred sexual union. They still visualize themselves as Queen and King, and during the whole union they are aware of their connection to the Shechinah and the Holy One, blessed be He. They do not perform the sexual union to fulfill their own desire, but rather to offer the joy and pleasure of sexual union as a gift to the Shechinah and her heavenly Spouse. This intention must be kept in mind all the time! Through their union they participate in the Divine Union of the Shechinah (i.e., the Shabbat Queen) and Ze'ir Anpin (i.e., the Holy King), and by doing so, both receive their portion of the divine blessing.

After a while—when she feels the moment is right—the woman speaks:

> BRIDE: Oh that thou wert as my brother, that sucked the breasts of my mother! When I should find thee without, I would kiss thee; yea, and none would despise me.[71] I would lead thee, and bring thee into my mother's house, that thou mightest instruct me; I would cause thee to drink of spiced wine, of the juice of my pomegranate. His left hand should be under my head, and his right hand should embrace me. "I adjure ye, O daughters of Jerusalem:

---

[71] According to Qabbalistic symbolism, the Shechinah can rest only one night each week (during Shabbat) in the arms of the Holy King. During the other days, She is in exile.

Why should ye awaken, or stir up love, until it please?"

BRIDEGROOM: Who is this that cometh up from the wilderness, leaning upon her beloved? Under the apple tree I awakened thee; there thy mother was in travail with thee; there was she in travail and brought thee forth.

BRIDE: Set me as a seal upon thy heart, and as a seal upon thine arm; for love is as strong as death, fervor is as cruel as the grave; the blaze thereof is a blaze of fire, a flame of YAH.

BRIDEGROOM: Many waters cannot quench love, neither can the floods drown it; if a man would give all the goods of his house for love, he would utterly be condemned.[72]

BOTH: So mote it be! Amen.

Now both wholeheartedly thank the Queen and King inside them. It is now time to let the image be removed again. Every time you breathe in, the image becomes smaller, until only a pinpoint of light is left. Keep this point of light inside your heart to remain as a lasting connection to the Divine. Thus every time you repeat this technique, it will become easier and more powerful. (When this is done the rite is closed.)

BRIDE *[goes to the altar and says]:*
With our souls and with our hearts we thank the Divine Powers that have shared Their delight and Their blessings with us in this night. Amen.

[She goes to the east and makes a gesture of removing the seal—as if she takes something and draws it back to her.]

I take back the seal of YOD HEH VAV HEH from the gate of mizrach (east).
I thank ye powers of heaven.
Return to thy abode and be blessed in the Name of the Lord of the Heavens.

[She makes the gesture of closing a veil.]
I close the mizrach.

[She goes to the south and makes a gesture of removing the seal—as if she takes something and draws it back to her.]

---

[72] Because love cannot be bought, nothing compares with love.

I take back the seal of ELOHIM from the gate of darom (south).
I thank ye powers of heaven.
Return to thy abode and be blessed in the Name of the Lord of the divine fire.

[She makes the gesture of closing a veil.]
I close the darom.

[She goes to the west and makes a gesture of removing the seal—as if she takes something and draws it back to her.]
I take back the seal of EL SHADDAI from the gate of Ma'arav (west).
I thank ye powers of the upper sea.
Return to thy abode and be blessed in the Name of the Lord of the waters.

[She makes the gesture of closing a veil.]
I close the ma'arav.

[She goes to the northwest and makes a gesture of removing the seal—as if she takes something and draws it back to her.]
I take back the seal of ADONAI from the gate of tzafon (north).
I thank ye powers of the earth.
Return to thy abode and be blessed in the Name of the Lord of the Universe.

[She makes the gesture of closing a veil.]
I close the tzafon.

Blessing of the Second Meal (Qiddusha Rabbah)

Before the second meal, the head of the house performs a short rite which, in the Talmud, was ironically called the *Qiddusha Rabbah*, the Great Qiddush.[73] For this rite, you will need a chalice filled with wine and two challah loaves—covered, as they were on Shabbat evening.

Read aloud these passages from the Bible.

From *Im Tashiv* (Isaiah 58:13–14):
If thou turn away thy foot because of the Shabbat, from pursuing thy

---

[73] Pesachim 106a.

business on My holy day; and call the Shabbat a delight, and the holy of YHVH (say: Adonai) honourable; and shalt honour it, not doing thy wonted ways, nor pursuing thy business, nor speaking thereof; Then shalt thou delight thyself in YHVH, and I will make thee to ride upon the high places of the earth, and I will feed thee with the heritage of Jacob thy father; for the mouth of YHVH (say: Adonai) hath spoken it.

From *Ve-shamru* (Exodus 31:16–17):

Wherefore the children of Israel shall keep the Shabbat, to observe the Shabbat throughout their generations, for a perpetual covenant. It is a sign between Me and the children of Israel forever; for in six days YHVH (say: Adonai) made heaven and earth, and on the seventh day He ceased from work and rested.

From *Zachor* (Exodus 20:8–11):

Six days shalt thou labour, and do all thy work; but the seventh day is a Shabbat unto YHVH (say: Adonai) thy God, in it thou shalt not do any manner of work, thou, nor thy son, nor thy daughter, nor thy man-servant, nor thy maid-servant, nor thy cattle, nor thy stranger that is within thy gates; for in six days YHVH (say: Adonai) made Heaven and earth, the sea, and all that in them is, and rested on the seventh day; wherefore YHVH (say Adonai) blessed the Shabbat day, and hallowed it. Honour thy father and thy mother, that thy days may be long upon the land which YHVH (say: Adonai) thy God giveth thee.

Then say the blessing over the wine:

Savri maranan ve-rabanan ve-rabotai
(By your leave, my masters and teachers)

Baruch Atah Adonai Eloheynu Melech ha-Olam, Borey pri ha-gafen.
(Blessed art Thou, Lord, our God, King of the Universe,
Creator of the fruit of the vine.)

The woman and other people present may reply "Amen." The man drinks at least 2 to 3 ounces of the wine, and then he passes the chalice to all others present and shares the wine with them. Then the washing of the hands is performed, and the blessing over the bread is spoken, as described earlier in this chapter.

Baruch Atah Adonai Eloheynu Melech ha-Olam,

> asher qidshanu be-mitzvotav,
> ve-tzivanu al netilat yadayim.
> (Blessed art Thou, Lord, our God, King of the Universe,
> who has blessed us with His commandments
> and who commands us to ritually purify our hands.)
>
> **Baruch Atah Adonai Eloheynu Melech ha-Olam**
> **Ha-Motzi lechem min ha-aretz.**
> (Blessed art Thou, Lord, our God, King of the Universe,
> who brings forth bread from the earth.)

The woman and other people present may reply "Amen."

Blessing of the Third Meal (Seudah Shlishit)

The third meal is called Seudah Shlishit (Hebrew: "third meal") and is served in the afternoon before sundown. This meal often consists of bread, cake, and salads or gefilte fish (i.e., filled fish). It may be the smallest meal, but it is very important, because by eating this meal, we fulfill the commandment to have three meals on Shabbat.

Seudah Shlishit is often celebrated with spiritual songs (zemirot) such as "Yedid Nefesh" and "Mizmor Le-David" (i.e., the Psalm 23).

The last two blessings of the second meal are also repeated before the third meal. First, the washing of the hands is performed, and then the blessing over the bread is spoken as described earlier in this chapter:

> **Baruch Atah Adonai Eloheynu Melech ha-Olam,**
> **asher qidshanu be-mitzvotav,**
> **ve-tzivanu al netilat yadayim.**
> (Blessed art Thou, Lord, our God, King of the Universe,
> who has blessed us with His commandments
> and who commands us to ritually purify our hands.)
>
> **Baruch Atah Adonai Eloheynu Melech ha-Olam**
> **Ha-Motzi lechem min ha-aretz.**
> (Blessed art Thou, Lord, our God, King of the Universe,
> who brings forth bread from the earth.)

The woman and other people present may reply "Amen."

Woodcut of Havdalah

The Ritual of Separation (Havdalah)

When we open the quarters in a magical ritual, and thus open our soul for a sacred moment, we must close when the sacred moment is over. The same applies to the Shabbat.

The Havdalah ritual marks the end of Shabbat. (Havdalah means "separation"—the departure of Shabbat and the distinction between the holy and the profane.) Traditionally, it should be performed on Saturday night when three stars can be seen in the sky, or about forty-five minutes after sundown.[74] The Chassidim, in particular, perform the Havdalah as late as possible, in order to make Shabbat last as long as possible: "When Shabbat comes to an end, Israel below must delay it, because this is a great and high day, and on that day a great and precious Guest is present. For that reason one should detain it and show that there is no hurry to press the Holy Guest" (Zohar II:207a).

Chassidic stories emphasize the point that we should delay Havdalah as long as possible. The following amusing tale was meant to inspire the reader to honor Shabbat and not waste this precious gift.

> The holy Reb Shmelke lived next door to a mitnaged, a fierce opponent of the Chassidim, who understood the letter of the Law in the most rigid way. He therefore performed Havdalah as soon as three

---

[74] Consult any Jewish calendar for the precise times of the Havdalah ritual.

stars appeared in the sky. Reb Shmelke, on the other hand, continued to observe the Shabbat far into the night. And this bothered his neighbor to no end.

This neighbor took it upon himself to save Reb Shmelke from this transgression. As soon as three stars appeared, he would open his window and shout: "Three stars! Time for Havdalah!" These shouts would disturb Reb Shmelke's reveries. Nonetheless, Reb Shmelke restrained himself and never said anything about it to his neighbor. Instead, he continued to savor the Shabbat for many hours after his neighbor had reminded him that the Shabbat was over.

Seeing that he had failed to convince Reb Shmelke to change his ways, the neighbor decided on a more drastic approach. As soon as the three stars appeared, he went outside, picked up some pebbles, and threw them through Reb Shmelke's window. One of those pebbles struck Reb Shmelke, tearing him from the arms of the Shabbat Queen. And Reb Shmelke not only felt the pain of his own loss, but also knew that his neighbor had made a terrible mistake. And before many months had passed, the neighbor became sick and died.

Some months later, when Reb Shmelke was sitting at the Shabbat table, about the time the three stars first appeared, he suddenly smiled mysteriously. And he mumbled the words "From below they look above, from above, below." None of his Chassidim understood what he meant, but Reb Shmelke refused to tell them until the end of the Shabbat. Then he said: "The soul of our neighbor was sent to Gehenna for his sins, where he is punished all week long but spared on the Shabbat. But as soon as three stars appear, the angels drag him back to Gehenna. And all the way there he shouts 'But Reb Shmelke is still celebrating the Shabbat!'"[75]

To perform the ritual, you will need a cup of wine, some fragrant spices (called *bessamim*), and a Havdalah candle, which is a candle with several wicks. The whole ceremony is usually performed by the head of the house.

---

[75] Eastern Europe, nineteenth century. This story is attributed to Miriam of Mohilev, the sister of Reb Shmelke, who is said to have told it to Reb Abraham Yehoshua Heschel, the Apter Rebbe. Quoted from Howard Schwartz, *Gabriel's Palace: Jewish Mystical Tales* (New York: Oxford University Press, 1993), "The Three Stars," 227.

Hineh El yishuati, evtach ve-lo efchad.
(Behold, God is my salvation, I will trust and will not be afraid.)

Ki azi ve-zimrat Yah, Adonai va-yehi li le-yeshuah.
(For my strength and song is Yah. Adonai has come to my salvation.)

U-shavtem mayim be-sasson mi-maayeni ha-yeshuah.
(With joy shalt thou draw water out of the wells of salvation.)

La-Adonai ha-yeshuah al amcha birchatecha selah.
(In Adonai is our salvation; over Thy people give Thy Blessing, Selah.)

Adonai Tzevaot imanu missgav lanu Elohei Yaakov selah.
(The Lord of Hosts is with us; our protection is the God of Jacob, Selah.

Adonai Tzevaot ashrey Adam botech be-cha
(Lord of Hosts, lucky is the man who trusts in Thee.)

Adonai Hoshiyah, ha-Melech yaanenu va-yom qarenu
(Adonai, who redeems, may the King hear us on the day of our calling.)

All others answer:

La-yehudim haytah orah ve-simcha ve-sasson vi-kar, ken tihyeh lanu.
(For the Jewish people there was light and joy, gladness and honor.
So may it be for us.)

The head of the house continues and lifts the cup filled with wine:

Kos yeshuot essa u-be-Shem Adonai ekra.
(I will lift the cup of salvation, and call upon the Name of Adonai.)

The Blessing of the Wine

The wine is a symbol of the joy of the Shabbat, which is soon going to be over. The cup should be filled to overflowing to symbolize the overflowing of good things for the coming week. Lift the wine with the right hand and bless it, but do not yet drink from the wine.

**Baruch Atah Adonai Eloheynu Melech ha-Olam,
Borey pri ha-gafen.**
(Blessed art Thou, Lord, our God, King of the Universe,
Creator of the fruit of the vine.)

The woman and other people present may reply "Amen."

The Blessing of the Spices

The spices (bessamim) are a symbol of the sweetness of the Shabbat, and when we smell them, they are meant to comfort us, for the Shabbat will soon be over, and the additional soul (Neshamah Yetera) that man is given on Shabbat will leave us: "Hence, at the conclusion of Shabbat, we should smell spices (Bessamim) to restore the Nefesh by the fragrance, instead of the high and holy fragrance[76] that left it. And the best spice [to do so] is myrtle. For the sustenance of the holy place, from which the souls emanate, is the myrtle. It also gives sustenance to the Nefesh of man, which is above, so it may be maintained when it is left naked (i.e., without the additional soul)" (Zohar 2, 208 b).

We breathe in the spices and keep in our minds throughout the week the memory of the pleasant aroma of Shabbat, until the next Shabbat. In addition to myrtle, the spices also often include cloves, cinnamon, and bay leaves, and they are often kept in a decorated container called a bessamim box. When everybody has had a chance to smell the scent, say:

> **Baruch Atah Adonai, Eloheynu Melech ha-Olam, Borey miney vessamim.**
> (Blessed art Thou, Lord, our God, King of the Universe,
> Creator of varieties of spices.)

The woman and other people present may reply "Amen."

The Blessing of the Fire

Because making fire is forbidden on Shabbat,[77] the lighting of a candle is a symbol for the end of Shabbat. For this purpose, we light the Havdalah candle, which has two (or more) wicks.[78] The wicks are twisted together and symbolize the union of the two principles, which were represented by two separate candles at the beginning of Shabbat.[79] The Bride and the Bridegroom are now united.[80]

---

[76] A play on words: *recha* = fragrance/Ruach = spirit. This means the Holy Spirit, which is the additional soul.

[77] This has been mentioned before. Lighting a fire is forbidden on Shabbat also because it is seen as an act of creation. Because God has rested from his creative work on Shabbat, so man should refrain from performing acts of creation on Shabbat.

[78] Some say it should have at least three wicks, while others consider two wicks sufficient.

[79] They are sometimes also interpreted as Creation and Redemption becoming one.

[80] Compare to the blessing that many Qabbalists say when donning the *tallit* (prayer shawl): "[I do this] For the sake of the unification of the Holy One, blessed be He, and His Shechinah, in awe and in love to unify the *Yod-Heh* and *Vav-Heh* in perfect unity, in the name of all Israel."

God created light on the first day of the week (Genesis 1:3), and He created fire on the first day of the second week and gave it to Adam.[81] Both events are remembered by the blessing of the fire.[82]

To perform the second benediction, light the Havdalah candle[83] and say the blessing:

> **Baruch Atah Adonai, Eloheynu Melech ha-Olam,**
> **Borey meorey ha-esh.**
> (Blessed art Thou, Lord, our God, King of the Universe,
> Creator of the lights of fire.)

The woman and others present may reply "Amen." Then everybody holds their hand up to the flame with curved fingers, so that the light falls on the fingernails, casting a shadow on the palms of their hands. Thus we make use of the light,[84] and the distinction between light and shadow is visible.[85]

This is the secret meaning of the fingernails at the back of the fingers, and the tips of the fingers on the inside. The fingernails at the back of the fingers are the "Outer Countenance" (Anpin Aacherim) that needs to be illuminated from within, that is from the candle. This Countenance is called "Back" (Achoraim). The fingers inside

---

[81] This is, of course, a parallel to Prometheus in Greek mythology. Fire is a symbol of knowledge and enlightenment.

[82] Also note that the blessing is made over the lights (plural!) of fire. The Havdalah candle must have two wicks, just as the lights of the sun and the moon are two, male and female. "There were two things God thought to create on Shabbat Eve, but they were not created until the Shabbat ended. At the ending of Shabbat, the Holy One, Blessed be He, inspired the first man (Adam ha-Rishon) with knowledge similar to the higher doctrine, and he brought two stones, rubbed them together, and created fire" (Babylonian Talmud, Pesachim 54a.

[83] A Havdalah candle can easily be made by placing two ordinary candles in a clean can, and pouring hot water over them. When they are soft, remove them and twist them together. If you dip them a few times in the can with the melted wax, a new layer of wax will form on the outside and make them appear as one. (Between dipping them, always cool them, by air or cold water.)

[84] The Talmud does not permit a blessing to be made over a light, unless that light is used afterward (Berachot 53b).

[85] The exoteric explanation is to show that the fingernails are clean and to thereby prove that no work has been done on Shabbat.

without nails are the "Inner Countenance" (Anpin Penimiyim) that is hidden. This is the secret of the verse "and thou shalt see My Back (Achorai), but My Face (Panai) shall not be seen" (Exodus 33:23). For "My Back" is represented by the nails at the back of the fingers and "My Face" is represented by the fingers on the inside the part without nails, the "Inner Countenance." When we say the blessing over the candle, we should let the nails at the back of the fingers be illumined (illuminated) from within, that is from the candle. But the inner side of the fingers must not be presented to the light of the candle, [but] be illumined (illuminated) from within, that is from the candle, for they do not need any illumination other then the most high of the Highest Candle (i.e., the Divine Light) which is hidden, and concealed and not revealed in any way. Thus, the nails at the back of the fingers should be presented, but the inner side of the fingers must not be presented to the candle, as it is hidden and is illuminated from [its] hiding. It is innermost and from inside it is illuminated. It is above and from above it is illuminated. Happy is Israel in this world and in the world to come.[86]

Think about the visible and the hidden aspect of the Divine Light.

Blessing of the Havdalah

The fourth and final blessing is the Havdalah itself, the symbolic separation of the sacred and the profane. Lift the cup again and say:

> **Baruch Atah Adonai Eloheynu Melech ha-Olam,**
> (Blessed art Thou, Lord, our God, King of the Universe)
>
> **ha-mavdil beyn qodesh le-chol**
> (who distinguishes between the holy and the profane)
>
> **beyn or le-choshech, beyn Yisrael la-amim,**
> (between light and dark, between Israel and the nations)
>
> **beyn yom ha-shevi'i le-sheshet yemey ha-maasseh**
> (between the seventh day and the six days of labor)
>
> **Baruch Atah Adonai, ha-mavdil beyn qodesh le-chol.**
> (Blessed art Thou, Lord, who distinguishes between the holy and the profane.)

---

[86] Zohar II:208b–209a.

The woman and others present may reply "Amen." Now the head of the house drinks from the cup. Unlike Qiddush, according to tradition, the cup is not passed around in the ritual of Havdalah.[87]

The Havdalah candle is then extinguished in the wine.[88] The traditional method is to pour some wine onto a plate and dowse the candle in it. Yet some just turn the candle upside down and dowse the candle directly in the wine.[89]

Some follow the custom of dipping a finger into the spilled wine, and putting some drops onto the eyelids or ears as a spell or blessing to see and hear good things during the coming week.

Each turns to his beloved and says, "Shavua tov" (a good week). Then all sing together the song of Elijah:

> *Eliyahu ha-Navi,*
> *Eliyahu ha-Tishbi,*
> *Eliyahu, Eliyahu,*
> *Eliyahu ha-Giladi.*
> *Bi-m'herah ve-yameynu yavo eleynu,*
> *Im Mashiach ben David,*
> *Im Mashiach ben David.*
>
> (Elijah the prophet,
> Elijah the Tishbite,
> Elijah, Elijah,
> Elijah the Giladite.
> Soon, may he come in our days,
> may he come to us
> with the Messiah, son of David,
> with the Messiah, son of David.)

---

[87] Sometimes, all the men drink from the cup; sometimes, only the head of the house drinks. Women traditionally do not drink from the cup, because this ritual is related to Eve eating from the Tree of Knowledge (which, according to some sources, grew grapes to make wine). The end of the Shabbat can be associated with the expulsion from Paradise. Because it is seen to be unlucky to "repeat" the eating from the Tree of Knowledge, women do not drink the wine. Another popular superstition says that a woman who drinks from the Havdalah cup will grow a moustache.

[88] There is a custom of lighting two new candles from the Havdalah candle before it is extinguished so that the light and blessing of Shabbat lasts throughout the week.

[89] In any case, the male principle (fire/candle) is united with the female principle (wine, i.e., water/cup).

Melaveh Malka: The Meal after Shabbat

King David asked God to tell him when he would die. When God refused to answer, David asked if he could let him know what day of the week it would be. So God told David that he would die on Shabbat. From that time on, David spent every Shabbat studying the Torah, for he knew that the angel of death cannot take away someone while he is studying the Torah. After every Shabbat was over, he celebrated that he was still alive. This celebration is the origin of Melaveh Malka.

Melaveh Malka means "escorting the Queen." We must honor the departure of the Queen Shabbat as we honor Her arrival. In the Jewish tradition, hospitality is taken very seriously, and it is customary to accompany a guest to the door—or even further if there is a potential source of danger. The Talmud clearly states this need to escort a traveler (Sotah 46b). Therefore, at least the same courtesy must be accorded the Divine Guest, the Queen Shabbat herself. To honor and escort Her, we prepare and eat the meal of Melaveh Malka.

If we do not have a meal after Havdalah, we would only have two meals between morning and midnight, thus we have not done more than on weekdays.[90] Thus this additional meal ensures that we have truly kept the commandment to celebrate Shabbat.

Melaveh Malka should be held during the first four hours after Havdalah and before midnight (*chatzot*). No major work should be done before Melaveh Malka.

Usually, candles are lit for this meal, and it would be ideal to use those candles that were lit from the Havdalah candle. The meal itself usually consists of the remains of the Shabbat challah, bread, and some cooked food or a light dish. Among the Chassidim is a custom to tell stories about the Baal-Shem-Tov during this meal.

---

[90] Two meals were considered normal in ancient times; three meals were seen as something special, thus the commandment to have three meals on Shabbat.

23

Tu B'Shevat

The New Year of the Trees

> *And there are four new year dates: The first of Nissan, new year for kings and festivals; the first of Ellul, new year for animal tithes; Rabbi Elazar and Rabbi Shimon say: the first of Tishrey, new year for calculation of the calendar, sabbatical years and jubilees, for planting and sowing; the first of Shevat—new year for trees, according to the school of Shammai; the school of Hillel says: the fifteenth of Shevat.*
>
> MISHNAH, ROSH HA-SHANAH 1,1

Tu B'Shevat means simply "the fifteenth day of the month Shevat." Fifteen is written in Hebrew with the letters *Tet* (ט) and *Vav* (ו) to avoid using *Yod* and *Heh,* the letters of the Divine Name, for profane purposes.

Because the Jewish calendar is a moon calendar, every month starts with

Woodcut of Tu B'Shevat

the new moon, and, therefore, the fifteenth day will always be a full moon. Shevat is the month corresponding to the sign of Aquarius and the fifteenth day of the month. Shevat is the full moon in late January or early February. Most of the annual rain in Israel falls before Tu B'Shevat, when the resources of the old year have been used up, and the new are on their way.

According to tradition, it is the time when the Court in Heaven decides which trees stay alive and which shall die in the coming year, in the same way as this is decided on Rosh ha-Shanah (first day of the month Tishrey) for human beings. This makes Tu B'Shevat a time of clearing out the old and preparing for the new awakening of plant life, comparable to the Celtic Imbolg (Candlemas) or the German Fasnacht or Karneval.

The fifteenth Shevat is a counterpart of the fifteenth Av (six months later), when the last of nine wood sacrifices for the Levites is made.[1]

This festival is of great significance to the Qabbalists, and a special *seder*—a ritual meal—is celebrated. The basic concept of this ritual was composed by the great Qabbalist Isaac Luria, called the Ari (1534–1572), who is also supposed to be the original compiler of a collection of readings published in 1753 from the scriptures and Midrashic literature and meant to be recited during and after this celebration: *Pri Etz Hadar* (Fruit of the Goodly Tree—meaning the etrog, or citron).

---

[1] There is also a custom to light fires on this day. This may be compared to the fire celebrations of Midsummer and Lughnasah in the Celtic tradition.

Preparation

This is a ritual that can be either celebrated on a simple level with your whole family or brought to a higher and more spiritual level with a dedicated group. (For this reason, I have assigned the roles of this ritual to the four officers used in ceremonial magic.) There is much more spiritual potential in this ritual than a first impression might reveal. (One person who once took part in it for the first time, and who was rather skeptical about the choice of symbolism, told me that once he had performed it, the effect was amazing. He had so many deep realizations that he was still busy writing notes more than one hour after the ritual.) Please note that this ritual is not only about trees, but is also about the soul of man: "For man is [like] a tree of the field" (Deuteronomy 20:19). Wear white garments to perform it, if possible, and prepare a variety of different fruits. (A list of possible fruits can be found on page 364 at the end of this chapter.) Look for suitable passages from the Bible, Talmud, and Zohar to be read after the ceremony. I leave up to you if and how you will ritually open and close the quarters for this ritual.

The Opening

OFFICER OF THE EAST: **This is the day on which Adonai our God will sit in judgment on all trees on earth.**
In Heaven will be decided which trees are good and which are bad, which trees will blossom in the coming year, and which will wither, which trees will be cut down and which will be planted.
All this will be decided by God's Wisdom
Let us therefore think of all the trees and let us think of the Tree of Trees, the Etz Chaim, the Tree of Life, which has its roots in Heaven and its fruits down here in our world. Let us now contact the higher spheres and strengthen the flow of the Shefa by eating the fruit.
By this action we will do Tiqqun and heal that which broke and came out of balance.

Shefa is the flow of Divine Influx, which may be seen symbolically as the sap of the Tree of Life. Tiqqun is the process of repairing the broken vessels of the lower Sefirot. By connecting ourselves to the Divine, sending our positive thoughts upward, and becoming aware of our sins—especially the first sin of Adam and Eve—we lift the spiritual level of humanity and the entire world.

Hand Washing

The officer of the west fills a large bowl with flower-scented water that is not too cold. Then he takes a small cup to pour the water over everyone's hands. Have towels ready. Say this blessing based on that which is traditionally recited when washing the hands before eating bread.[2]

> **Baruch Atah Adonai Eloheynu Melech ha-Olam,**
> **asher kidshanu be-mitzvotav, ve-tzivanu al netilat yadayim.**
> (Blessed art Thou, Lord, our God, King of the World, who has
> blessed us with His commandments and who commands us to
> ritually purify our hands.)

The First Cup of Wine

OFFICER OF THE NORTH *[fills the cup with white wine and speaks the blessing over the wine]:*

Baruch Atah Adonai Eloheynu Melech ha-Olam Borey pri ha-gafen.
[Blessed art Thou, Lord, our God, King of the World,
Creator of the fruit of the vine.]

THE OFFICER OF THE NORTH *[lifts the wine and says]:*
   This is the first cup of wine
   The symbol of the whiteness of the winter of Assiah

OFFICER OF THE SOUTH: **For YHVH thy God, bringeth thee into a good land, a land of brooks of water, fountains and depths, springing forth in valleys and hills, a land of wheat and barley, and vines and fig trees and pomegranates, a land of olive trees and honey, a land wherein thou shalt eat bread without scarceness, thou shalt not lack anything in it, a land whose stones are iron, and out of whose hills thou mayest dig brass. And thou shalt eat and be satisfied, and bless YHVH thy God for the good land which He hath given thee. (Deuteronomy 8:7–10)**

The First Fruit: Walnut

OFFICER OF THE NORTH *[speaks the blessing over the walnut]:*

Baruch Atah Adonai Eloheynu Melech ha-Olam Borey pri ha-etz.

---

[2] See chapter 22, Shabbat.

> (Blessed art Thou, Lord, our God, King of the World,
> Creator of the fruits of the tree.)

This is the first fruit of the tree.
Hidden within a hard shell is a nourishing fruit.
Therefore, the walnut is the symbol of Assiah,
for the World of Making is outwardly hard,
but hidden therein is spiritual nourishment.

The officer of the north offers the walnut to everyone present.

ALL [*take the walnut and say*]: **Awake, O north wind; and come, thou south; blow upon my garden, that the spices thereof may flow out. Let my beloved come into his garden, and eat his precious fruits.** (Song of Songs 4:16)

The beloved is God and the garden is a symbol for the world of Assiah. Thus we have an invocation to God to come to us and our world.

ALL: **By eating these fruit, we connect ourselves to the Tree of Life.**

Everyone eats thereof and contemplates the meaning of this symbol.

OFFICER OF THE NORTH: **Rabbi Tarfon likened the people of Israel to a pile of walnuts. He would say: If one walnut is removed, each and every walnut in the pile will be shaken.** (Midrash, Avot de Rabbi Nathan 18:1)

The people of Israel are spiritually Yisra-El—Men of God. In other words, they are Qabbalists or servants of God.

The Second Cup of Wine

OFFICER OF THE SOUTH [*fills the cup with white wine and a bit of red wine and speaks the blessing over the wine*]:

Baruch Atah Adonai Eloheynu Melech ha-Olam Borey pri ha-gafen.
> (Blessed art Thou, Lord, our God, King of the World,
> Creator of the fruit of the vine.)

OFFICER OF THE SOUTH [*lifts the wine and says*]:
This is the second cup of wine.
To the whiteness of the winter cometh the warm redness of Yetzirah.
The dawn of spring is breaking through the icy coldness.[3]

---

[3] Yetzirah is the "mold" of Assiah. Therefore, the spring to come in Assiah will be anticipated in Yetzirah.

OFFICER OF THE NORTH: And all these blessings shall come upon thee, and overtake thee, if thou shalt hearken unto the voice of YHVH thy God. Blessed shalt thou be in the city, and blessed shalt thou be in the field. Blessed shall be the fruit of thy body, and the fruit of thy land, and the fruit of thy cattle, the increase of thy kine, and the young of thy flock. Blessed shall be thy basket and thy kneading trough. Blessed shalt thou be when thou comest in, and blessed shalt thou be when thou goest out. (Deuteronomy 28:2–6)

The Second Fruit: Date

OFFICER OF THE SOUTH *[speaks the blessing over the date]*:

Baruch Atah Adonai Eloheynu Melech ha-Olam Borey pri ha-etz.
(Blessed art Thou, Lord, our God, King of the World,
Creator of the fruits of the tree.)

This is the second fruit of the tree.
Hidden within a nurturing fruit is a hard stone.
Therefore, the date is the symbol of Yetzirah,
for the World of Formation is outwardly soft and formable,
but hidden therein is the stone of our ego.

The officer of the south offers the date to everyone present.

ALL *[take the date and say]*: May it be His Will that we should be as upright as the date palm, as it is written: "The righteous shall flourish as the date-palm." (Psalm 92:13)
By eating this fruit, we connect ourselves to the Tree of Life.

Everyone eats thereof and contemplates the meaning of this symbol.

OFFICER OF THE SOUTH: No part of the palm tree is wasted. The dates are for eatin, the lulav branches are for waving in praise on Sukkot, the dried thatch is for roofing, the fibers are for ropes, the palm fronds are for sieves, and the trunk is for house beams. Similarly, no one is worthless in Israel. Some are scholars, some do Mitzvot (good deeds/religious duties), and some give for charity. (Midrash, Bamidbar Rabbah 3:1)

The Third Cup of Wine

OFFICER OF THE WEST *[fills the cup with half white wine and half red wine and speaks the blessing over the wine]:*

Baruch Atah Adonai Eloheynu Melech ha-Olam Borey pri ha-gafen.
(Blessed art Thou, Lord, our God, King of the World,
Creator of the fruit of the vine.)

OFFICER OF THE WEST *[lifts the wine]:*
This is the third cup of wine.
The redness and the whiteness are in balance,
and from this polarity emerges the creative power of Beriah

OFFICER OF THE EAST: **And God said: "Let the earth put forth grass, herb yielding seed, and fruit-tree bearing fruit after its kind, wherein is the seed thereof, upon the earth." And it was so.** (Genesis 1:11)

The Third Fruit: Fig

OFFICER OF THE WEST *[speaks the blessing over the fig]:*

Baruch Atah Adonai Eloheynu Melech ha-Olam Borey pri ha-etz.
(Blessed art Thou, Lord, our God, King of the World,
Creator of the fruits of the tree.)

This is the third fruit of the tree.
Nurturing and edible is the whole fruit.
Therefore, the fig is the symbol of Beriah,
For the World of Creation in which our Higher Soul liveth
is pure and exalted and above all matter.

The officer of the west offers the fig to everyone present.

ALL *[take a fig and say]:* **Be not afraid, ye beasts of the field; for the pastures of the wilderness do spring, for the tree beareth its fruit, the fig tree and the vine do yield their strength.** (Joel 2:22)
By eating these fruit, we connect ourselves to the Tree of Life.

Everyone eats thereof and contemplates the meaning of this symbol.

OFFICER OF THE WEST: Why are the words of the Torah compared to a fig tree? As a fig tree yields its fruit whenever it is shaken, so does the Torah always yield new teachings whenever it is repeated. (Babylonian Talmud, Eruwin 54 a/b) [Because all the figs do not ripen at the same time, the more we search the tree, the more figs we find in it. So it is with the words of Torah. The more they are studied, the more delight that is taken in them.]

The Fourth Cup of Wine

OFFICER OF THE EAST [fills the cup with red wine and speaks the blessing over the wine]:

Baruch Atah Adonai Eloheynu Melech ha-Olam Borey pri ha-gafen.
(Blessed art Thou, Lord, our God, King of the World,
Creator of the fruit of the vine.)

OFFICER OF THE EAST [lifts the wine]:
This is the fourth cup of wine,
The pure redness of the spiritual power of Atzilut.

OFFICER OF THE WEST: And the angel of YHVH appeared unto him in a flame of fire out of the midst of a bush; and he looked, and, behold, the bush burned with fire, and the bush was not consumed. (Exodus 3:2)

The Fourth Fruit: Etrog (Citron)

The etrog—from the root תרג—is literally "the bright one," a fruit with special significance in the Jewish religion.

OFFICER OF THE EAST [speaks the blessing over the etrog]:

Baruch Atah Adonai Eloheynu Melech ha-Olam Borey pri ha-etz.
(Blessed art Thou, Lord, our God, King of the World,
Creator of the fruits of the tree.)

This is the fourth fruit of the tree
Yet there is none among the fruits that suits Atzilut,
But closest to the World of Emanations is the one that is called
Fruit of the Goodly Tree,
the etrog is "the bright one."

When man ate from the Tree of Knowledge,
he separated himself from his Divine Origin.
And therefore, it is said that the sour taste of the etrog
corresponds to the taste of the fruit of the Tree of Knowledge.
Therefore, let us remember this,
and by eating this fruit let us renew the dedication to our Creator.

The officer of the east offers the etrog to everyone present.

ALL [take an etrog and say]: Blessed is the man that trusteth in YHVH, and whose trust YHVH is. For he shall be as a tree planted by the waters, and that spreadeth out its roots by the river, and shall not see when heat cometh, but its foliage shall be luxuriant; and shall not be anxious in the year of drought, neither shall cease from yielding fruit. (Jeremiah 17:7–8)

By eating these fruit, we connect ourselves to the Tree of Life.

Everyone eats thereof and contemplates the meaning of this symbol.

OFFICER OF THE EAST: "Rabbi Yochanan used to say: If you happen to be standing with a sapling in your hand and someone says to you: 'Behold the Messiah has come!' first plant the tree, and then go out to greet the Messiah." (Midrash, Avot de Rabbi Nathan 8,31)

ALL: Go thy way, eat thy bread with joy, and drink thy wine with a merry heart; for God hath already accepted thy works. (Ecclesiastes 9:7)

All stay for a while and contemplate the symbolism of this festival. At the end of the seder, everyone plants an etrog seed. The tree will then provide fruits for the Sukkot festival.

On this day, greet all trees when you see them, and wish them a happy new year. This may feel a bit strange in the beginning, but never mind—do it silently if you wish. This is a chance to communicate with these beings. Remember that tradition says that King Solomon himself used to speak with plants and animals, and you may well get an answer if you listen with an open heart. Note that trees are simple but pure beings, and their aspiration to the light can be a source of great spiritual inspiration to us.

Fruits for the New Year of the Trees

- Fruits with shells (Assiah): walnut, hazelnut, coconut, almond, pistachio, sharon, orange, tangerine, grapefruit, starfruit, pomegranate, papaya, pineapple, banana
- Fruits with a stone (Yetzirah): date, olive, cherry, peach, plum, apricot, avocado, mango
- Pure fruits (Beriah): fig, grape, apple, pear, strawberry, raspberry, blueberry, kiwi
- Special fruit (Atzilut): etrog (citron)

Contacting the Maggid

The Inner Plane Teacher

The word *Maggid* (מגיד) means "one who speaks or tells."[1] Though in exoteric language it is used for a preacher, the esoteric meaning of the word *Maggid* is that of an Inner Plane Teacher—that is, a higher being of angelic or divine origin in telepathic contact with an incarnated human being in order to teach humanity. Some *Maggidim* (plural of Maggid), such as Elijah or Henoch (Chanoch), were once incarnated human beings. Others are divine beings or principles, such as the Shechinah, the Divine Mother or the spirit of the Mishnah (i.e., the oral Torah).

Higher guidance is essential on the spiritual path. Not every type of higher guidance, however, is the same. A person who has established a conscious contact with an Inner Plane Teacher is called a *mediator* in modern occult terminology.[2] If the person can contact the Inner Plane Teacher

---

[1] From *higid* (hifil of נגד), which means "to tell," "to inform," "to say."

[2] If he or she is in contact with more than one Inner Plane Teacher, we speak of a cosmic mediator.

only in trance, he or she is called a *medium*. Unlike a mediator, a medium is totally unaware of the message that comes through.

Not every reader of this book will become a high-level mediator, but the majority will be able to make a certain amount of contact. The first higher contact will always be the Higher Self of the individual. If the seeker's dedication is strong enough, he may further contact another Inner Plane Teacher. The three most important contacts in the Qabbalah are Elijah, Metatron (i.e., Henoch or Chanoch), and the Shechinah.[3] Yet there are many other (lesser) Inner Plane Teachers that will help the student of the Qabbalah on his spiritual path.

The most well-known mediator in the Qabbalistic tradition was Joseph Qaro (1488–1575), chief rabbi of Safed (Tzefat) from 1546. He is most famous for being the author of the *Shulchan Aruch* (Set Table), the most well-known and the main authoritative source of the Halachah (Jewish Law) after the Talmud. He was also the halachic teacher of the famous Qabbalist Moses Qordovero, who founded the famous Qabbalistic Academy in Safed, where later the great Isaak Luria taught.

Joseph Qaro's Maggid identified itself as the Spirit of the Mishnah. The Mishnah was called the oral Torah, and it is considered to have been given to Moses together with the written Torah. It must be understood, however, that the corpus of texts commonly known as the Mishnah (as written down by Yehudah ha-Nasi around the year 200 CE) does not contain the entire oral Torah. The mystical teachings were considered too holy and were said to be deliberately excluded from the written texts. Therefore, when Joseph Qaro's Maggid is called the Spirit of the Mishnah, we must not only think of the well-known halachic text, but also of the corpus of mystical teachings that remained oral. Joseph Qaro's Maggid also identifies itself in other passages as the Shechinah, which here can be seen as the Divine Presence behind the Torah.

The Qabbalist Shlomo ben Moshe Halevi Alqabetz (ca. 1505–1576), composer of the mystical song "Lecha Dodi"[4] and brother-in-law of Moses Qordovero—and one who studied the Qabbalah with Qordovero—wrote an eyewitness report of how Joseph Qaro's Maggid spoke through Qaro's mouth. His report is very valuable, for he gives us a very accurate idea of what can be experienced if a true Maggid speaks through a trained mediator.

---

[3] These were known in other cultures as well. The Egyptians called Metatron by the name of Horus, the Shechinah by the name of Isis, and Elijah by the name of Anubis.

[4] See chapter 22, Shabbat.

He describes how the tone of voice changed significantly, and, most important, the awe that the presence of the Maggid inspired in the audience.

The Chassid [Joseph Qaro] and I his servant and your servants amongst the Chaverim (the Qabbalists) we agreed to stay awake on the night of Shavuot[5] and keep the sleep from our eyes. And thanks to God we did so, we took care that we did not interrupt [this] one moment. Even if you hear it, your souls will be enlivened by it. And this is the order of the Tiqqunim (recitations to bring about the healing of the world) I did in this night:

First we read the Torah from Parashah (section) Bereshit (Genesis 1:1–6, 8) to "And [the Heaven and the earth] were finished" (Genesis 2:1) in a melody in a great voice. After that "In the third month" (Exodus 19:1) until the end of the sequence. More from the Parashah Mishpatim (Exodus 21:1–24:18) "And unto Moses He said" (Exodus 24:1) until the end of the sequence. More from the Parashah Va-Etchanan (Deuteronomy 3:23–7:11) "And Moses called all Israel" (Deuteronomy 5:1) until the end of the Parashah "Hear, O Israel" (Deuteronomy 6:4). More from the Parashah Ve-sot Ha-Berachah (Deuteronomy 33:1–34:12) "And Moses goeth up" (Deuteronomy 34:1) until "before the eyes of all Israel" (Deuteronomy 34:12). More the Haftarah (section from the Prophets) "Now it came to pass in the thirtieth year" (Ezekiel 1:1) and the Haftarah "A prayer" from Habakkuk the prophet (3:1). After that the psalm "The heavens declare" (Psalm 19) and psalm "Let God arise" (Psalm 68). After that the alphabet without singing. After that the Megilah (scroll) of the Song of Songs and the entire Megilah of Ruth. And after that the last passages from Chronicles. And all this [we did] with awe, reverence, melody and appreciation. No one will believe what will be told [about what happened then].

And after this we learned according to the way of truth. And at the time that we began to learn the Mishnah and [after] we learned two tractates, our Creator granted us that we could hear a voice that spoke (alternative translation: "the voice of the speaker," i.e., the communicator from the inner levels) out of the mouth of the Chassid

---

[5] Shavuot is the Jewish Festival of Weeks. According to the Jewish tradition, this is the time when the Torah was given to Moses. It is customary to stay up the first night of Shavuot and study the Torah.

[Joseph Qaro], may his light shine. A great voice with clearly cut letters (i.e., clearly enunciated syllables), and all the neighbours (i.e., the chaverim) listened but did not understand [the deeper meaning]. And it was very pleasant [to hear the voice]. And the voice continued and grew stronger. And we fell on our faces. And there was no one who dared to lift his eyes or face to look [at him], because of great fear (awe). And he began the speech he spoke to us:

"Listen my friends exalted among the exalted ones, my beloved friends, peace upon you. Happy art ye and happy are those who bore you. Happy in this world and happy in the world to come, that ye have put it upon thyselves to crown me in this night. For it has been some years that the crown of my head fell down and there has been no one to comfort me.

"And I was cast into the dust and enclosed in filth. And now ye have returned the crown of old. Strengthen thyselves my friends fortify thyselves my beloved and rejoice and reinforce thyselves. And know that ye are among the exalted. Ye deserve to be in the Palace (Hechal) of the King. And the voice of thy Torah and speech of thy mouths have ascended before the Holy One blessed be He. And it broke through a few layers of air and a few firmaments until it ascended and the Malachim (messenger angels) were silent, and the Serafim (fire angels) were quiet and the Chayot (Holy Creatures) stood still and all the hosts on high of the Holy One blessed be He heard thy voices.

"Behold I am the Mishnah (the oral Torah), the first one, that admonishes mankind; I have come to speak to you, and if ye were ten[6] ye would have ascended even higher and higher. But even though [ye art not ten] ye have ascended so far. Happy art ye and happy those who bore you my friends for ye kept the sleep from your eyes; and through you I ascended in this night; and through the Chaverim that are in the great city (i.e., Jerusalem; others say Safed), that is the city and mother in Israel. And ye art not like them, who lie in their beds sleeping the sleep, that is the sixtieth part of death, stretched out on their beds. And ye have been adjoined to YHVH and He is pleased with you. Therefore my children strengthen, fortify and reinforce thyselves with my love, with my Torah and with awe for me.

---

[6] Ten Jews (over the age of Bar Mitzvah) are needed to form a *minyan,* that is a quorum sufficient for communal prayer service (in a synagogue). According to the Babylonian Talmud, upon every gathering of ten Jews, the Shechinah dwells among them (Sanhedrin 39a).

"However imagine one thousandth of a thousandth of a thousandth of a myrriadth of a myrriadth of a myrriadth of the sadness that I am in; no happiness would enter into your hearts and no laughter would be in thy mouths; remember because of you I was cast into the dust. Therefore strengthen, fortify and reinforce thyselves, my honoured friends, and do not interrupt thy studies. For the thread of Chesed (Mercy, Love) is drawn to you and your Torah [studies] are pleasant before the Holy One, blessed be He. Therefore stand up my children my friends on thy feet and elevate me."

And we said with a loud voice as on Yom Kippur: "Baruch Shem Kavod Malchuto le-Olam Va-ed" (Blesssed is the Name of the Glory of His Kingdom forever and ever.) And we stood on our feet and we spoke with a voice as if on command.

And he [i.e. the Maggid] returned and spoke:

"You are happy my children, return to your studies and do not interrupt them for one moment and go up to the land of Israel; for not all the times are equal. And there is no inhibition to the salvation by much or by a little. And your eyes shall not spare on your belongings; for you will receive the good things of the Land thou willeth go up to. And if you are willing and hear (obey) you will receive the good things of the Land. Therefore hurry and go up; for I am the sustainer, for you I will sustain you. And peace upon you and peace to your houses and peace to all that are with you. YHVH will give strength unto His people; [YHVH will bless his people with peace] (Psalm 29:11)."

All these words he spoke to us and our ears did hear this and many other important matters of wisdom and great promises that each of us was weeping from happiness. And we also heard about the sorrows of the Shechinah through our sins. And [at this moment] the voice was like the voice of a sick person beseeching us. And then we strengthened us until the light of the morning and we did not interrupt reading [the scriptures] aloud and with joy and trembling.[7]

The account of Shlomo Alqabetz gives quite a realistic idea of what happens when a Maggid speaks though an experienced mediator. The effect this has on both the mediator and the audience is not very much different in our times.

---

[7] See: *Maggid Mesharim,* Introduction

I always feel a sensation of awe and trembling in the presence of my Inner Plane Teacher, even though over the years he has become a trusted guide and companion. The first time I consciously experienced his presence he spoke through the mouth of my own (human) teacher, who is a very gifted mediator and a great occultist. Later on I learned how to contact him myself in meditation and even in waking consciousness.

The signs and sensations every person experiences may vary, but they will always be accompanied by awe and a feeling of spiritual intensity. One person described to me a significant increase of heat in the presence of the Maggid, as if heat were radiating from the mediator.

What Happens When We Contact an Inner Plane Being

Let us look more closely at what happens when we contact an inner plane being. If you initiate the contact, you will visualize the being you want to contact. It may be one of the traditional teachers, such as Elijah or Metatron. This image will be a thought-form built in the way you imagine the being to appear. If you are well trained, this image will be built in the way this being is seen traditionally, and thus it will be ideal for containing the essence of the inner plane being. (Do not make the mistake, however, of thinking that this image is the real appearance of this being. Inner plane beings live on a level of existence that is beyond our ability to imagine. Some thought-forms are very useful, because they have been used over many generations by the masters of the tradition to contact those beings, but they are only a symbolic representation of the beings' true nature.) Then empower this image with your own emotions, filling it with that aspect of your energy that corresponds to the being. This will be easier if you have already contacted the being before, because you will be able to recall the emotions you experienced when you first met this being. It may also help if you are guided by an experienced master of the tradition. The thought-form, empowered by the desire to contact the being and the vibration of the magical name of this being, will ring a bell on the astral level (Yetzirah).[8] The being will be aware of your call, and if you have done your work well, it will fill up the form to the degree that you are able to make the contact. This degree will not be the same for everybody and depends on:

- how well you are trained in the art of building thought-forms

---

[8] This is so even if the being itself does not come from the level of Yetzirah.

- how well you understand the nature of the being
- how much you are able to endure the presence of the being
- how deep the degree of your devotion is

If the contact is initiated from the inner levels, the process will not be very different. The being will appear to you in a thought-form that you will be able to accept.

Every inner plane being consists of a multitude of particles, just as we do. And just as every particle of our body contains our complete DNA, every particle of such a being is holographic and contains its complete essence. Thus it can send a true particle of itself and be present at many different places at the same time.

It, however, must adjust its vibration to our level and communicate with us in a way that we can understand. If I wish to communicate with you through the medium of this book, I must use words or symbols that you can understand, and this means that mainly I will have to use those words or symbols that you already know—but the information is contained in the way I use them. In the same way, the inner plane being will use not only words and symbols, but also ideas that you already know. Every communication with the inner plane will have to pass through your own subconscious mind. In order to communicate with you, the inner plane being will use those words, symbols, and ideas that it can find in your own (subconscious) mind. It will therefore speak with you in your language (although tradition says the angels will always speak Hebrew to those who understand this language well enough). The inner plane being will not usually use ideas that are very foreign to your mind. A certain number of the answers received will always originate in your own mind, but if the contact is more than wishful thinking, and if your desire to contact the being is motivated by true devotion, the answers will always contain some true information. Do not be confused if some of the things that are said sound familiar, but beware making up answers you would like to hear. The Maggid is real. It may not be our level of reality, but he is real on his own level. The image that you see is a thought-form, but behind this thought-form is a real consciousness. The thought-form and the symbols and ideas used for communication may seem to come from your mind, but they are being used by another being to communicate with you.

You can ask your Maggid any question you wish, but he will always give you an answer that is based on the spiritual point of view. He will not make your decisions for you, and he will not give you answers to questions that you could or should find out for yourself, but he may give you a hint as to how to find these answers. His answers will lift up your awareness to the spiritual level, which is the source of all things. He will help you realize the hidden causes of your problems, and he will help you to understand how to learn from your mistakes, how to balance your personality, and how to become a better human being. He will also teach you, giving you advice in all kinds of spiritual work, and it will explain the secret meanings of the Holy Scriptures. He will always insist that your path be the Path of Light. If you step on the dark path, he will leave you (although he may come back and help you, if you honestly regret leaving the path of light and want to make amends for what you have done).

Your Maggid can be an aspect or a form of your Higher Self, or he could be a teacher from the inner planes of existence, a sage who passed away, an angelic being, an aspect of the Tree of Life, or the Spirit of the Holy Scriptures. It may also happen that one day—maybe after many years—your Maggid hands you over to another Maggid.

Try to work with your inner Maggid and ask regularly for its advice or teaching. If possible, contact it at least once a week. You have the right to ask it for a proof or sign of its words, but do this respectfully, and always take its advice seriously!

No Mediator Is Infallible

Joseph Qaro has recorded the teachings and messages of his Maggid in a book called *Maggid Mesharim* (Speaker of Upright Words). It was written in the form of a diary over fifty years.

> Fourth day (Wednesday): 5th of the Month Shevat at the time of the Mincha (afternoon prayer service). [The Maggid said:] "I maintain the Mishnayot (i.e., the passages from the Mishnah). Strenghten and fortifiy [thyself] with my Torah and dedicate thy heart that thy thoughts do not separate from my Torah and my awe (i.e., thy awe for me). Be [emotionally and spiritually] attached to my Netzach (Eternity) to my Purity to my Mystery to my Strength, and so forth, to my Tiferet (Beauty) to my Torah to my salvation and to my Answer (Teshuvah; alternative translation: "my repentance"). For that is what thou seeketh from the Holy One blessed be He, that He guideth thee on the Ways of His Salvation (Teshuvah; alternative translation: "His repentance"

or "His answer"). These are the ways that I teach thee and these are also the ways of His Salvation (Teshuvah—see previous bracketed text). And strengthen thyself with them not to separate thy thoughts even for one moment from my Torah and my awe (i.e., thy awe for me) and annul from thy heart all passing thoughts that come to thee from the Yetzer ha-Ra (Evil Urge); and the snake and Samael insert them in thy heart to doom thee, to stun thee, to annihilate thee, and thou shalt stand against them and annul them from thy heart. And do not let them insert their speech in thy ear and thus thou doometh them, thou stunneth them, thou annihilateth them, for after thee is their lust and thou shalt rule over them. [. . .] And further let not even passing thoughts come into thy heart and cause that all my words do not come up [correctly in thy mind] and also cause me to stutter (or hesitate in my speech) and then I cannot reveal to thee all the words (and matters) therefore, be warned, be on thy guard from passing thoughts and in particular in the time of prayer neutralize all the thoughts and dedicate thy heart to my prayer and my service and thou needeth to ensure that thou be not distracted from thy attention (Daat)[9] completely. For in the one moment that thou art distracted from thy attention (Daat), the Yetzer ha-Ra (Evil Urge) will doom thee, stun thee, degrade thee, annihilate thee, bring thee down into the lowest pit.[10]

As mentioned before, the Yetzer ha-Ra mentioned in the text is the Evil Urge—that is, the selfish, sinful, and destructive ego within ourselves that tries to hinder us from following the path of righteousness and tries to lead us astray, irritate us, and give us false information. (It is seen as identical to the Snake and Samael.)

The Maggid never tires of emphasizing how important, true, and constant is dedication. You must seek the contact with your entire heart, and all your thoughts must be directed toward the contact. Even a great mediator such as Joseph Qaro, however, was never sure of bringing through the words of the Maggid 100 percent correctly. It is always possible that passing thoughts will enter the mind of the mediator and become mixed up with the message of the Maggid. The Maggid warned him that this may happen, and admonished him to avoid it as much as possible. Experience shows that a very good mediator can get about 70 percent to 80 percent of the

---

[9] Alternative translations for Daat are: "cognition," "gnosis," "realization."
[10] Joseph Qaro, *Maggid Mesharim,* Parashah Va-Era.

message correctly—but there is always a bit that comes from the (conscious or subconscious) mind of the mediator, so no human being is able to bring through a message perfectly. It is therefore important never to stop being critical about the information that you bring through. On the other hand, if you have made a true contact with a Maggid, follow his advice and trust him as you would trust an incarnated teacher—or even more so, because he is beyond human weaknesses.

There are some who believe that perfect contact with the higher worlds was possible only in biblical times, and that this level of prophecy has never been attained since. After the prophets came the early saints (*Chassidim rishonim*) who concerned themselves with the Vision of the Merkavah. And again there are those who believe that their level is unattainable today. There is a natural tendency to glorify the past and to think that whatever happened a long time ago must be better than what we can achieve today. I do not think that this is necessarily true. There have always been great holy men and women with the gift of prophecy and/or divine insight. They have always been rare, but nevertheless, they have existed throughout all the ages. I think modesty of the individual is a virtue, but there is no reason why we should think of ourselves as more limited than our ancestors. If we do not reach the same level as our ancestors, this is due to lack of devotion, not due to living in the wrong time.

Today, many people claim to be in contact with the higher worlds. They say that they are "channelling" messages they receive from angels or other high beings. Very often, what comes through is only the suppressed contents of their own subconscious mind. This phenomenon is not new; there have been always false prophets—even in biblical times.

Purification and dedication of the soul must come first, otherwise we will not be able to contact a true Maggid. A person will attract only such beings that match his own soul. If the soul is pure, he will attract pure beings of angelic, divine, or saintly nature, and if the soul is not pure, he will attract—if he attracts anything at all—impure or lesser beings who may be impersonating someone else.

The very fact that there is an incorporeal being that communicates does not mean that everything that being tells you is the truth. It entirely depends on the nature of the being. If you communicate with the soul of a deceased person, the person will have the same character faults that he had when he was alive. If he was a liar, he will most likely still be a liar. If he was a saint, he will, of course, speak the truth.

A true Maggid will always speak the truth, but even if we are in contact with a true Maggid, the communication is limited by the mediator's ability to understand (and the adulteration by passing thoughts of the mediator's mind, as mentioned earlier in this chapter).[11] You must realize that the contact to the Inner Plane Teacher is made via the abstract aspect of the Ruach (the higher mental level). The Maggid transmits not words, but concepts. (Sometimes there occurs the strange experience of the mediator hesitating while the Maggid seems to search the mind of the mediator for an expression that matches the concept he wants to communicate.) Consequently, the Maggid can express only such concepts that the mind of the mediator has as corresponding knowledge.

Qaro's Maggid often quoted the Torah and Mishnah, for Qaro was a leading expert on rabbinical law. These passages were part of Qaro's mind and could be used by the contact to illustrate certain ideas. If the mediator does not know biblical quotes, ideas might still be expressed, but they are unlikely to be explained via biblical quotations. This may, however, result in a loss of precision. For this reason it was very important for Qaro to study the Mishnah continually, for it was the basic set of ideas though which he could understand his Maggid, who, after all, was the Spirit of the Mishnah. On the other hand, Qaro was not an eminent student of the Qabbalah, and therefore, information concerning this subject revealed through him did not have the same quality as, for example, the teachings of Isaak Luria. Qaro's Maggid did not find the right "vocabulary" in Qaro's mind that would have enabled him to express more advanced Qabbalistic concepts with the required precision.[12]

For this reason, the importance of deeply and thoroughly studying the Qabbalah cannot be overemphasized if you want to become an advanced Qabbalistic mediator, because the Qabbalah is the most universal system of

---

[11] This is one of the reasons why self-knowledge is so important in spiritual work. If you know yourself, you have a fair chance of recognizing most of the contents of the information that come from your own thoughts. No one, however, is likely to get a perfect result—even with all the self-knowledge to be expected in a saintly person.

[12] Dion Fortune is a modern example of a mediator. Her Inner Plane Teacher dictated a book called *The Cosmic Doctrine*. Dion Fortune had a basic knowledge of physics, and her mind held information unknown in Qaro's time. Her contact would have been unlikely to quote the Torah or even the Mishnah, for she knew very little about either, but her knowledge about physics was used to express the ideas in many passages of *The Cosmic Doctrine*. Yet even her knowledge of physics was quite limited from that of a modern scientific perspective, and consequently there may be some errors in the text due to this fact.

symbolism that will enable your mind to bring through the most complex spiritual concepts.

How to Contact the Maggid

Devotion, dedication, and purity of character are the keys to contacting a Maggid. Qaro's Maggid was the Spirit of the Mishnah, which is also the oral Torah. This means that in order to contact his Maggid, devotion to the study of the Torah and the Mishnah was an important precondition for Qaro. To fulfill the commandments of the Torah was important to show that his dedication was honest and that Qaro's character was worthy of receiving the teachings of the Maggid. Nevertheless, the most essential condition was, and is, the selfless desire to serve. Therefore, service and dedication are mentioned again and again in the teachings of Qaro's Maggid:

> [...] think constantly about my Torah and about my awe (i.e. thy awe for me) and about my Mishnah, and do not separate for one moment from my Torah and from my awe, even in the time you eat or speak thy tongue there be a heavy limb in thy body as it was [in Qaro's life] in the few days that passed. And do not even speak of unimportant matters (literally, small speech) if there is not an extreme need to do so. And dedicate thy heart and thy tongue and thy limbs completely to my service and to my awe and to my Torah. And remember what is said [in the Talmud] about Rav who did not speak trivial talk on the journey of his days (i.e., all his life).
>
> And so must a man do to dedicate his thoughts completely to the awe of YHVH and His service. As the scripture says: "My son, give me thy heart, and let thine eyes observe my ways" (Proverbs 23:26). That is to say: as thou doeth Mitzvah (good deed) or be involved with the Torah, thy heart shall be dedicated to me. And do not think of any other thing. As is similarly written: "And that ye go not about after thy own heart and thy own eyes" (Numbers 15:39).
>
> And when thy heart is definitely and completely dedicated to me, that thine eyes seek not other things, then that is as is said: "let thine eyes observe my ways" (Proverbs 23:26). Especially in the time of prayer, nullify from thee every kind of passing thoughts that try to enter thy heart. [They are the] Yetzer ha-Ra (Evil Urge), thy fears with the powers that are upon them for they are the [the real meaning of] the snake and Samael and their armies.

And dedicate thy heart completely and all the time and in every hour and in every moment (minute) that thou dost not think [of anything else] but of me and of my Torah and of my service, for this is the mystery of a man who dedicates himself to commune truly in unity with his Creator, for the soul attaches and unites with Him and he will be blessed and his body and his limbs (organs) become truly an encampment of the Shechinah (Divine Presence), as is said in the Torah: "Thou shalt fear YHVH thy God; Him shalt thou serve; and to Him shalt thou cleave." (Deuteronomy 10:20)[13]

It must be understood that the Maggidim (Inner Plane Teachers) are there to enhance the spiritual development of humanity. They are always willing to help and guide those who themselves are willing to serve them, and have their part in the spiritual development of humankind. It is for this reason, and only for this reason, that a Maggid chooses to teach and train a human being: "The Masters receive souls as pupils, not for the benefit of the soul, but for the benefit of the Great Work; a man is not trained for the sake of his curiosity or enthusiasm, but only in so far as he is of value as a servant; it is for this reason that a selfless desire to serve is the surest path to the Master."[14]

In the writings of the Qabbalist Chaim ben Joseph Vital (1543–1620) we find detailed descriptions of how to contact the inner planes and communicate with a true Maggid. Chaim Vital was a student of Moses Qordovero, and later became the leading student and foremost interpreter of Isaak Luria (the Arizal). It is also said that Joseph Qaro had some influence on the early years of Chaim Vital's education.

Several times in his book *Shaarey Qedushah* (Gates of Holiness), Chaim Vital describes having found three occult methods of obtaining higher knowledge:

1. The first and lowest of them is dream.
2. The second is the communication with a teacher from the inner planes. This can be the soul of a Tzaddiq (a saint) who has passed away, or it may be the prophet Elijah, who will reveal himself to you if you have developed to a very high degree within you the virtue of

---

[13] Joseph Qaro, *Maggid Mesharim*, Parashah Beshalach.
[14] Dion Fortune, *Esoteric Orders and Their Work and the Training and Work of an Initiate* (Glasgow: Thorsons, 1995), 78.

Chassidut. It is also possible that the Inner Plane Teacher is a being of angelic origin.[15]

3. The third, and highest, is to cloak yourself in the Ruach ha-Qodesh (Holy Spirit), which is described as an attraction of the Highest Light (Or Eliyon) to the [lower] soul (Nefesh) from the root of the highest [aspect of the] soul (i.e., this is the highest form of communication with the Higher Self of the individual).

Before we go on to more advanced methods of contacting the inner planes, let us first have a look at what Chaim Vital says about obtaining information through dreams:

It was testified to me by Rabbi Elijah [De] Vidas Z"L,[16] author of Sefer Reshit Chochmah, in the name of his teacher Rabbi Moses Qordovero Z"L, author of Sefer Pardes Rimonim, that everyone who wants to know [the answer to] a question shall accustom himself to holiness, purity and fear of sin. And this especially on the concerned day. And at night after he recites the order of the *Qriyat Shma*[17] on his bed, he shall seclude himself (i.e., meditate) [for] a little [while] in his consciousness without any other thoughts at all. And then he shall ponder and think about his question until he falls to sleep and sleeps [deeply]. And he shall be alone in the house at a place where no one wakes him up or [accidentally] awakens him. And when his question is answered in his sleep, he should ensure that his sleep is not interrupted [until he has received the entire answer].[18]

I will not expand on this method, because a more magical and very effective method to achieve divine inspiration through a dream is described in detail in chapter 15.

The use of any kind of magical invocation is often rejected by those following the Lurianic Qabbalah system. Isaak Luria, the Ari, was a deeply mystical person who—despite his high spiritual qualities—did not, unfor-

---

[15] In the teachings of the Ari, only the angels or souls that had gained or created the personification of good Karma by studying the Torah or keeping the commandments were called Maggidim. Other inner level teachers such as Elijah were not called Maggidim by the Ari.

[16] Zichrono Livrocho (Of Blessed Memory).

[17] The well-known prayer Shma Yisrael (Hear Israel).

[18] Chaim Vital, *Shaarey Qedushah,* part 4, chapter 1:9.

tunately, have any understanding of magic. He rejected the use of invocations, and in his opinion, the only way to contact the inner planes was piety and asceticism. When a person has a deep predisposition toward mysticism, it may happen that any other spiritual path seems a detour that may lead the student astray. All true magicians will become mystics in the end, because both have the same goal, but, unlike the mystic, who considers such knowledge obsolete or unnecessary, the magician will learn a great deal about the wisdom of how to use the powers of the soul.[19]

Chaim Vital was a very devout student of Luria, whom he considered a saint *par excellence.* While he was Luria's student, he kept very strictly to the rules laid down by Luria. Many years later, however, he seems to have reconsidered his point of view to a certain degree, for in his book *Shaarey Qedushah* he describes methods that show a much more occult approach than those taught by Luria. On the other hand, Chaim Vital kept to Luria's ideas insofar as he never thought very much of methods such as spells and amulets.

I know from personal experience that a powerful ritual is a very potent method of opening human awareness to the inner planes. I also know that ritual is not needed to contact the higher levels of existence, but it can very much help in the process. Even though we respect the Ari, let us not reject a very potent method that will enable us to develop our spiritual potential in a very effective way.

Whether we use magical or mystical methods, what cannot be overemphasized is how important it is to ensure that before any such attempt is undertaken, we must reach a high level of inner purity and true dedication.

---

[19] I can describe the difference in this way: Both the mystic and the magician want to rise from Malchut to Keter on the Tree of Life. The mystic travels the straight way along the middle pillar, while the magician moves along the Path of the Lightning Flash. This may seem to be the longer way, but when the magician arrives, he comes with a much more complete experience, and he has learned to control the powers of polarity inside and outside himself. Further, due to the extra knowledge, wisdom, and power he gains, it may be that he travels more effectively and does not even arrive any later than the mystic. Compare this to two men who want to travel from one city to another. One goes the direct way, and the other first goes to a place where he can get a horse. Even though he may not be able to take the direct route with the horse (for it cannot cross mountains or other obstacles) he may still arrive at the destination at the same time or even faster. On the other hand, the magician must make sure that his devotion and love are as strong as those of the mystic, otherwise he may indeed be led astray, like the man on the horse who will lose his path if he likes riding so much that he forgets where he wants to go.

The Ari was therefore partly right to warn against attempting any occult methods, for unless they are performed with deep devotion and pure intention, they will cause imbalance in the ego and confuse the soul with falsehood.

Chaim Vital, in a similar way to Qaro's Maggid, emphasizes that purity of character and resistance to sin are very important preconditions for the successful practice of meditation/seclusion (*hitbodedut*). Unless we resist the powers of sin from Yetzirah (the World of Formation), we are unable to contact the higher worlds: "[Concerning meditation]: For at first he shall do Teshuvah (repentance) from all sin. And after this he shall take care not to add another sin to them. And after that he shall accustom himself to removing from himself the bad attributes that are impressed in him (i.e., in his soul), such as the attributes of wrath, anger, over-meticulousness, and idle conversation, et cetera. . . . And after that heal (do Tiqqun) the disease of the Nefesh (lower soul), which consists of sins and [bad] attributes. Then there is no power in the impure mind (Ruach) to interrupt his Devequt (i.e., state of being attached) with the Eliyonim (higher beings).[20]

Only if we develop our soul to a very high ethical level and guard ourselves from being affected by pride, egoism, hate, or anger, and further, constantly purify our character from all vices to the best of our ability, may we have any hope of ever contacting a true Maggid. The Maggid will look into our hearts, and unless he finds a good character, true devotion to the Divine Light, and love for our fellow human beings (in fact, for all life on this planet), he will refuse to speak to us.

Now providing that we have purified ourselves to the necessary degree and that our devotion is deep and absolutely honest, and that we act responsibly and with the best of intentions, we may try to contact the inner planes. Chaim Vital describes the method of contacting the Inner Plane Teacher:

Meditation: In the house alone (i.e., make sure you are undisturbed), as mentioned above, wrap thyself in the Tallit (prayer shawl) and sit and close thy eyes. And undress from the [physical] matter as if thy Nefesh (astral/emotional soul) goeth out of thy body and ascendeth to the firmament. And after the "undressing," recite one Mishnah (i.e., one passage from the Mishnah—that is, the oral Torah) that thou wanteth many times again and again (i.e., like a mantra). With great

---

[20] Chaim Vital, *Shaarey Qedushah*, part 4, chapter 2, Introduction.

speed as much as thou art able to do well with clear speech and without omission of one word. And concentrate on attaching thy Nefesh with the Nefesh of the Tanna (rabbinic authority in time of Mishnah) who is mentioned in this Mishnah (i.e., the Rabbi who wrote this particular passage). And this is [done] by concentrating [on the idea] that thy mouth is a vessel that puts forth letters of the language of the Mishnah. And the voice that thou expelleth is from the vessel of the mouth, that is the sparks of thy inner Nefesh, which come out and recite this Mishnah. And it becomes a Merkavah (i.e., a vehicle) that coateth inside itself the Nefesh of the Tanna who is the Master of this Mishnah (i.e., about whom the Mishnah is written). And his Nefesh will coat itself in thy Nefesh (alternative translation: "And thou wilt coat his Nefesh in thy Nefesh"). And [at the time] when thou art tired from thy speaking the language of the Mishnah, if thou art worthy for such a purpose, it is possible that the Nefesh of this Tanna is true in thy mouth. And he will be coated there with thy strength reciting the Mishnah. And then [after] with thy strength [thou art] speaking the Mishnah, he will speak with thy mouth. And he will give thee "Shalom" (i.e., greetings, peace). And all that thou will think at that time in thy thoughts to ask him he will answer thee. And he will speak with thy mouth. And thy ears will hear his speech. And thou wilt not speak thyself, but he is the one who speaks. And this is the secret [of the verse] "The Ruach YHVH (Spirit of God) spoke through me, and His Word was upon my tongue." (2 Samuel 23:2)[21]

The Technique

Make sure you are undisturbed for several hours. Wear your prayer shawl or white robes, or both if possible. Sit in your meditation position, close your eyes, and visualize your astral body leaving your physical body.[22] See and feel how you ascend to Heaven. Now you must focus your mind on the teacher you wish to contact. Use the Mishnah as a point of contact by reciting one passage of it in which the teacher is mentioned. (In order to recite this passage with closed eyes, you should know it by heart.) Start slowly, speeding up until the recitation is as fast as possible. Like a mantra, the

---

[21] Chaim Vital, *Shaarey Qedushah*, part 4, chapter 2:1.

[22] It may help if you start the meditation by imagining that you are in the place where the teacher lived and at the time when he was alive. By doing so, you will help your mind to focus on the teacher, which may help in making the contact.

recitation should go without thinking, while imagining that your mouth ejects the letters of the Mishnah, sending them out into Heaven.

If you are successful, you will see the astral image of the teacher approach or appear before you. Continue speaking the Mishnah, until your mouth is tired and you achieve a deep level of trance. Let the astral image of the teacher come closer, and then let it enter your own astral body, and surround it with your own astral body. Let its astral image fill the same space as your astral body and be inside it—its arms and legs inside your arms and legs, its head inside your head, and so on. . . . Feel it, feel its heartbeat and its breath, and adjust your heartbeat and your breath to them. There will be a feeling of great peace and spiritual intensity. Feel his presence and thoughts, and then let him take over your mouth and lips and tongue, and let him speak through your mouth. At some point, he will say "Shalom" to you. Do not force this, but simply let it happen. Continue speaking the Mishnah until he takes over. Now in your mind you can ask a question, and he will answer through your mouth. (This may or may not be physical speech. If no one else is present, it does not matter if he answers only in your mind.) When he has answered (and even if you did not get an answer), thank and bless him. Separate from him, and let his astral image out of your astral body. Say goodbye and descend to your physical body.

Next you will find two Mishnayot to choose from if you do not know the Mishnah:

> Mishnah Sotah 3:2—He giveth her to drink [from the Water of Bitterness] and after that he offers up her grain-offering. Rabbi Simeon [ben Yochai] sayeth: He offers up her grain-offering and after that he giveth her to drink, as it is said: 'And afterwards [he] shall make the woman drink the water' (Numbers 5:26). And if he giveth her to drink and after that offers up her grain-offering, [it is] kosher (i.e., valid)."

This Mishnah is about the exact order of the procedure of giving the Water of Bitterness (see Numbers 5:11–31), an ancient occult practice of forfeit and purification from sin (in this case, adultery). I have chosen this passage because purification from sin is an important part of this work. The sage mentioned is Rabbi Simeon ben Yochai (also called Shimon bar Yochai), a third-generation Tanna and a student of Rabbi Aqiva. He lived in the second century and is supposed to have reached the age of 120. According to one legend he lived for thirteen years in a cave to hide from the Romans and was freed by the prophet Elijah himself. He was a great mystic, magician, and exorcist, and the authorship of the Zohar is ascribed to him.

The second Mishnah refers to a number of sages, and thus offers the potential to contact several different Tannas and prophets:

> Mishnah Edujot 8:7: [Thus] spoke Rabbi Yoshuah: I have a tradition from Rabban Yochanan ben Zakkai who heard it from his teacher and his teacher [heard it] from his teacher. A Halachah (rule, law, theory) of Moses from Sinai, that Elijah doth not come [to decide what is] impure and pure, [what is] to be distanced and to be brought close, except to distance what is brought close by violence and to bring close what is distanced by violence. The family of Bet Tzerifah was forcefully distanced to the other side of the [river] Jordan by Ben Tzion (Zion). And another one (i.e., a family) was there and was forcefully brought close by Ben Tzion. For example [in] this one (i.e., in this case)—Eliah cometh [to decide what is] impure and pure, [what is] to be distanced and to be brought close. Rabbi Yehudah sayeth: To be brought close but not to be distanced. Rabbi Simeon [ben Yochai] sayeth: To make equal what is different. And the sages say: not to be distanced and not to be brought close but to create peace in the world. As is said: "Behold, I will send you Elijah the prophet before the coming of the great and terrible day of YHVH. And he shall turn the heart of the fathers to the children, and the heart of the children to their fathers; lest I come and smite the land with utter destruction."[23]

This Mishnah describes that Elijah will decide in the world to come which families are of proper lineage and which are not, and whether or not the improper ones will be removed. It further describes Elijah's general function as a judge and bringer of peace. A number of important sages are mentioned in this passage:

- Rabbi Yoshuah ben Chananya: a second-generation Tanna and a student of Rabbi Yochanan ben Zakkai. He was known to be a man of great wit and wisdom and opposed asceticism.
- Rabban Yochanan ben Zakkai: a student of Hillel and a first-generation Tanna who died about 80 CE. He was founder of the academy at

---

[23] Malachi 3:23–24.

Yawneh/Jabneh and a great mystic and teacher of occult knowledge. Rabbi Aqiva is supposed to have learned the esoteric doctrines from him.

- Rabbi Yehudah ben Ilai: a third-generation Tanna, known to be a pious and compassionate man as well as being a very strict ascetic. He lived in poverty, drank almost no wine, and was a vegetarian.
- Rabbi Simeon ben Yochai: see the description on page 382.

Furthermore, Moses is named as being the source of this Mishnah, and the prophet Elijah is the subject of the entire Mishnah. Thus this Mishnah offers potential for contacting quite a number of important sages, including the two most important prophets. Like the previous one, it is about the undoing of past injustice, and is also about the secrets of the future.

If you perform the technique as described, what kind of results should you expect? The contact may be present immediately, but more likely, at first you might not seem to get any results at all. This will change after a while, depending on your spiritual progress. Once the contact is well established you will get answers, advice, and guidance in all kinds of spiritual matters.

If you have a personal (incarnated) teacher, he or she will often be able to see the effects of the contact much earlier than you. A while before I was fully aware of the influence of my Maggid in my spiritual life, my teacher told me that certain spiritual ideas I had were signs of the contact. She told me that the contact was already very deep, and I had not yet even learned how to contact him at will (at least, it did not seem to be very efficient at that time). This, however, is not unusual. You must understand that very often the maggid is aware of the student long before the student is aware of the Maggid.

Another Technique

Chaim Vital explains to his readers that if we are not yet worthy of (or ready for) this great level, it is possible that we will be more successful with another technique. He further describes that some people will be more likely to contact the inner planes in a mediumistic way—that is, in deep trance: "And thou will fall into slumber (i.e., trance) but thou will not slumber [in a normal way]. And as [you fall] into this slumber, thou will see that the answer to thy question will be given to thee, either by hints or clarification, all of which depends on thy preparation. And if thou dost not get [results] by one of the two mentioned techniques, know that thou art not worthy (or ready) yet, or that [thy] ability to undress from the [physical] matter is not good enough" (Chaim Vital, *Shaarey Qedushah,* part 4, chapter 2:1).

Chaim Vital describes the following alternative technique, which can be used after having purified and sanctified the body from impurity and having cleansed the hands of all kinds of crime or sin. As it is written: "He that hath clean hands, and a pure heart; who hath not taken My Name in vain, and hath not sworn deceitfully" (Psalm 24:4). And then we must purify the soul and heart. As it is written: "and a pure heart" (Psalm 24:4).

One should further study the Torah. To do so deliver a blessing to God, for this is [an attempt to reach] the level of prophesy. Then connect your mind (Ruach) to the higher levels; and after that continue to your learning. And in the beginning you may find logical thought and inner disputes appearing, but when that happens immerse yourself (i.e., your mind) in the Mysteries of HaShem—blessed be Elohim. You should further do Mitzvot (good deeds/religious duties) and distance yourself from idle talking all of your day. You should undergo ritual immersion and dress in white garments and go to a pure place, far from all kinds of impurity, and far from dead things and from the graveyard, and be far from all grief and moaning and irritation, and dress yourself in great joy. . . .

Meditation: In the house alone (i.e., make sure you are undisturbed), close thy eyes. And if thou were to wrap thyself in the Tallit (prayer shawl) and the Tefilin (phylacteries) it would be even better. And after thou hast tuned thy thoughts entirely [toward this work], combine (tzeref) in thy thoughts one word that thou want with all the Combinations (*tzerufim*), for there is no objection in any word thou will combine, only [to use] that which thou want. For example: Aretz "Earth"(ארץ), Atzar (אצר), Ratza (רצא), Raatz (ראץ), Tzaar (צאר), Tzara (צרא). And in this way [act] with all words which thou want [to use]. Ensure that it is in the way of Righteousness in the well-known [method of] Combination (tzeruf).[24] And then undress thyself from matter and from this world (Olam Hazeh) as if thy soul (Nefesh) goes out of the midst of thy body (Guf), and it ascends and dresses itself in the six aforementioned Tzerufim. And it ascends from Firmament to Firmament until the seventh Firmament that is called Aravot. And thou will imagine (i.e., visualize) that above the

---

[24] Compare the chapter concerning tzeruf in *Pardes Rimonim.*

Firmament Aravot there is a sheet (parchment), white as snow, spread out on the exterior (i.e., the upper part) of the Firmament Aravot. And on it are the images of these Letters of the aforementioned Tzerufim. And they are written in Hebrew Letters[25] in the colour of white fire, huge Letters, each Letter like a mountain or hill. And visualize in thy thoughts asking thy question to them, the Tzerufim, that are written there. And they will answer thy question. Either that thou resteth their spirits (Ruach) in thy mouth, or that thou sleep and returneth like from a dream as aforementioned in paragraph 1.[26]

Make sure you are undisturbed for several hours. As before, wear your prayer shawl and *tefilin* (phylacteries) or white robes, or all together if possible. Sit in your meditation position and close your eyes. Now concentrate totally on what you want to achieve. Form a sentence in your mind, and then permute the letters of the words as shown in Vital's example. If the word is *aretz,* "earth" (ארץ), then these are all the possible permutations:

aretz (ארץ), atzar (אצר), ratza (רצא), raatz (ראץ), tzaar (צאר), Tzara (צרא)

Do so with all the words. For example, if you want wisdom, you say: "I want wisdom": Ani rotzeh chochmah (אני רוצה חכמה). These would be the combinations (tzerufim) of the letters:

ani (אני), ain (אין), nia (ניא), naai (נאי), yaan (יאן), yana (ינא)

rotzeh (רוצה), rohetz (רוהץ), retzho (רצהו), retzoh (רצוה), rehotz (רהוץ), rehtzo (רהצו)

vatzher (וצהר), vatzreh (וצרה), vahretz (והרץ), vahtzer (והצר), vartzeh (ורצה), varhetz (ורהץ)

tzehro (צהרו), tzehor (צהור), tzeroh (צרוה), tzerho (צרהו), tzoher (צוהר), tzoreh (צורה)

harotz (הרוץ), hartzo (הרצו), hotzer (הוצר), horetz (הורץ), hetzro (הצרו), hetzor (הצור)

chochmah (חכמה), chochham (חכהם), chomhach (חמהך)
chomchah (חמכה), chohcham (חהכם), chohmach (חהמך)

---

[25] Hebrew: *ashurit,* which is the name for the "modern" (square) Hebrew script. It is supposed to have been brought along by the returning Babylonian (Assurian) captives, and then replaced the older Hebrew letters.

[26] Chaim Vital, *Shaarey Qedushah,* part 4, chapter 2:3.

komhach (כמהח), komchah (כמחה), kohcham (כהחם)
kohmach (כהמח), kochmah (כחמה), kochham (כחהם)
mohchach (מהחך), mohchach (מהכח), mochchah (מחכה)
mochhach (מחהך), mochhach (מכהח), mochchah (מכחה)
hochcham (החכם), hochmach (החמך), hochmach (הכמח)
hochcham (הכחם), homchach (המחך), homchach (המכח)

As you can see, six permutations (1 × 2 × 3) are possible if the word has three letters, twenty-four permutations (1 × 2 × 3 × 4) if the word has four letters, one hundred twenty permutations (1 × 2 × 3 × 4 × 5) if the word has five letters, and so forth. (Fortunately, very few Hebrew words have more than five letters.)[27]

Now visualize your astral body leaving your physical body. Then visualize the aforementioned combinations (tzerufim) of the letters, like a garment or robe around your body (or if you prefer, imagine wearing a garment or robe on which these combinations of the letters are written). Then see and feel how you ascend from Firmament to Firmament, until the seventh Firmament that is called Aravot.

There, you see a parchment spread out on the upper part of the Firmament Aravot. The parchment is white like snow. Written on the parchment in Hebrew script, and the color of white fire, are the aforementioned combinations (tzerufim) of the letters. Each letter is huge, like a mountain. Imagine asking your question to the combinations (tzerufim) of the Holy Letters. (Note that the Hebrew letters are beings in themselves.) The letters will either answer your question or their spirits (Ruach) will rest in your mouth and answer with your voice or you will sleep [after the meditation] and wake up (as described above) with a dream that gives an answer through the use of symbols. After this, thank and bless the letters and descend to your physical body.

In another description that Vital gives directly before this one, the aforementioned permutations are not included. Instead, he instructs the reader that once he has reached the seventh firmament, he should visualize combinations of the letters of the Divine Name:

[27] "Two stones (other versions: two letters) build two houses, three build six houses, four stones build twenty-four houses, five build one-hundred-and-twenty houses, six build seven-hundred-and-twenty houses, seven build five-thousand-and-forty houses. From here onward go forth and consider (or calculate) that which the mouth cannot speak and the ear cannot hear" (*Sefer Yetzirah* 4:12).

And he will imagine (i.e., visualize)that on the Firmament Aravot there being a very big white sheet. And on it he imagines the Name HAVAYAH (הוי״ה = Existence = YHVH) written in Hebrew letters in the known colour; in very coarse script; each letter like a mountain, with an image white like snow. And he will connect the letters: Yod with Heh, Heh with Yod, Vav with Heh, Heh with Vav. Different formula: And he will connect the letters: Yod with Heh, Heh with Yod, Vav with First-Heh, and First-Heh with Vav, Vav with End-Heh, and End-Heh with Vav. (Original text says *Yod,* but it should be *Vav!*)[28]

Chaim Vital does not give any detailed information about how to perform the connections. If you want to use this method, you may read, for inspiration, the descriptions on letter permutations in chapter 21, Creating a Golem with the *Sefer Yetzirah* (Book of Formation), or alternately permute them as described above.

---

[28] Chaim Vital writes literally: "with Yod (maybe it should be VAV)"; Chaim Vital, *Shaarey Qedushah,* part 4, chapter 2:2.

צא אתה
וכל העם אשר
ברגליך
בשם קוף קפו וקף
ופק פסי
פוק

The Invocation of Elijah, the Prophet

The Prophet Elijah (Hebrew, Eliyahu or Eliyah) is a central figure in the Hebrew tradition. He gives hope to the desperate and advice to the scholar and reveals the mysteries to the Qabbalist.

His invisible presence is a part of many customs in the Jewish faith; he is often the invisible guest. There is, for example, an empty chair for him at every circumcision ceremony, and during the Seder meal, the door is opened so that he can enter, and a cup of wine is provided for him.

His name means "My God is Yahu" or "My God is Yah." Thus we can interpret this name in the same way as the magical name used by modern magicians, describing the motto of his spiritual work. In the Bible he performs many miracles, such as casting divine fire, falling from Heaven to destroy troops sent to capture him, splitting the waters of the river Jordan, reviving a dead boy, and acting as a defender of the Divine Law. He is judge, advocate, and peacemaker in one person. "Behold, I will send you Elijah the prophet before the coming of the great and dreadful day of

YHVH: And he shall turn the heart of the fathers to the children, and the heart of the children to their fathers, lest I come and smite the earth with a curse" (Malachi 3:23–24).

Elijah never died. He is one of the two men who entered Heaven without dying, ascending to Heaven in a fiery chariot: "And it came to pass, as they still went on, and talked, that, behold, there appeared a chariot of fire, and horses of fire, and parted them both asunder; and Elijah went up by a storm (saarah) into heaven" (2 Kings 2:11).

The Angel of Death, exercising jurisdiction over all humankind, refused to let him enter Heaven, claiming that other men would complain if Elijah was an exception. Although God said that Elijah is unlike other men, the Angel of Death still refused to let him enter. Elijah and Death fought until God stopped the battle after Elijah had almost annihilated Death.

After his ascent to Heaven, he was transformed into the archangel Sandalfon. In Heaven he records the deeds of men and the chronicles of the world, guiding the souls of the pious to their place in Paradise.

Many legends describe how he helped those in need: He told Rabbi Simeon ben Yochai, who hid for thirteen years in a cave, that he need not fear the Romans any longer, and thus helped him out of this uncomfortable situation.

Rabbi bar Abbahu was so poor that he could not spend any time on

Elijah Ascending to Heaven *by Julius Schnoor von Carolsfeld*

his studies. Elijah helped him obtain the financial means to be able to continue his studies.

He helped the poor father of a family to acquire money for food: The poor man was permitted to sell Elijah as a slave. Elijah built a palace overnight for the prince who bought him.

Elijah predicted seven wealthy years to a man who had lost his fortune, offering them either immediately, or at the end of the man's life. They were wanted immediately, and the man practiced so much charity that when Elijah came to take back the wealth he had given, no one could be found who was worthier of the money. The man therefore stayed wealthy forever.

He helped a pious but poor man to become rich. When the man turned his desires to material gain, forgetting to be pious and neglecting deeds of charity, Elijah took away the riches. When the man complained about his loss, Elijah promised to give him back his riches if they did not ruin his character—which is what happened.

If he could not ease a situation because a lesson had to be learned or someone had to go through a certain experience, he tried to help people to look at the situation in a more positive way, as happened in the case of Rabbi Aqiva. Before Rabbi Aqiva was famous, he lived in poverty. On a cold winter night Elijah visited him in disguise and asked for some straw to sleep on. Aqiva replied that he did not even have enough straw for his wife, but Rabbi Aqiva realized that his lot was not as bad as it could have been, for the stranger (Elijah) did not have any straw at all.

He healed Rabbi Yehudah's toothache by appearing as Rabbi Chayah. Rabbi Yehudah was thankful to Rabbi Chayah, even though they were at odds with each other before. Thus he helped to create peace between the two Rabbis.

He helped to create peace and harmony between a jealous man and his innocent wife.

Three sons of a pious man had inherited only a spice garden. Elijah gave them three alternative possibilities from which to chose. The first one took great wealth, the second one took knowledge of the Torah, and the third one took a beautiful and pious woman.

Other legends give a more complete picture of him:

Elijah helps the innocent.

Once upon a time it happened that when Nahum, the great and pious teacher, was journeying to Rome on a political mission, he was, without knowledge, robbed of the gift he bore to the emperor as an offering from the Jews. When he handed the casket to the ruler, it was found to contain common earth, which the thieves had substituted for the jewels they had abstracted. The emperor thought the Jews were mocking him, and their representative, Nahum, was condemned to suffer death. In his piety the Rabbi did not lose confidence in God; he said only: "This too is for good." And so it turned out to be. Suddenly, Elijah appeared, and, assuming the guise of a court official, he said: "Perhaps the earth in this casket is like that used by Abraham for purposes of war. A handful will do the work of swords and bows." At his insistence, the virtues of the earth were tested in the attack upon a city that had long resisted Roman courage and strength. His supposition was verified. The contents of the casket proved more efficacious than all the weapons of the army, and the Romans were victorious. Nahum was dismissed, laden with honors and treasures, and the thieves, who had betrayed themselves by claiming the precious earth, were executed, for, naturally enough, Elijah works no wonder for evildoers.

Elijah helps to maintain a happy marriage.

On another occasion, Elijah re-established harmony between a husband and his wife. The woman had come home very late on Friday evening, having allowed herself to be detained by the sermon preached by Rabbi Meir. Her autocratic husband swore she should not enter the house until she had spat in the very face of the highly esteemed Rabbi. Meanwhile, Elijah went to Rabbi Meir and told him a pious woman had fallen into a sore predicament on his account. To help the poor woman, the Rabbi resorted to a ruse. He announced that he was looking for someone who knew how to cast spells accomplished by spitting into the eye of the afflicted one. When he caught sight of the woman designated by Elijah, he asked her to try her power upon him. Thus she was able to comply with her husband's requirement without disrespect to the Rabbi; and through the instrumentality of Elijah, conjugal happiness was restored to an innocent wife.

He enables the studies of those who devote their lives to the spiritual path.

Rabba bar Abbahu [. . .] was a victim of poverty. He admitted to Elijah that on account of his small means, he had no time to devote to his studies. Thereupon, Elijah led him into Paradise, where he bade him remove his mantle and fill it with leaves grown in the regions of the blessed. When the Rabbi was about to quit Paradise, his garment full of leaves, a voice was heard to say: "Who desires to anticipate his share in the world to come during his earthly days, as Rabba bar Abbahu is doing?" The Rabbi quickly cast away the leaves. Nevertheless, he received twelve thousand denarii for his upper garment, because it retained the wondrous fragrance of the leaves of Paradise.

Elijah rewards the pious.

A similar thing happened to a well-to-do man who lost his fortune and became so poor that he had to do manual labor in the field of another. Once, when he was at work, he was accosted by Elijah, who had assumed the appearance of an Arab: "Thou art destined to enjoy seven good years. When dost thou want them—now, or as the closing years of thy life?" The man replied: "Thou art a wizard; go in peace, I have nothing for thee." Three times the same question was put, three times the same reply was given. Finally, the man said: "I shall ask the advice of my wife." When Elijah came again, and repeated his question, the man, following the counsel of his wife, said: "See to it that seven good years come to us at once." Elijah replied: "Go home. Before thou crossest thy threshold, thy good fortune will have filled thy house." And so it was. His children had found a treasure in the ground, and, as he was about to enter his house, his wife met him and reported the lucky find. His wife was an estimable, pious woman, and she said to her husband: "We shall enjoy seven good years. Let us use this time to practice as much charity as possible; perhaps God will lengthen our period of prosperity." After the lapse of seven years, during which man and wife used every opportunity of doing good, Elijah appeared again, and announced to the man that the time had come to take away what he had given him. The man responded: "When I accepted thy gift, it was after consultation with my wife. I should not like to return it without first acquainting her with what is about to happen." His wife charged him to say to the old man who had come to resume possession of his property: "If thou canst find any who will be more conscientious stewards of the pledges entrusted to us than we have been, I shall willingly yield them up to thee." God recognized that these people had made a proper use of their wealth, and He granted it to them as a perpetual possession.

Elijah helps only the pious.

In the form of an Arab, he once appeared before a very poor man whose piety equaled his poverty. He gave the man two shekels. These two coins brought the poor such good fortune that he attained great wealth. But in his zeal to gather worldly treasures, he had no time for deeds of piety and charity. Elijah again appeared before him and took away the two shekels. In a short time, the man was as poor as before. A third time Elijah came to him. The man was crying bitterly and complaining of his misfortune, and the prophet said: "I shall make thee rich once more, if thou wilt promise me under oath thou wilt not let wealth ruin thy character." The man promised, the two shekels were restored to him, he regained his wealth, and he remained in possession of it for all time, because his piety was not curtailed by his riches.

He will reward the good and punish the evil.

There were two brothers, one of them rich and miserly, the other poor and kind-hearted. Elijah, in the garb of an old beggar, approached the rich man, and asked him for alms. Repulsed by this man, Elijah turned to the poor brother, who received him kindly and shared his meager supper with him. On bidding farewell to him and to his equally hospitable wife, Elijah said: "May God reward you! The first thing you undertake shall be blessed and shall take no end until you yourselves cry out Enough!" Presently, the poor man began to count the few pennies he had, in order to convince himself that they sufficed to purchase bread for his next meal. But the few became many, and he counted and counted, and still their number increased. He counted a whole day, and the following night, until he was exhausted, and had to cry out "Enough!" And, indeed, it was enough, for he had become a very wealthy man. His brother was not a little astonished to see the fortunate change in his kinsman's circumstances, and when he heard how it had come about, he determined that if the opportunity should present itself again, he would show his most amiable side to the old beggar with the miraculous power of blessing. He had not long to wait. A few days later he saw the old man pass by. He hastened to accost him, and, excusing himself for his unfriendliness at their former meeting, begged him to come into his house. All that the larder afforded was put before Elijah, who pretended to eat of the dainties. At his departure, he pronounced a blessing upon his hosts: "May the first thing you do have no end, until it is enough." The mistress of the house thereupon said to her husband: "That we may count gold upon gold undisturbed, let us first attend to our most urgent physical needs." So they did, and they had to continue to do it until life was extinct.

Elijah may try to encourage man to be more devotional.

Sometimes Elijah considered it his duty to force people into abandoning a bad habit. A rich man was once going to a cattle sale, and he carried a snug sum of money to buy oxen. He was accosted by a stranger none other than Elijah, who inquired as to the purpose of his journey. "I go to buy cattle," replied the would-be purchaser. "Say, if it please God," urged Elijah. "Fiddlesticks! I shall buy cattle whether it please God or not! I carry the money with me, and the business will be dispatched." "But not with good fortune," said the stranger, and he went off. When he arrived at the market, the cattle buyer discovered the loss of his purse, and he had to return home to provide himself with other money. He again set forth on his journey, but this time he took another road to avoid the stranger of ill omen. To his amazement he met an old man with whom he had precisely the same adventure as with the first stranger. Again, he had to return home to fetch money. By this time had learned his lesson. When a third stranger questioned him about the object of his journey, he answered: "If it please God, I intend to buy oxen." The stranger wished him success, and the wish was fulfilled. To the merchant's surprise, when a pair of fine cattle were offered him, and their price exceeded the sum of money he had about his person, he found the two purses he had lost on his first and second trips. Later he sold the same pair of oxen to the king for a considerable price, and he became very wealthy.

If some hardship is necessary for someone's spiritual path, he may at least give consolation.

> If Elijah was not able to lighten the poverty of the pious, he at least sought to inspire them with hope and confidence. Rabbi Aqiva, the great scholar, lived in dire poverty before he became a famous Rabbi. His rich father-in-law would have nothing to do with him or his wife, because the daughter had married Aqiva against her father's will. On a bitter cold winter night, Aqiva could offer his wife, who had been accustomed to the luxuries wealth can buy, nothing but straw as a bed to sleep upon, and he tried to comfort her with assurances of his love for the privations she was suffering. At that moment Elijah appeared before their hut, and cried out in supplicating tones: "O good people, give me, I pray you, a little bundle of straw. My wife has been delivered of a child, and I am so poor I haven't even enough straw to make a bed for her." Now Aqiva could console his wife with the fact that their own misery was not so great as it might have been, and thus Elijah had attained his end, to sustain the courage of the pious.

Elijah expects more responsibility from those who have progressed further in spiritual work.

> Elijah displayed the extreme of his rigor toward teachers of the Law. From them he demanded more than obedience to the mere letter of a commandment. For instance, he pronounced severe censure upon Rabbi Ishmael ben Jose because the Rabbi was willing to act as bailiff in prosecuting Jewish thieves and criminals. He advised Rabbi Ishmael to follow the example of his father and leave the country.
>
> His estrangement from his friend Rabbi Yoshuah ben Levi is characteristic. One who was sought by the officers of the law took refuge with Rabbi Yoshuah. His pursuers were informed of his place of concealment. Threatening to put all the inhabitants of the city to the sword if he was not delivered up, they demanded his surrender. The Rabbi urged the fugitive from justice to resign himself to his fate. It is better for one individual to die, he said, than for a whole community to be exposed to peril. The fugitive yielded to the Rabbi's argument and gave himself up to the bailiffs. Thereafter, Elijah, who had been in the habit of visiting Rabbi Yoshuah frequently, stayed away from his house, and he was

induced to come back only by the Rabbi's long fasts and earnest prayers. In reply to the Rabbi's question of why Elijah had shunned him, he said: "Dost thou suppose I care to have intercourse with informers?" The Rabbi quoted a passage from the Mishnah to justify his conduct, but Elijah remained unconvinced. "Dost thou consider this a law for a pious man?" he said. "Other people might have been right in doing as thou didst; thou shouldst have done otherwise."

The story told of Elijah and Rabbi Anan forms the most striking illustration of the severity of the prophet. Someone brought Rabbi Anan a mess of little fish as a present, and at the same time the gifter asked the Rabbi to act as judge in a lawsuit he was interested in. Anan refused, in these circumstances, to accept a gift from the litigant. To demonstrate his single-mindedness, the applicant urged the Rabbi to take the fish and assign the case to another judge. Anan acquiesced, and he requested one of his colleagues to act for him, because he was recused from serving as a judge. His legal friend drew the inference that the litigant introduced to him was a kinsman of Rabbi Anan's, and accordingly, he showed himself particularly complacent toward him. As a result, the other party to the suit was intimidated. He failed to present his side as convincingly as he might otherwise have done, and so lost the case. Elijah, who had been the friend of Anan and his teacher as well, thenceforth shunned his presence, because he considered that the injury done the second party to the suit was due to Anan's carelessness. Anan, in his distress, kept many fasts and offered up many prayers before Elijah would return to him. Even then, the Rabbi could not endure the sight of the prophet; he had to content himself with listening to Elijah's words without looking upon his face.

Sometimes, tradition tends to look at Elijah's rigor with an attitude of humor (even an angel may err).

The rigor practiced by Elijah toward his friends caused one of them, the Tanna Rabbi Jose, to accuse him of being passionate and irascible. As a consequence, Elijah would have nothing to do with him for a long time. When he reappeared and confessed the cause of his withdrawal, Rabbi Jose said he felt justified, for his charge could not have received a more striking verification.

Elijah encourages people to engage in spiritual studies.

> The prophet once met a man who mocked Elijah's exhortations
> to study, and he said that on the great day of reckoning he would
> excuse himself for his neglect of intellectual pursuits by the fact that
> he had been granted neither intelligence nor wisdom. Elijah asked
> him what his calling was. "I am a fisherman," was the reply. "Well,
> my son," questioned Elijah, "who taught thee to take flax and make
> nets and throw them into the sea to catch fish?" The man replied:
> "For this Heaven gave me intelligence and insight." Hereupon, Elijah
> responded: "If thou possessest intelligence and insight to cast nets
> and catch fish, why should these qualities desert thee when thou deal-
> est with the Torah, which, thou knowest, is very nigh unto man that
> he may do it?" The fisherman was touched, and he began to weep.
> Elijah pacified him by telling the man that what he had said applied
> to many another beside him.

He sometimes tries to broaden the outlook of those he teaches.

> How difficult it is to form a true judgment with nothing but external
> appearances as a guide, Elijah proved to Rabbi Baroka. They were once
> walking in a crowded street, and the Rabbi requested that Elijah point
> out any in the throng who were destined to occupy places in Paradise.
> Elijah answered that there was none, only to contradict himself the very
> next minute and point to a passer-by. The man's appearance was such
> that in him least of all the Rabbi would have suspected a pious man.
> His garb did not even indicate that he was a Jew. Later, Rabbi Baroka
> discovered by questioning the man that he was a prison guard. In the
> fulfillment of his duties as such he was particularly careful that the vir-
> tue of chastity should not be violated in the prison in which both men
> and women were kept in detention. Also, his position often brought
> him into relations with the heathen authorities, and so he was able to
> keep the Jews informed of the disposition entertained toward them by
> the powers that be. The Rabbi was thus taught that no station in life
> precluded its occupant from doing good and acting nobly.

Tradition has always considered Elijah to be a great teacher of the
Qabbalah.

The frequent meetings between Elijah and the teachers of the Law of the Talmudic time were invested with personal interest only. Upon the development of the Torah, they had no influence whatsoever. His relation to the mystic science was of quite other character. It is safe to say that what Moses was to the Torah, Elijah was to the Qabbalah. His earliest relation to it was established through Rabbi Shimon ben Yohai and his son Rabbi Eliezer. For thirteen years he visited them twice daily in their subterranean hiding place, and imparted to them the secrets of the Torah. A thousand years later, Elijah again gave the impetus to the development of the Qabbalah, for it was he that revealed mysteries, first to the Nazarite Rabbi Jacob, then to his disciple of the latter, Abraham ben David. The mysteries in the books Peliah and Kanah the author Elkanah owed wholly to Elijah. He had appeared to him Elkanah in the form of a venerable old man, and had imparted to him the secret lore taught in the heavenly academy. Besides, he led him to a fiery rock whereon mysterious characters were engraved, and these were deciphered by Elkanah.

After Elkanah had thus become thoroughly impregnated with mystical teachings, Elijah took him to the tomb of the patriarchs, and thence to the heavenly academy. But the angels, little pleased by the intrusion of one "born of woman," inspired Elkanah with such terror that he asked Elijah to carry him back to earth. His mentor allayed his fears and long continued to instruct him in the mystical science, according to the system his disciple has recorded in his two works.

The prophet Elijah can be invoked, either in human form or in the form of Sandalfon, his angelic aspect.

The Qabbalists in general were possessed of the power to conjure up Elijah by means of certain formulas. One of them, Rabbi Joseph della Reyna, once called upon Elijah in this way, but it proved his own undoing. He was a saintly scholar, and he had conceived no less a purpose than to bring about the redemption of man by the conquest of the angel Samael, the Prince of Evil. After many prayers and vigils and long indulgence in fasting and other ascetic practices, Rabbi Joseph united himself with his five disciples for the purpose of conjuring up Elijah. When the prophet, obeying the summons, suddenly stood before him, Rabbi Joseph spoke: "Peace be with thee, our master! True prophet, bearer of salvation, be not displeased with me that I have troubled thee to come hither. God knows, I have not done it for myself, and not for mine own honor. I am zealous for the name and the honor of God, and I know thy desire is the same as mine, for it is thy vocation to make the glory of God prevail on earth. I pray thee, therefore, to grant my petition. Tell me with what means I can conquer Satan." Elijah at first endeavored to dissuade the Rabbi from his enterprise. He described the great power of Satan, ever growing as it feeds upon the sins of mankind. But Rabbi Joseph could not be made to desist. Elijah then enumerated what measures and tactics the Rabbi would have to observe in his combat with the fallen angel. He enumerated the pious, saintly deeds that would win the interest of the archangel Sandalphon in his undertaking, and from this angel he would learn the method of warfare to be pursued. The Rabbi followed Elijah's directions carefully, and succeeded in summoning Sandalphon to his assistance. If he had continued to obey instructions implicitly, and had carried out all Sandalphon advised, the Rabbi would have triumphed over Satan and hastened the redemption of the world. Unfortunately, at one point the Rabbi committed an indiscretion, and he lost the great advantages he had gained over Satan, who used his restored power to bring ruin upon him and his disciples.

Elijah reveals divine mysteries.

On one occasion, Elijah fared badly for having betrayed celestial events to his scholars. He was a daily attendant at the academy of Rabbi Yehudah ha-Nasi. One day, it was the New Moon Day, he was late. The reason for his tardiness, he said, was that it was his daily duty to awaken the three patriarchs, wash their hands for them so that they might offer up their prayers, and after their devotions, lead them back to their resting places. On this day their prayers took very long, because they were increased by the Musaf service on account of the New Moon celebration, and hence he did not make his appearance at the academy in good time. Elijah did not end his narrative at this point, but went on to tell the Rabbi that this occupation of his was rather tedious, for the three patriarchs were not permitted to offer up their payers at the same time. Abraham prayed first, then came Isaac, and finally Jacob. If they all were to pray together, the united petitions of three such paragons of piety would be so efficacious as to force God to fulfill them, and God would be induced to bring the Messiah before his time. Then Rabbi Yehudah wanted to know whether there were any among the pious on earth whose prayer possessed equal efficacy. Elijah admitted that the same power resided in the prayers of Rabbi Hayyah and his two sons. Rabbi Yehudah lost no time in proclaiming a day of prayer and fasting and summoning Rabbi Hayyah and his sons to officiate as the leaders in prayer. They began to chant the Eighteen Benedictions. When they uttered the word for wind, a storm arose; when they continued and made petition for rain, the rain descended at once. But as the readers approached the passage relating to the revival of the dead, great excitement arose in heaven, and when it became known that Elijah had revealed the secret of the marvelous power attached to the prayers of the three men, he was punished with fiery blows. To thwart Rabbi Yehudah's purpose, Elijah assumed the form of a bear, and put the praying congregation to flight.[1]

These legends are not merely fairy tales. I have experienced his help several times in my life.

In one case, I had a professor at university who was so strict that every student feared her. One young woman got stomach cramps at the mere thought of the next lesson with her. No matter how much we learned, it was never enough. As a result, I decided that this was unacceptable—learning should be joyful, not painful. I asked Elijah to help, but not to punish, for I believed this professor was a very poor, lonely, and maybe frustrated woman who had no friends and no human contact outside of university (where, incidentally, everybody hated her). Elijah promised help, and the next day, she was extremely friendly. I cannot say what happened to her, but everybody noticed the change. It did not last very long, but during the years of my studies, she started to be friendlier toward the students. She never turned out to be very popular, but she tried her best, which is all we can ask.

In another case, I had some trouble with the local authorities while trying to file an application. The officer tried to follow the law very strictly

---

[1] If not stated otherwise, all quotations and extracts in this chapter are taken from Louis Ginzberg, *Legends of the Jews* (Philadelphia: Jewish Publication Society of America, 1909). [The previous extracts have been edited for consistency, clarity, and ease of reading. —*Editor*]

and was about to refuse my application. I had moral right on my side, but I could not prove it—so I asked Elijah for help. Things turned out well, and the application was accepted.

(For the result in both cases I am very thankful to Elijah and to the Holy One, blessed be He, who sent Elijah to me.)

Invoking Elijah

If you need help, Elijah can be invoked to ease your need. To call Elijah, say:

> Elijah the prophet, Elijah the friend,
> come and help me, lawful judge.
> Save my life, for you defend
> those who've been mistreated much.
> Bring harmony and peace to me.
> In Yahu's Name, so mote it be.

Sit down in meditation, close your eyes, and visualize your meditation room. See the image of your room clearly with your inner eye. After a while, hear the sound of someone knocking at the door. Stand up in your astral body and go to the door. Upon opening the door, someone will stand in front of you. I cannot tell you how the person in front of you will look. To most people Elijah appears as he really is: a middle-aged man with a long beard and white Jewish garments. Tradition says, however, that he may appear in every possible shape, and the legends of the Talmud describe some of them. Sometimes, he appears as an ordinary old man or someone known to the person to whom he appears—an Arab, a horseman, a court official, or a harlot. Once, he even appeared to Rabbi Chiya in the form of a fiery bear to prevent him performing the great miracles. Welcome Elijah in whatever shape he appears to you and whatever name he may use. Offer him something to eat and to drink. He will talk to you in a way that fits his appearance. Tell him about your problem and listen to his advice. If you ask him to administer justice, he will do so, but he will always judge YOU first. He will be very strict, so it would be wise to ask for his judgment only in cases where you are absolutely certain that you have done nothing wrong. If you are right to ask for judgment, he will make sure that the affairs on the physical plane will be affected in such a way that justice will be re-established and that the person who mistreated you will have to learn his lesson. If you are not right, you will first have to pay your dues. He will not be concerned with local laws, but will judge only according to Divine Law. If you think that both you and others have done something wrong, you may ask him to act as a peacemaker. In this way, you will ensure that you will not be punished for your mistakes, although you may have to accept responsibility for your past actions.

You can also ask Elijah to come to you as a teacher and interpreter of the Holy Scriptures and the mysteries. In this case, you can call upon him with your own words. He will appear to you in his true form and answer your questions. He will, however, come only if you are a dedicated student of the tradition, and he will insist that you continue to go on with your studies and learn more about what he has taught you.

26

Chassidut and Hishtavvut
Mystical Devotion and Equanimity

> . . . [T]he control of environment must begin with self-control, and until we cease to be influenced by surrounding conditions we cannot hope to exercise any mental influence over them. Paradoxically, it is only when our environment ceases to matter to us that we have the power to change it by mental means.
>
> DION FORTUNE, *SANE OCCULTISM*

Every magical work starts within the soul of the magician. If he is not in control of the elements within his soul, he cannot hope to control the elements without. Thus the development of his soul is an important factor both in high and low magic. For this reason, the Chassidey Ashkenaz (a medieval group of powerful occultists who lived in Germany) developed a highly ascetic lifestyle and a very high standard of ethics, based of the idea of *Chassidut* (חסידות), as can be seen in their name.

404

Chassidut is a very important concept in the Qabbalah, so important that it also gave its name to the most well known Qabbalistic movement to date.[1] Chassidut is often translated as "piety" or "righteousness." Literally, it means "chassid-ness"—that is, being like a Chassid. But what is a Chassid? A Chassid is one whose heart is filled with Chesed—with love for God, with mercy for his fellow men, and with inner peace.

Chassidut is closely linked to *Hishtavvut* (השתוות), "equanimity." The Qabbalist Isaac ben Samuel of Acre/Acco (fourteenth century) considers Hishtavvut to be an important step in the attainment of the mental union with God.[2] Chaim Vital quotes his description of the process of spiritual attainment: "And behold, after a man has attained the mystery (sod) of the *Hitdabqut* (adherence to God) which was mentioned, he can attain the mystery (sod) of the *Hishtavvut* (equanimity), and if he has attained the mystery (sod) of the Hishtavvut (equanimity), he can attain the mystery (sod) of the *Hitbodedut* (seclusion), And after he has attained the mystery (sod) of the Hitbodedut (seclusion), he can attain the *Ruach ha-Qodesh* (Holy Spirit). And from there he may attain *Nevuah* (prophesy); that is to say he will prophesy and predict the future" (Chaim Vital, *Shaarey Qedushah,* part 4, chapter 2:5).

Let us have a closer look at the levels (or degrees) of spiritual development as described in the Qabbalistic tradition:[3]

Sod ha-Hitdabqut (mystery of adherence to God) refers to having attained the level of Malchut and Yesod—that is, the material and the astral plane. In Malchut the seeker experiences the Vision of the Holy Guardian Angel, which is the spiritual experience of Malchut and which reveals to him the deeper meaning of life in the manifested world. It also inspires in his soul a deep understanding of the consequences of his actions, resulting in a higher sense of responsibility for his deeds. In Yesod the seeker develops the virtue of emotional independence and overcomes the vice of idleness. Thus his entire Nefesh is focused on the spiritual path. This is the mystery

---

[1] This refers to modern Chassidism, which originated in Eastern Europe and should not be mixed up with the Chassidey Ashkenaz of medieval Germany.

[2] See Isaac ben Samuel, *Meirat Eneyim* (Illumination of the Eyes), passage "Eqev" (cod. Beer 195 a b).

[3] Here, I can of course present only a rough outline, for a more detailed description would go beyond the scope of this book. I will, however, describe these levels in much greater detail in my next book, *The Wisdom of the Holy Qabbalah.*

of adherence to God. The seeker who has attained Sod ha-Hitdabqut is traditionally called a *Chassid*.

The next level is the level of the *Ish Chacham* (wise one) who has mastered the lower mental plane that is Hod and Netzach. This level is not mentioned in the preceding text—the quote of Isaac ben Samuel of Acre/ Acco—because this text focuses on the major stations related to the five Partzufim (Keter, Chochmah, Binah, Tiferet, and Malchut). On the other hand, Chaim Vital may not have mentioned this level because Hod and Netzach do not belong to the middle pillar, and are seen as being less important for the path of the mystic, which is Chaim Vital's main interest.

Sod ha-Hishtavvut (mystery of equanimity) refers to having attained the level of Tiferet, which is the first stage of adepthood. In order to attain this level, the seeker must overcome his pride, the vice of Tiferet, and he must develop equanimity, which is the natural result of having attained the spiritual experience of Tiferet: the Vision of the Harmony of Things. This vision will enable him to accept all the events of life, both good and bad, with equanimity, for he knows about the underlying harmony of all things, and he has realized that all events are just stages of the manifestation of the Divine Plan.

Now we can also understand why the mystery of adherence to God must precede the mystery of equanimity. Unless we have gained an understanding of the spiritual meaning of life and gained emotional independence, we have no hope of overcoming our pride and thus gaining independence from our ego.

Though again not mentioned in the above text, between Tiferet and Binah lies the level of Gevurah and Chesed, which is the level of the true Baal-Shem (Master of the Name), the greater adept who has attained both the Vision of Power and the vision of Love, and thus uses his magical power with altruistic love.

Sod ha-Hitbodedut (mystery of seclusion) refers to having attained the level of Binah. Here the adept attains the virtue of Binah, which is called "silence," and which does not so much refer to living in a hermitage as to means having achieved inner silence—that is, the silence of the ego. The *Mitboded* (secluded one) is a high adept who secludes himself from the egoistic noise of worldly affairs in order to gain inner silence. Only when this inner silence is attained can the voice of the Ruach ha-Qodesh (Holy Spirit) be heard. Thus, at this level, true and untainted communication with the spiritual plane is possible.

Obviously, the mystery of equanimity must precede the mystery of seclusion, for unless we have overcome our pride and gained independence from our ego, we may not hope to experience moments of complete silence from our ego.

Nevuah (prophesy) refers to having attained the level of Chochmah. This is the level where the Prophet attains—like Moses—"the Vision of God face to face" (Exodus 33:11).

The highest level is that of Keter, the level of the complete Tzaddiq (Tzaddiq gamur). *Tzaddiq* means "righteous one" or, less literally, "saint," for those who have reached this level are free of sin (i.e., free of the Evil Urge). The complete Tzaddiq is a potential Messiah who has attained the Vision of unity with God, which is sometimes called *Devequt* (literally, "being adjoined to God") in the Qabbalistic tradition.[4] This level is also called Completion of the Great Work.

Chaim Vital explains the idea of Hishtavvut by telling a story of a person seeking admission to the higher levels of mystical wisdom.[5]

And about the meaning (perush) of the mystery of equanimity (Sod ha-hishtavut):

Rabbi Avner Z"L[6] said to me that a wise man (Ish Chacham) came to one of the Mitbodedim (secluded ones) and he asked him that he be accepted[7] to be amongst the Mitbodedim. And the Mitboded said to him: Blessd art thou, my son, to God for thy intention (Kavvanah), it is good! Honestly, let me know, art thou equanimous or not? He said to him: Rabbi, explain thy words! He said to him: If [there are] two men, one of whom honours thee and the second one humiliates thee, are they equal in thy eyes or not? He said to him: No Sir, for I feel delight and satisfaction[8] by the one who honours me, and sadness by the one who humiliates [me]. But I do not avenge or bear a grudge. He said to him: My son, go in peace!

---

[4] Quite often, however, the term *Devequt* is used as a synonym for Sod ha-Hitdabqut.

[5] Like the previous passage, this description of Chaim Vital's is a quote from *Meirat Eneyim* by Isaac ben Samuel of Acre/Acco.

[6] Zichrono Livrocho (Of Blessed Memory).

[7] The verb used for "to be accepted" is *qibbel,* from the same root as Qabbalah. He wishes to become a *Mequbbal,* a Qabbalist (literally, "one who has been accepted")—in other words, an adept (from Latin, *adeptus,* "having reached, attained").

[8] The Hebrew term is *nachat ruach* (literally, "pleasure of the Ruach /mental soul"). This may be interpreted as pleasure of the ego.

For as long as thou art not equanimous—until thy Nefesh neither feels the honour of the one who honours [thee] nor the humiliation of the one who humiliates [thee]—it is not for thee to be invited to have thy thought[s] connected with the Highest One (Eliyon), to be taken captive [by the Highest One], and seclude thyself [from the lower influences]. And truly, go and further subdue thy heart into true surrender until thou art equanimous, and then thou art capable of seclusion.[9]

What keeps us from attaining true spiritual union with the Divine is tension in different parts of ourself. Think of your physical body. When it is tense, you feel physically uncomfortable, and this may hinder your spiritual work, a fact most obvious in meditation, where every tension in the physical body hinders relaxation and achieving any higher level of meditation in which closeness or union with the Divine is possible. Not only your physical body, but also your emotional body (Nefesh) or your mind (Ruach) can be tense. This emotional or mental tension is different from physical tension, but like it, both emotional and mental tension hinder occult exercises, spiritual work, and inner happiness.

If the emotions are tense, they create anger, fear, sadness, and imbalanced desires. It may seem strange to describe anger as an emotional tension, but try to recall this feeling. The tension even expands to the physical body, doesn't it? A typical reaction is that people grit their teeth. Fear is a different tension, felt in the shoulders and in the stomach. Sadness is felt in the heart area, and desire in the genitals or other sensual parts of the body.

Even subtler is mental tension. This creates an imbalanced ego. It makes our mind so stiff that clear thought becomes difficult or impossible,[10] and every idea is influenced by the ego in such a way that either the person tends to think of himself as "the greatest" or even the center of the universe, or he may consider himself unworthy and inferior, depending on the type of tension. Also, the effect that other people's praise or blame has on our thoughts, as described by Rabbi Awner in his anecdote, is a result of mental tension and an imbalanced ego.

---

[9] Chaim Vital, *Shaarey Qedushah,* part 4, chapter 2:5.
[10] This is why clear thought is seldom found in our selfish society.

SOUL	RELAXATION	TENSION
Higher Soul (Neshamah)	union with the Divine	(no tension)[11]
mental soul (Ruach)	altruism and clear thought	imbalanced ego
emotional soul (Nefesh)	true happiness	bad emotions
physical body (Guf)	bodily pleasure	tight muscles

[11] If the physical, emotional, and mental levels are free of tension, then devequt, closeness, or union with the Divine follows automatically, for our Higher Self constantly seeks union with us. Only the fact that we have put things in the way hinders this union.

But how can we learn to avoid tension? Let us first have a closer look at the emotions. The first rule is: Do not try to suppress your negative emotions, for this will only cause them to withdraw into the subconscious mind. There, they will have the power to control you without your awareness of this control. Never suppress anything, because pressure will cause resistance.

Think of pressure in a boiler. If it is not restricted, the steam simply dissipates into the air, but if it is kept within the boiler, it might build up so much pressure that eventually it could even cause the boiler to explode. It is a well known fact among psychoanalysists that suppressed desires can cause severe psychotic disturbances.

Instead of suppressing these feelings, you should strive to let go of all the negativity in your emotions. The result should be a feeling of emotional relaxation comparable to relaxation of the muscles in the physical body. It will remove tensions in your emotional body (Nefesh), and increases the emotional body's ability to experience true happiness in the same way that physical relaxation enables bodily pleasure.

You should try to develop an attitude of constant inner happiness. Again, never force your emotions to do something. If you force yourself to be happy, the result will be false happiness, which will not give you any inner satisfaction. Do not make up anything, but try to become aware of the eternal delight of our Higher Self that is present all the time.

I could write an entire book about the mystical states of Chassidut and hishtavvut, but no matter how much you read about it, you will not become a Chassid unless you start practicing. Therefore, I suggest that we start with a simple exercise.

First Exercise: Observe Your Emotions

Have a look at your emotional state. Do you find any traces of bad feelings? If so,[12] can you try to let it go? If this is difficult, can you think of any reason why this emotion is not good for you?[13] Let us assume you are angry. Someone might have done something wrong to you, and you may feel that you have a right to be angry. This may be so, but your anger will probably prevent the best possible reaction to the situation. How does it help you to be right if, as a result, it is also disadvantageous for you? Think of a possible negative outcome caused by your anger. Imagine this very vividly. (Try several outcomes if you like!) You will realize that anger is not good for you. You may feel unhappy about being angry. Fine! Now let the anger go!

Do the same if you are sad. Something has happened that you hoped would be different. Your sadness will make you stick to your head's idea of how it should have been, and it will keep you from seeing the potential of the actual situation. Fear will also limit your perspective, but in a different way from how sadness will limit you. And imbalanced desire for something you do not have prevents you from enjoying what you already do have.

Anger and sadness limit you because of what has occurred in the past, while fear and imbalanced desire limit you because of what may happen in the future. What all these emotions have in common is that they make it impossible for you to enjoy the present moment.

Anger, fear, sadness, and even desire do have a reason to exist, and we may well ask if it would be good to be without them. Note, however, that you can be courageous, and even a warrior with all the adrenaline you need to defend your beloved ones—but with no inner feeling of anger. You can be careful and alert to danger without any feeling of fear. You can even learn to accept a difficult situation without any bitterness or lengthy mourning. Your ability to understand and to trust in God and in your destiny will enable you to do so, even though this is far from easy. Finally, you can get to the point where the Divine Will of your Higher Self is your primary motivation, and then you can let go of lower desires

---

[12] If the answer is always no, you have no bad feelings—you are either a tzaddiq (saint) of the highest level, and you will soon ascend to heaven to be transformed into an immortal angel . . . congratulations! Or you are simply deceiving yourself.

[13] Note that the Higher Soul always rules over the lower. Our mind and our thoughts can help us to influence our emotions if—and only IF—we use our mind wisely.

without becoming unmotivated, inert, or apathetic. You will not lose any joy by letting go of your imbalanced desire, but you will gain the ability to enjoy your senses without the restless urge that makes you hunt stimulus after stimulus, without any hope of satisfaction.[14]

Repeat this exercise as often as possible, so that eventually you become used to noticing and removing any unwanted tension from your emotions. If an emotional impulse is too strong to influence this tension immediately, try to assume the perspective of an unaffected observer. This may be difficult at first, but with practice, it will become easier.

Second Exercise: Create Happiness

Now that we have begun to let go of bad emotions, we must replace them with something else. Start by trying to find something that is good right now. Let us take an example of a very bad situation: You have had a car accident, but you are still alive, and the damage is not beyond repair. No broken bones. So be happy about that. You could be dead, so thank God for the second chance you were given.

Let us take another example. It does not have to be dramatic: You are sitting here, simply reading this book. Be thankful for the chance to do so. A few hundred years ago, it would have been very difficult to obtain a book like this. Also, you have obviously found the time to read. Not everybody is able to do so—some people have to work so hard that they find it difficult to take the time to read a book that has nothing to do with their work. You may also look at physical things. Are you sitting on a comfortable couch? Be happy about that. Is whatever you are sitting on not very comfortable? Well, at least you are not outside in the cold rain. Whatever the situation, find something to be happy about. Don't worry if you are happy about simple or even silly things. It does not matter, and it does not make you less happy if the reason for your happiness is trivial.

As with the first exercise, repeat this exercise as often as possible. Do it during odd moments: when you get up in the morning, when you are waiting for the bus, or when you have to do the laundry. Learn to be happy about as many things as possible until you develop an attitude of constant inner happiness—independent of external matters.

---

[14] Modern psychology may tell you that all this is impossible, but modern psychology is the study of the psyche of the majority of people based on statistics. If you attempt the path outlined in this chapter, you will leave the majority behind you, for you are on the journey to becoming a Chassid, and maybe even a Tzaddiq (saint).

Inner happiness does not mean that you should lose your concern for the world. If something tragic happens, it is quite all right—in fact, very important—to be aware of the sorrow it causes others. Yet you can help others much more effectively if you have faith in God and in the fact that anything that happens has a reason. Your faith and confidence in the future will encourage those who may feel that the world as they have known it has just ended. If you collapse in sadness, you will not be a help to anyone, but if you can give others the feeling that life is still worth living, this may be a great help to them. You must be strong to help those who are weak or in need.

Third Exercise: Observe Your Ego

In the previous two exercises, we used the power of the mental soul (Ruach) to influence our emotional soul (Nefesh). We used thought to influence feelings as the higher controls the lower. Most people will find this possible, but someone with an untrained and undisciplined mind may find this more difficult than would a person with advanced mental training. In this exercise we want to influence our mental soul (Ruach), and thus we need the help of our Higher Soul (Neshamah). Here, we face a difficulty. Nearly every human being has a fully functioning emotional soul. It may be imbalanced, but it is usually fully functioning—except, maybe, in cases of severely retarded souls. Most people have a minimum mental capacity, yet only a few have developed a sharp mind. Even so, the number of those who can call on the Higher Soul, even to the slightest degree, is very few indeed, and unless you have developed to the point that the influence of the Higher Soul can be felt to a certain extent, the third and fourth exercises in this chapter may be impossible to perform. Fortunately, the very fact that you are reading this book indicates that you may have developed a certain awareness that there are more things between Heaven and earth than most people realize, so the chances are not too poor!

Spiritual arrogance, false pride, vanity, envy, greed, egoism, megalomania, or an inferiority complex are the vices that we must overcome in this exercise. To do so, we must look beyond the viewpoint of the mortal self; we must raise our consciousness to the Neshamah, our immortal Higher Soul. If we look at our life from the perspective of our Neshamah, we understand that the only thing that matters when we leave this world is how well we have served the Light: "I have seen all the works that are done under the sun; and, behold, all is vanity and a striving after wind" (Ecclesiastes 1:14).

Everything below the level of Tiferet (i.e., the sun) is determined by the ego. Arrogance, false pride, vanity, and envy are based on the idea that we want to be better than others. We want to feel more important, and we want think of ourselves as special. We want others to praise us and think that we are superior.

Once we look at our life from the point of view of the higher soul, it does not matter what others think of us. Nor does it matter what we think of ourselves. All that matters is the amount of light and love in our heart and the good things we have done in our life. Once we have realized that, praise of others or of ourselves does not matter; we no longer care about such praise.

You may want to feel worthy and loved, but the eternal love of the Creator is omnipresent. His love does not depend on anything; you do not have to do anything to earn it, nor can you do anything to lose it. His love is the unconditional love of a parent for His children. All you must do is let go of the tension in your ego, so that you can open your heart and feel His limitless love.

Greed and egoism are based on the idea that we must compete with others to make sure we get as much as possible from life, but from the point of view of the higher soul, we all serve the one Creator. We are all a part of His universe, which is, in a way, His body. We must compete with each other no more than the organs in your body must compete. Would you want your liver to try to defeat your lungs? It is ridiculous, isn't it? We all have a task in this universe, and this task is a part of the Creator's Divine Plan. So why should we compete? Why should it matter who appears to be better or more successful, or who has more of something? Instead, let us work together!

Megalomania and inferiority complexes also do nothing but hinder your Higher Soul in the service of God. If you think you are the best or the most unworthy one, you are preventing yourself from serving God in the best possible way. Either you attempt tasks that are too big for you or you shy away from work that you could do successfully.

A great deal of pain and suffering is also the result of the tension of the ego. The ego identifies itself with certain things or ideas, and suffers when it has to let go of them. Even when we still have them, the ego is constantly busy worrying about losing them and suffers because it fears losing a part of itself, because it has identified itself with them. As a consequence, the ego tenses and clings to these things as much as possible, and this tension and stubborness makes the ego impenetrable to the inspiration of the Higher Self. The things and ideas with which the ego identifies can be anything: the new car that makes us feel more important, our social status, our occult degree as a member of an esoteric organization, our family or friends, or even a philosophical idea that we identify with. It is important to understand that none of these things is really a part of us, and that we do not lose a part of us if any of these has to go.

Everything will eventually decay, glory will be forgotten, and people will die. What remains is the inner experience, which is remembered and absorbed into the depths of our soul and which cannot be taken from us. The love we have shared with our dear ones will still connect us to them when we meet them again after this life. Remember: That which really belongs to us can never be lost, and that which can be lost does not really belong to us. Thus the pain of losing something is really nothing but an aberration or tension of the ego. (Of course, an emotional tension may also add to the tensions of the ego.) We even sometimes suffer because we cannot accept that the world is not as we think it should be. This is often nothing but the ego suffering, because it believes that what it considers right is better than what God has decreed in order to fulfill His Divine Plan—hubris at its worst. If we discover that we have identified ourselves with things, ideas, or even people, then we must let these go and become aware that there is no need to cling to anything. Learn to relax the tension in your ego and live a much happier life![15]

Observe your thoughts and try to detect even the slightest note of selfishness. Is your ego ever effected by what others think of you? If yes, try to assume the point of view of your immortal soul. If what you do is good, what does it matter if others like it or not? If what you do is not good, well,

---

[15] Once we have learned to relax our emotions, we sometimes still experience feelings of desire, fear, anger, or sadness that we cannot avoid completely. We may be able to let go of such feelings for a short while by using sheer willpower, but they keep popping up again. These emotions have their cause not in the astral plane, but in the mental plane, for each plane is ruled by the plane above it. These emotions are sometimes the result of the ego identifying itself with certain things—it desires more of them or is afraid to lose them or is angry or sad if it has already lost them. In order to release the tension of these emotions, we must first release the tension of the ego. Only when we stop identifying with these things can we let go of them. In order to release the tension of the ego, however, it is necessary to be able temporarily to relax the emotions to such a degree that we can observe and influence our ego. This is why we must master Yesod before we can master Tiferet.

even the best feedback will not make it better. If it does not make a difference, then, let go of the pain or pride that the words of others cause you. Observe your ego until you are adept at discovering the slightest effects of imbalance. Once you understand how useless they are, let them go. The feeling you experience should always be one of relaxation, not one of guilt, sin, or suppression, for this will only create neuroses.

Overcoming egoism and greed does not mean that you do not care for what you need in this life. Remember, however, that what you need is not always the thing you like or desire. Try to accept that things in life may turn out different from how you hoped. Change them if you can, and do not fall into the other extreme of fatalism. In any case, whether or not you succeed in changing them, have faith in the wisdom of the Divine Plan.

Note that blame or praise may also include useful information. If you did something wrong, the person who tells you off may have some hints as to how you can avoid the mistake next time. Listen to the advice, but be unaffected by the blame.

Equanimity does not mean that you are unaware of the difference between praise or blame. Of course, someone who insults you may cause you trouble in the physical world, and it would be foolish not to take the necessary precautions. Instead, equanimity means that you neither feel hurt by someone who blames you nor flattered by someone who praises you. Both hurt and a sense of being flattered may keep you from making an objective judgment.

Once you make a certain progress in the development of equanimity, there is the danger that you will fall into the trap of being proud of your achievement. You may be insulted and may be seemingly unaffected, because you think yourself better than the insulter due to developing equanimity. Thus, once again, your ego tenses with pride and arrogance. This is an "advanced" and more subtle form of pride, but it is nevertheless an expression of an imbalanced and tense ego that must be avoided in order to develop true equanimity. As long as we still worry about who is better, we are still dominated by the ego, for once we have developed equanimity, our self-esteem is no longer affected.

Fourth Exercise: Create Altruism

Whatever you feel you have developed—whatever your development of equanimity—it is not enough to make an objective judgment. You will also need to have love and mercy for the person who praises or blames you. If your hand hurts, do you hate it? No, you know it is ill and needs healing. You care for it and wish to help it. If your fellow human hurts you, do the same. This healing may involve the use of Din (Justice) or Gevurah (Power), but even if this is the case, act with love.

In all beings are hidden Divine Sparks (*Netzotzim*) which come from the Creator himself. Some of these Sparks are aware of their Divine Origin, but most of them still wait to be redeemed.[16] Try to see the Divine Spark in every being, and even if the shell of this spark looks disgusting, love it, for it is a vessel of the Divine.[17]

The more love you give to others, the more love comes back into your own life. Learn to think of yourself as a servant of the Light who lives to serve the Divine Will, and who does not live for his own sake.

According to tradition, there are thirty-six[18] (ל"ו) hidden Tzaddiqim[19] (righteous ones) in every generation who carry on their shoulders the burden of the world and thus lift the burden of the Shechinah. They live not for their own sake, but for the sake of the world.[20] No one knows who they are, and according to one branch of the tradition, even they do not know that they are one of the *Lamed-Vav:* the thirty-six. When one of them dies, another one is chosen for this task. Tradition also says that the Messiah (the savior of the age) hides among them, carrying the greatest burden.

Think of the idea that somewhere there are thirty-six just men or women helping to carry the burden of your sins and of the pain and sorrows you have caused the world. Try to fill your heart with true altruism in order to lift their burden.

Sefer Chassidim (Book of the Chassidim) describes the allegory of a Chassid who, in summer, used to sleep on the ground among the fleas and

---

[16] The act of redeeming these Sparks is called Tiqqun (healing) in Qabbalistic philosophy.

[17] The great occultist Walter Ernest Butler, who may well have been one of the thirty-six Tzaddiqim (righteous ones or saints), once said: "If you want to see God, look into the eyes of the person next to you."

[18] The number thirty-six is symbolic for a complete circle. Thirty-six is two times eighteen, the number of life—eighteen men and eighteen women.

[19] Also called *Tzaddiqim Nistarim* in Hebrew, or *Lamed-Vav-niks* in Yiddish.

[20] "The world [must contain] not less than thirty-six righteous men in each generation who are granted to see the countenance of the Shechinah, for it is written: 'Blessed are all they that wait for Him' (Isajah 30:18). The Gematria of "for Him" (Hebrew: לו) is thirty-six" (Babylonian Talmud Sanhedrin 97b).

ants, and, in winter, on the snow, putting his feet into a vessel filled with water until the water froze to ice. One of his disciples asked him: "Why do you do this? Because every human being is responsible for his own life, why do you endanger yourself in such a way?" The Chassid answered: "I have certainly not committed a mortal sin, and even though I may have committed some minor sins, these torments may not seem necessary [in order to undergo the process of Teshuvah, "repentance"]. But in the *Midrash* (Jewish legends) is written that the Messiah suffers for our sins as it is written: 'But he was wounded because of our transgressions' (Isaiah 53:5), and also the Tzaddiqim suffer for the sins of their generation. Yet I do not want anyone but me to suffer for my own sins."[21]

This story is certainly not to be taken literally, but it does describe the inner attitude of a man whose altruism is stronger than his selfish desires. He is aware of the effect that his actions have, and he is willing to accept responsibility for his own Karma. He wants to make sure that the sum total of his deeds makes the world a better place.

After all this, however, remember that love, mercy, altruism, and self-lessness do not mean that you are unaware of the motives of others. You may love them and have mercy, and your aims may be selfless and altruistic, but other people's aims may or may not be as good as yours. Do not lose your common sense. Be prepared, but love them anyway, and if they do wrong, forgive them, for they may have their own lessons to learn. No matter what happens in your life, keep peace in your heart and be thankful for the help given by God.

Gadlut and Qatnut:
The Greater and the Lesser State

According to the Qabbalah, no mortal human being can continuously be in perfect harmony. Qabbalists distinguish between two kinds of awareness:

Gadlut (the greater state) refers to a state of higher awareness in which we experience inner harmony and in which we are in contact with our Higher Soul.

Qatnut (the lesser state) refers to a state of awareness that is separated from true higher awareness. This is the viewpoint of the ego that is bound by the material world.

---

[21] *Sefer Chassidim*, § I 556.

Rabbi Levi Isaak of Berdichev (1740–1810), a disciple of Rabbi Dov Baer (the successor of the Besht) taught that some people serve the Creator, blessed be He, because of the great reward that is bestowed upon them for their service. This is called Qatnut (the lesser state). This is service to God with a small degree of consciousness. Others serve Him because He is Master, Ruler, and King, paying no attention to the blessings or rewards that God may give them. All such benefits and pleasures are as nothing to them compared with the true joy of serving their Creator, blessed be He. Such a one is said to be serving God with Gadlut (the greater state).[22]

Qabbalistic teachings say that we cannot stay in a state of Gadlut all the time. There must be a time of Qatnut. (Both are necessary—like the two pillars in the Tree of Life.) Qabbalists do not condemn this state or a being in this state. From time to time, we must turn our attention to the Path of the Hearth-Fire and be concerned with material problems. We cannot live permanently in higher consciousness. There will be times when we cannot access the wisdom of our Higher Soul, and at those times, our souls are tested.[23] Yet even the mistakes that may occur if we are in a limited state of consciousness are not to be condemned, for it is from these that we learn and grow. So do not be irritated if you find it impossible to maintain your inner harmony uninterruptedly—just keep trying.

As I said earlier, mysticism is about practice. It is no good reading these lines and saying to yourself, "Well, that sounds good. Now I know all about mysticism." You must practice it again and again until it becomes natural and without conscious thought. You may find that in the beginning there is little success, and you may find that after a while, when you thought you were making good progress, something happens that seems to throw you back for months or even years. You must not falter, and you must go on without diminishing your devotion. Then—and only then—will you become a true Chassid.[24]

---

[22] See: Sefer Qedushat Levi.

[23] As described by St. John of the Cross in "The Dark Night of the Soul."

[24] The traditional Qabbalistic terms for the stages of relaxation as described in this chapter are: Bitul ha-Hargashot (annulment of the feelings) for the emotional level, and Bitul ha-Yesh (annulment of the somethingness; i.e., the lower ego) for the mental level. Above them is the stage of Bitul be-Metziut (annulment in reality; i.e., the union with Keter).

27

Tiqqun ha-Olam

Healing the World

Chapter 26 mentions the thirty-six tzaddiqim. Even though the general opinion is that no one knows who they are, there is a Chassidic story about a man who knows that one of them lives in his town as a tailor. The man rips his trousers in order to have a reason to meet the tailor, enters the tailor's shop, and asks him for help. The tailor offers him a bench to sit on and then threads a needle. He begins to sew, and just as his needle pierces the cloth, the man feels a pricking sensation. The needle and thread pull together the two edges of the ripped trousers, and in the very moment when the edges merge, the man feels a wonderful sense of relief and inner peace. As the tailor goes on sewing, the man continues to feel the pricks and the feeling of relief and peace. The man thinks: "This tailor is not just mending my trousers; he is mending my soul."

His thoughts are interrupted by a young Chassid who enters the tailor's shop and greets the tailor with great respect. The tailor smiles at him, and the Chassid takes a seat on the bench next to the man. When the tailor is finished the Chassid stands up and bows to the tailor, saying: "Thank you for letting me watch you heal the world." And the man thinks: "Oh, what a fool I have been! Here I was thinking he was healing my soul, when he was really healing the entire world."

Another Chassidic legend[1] describes the life of Henoch (Chanoch), who is mentioned only briefly in the Torah: "And Henoch (Chanoch) walked with God, and he was not; for God took him" (Genesis 5:24).

The Qabbalah teaches us that he did not die, but was instead transformed into Metatron, the highest of the archangels. But what did he do to earn such a high reward? The legend says that he was a shoemaker, and whenever he joined the upper leather of a shoe with its sole, he also united the upper world with the lower world to enable the union of the Holy One, blessed be He, and the Shechinah.

Both the tailor and Henoch (Chanoch) did ordinary work, and at the same time, they changed the world.

Tibetan lamas perform specific rituals in order to bless the world. The Jewish Tzaddiqim bless the world during their everyday work. The redemption of the world from the imbalanced Qlippotic influences is what the Qabbalah calls *Tiqqun ha-Olam* (healing the world).

We all spend a great deal of time every day with work that neither requires all our attention nor asks for our full mental or emotional capacities. These times can be used to send out to the world positive influences. We do so by identifying our work with an aspect of the world that needs healing. The tailor in the story identified the cloth with the world and the tear with the wounds of this world. By bringing together the edges and mending them, the world is healed. Technically speaking, if performed correctly, this is an act of sympathetic magic on a very high level.[2]

There is a danger to this exercise: spiritual pride. Never be tempted to think that you are a Tzaddiq or that the world depends on you. Many sages believe that a true Tzaddiq would never think of himself as being one of the thirty-six, simply because he would be too humble to consider himself as

---

[1] This story seems to originate in Germany in the thirteenth century and came via Isaac ben Samuel of Acre to Moses Qordovero.

[2] A more complex variation of this principle is found in the Kavvanot (Intentions) and Yichudim (Unifications) used in the Lurianic Qabbalah. These were specific (mainly numerological) meditations based on doing certain (religious) acts with intention (Kavvanah), or meditations on the unification of two or more Divine Names to bring about the reunion of the Holy King and the Shechinah (Yichudim).

one of them. Furthermore, tradition says that even though we never know who is a Tzaddiq, anyone who claims to be a Tzaddiq is certainly a liar—a true Tzaddiq would never reveal himself. Perform this exercise with love, compassion, and altruism—and not in order to feel important. Here you will find a few ideas for the application of this exercise to your daily life:

- When you do creative work, create good things in the world. For example, when you make food, imagine that you are giving food to all who are hungry, and that you are giving spiritual nourishment to those who are experiencing spiritual dryness.
- When you do work that causes growth, let goodness grow. For example, when you work in the garden growing roses, imagine that at the same time, you are letting love and compassion grow in the world at the same time.
- When you do organizational work, or you rearrange something, let the world be put in order. For example, when you tidy your house, imagine that the whole world is being harmoniously balanced.
- If you are cleaning, cleanse the world from evil or imbalance. For example, when you wash the dishes, imagine that you are wiping away the sorrows of the world.
- If you are repairing something, heal the world. For example, when you repair the motor of your car, imagine that, as you put together the pieces of the motor, you are putting together the people that need to work together, or that you are healing the broken relationships among people who should be in harmony with each other.
- If you enjoy something, let the world share your joy. For example, when you enjoy a good meal, share your delight and thankfulness with all life forms on this planet, so that all beings and the earth itself is blessed.

It is always better to choose a kind of positive influence that is related to your work. Be specific about the kind of positive change you want to make, but do not be specific about where you want to make this change. Leave this to the Shechinah Herself. If you want to feed the hungry, do not state a particular region, but feed the whole world. (You may hear in the news about big catastrophes in other countries and wish to do something for the people who have experienced them, but to help cure the small tragedies in your neighborhood is just as important.) If you want to change society, do not try to influence the politics of a particular country, for this will mean that in the end you will try to influence the leader of this country. You would, therefore, exert an influence over his free will, which is absolutely forbidden. If, for any reason, you feel that a specific area needs help, then heal the land itself. You may wish to send a positive influence to Israel, but do not try to influence the leaders of Israel or Palestine. Instead, work to heal the anger and the pain of both Israelis and Arabs and of the Holy Land itself.

It is, however, best to heal the entire world, because then you will not be tempted to look for a specific result. Remember that you must not expect the world to change instantly. The amount of change you bring to the world depends on the clarity of your concentration and the strength of your faith and especially on the intensity and purity of your love for the world. Further, be aware that, as you heal the world, your own soul will be healed in the same way.

28

The Mystical Prayer
of the Four Sages

A Chassidic tale describes how we can bring the ancient ways back to life, and how we can mentally reenact the physical actions of olden times. Remember that the art of storytelling is the art of pathworking.

> When the Baal Shem had a difficult task before him [a secret work to the benefit of all creatures],[1] he would go to a certain place in the woods, light a fire and meditate in prayer—and what he had set out to perform was done. When a generation later the Maggid of Meseritz was faced with the same task he would go to the same place in the woods and say: We can no longer light the fire, but we can still speak the prayers—and what he wanted done became reality. Again a generation later Rabbi Moshe Leib of Sassov had to perform this task. And he too went into the woods and said: We can no longer light the fire,

---

[1] This explanation can be found in the German edition of Scholem's work.

nor do we know the secret meditations belonging to the prayer, but we do know the place in the woods to which it all belongs—and that must be sufficient; and sufficient it was. But when another generation has passed and Rabbi Israel of Rishin was called upon to perform the task, he sat down on his golden chair in his castle and said: We cannot light the fire, we cannot speak the prayers, we do not know the place, but we can tell the story of how it was done. And the story he told had the same effect as the actions of the other three.[2]

These are the four sages of the tale:

Israel Ben Eliezer Baal-Shem-Tov (ca. 1700–1760): Israel Baal Shem Tov was called the Besht, which is a notarikon of Baal Shem Tov (Master of the Good Name). The Besht was the founder and first leader of Chassidism in Eastern Europe. He was a charismatic person and was considered to be a great saint and a healer, accomplishing many miracles by the use of spells and by the writing of amulets. He was the subject of many legends collected in a text called *Shivhey ha-Besht*.

This portrait is often believed to be of the Besht, but in fact it shows Chaim Samuel Jacob Falk, the Baal Shem of London.

Dov Baer, the Maggid of Meseritz (1710–1772): Dov Baer studied the Qabbalah and lived a very ascetic life, which included mortifications that made him ill and affected his legs. He went to the Besht and asked for healing, and became one of his foremost disciples. He was an eloquent preacher and teacher who eventually became the successor of the Besht and the leader of the Chassidic movement.

---

[2] Gershom Scholem, *Major Trends in Jewish Mysticism* (New York: Schocken Books, 1941).

Rabbi Moshe Leib of Sassov (1745–1807): Moshe Leib of Sassov was a Chassidic rabbi and a pupil of Dov Baer, the Maggid of Meseritz. He was famous for his selfless love for others and for his charity, which earned him the title Father of Widows and Orphans.

Israel Friedmann of Rishin/Ruzhin (1797–1850): Israel Friedmann of Rishin was a great-grandson of Dov Baer. He had a naturally keen mind and was famous for his expensive garments. He lived in great luxury and unusual splendor. His residence was a castle or palace with all its opulence.

The Mystical Prayer

This ritual pathworking is meant to bring about a change to benefit all creatures. Do not ask for something you need for yourself. If you need help for yourself, perform the invocation of Elijah described in chapter 25, The Invocation of Elijah, the Prophet.

If you can, go into a forest and look for a special and secret place to do this ritual. If this is not possible, however, it can also be performed at home. Light a fire if possible, or use a tea light candle holder instead if a fire is not possible or is forbidden. (If you make a fire in the woods, take care that you do not cause a forest fire: Clean the fire area and lay big stones around the firepit to keep the fire contained. Use only dry wood so that the fire does not create too much smoke.) Contemplate the Divine Light for a short while, and then speak a suitable prayer, or simply state what you hope to accomplish.

Then close your eyes and see the flame in front of you growing bigger and higher. It expands and becomes ever wider and turns into a huge gate of pure fire. Rise with your inner body leaving your physical body behind. Slowly and carefully, move forward. You can feel the heat of the fire, but it is not uncomfortable. It neither burns nor hurts you. You move right through the gate of fire. . . . For a moment you feel as though you are being drawn through a long tunnel, connecting different places in different times, leading to another gate of fire. On the other side there is a wide landscape. The sun has already set and the night is beginning to lay her dark cloak over everything, and the full moon begins to rise. You can see the farmers' fields and some lonely trees.

From somewhere behind you there is the sound of rippling water: a small river. You cannot see any buildings, nor can you hear the sound of modern civilization. Only some birds are singing their evening songs. You enjoy the peaceful atmosphere of this area. You feel that this is an ancient place, maybe Eastern Europe as it was hundreds of years ago.

In front of you, there is a pathway that leads into a forest. It takes you a while to reach the forest. As you come closer to it, you see how huge the trees are. Their long boughs appear like giant arms with clawlike fingers. Everything seems a bit eerie. You follow the pathway leading directly into the forest, and after a while, the forest surrounds you. Above you is a roof of branches through which you can still see the fading light of the late evening, although when you look into the woods, you face a solid wall of darkness.

As the night begins, the air becomes colder. The only light is the moon shining through the trees every now and then. After a while you see a glow worm appearing somewhere out of the darkness, crossing toward you and flying away until it disappears again in the far distance. As you walk through the forest, somehow the atmosphere seems to change. You feel a strange energy that grows stronger as you move forward. It seems that you are approaching a very special place.

In the far distance, you see a light. As you grow closer, you see, standing in front of the fire, an old, slightly stocky man who who wears an old black coat and a black hat. His hair is gray and he has a long, gray beard. His round face looks very friendly and kind. He is muttering what seems to be an ancient invocation or prayer. It sounds like Hebrew or Yiddish. He does not seem to notice you as you come closer. He might be in a light trance, for he is deep in prayer. You feel the great spiritual power of his prayer and realize that his prayer can accomplish great miracles.

When he is finished, he turns around and looks at you with friendly eyes full of love and compassion. He smiles. "Shalom Alecha—Peace to you," he says. "Shalom Alecha Rebbe," you answer. As you look into his loving eyes, you recognize him as Israel Baal-Shem-Tov, the Besht.

He offers you a place by the fire, where you feel warm and comfortable. He then fills his pipe with tobacco, takes a long puff, and makes himself comfortable. If you wish, you may speak to him about the task ahead. His answer may be that he tells you a seemingly secular tale. Yet in doing so he will teach you of higher mysteries, for the tale gives you an answer to your problem. He may explain that all things come from God and that the power of prayer lies in attaching ourselves to the spirituality of the Light of the Eyn Sof. He may also tell you to pray joyfully with your whole heart. He may even sing with you. (You may learn about what later generations called the wisdom of the Besht—the secret of finding and sublimating the Divine Spark within undesirable thoughts that come up during prayer. This can be accomplished either by joining the Qlippotic[3] thought with a good thought or by removing them if there is nothing good within them.)[4] When you have finished, he blesses you and sends you forth to continue your journey.

Again, you walk deep into the forest. You hear the leaves of the trees rustling in the wind. The woods seem to change again and you feel as if time passes very quickly with every step. After a while, the forest seems to be less private. You think it would not be wise to make a fire here; someone might ask what you are doing here. Someone caught here by a fire might be accused of being a criminal or of being involved in the dark arts. The need to hide yourself overshadows your thoughts. Yet the forest is lonesome. After some time has passed, somewhere in the far distance you can hear someone muttering an ancient invocation. As you come closer, you see a faint light. You walk toward the light, and it seems as if you remember the place. Is this the same place where you met the Besht? Have you walked in a circle? It is the place where you came from, and yet it is not. The place has changed. Some of the trees surrounding it have grown taller, and the firepit is gone. Only a small candle stands on a large stone.

Before the candle stands an old man who is rather like the Besht. He wears an old black coat and a black hat. He leans on a walking staff, and it appears as if his legs are weakened. His hair and his long beard are gray, like those of the Besht. He is Dov Baer, the Maggid of Meseritz, the successor of the Besht. You listen to his voice as he mutters the same prayer you have heard before. As you watch the candle flame, you see within it all that could be found in the bright fire of the Besht. You are deeply impressed by the effect of his prayer in front of the single flame. You realize that the spiritual power of this man is no less than that of the Besht. Further, his prayer, like that of the Besht, can accomplish great miracles.

When he has finished, he looks at you, and you feel the warmth of his heart. He says, "Shalom Alecha—Peace to you." You answer, "Shalom Alecha Rebbe." He offers you a place by the candlelight, and explains: "We can no longer light the fire, but we can still speak the old prayers." You nod

---

[3] The Qlippot are the unbalanced demonic forces.

[4] For example, if you see a weakness in another person, realize that this is just a reflection of your own weakness. Learn self-knowledge from this experience, and become a better and more compassionate person.

in understanding. If you wish, you may speak to him about the task ahead. He will help you to see the spiritual side of things, both religious and pro-fane. He may explain that according to his teachings, the secret of prayer is an attitude of indifference toward its results and a denial of all selfish thoughts. When you have finished, he too will bless you and send you forth to continue your journey.

You walk through the forest again. Time passes. After a long walk, you see a light in the distance. You come closer and arrive at the same place you have reached two times before. Again, it has changed as if some decades have passed. You notice that this time, there is deep silence. You see the light from a candle, and in front of it sits another old man with a gray beard who wears a black coat and a black hat. He is deep in silent meditation, sur-rounded by an aura of great spiritual power. Even though he does not say any prayer, you feel that the spiritual power of his meditation equals that of the first two men and that, like them, he can accomplish great miracles.

When he has finished, he turns around. It is Rabbi Moshe Leib of Sassov. You feel his spiritual love and compassion. He says, "Shalom Alecha—Peace to you." "Shalom Alecha Rebbe," you answer. He offers you a place by the candlelight. As he notices the unspoken question in your mind he says: "We can no longer light the fire, nor do we know the secret prayers, but we do know the place in the woods to which it all belongs—and that must be sufficient." As he speaks, you know that it is enough. If you wish, you may speak to him about the task ahead. He may tell you that prayer should be spoken with an attitude of love and compassion for those in need, and he may tell you about the power of love that brings healing and positive change. When you have finished, he too will bless you and send you forth to continue your journey.

You walk through the forest, and after a while you come to a small valley surrounded by fields. On the top of a hill you see a beautiful castle. Through the windows shines an inviting light. You come closer, and even-tually you knock on the door. A servant opens. He tells you that you are already expected, and he guides you through the castle. Everything inside is of the highest quality. You see all kinds of expensive furniture. After a while you arrive in a luxurious living room. On a golden chair sits Rabbi Israel of Rishin, dressed in immaculate and expensive garments in the man-ner of a Russian noble, and on his head he wears a hat embroidered in gold. From the tips of his toes to his head there is an elegance about his expen-sive clothes. He has no beard, only a moustache. His imposing presence and his stature make a pleasing impression upon the onlooker—he looks noble and refined. He is deep in silent meditation, and from the aura of spiritual power that surrounds him, it seems that in his mind he approaches the ancient sages, and that the tradition of the earlier sages has come alive again. You feel that, like the other sages, he can accomplish great miracles.

When he has finished, he turns to you, and as he looks at you, your heart is filled with spiritual love and friendship. You notice that all his movements are deliberate and that his eyes exercise a hypnotic charm. He says, "Shalom Alecha—Peace to you." "Shalom Alecha Rebbe," you answer. He offers you a place at the table, and then he says: "We cannot light the fire, we cannot speak the prayers, we do not know the place, but we can tell the story of how it was done." As he speaks, you suddenly realize that the tale and the corresponding inner journey include the whole mystery of this work. All the power of the sages lies within the tale.

If you wish, you may speak to him about the task ahead. He speaks little, confining his remarks to what is absolutely essential. Although not as highly educated as the others, he has a naturally keen mind. With his sharp eye and keen intellect, he immediately penetrates to the heart of any difficulty brought before him, however obscure and complicated, and arrives at a decision. When you have finished, he will bless you and send you back to the place where your journey began. You leave the castle, and through a gate of fire you return to the starting point of your journey.

As you watch the light in front of you, you remember all the experiences you have had. You feel around you the presence of the four great sages. You hear their voices: "Now companion, it is upon you to carry on the tradition. Our strength and our power is with you." As they speak, you feel their power filling your heart and soul, and how their potential to accomplish miracles will be added to your own spiritual power. Now approach the Light in your heart and ask for what needs to be done . . . and so it will happen.

Epilogue

As we have learned from the tale of the four sages in the chapter 28, a living tradition changes, yet at its core it remains the same. This will always be the case, because change is a part of life. Every tradition that stops evolving will die, but every tradition that does not remember its roots will eventually dissolve. The balance between stagnation and dissolution is also the balance between the two pillars of the Tree of Life—we are already applying the Qabbalah here, as we should, being part of a living tradition.

We do not need to do all things as they were done in the ancient times, but we can learn from the ancient sages and their teachings and apply them, with wisdom and understanding, to our times.

I would appreciate hearing from you—hearing how you have enjoyed this book and how it helped you in your own Qabbalistic work.

For more information about this book (including many additional resources and a discussion forum dedicated to this book), about Qabbalistic magic in general, about Qabbalistic training (either personally or by correspondence course), or for contact details, visit my website at: www.qabbalah.org (English) or www.qabbalah.de (German).

There are many fundamental Qabbalistic concepts that could not be explained here in detail, as they would have exceeded the scope of this book, but for those who wish to study the principles of the Holy Qabbalah in a systematic and profound way, my next book, *The Wisdom of the Holy Qabbalah,* will include important information about the Qabbalah never described before in a similar work.

APPENDIX I

Sefer Yetzirah
(Book of Formation)

ספר יצירה

Translated by Salomo Baal-Shem

Note: Text in brackets is omitted in some versions of the book, and text in parentheses provides an explanation, remark, or alternative translation.

פרק א'   Chapter 1

משנה א': בשלשים ושתים נתיבות פליאות חכמה חקק יה יהוה צבאות
אלהי ישראל אלהים חיים ומלך עולם אל שדי רחום וחנון רם ונשא שוכן
עד מרום וקדוש שמו וברא את עולמו בשלשה ספרים בספר וספר וספור:

Mishnah 1: With thirty-two Mystical Paths of Wisdom (Chochmah) engraved Yah YHVH Tzevaot (of Hosts) Elohey Yisrael (God of Israel) Elohim Chaim (God of Life) u-Melech Olam (King of the Universe) El Shaddai (God Almighty) Rachum ve-Chanun (Compassionate and Gracious) Ram ve-Nissa (High and Exalted) Shochen Ad (Dwelling Eternally) Marom ve-Qadosh Shemo (Lofty and Holy is His Name). And He created His universe with three books (sefarim), with text (sefer) and scribe (sofer) and narration (sippur; or "with number/sefar with counter/ sofer and with calculation/sippur").[1]

---

[1] Many versions have: שוכן עד וקדוש שמו מרום וקדוש הוא instead of שוכן עד מרום וקדוש שמו.

431

משנה ב': עשר ספירות בלימה ועשרים ושתים אותיות יסוד שלש אמות
ושבע כפולות ושתים עשרה פשוטות:

Mishnah 2: Ten Sefirot Blimah (ten "Holy Numbers" without anything)[2]
and twenty-two foundation letters (Otiyot Yesod): three mothers, seven
doubles, and twelve simples.

משנה ג': עשר ספירות בלימה במספר עשר אצבעות חמש כנגד חמש
וברית יחיד מכוון באמצע במילת הלשון ובמילת המעור:

Mishnah 3: Ten Sefirot Blimah (ten "Holy Numbers" without anything):
with the number (*mispar*) of ten fingers, five opposite five, with a single
covenant adjusted in the middle; in the circumcision (or "word") of the
tongue and in the circumcision (or "word") of the membrum.

משנה ד': עשר ספירות בלימה עשר ולא תשע עשר ולא אחת עשרה הבן
בחכמה וחכם בבינה בחון בהם וחקור מהם והעמד דבר על בוריו והשב
יוצר על מכונו:

Mishnah 4: Ten Sefirot Blimah (ten "Holy Numbers" without anything): ten and not nine, ten and not eleven, understand with Wisdom
(Chochmah), be wise with Understanding (Binah). Examine with them
and quest with them (literally, "from them") and make [the] thing (matter)
stand on its evidence; and make the Creator (Yotzer, literally, "Former" or
"Builder") sit on His base.

משנה ה': עשר ספירות בלימה מדתן עשר שאין להם סוף עומק ראשית
ועומק אחרית עומק טוב ועומק רע עומק רום ועומק תחת עומק מזרח
ועומק מערב עומק צפון ועומק דרום אדון יחיד אל מלך נאמן מושל
בכולם ממעון קדשו עד עדי עד:

Mishnah 5: Ten Sefirot Blimah (ten "Holy Numbers" without anything):
Their measurement is ten, for there is no end to them; a depth of beginning and a depth of end, a depth of good and a depth of evil, a depth of
above and a depth of below, a depth of east and a depth of west, a depth
of north and a depth of south. Adon yachid (the singular Lord) El Melech
ne'eman (God Faithful King) rules over them all from His Holy Dwelling
until eternal eternity of eternities.

---

[2] Blimah means "without anything," "without material substance."

משנה ו': עשר ספירות בלימה צפייתן כמראה הבזק ותכליתן אין להם קץ ודברו בהן ברצוא ושוב ולמאמרו כסופה ירדופו ולפני כסאו הם משתחוים:

Mishnah 6: Ten Sefirot Blimah (ten "Holy Numbers" without anything): Their vision is like the "appearance of a flash of lightning" (Ezekiel 1:14), and their purpose has no end (alternative translation: "their limit has no end"); and His Word in them is with "running and returning" (Ezekiel 1:14); and to His saying they rush like a whirlwind (*sufah*); and before His Throne they prostrate themselves.

משנה ז': עשר ספירות בלימה נעוץ סופן בתחלתן ותחלתן בסופן כשלהבת קשורה בגחלת שאדון יחיד ואין לו שני ולפני אחד מה אתה סופר:

Mishnah 7: Ten Sefirot Blimah (ten "Holy Numbers" without anything): Their end is affixed to their beginning and their beginning to their end, like a flame is tied to a [burning] coal; for the Lord (Adon) is singular (*yachid*). He has no second. And before One, what doth thou count?

משנה ח': עשר ספירות בלימה בלום פיך מלדבר ולבך מלהרהר ואם רץ לבך שוב למקום שלכך נאמר רצוא ושוב ועל דבר זה נכרת ברית:

Mishnah 8: Ten Sefirot Blimah (ten "Holy Numbers" without anything): Block thy mouth from speaking and thy heart from pondering; and if thy heart runs return to the Place (*Maqom*). It is therefore said: "running and returning" (Ezekiel 1:24). Concerning this matter a covenant was made.

משנה ט': עשר ספירות בלימה אחת רוח אלהים חיים ברוך ומבורך שמו של חי העולמים קול ורוח ודבור והוא רוח הקודש:

Mishnah 9: Ten Sefirot Blimah (ten "Holy Numbers" without anything): One is Ruach Elohim Chaim (the Spirit of the Living God), blessed and benedicted is His Name, of the life of universes (worlds); voice and spirit (Ruach) and speech; and this is the Holy Spirit (Ruach ha-Qodesh).

משנה י': שתים רוח מרוח חקק וחצב בה עשרים ושתים אותיות יסוד שלש אמות ושבע כפולות ושתים עשרה פשוטות ורוח אחת מהן:

Mishnah 10: Two: Spirit (Ruach) from spirit (Ruach): He engraved and carved with it twenty-two foundation letters (Otiyot Yesod): three mothers, seven doubles, and twelve simples; and one spirit (Ruach) is from them.

משנה יא׳: שלש מים מרוח חקק וחצב בהן תהו ובהו רפש וטיט חקקן
כמין ערוגה חצבן כמין חומה סככן כמין מעזיבה:

Mishnah 11: Three: Water (*mayim*) from spirit (Ruach): He engraved and
carved nothingness and emptiness (Tohu va-Vohu), loam (mud), and clay
with them. He engraved them like a kind of flowerbed, He carved them
like a kind of wall, He covered them like a kind of pavement.

משנה יב׳: ארבע אש ממים חקק וחצב בה כסא הכבוד שרפים ואופנים
וחיות הקודש ומלאכי השרת ומשלשתן יסד מעונו שנאמר עושה מלאכיו
רוחות משרתיו אש לוהט:

Mishnah 12: Four: Fire (*esh*) from water (mayim): He engraved and carved
with it the Throne of Glory (Kise Ha-Kavod), Serafim (Burning Angels),
and Ofanim (Wheels), and Chayot ha-Qodesh (Holy Creatures) and
Malachey ha-Sharet (Ministering Angels). From these three He founded
His Dwelling as it is said: "Who makest winds (or spirits; Hebrew: ruachot) Thy messengers, the flaming fire (Esh lohet) Thy ministers" (Psalm
104:4).

משנה יג׳: [בירר שלש אותיות מן הפשוטות בסוד שלש אמות אמ״ש
וקבעם בשמו הגדול וחתם בהם ששה קצוות] חמש חתם רום ופנה למעלה
וחתמו ביה״ו שש חתם תחת ופנה למטה וחתמו ביו״ה שבע חתם מזרח
ופנה לפניו וחתמו בהי״ו שמונה חתם מערב ופנה לאחריו וחתמו בהו״י
תשע חתם דרום ופנה לימינו וחתמו בוי״ה עשר חתם צפון ופנה לשמאלו
וחתמו בוה״י:

Mishnah 13: [He chose three letters from among the simples in the secret
of the three mothers AM"Sh (*Alef Mem Shin*) and He set them in His
great Name (Shem ha-gadol) and He sealed with them six extremities.]
Five: He sealed "above" and faced upward and He sealed it with YH"V
(*Yod Heh Vav*). Six: He sealed "below" and faced downward and He sealed
it with YV"H (*Yod Vav Heh*). Seven: He sealed [the] "east" and faced forward and He sealed it with HY"V (*Heh Yod Vav*). Eight: He sealed [the]
"west" and faced backward and He sealed it with HV"Y (*Heh Vav Yod*).
Nine: He sealed [the] "south" and faced to the right and He sealed it with
VY"H (*Vav Yod Heh*). Ten: He sealed [the] "north" and faced to the left
and He sealed it with VH"Y (*Vav Heh Yod*).

---

3 Alternative translation: Wind from Wind.

משנה יד': אלו עשר ספירות בלימה רוח אלהים חיים רוח מרוח מים
מרוח אש ממים רום ותחת מזרח ומערב צפון ודרום:

Mishnah 14: These are the ten Sefirot Blimah (ten "Holy Numbers" without anything): Ruach Elohim Chaim (Spirit of the Living God), spirit (Ruach) from spirit (Ruach),[3] water (mayim) from spirit (Ruach), fire (esh) from water (mayim), above and below, east and west, north and south.

Chapter 2   פרק ב'

משנה א': עשרים ושתים אותיות יסוד שלש אמות ושבע כפולות ושתים
עשרה פשוטות:

Mishnah 1: Twenty-two Otiyot Yesod (foundation letters): three mothers, seven doubles, and twelve simples.

משנה ב': עשרים ושתים אותיות יסוד חקקן חצבן צרפן שקלן והמירן
וצר בהם [נפש] כל היצור [ונפש] כל העתיד לצור:

Mishnah 2: Twenty-two Otiyot Yesod (foundation letters): He engraved them, He carved them, and He joined them, He weighed them, He permuted (i.e., exchanged) them, and He formed with them [the Nefesh of] all that was formed [and the Nefesh of] all that shall be formed.

משנה ג': עשרים ושתים אותיות יסוד חקקן בקול חצבן ברוח קבען בפה
בחמשה מקומות אחה"ע [בגרון] גיכ"ק [בחיך] דטלנ"ת [בלשון] זססר"ץ
[בשינים] בומ"ף [בשפתים]:

Mishnah 3: Twenty-two Otiyot Yesod (foundation letters): He engraved them in the voice (alternative translation: "with the voice"), He carved them in the Ruach (alternative translation: "with the Ruach"), and He set them in the mouth in five places: AChH"E (*Alef Chet Heh Eyin*) [in the throat], GYK"Q (*Gimel Yod Kaf Quf*) [on the palate], DTLN"T (*Dalet Tet Lamed Nun Tav*) [on the tongue], ZSShR"Tz (*Zayin Samech Shin Resh Tzadde*) [on the teeth], BVM"P (*Bet Vav Mem Peh*) [on the lips].

משנה ד': עשרים ושתים אותיות יסוד קבועות בגלגל ברל"א שערים
וחוזר הגלגל פנים ואחור וסימן לדבר אין בטובה למעלה מענג ואין ברעה
למטה מנגע:

Mishnah 4: Twenty-two Otiyot Yesod (foundation letters): Set in a circle with 231 gates. And the circle turns forth and back.[4] And the sign of this matter is this: There is nothing in good higher than delight (ONeG); and there is nothing in evil lower than plague (NeGA).

---

[4] Probably clockwise (deosil) and counterclockwise (widdershins).

משנה ה': כיצד [צרפן] שקלן והמירן א' עם כולם וכולם עם א' ב' עם
כולם וכולם עם ב' וחוזרות חלילה נמצא כל היצור וכל הדבור יוצא משם
אחד:

Mishnah 5: How? He [joined them,] weighed them, and permuted (i.e., exchanged) them: *Alef* with them all and all of them with *Alef*, *Bet* with them all and all of them with *Bet*. They repeat in turn (going round) and [thus] is found [that] all that is formed and all that is spoken emanates from one Name (i.e., the Divine Name).

משנה ו': יצר ממש מתהו ועשה את אינו ישנו וחצב עמודים גדולים
מאויר שאינו נתפש [וזה סימן צופה וממיר ועשה כל היצור ואת כל
הדברים בשם אחד וסימן לדבר עשרים ושתים חפצים בגוף אחד]:

Mishnah 6: He formed substance from the unmanifest and made be that which is not. He carved great pillars from air (*avir*) that cannot be grasped. [This is a sign: He visualizes and He permutes (exchanges). He makes all that is formed and all that is spoken with one Name. A sign for this matter: Twenty-two objects (alternative translation: "twenty-two desires") in a single body (Guf)].

Chapter 3   פרק ג'

משנה א': שלש אמות אמ"ש יסודן כף זכות וכף חובה ולשון חק מכריע
בינתים:

Mishnah 1: Three mothers: AM"Sh (*Alef Mem Shin*): Their foundation is a scale of merit and a scale of debt and the tongue of decree balancing between them.

משנה ב': שלש אמות אמ"ש סוד גדול מופלא ומכוסה וחתום בשש
טבעות ויצאו מהם אש ומים ומתחלקים זכר ונקבה שלש אמות אמ"ש
יסודן ומהן נולדו אבות שמהם נברא הכל:

Mishnah 2: Three mothers: AM"Sh (*Alef Mem Shin*): A great secret—mystical and covered (i.e., hidden) and sealed with six seals (literally, signet rings). And from them emanated fire (esh) and water (mayim), dividing themselves into male and female. Three mothers: AM"Sh (*Alef Mem Shin*) are their foundation and from them are born fathers and from them everything was created.

משנה ג': שלש אמות אמ"ש בעולם אויר מים אש שמים נבראו תחלה
מאש וארץ נבראת ממים והאויר מכריע בין האש ובין המים:

Mishnah 3: Three mothers: AM"Sh (*Alef Mem Shin*) in the universe—air (avir), water (mayim), fire (esh), Heaven was created at first from fire, and the earth was created from water, and the air balances between the fire and the water.

משנה ד׳: שלש אמות אמ״ש בשנה אש ומים ורוח חום נברא מאש קור נברא ממים ורויה מרוח מכריע בינתים:

Mishnah 4: Three mothers: AM"Sh (*Alef Mem Shin*) in the year—fire (esh) and water (mayim) and breath (Ruach; alternative: spirit)—heat was created from fire, cold was created from water and saturation (i.e., temperance) from wind (Ruach) balancing between them.

משנה ה׳: שלש אמות אמ״ש בנפש אש מים ורוח ראש נברא מאש ובטן נברא ממים וגויה נברא מרוח מכריע בינתים:

Mishnah 5: Three mothers: AM"Sh (*Alef Mem Shin*) in the soul (Nefesh)— fire (esh) water (mayim) and breath (Ruach; alternative: spirit)—[The] head was created from fire, [the] belly (abdomen) was created from water and [the] chest was created from breath balancing between them.

משנה ו׳: שלש אמות אמ״ש חקקן וחצבן וצרפן וחתם בהן שלש אמות בעולם ושלש אמות בשנה ושלש אמות בנפש זכר ונקבה:

Mishnah 6: Three mothers: AM"Sh (*Alef Mem Shin*): He engraved them, and He carved them, and He joined (tzerafan) them, and He sealed with them: three mothers in the universe, and three mothers in the year, and three mothers in the soul (Nefesh), male and female.

משנה ז׳: המליך אות אל״ף ברוח וקשר לו כתר וצרפן זה עם זה וחתם בהן אויר בעולם רויה בשנה גויה בנפש זכר באמ״ש ונקבה באש״מ:

Mishnah 7: He made the letter *Alef* king over breath and He bound a crown to it and he joined them one with another. And He sealed with them (other versions: "And He formed with them") air in the universe, saturation (i.e., temperance between the seasons) in the year, and [the] chest in the soul (Nefesh)—male with AM"Sh (*Alef Mem Shin*) and female with ASh"M (*Alef Shin Mem*).

משנה ח׳: המליך [אות] מ״ם במים וקשר לו כתר וצרפן זה עם זה וחתם [בהן] ארץ בעולם וקור בשנה ובטן בנפש זכר במא״ש ונקבה במש״א:

Mishnah 8: He made [the letter] *Mem* king over water and He bound a crown to it and he joined them one with another. And He sealed (other versions: "And He formed") [with them] earth in the universe, cold in the year, and the belly (abdomen) in the soul (Nefesh)—male with MA"Sh (*Mem Alef Shin*) and female with MSh"A (*Mem Shin Alef*).

משנה ט': המליך [אות] שי"ן באש וקשר לו כתר וצרפן זה עם זה וחתם
בו שמים בעולם וחום בשנה וראש בנפש זכר בשא"מ ונקבה בשמ"א:

Mishnah 9: He made [the letter] *Shin* king over fire and He bound a crown
to it and He joined them one with another. And He sealed (other versions:
"And He formed") with it Heaven in the universe, heat in the year, and
[the] head in the soul (Nefesh)—male with ShA"M (*Shin Alef Mem*) and
female with ShM"A (*Shin Mem Alef*).

פרק ד'   Chapter 4

משנה א': שבע כפולות בג"ד כפר"ת יסודן חיים ושלום וחכמה ועושר חן
וזרע וממשלה מתנהגות בשתי לשונות ב"ב ג"ג ד"ד כ"ך כ"ד פ"פ ר"ר ת"ת
תבנית רך וקשה תמורות גבור וחלש כפולות שהן תמורות תמורת חיים
מות תמורת שלום רע תמורת חכמה אולת תמורת עושר עוני תמורת חן
כיעור תמורת זרע שממה תמורת ממשלה עבדות:

Mishnah 1: Seven doubles: BG"D KPR"T (*Bet, Gimel, Dalet, Kaf, Peh,
Resh, Tav*). Their foundation is life, peace, wisdom, wealth, grace, seed, and
dominance. They are conducted by two tongues B"V G"G D"D K"Ch
P"F R"R T"T (*Bet-Vet, Gimel-Gimel, Dalet-Dalet, Kaf-Chaf, Peh-Feh,
Resh-Resh, Tav-Tav*—i.e., they all have two pronunciations. Yet not all of
them can still be distinguished). [They are] a pattern of soft and hard, a
pattern of strong and weak. [They are] doubles for they are permutations
(temurot). The permutation of life is death, the permutation of peace is
evil, the permutation of wisdom is foolishness, the permutation of wealth
is poverty, the permutation of grace is ugliness, the permutation of seed is
desolation, the permutation of domination is slavery.

[משנה ב': שבע כפולות בג"ד כפר"ת שבע ולא שש שבע ולא שמונה
בחון בהן וחקור בהן והעמד דבריל בורריו והשב יוצר על מכונו:]

[Mishnah 2: Seven doubles: BG"D KPR"T (*Bet, Gimel, Dalet, Kaf, Peh,
Resh, Tav*) seven and not six, seven and not eight. Examine with them and
quest with them. Make [every-]thing stand on its evidence and make the
Creator (Yotzer) sit on His base.]

משנה ג': שבע כפולות בג"ד כפר"ת [כנגד שבע קצוות מהן שש קצוות]
מעלה ומטה מזרח ומערב צפון ודרום והיכל הקודש [מכוון] באמצע
והוא נושא את כולן:

Mishnah 3: Seven doubles: BG"D KPR"T (*Bet, Gimel, Dalet, Kaf, Peh,
Resh, Tav*) [compared to seven extremities] (alternative translation: "as protection against seven ends") [from these are the six extremities] above and

below, east and west, north and south and the Holy Palace (Hechal ha-Qodesh) [precisely] in the middle and it bears them all.

משנה ד': שבע כפולות בג"ד כפר"ת [יסוד] חקקן וחצבן וצרפן וצר בהן [שבעה] כוכבים בעולם [שבעה] ימים בשנה [שבעה] שערים בנפש שמהן חקק שבעה רקיעין ושבע אדמות ושבע שבועות לפיכך חובב שביעי תחת כל השמים:

Mishnah 4: Seven doubles: BG"D KPR"T (*Bet, Gimel, Dalet, Kaf, Peh, Resh, Tav*) [of foundation/Yesod]: He engraved them, and He carved them, and He joined (tzerafan) them, and He formed with them [seven] planets (literally, stars) in the universe, [seven] days in the year, [seven] gates in the soul (Nefesh). For with (literally, from) them He engraved seven firmaments, seven lands, seven weeks. Therefore, seven is beloved under all the Heavens.

The following seven mishnayot do not appear in every manuscript. The assignment of the different attributes, planets, days of the week, and parts of the soul differs depending on the version used. Unlike any of the other assignments, the seven doubles have caused so much confusion—maybe due to their two-sided nature—that many Qabbalists have created their own system, with the result that there are about a dozen different systems. The following system is considered the oldest version. Yet it seems to be corrupt, for it is unlikely that anyone with even the faintest understanding of astrology would, for example, assign wisdom to Mars. In some versions these seven mishnayot have simply been left out to avoid the problem—and thus chapter four has only five mishnayot. If you are used to different correspondences than those described here, continue using them if they work for you.[5]

משנה ה': המליך אות ב בחיים וקשר לו כתר וצרפן זה בזה וצר בהם שבתאי בעולם יום ראשון בשנה ועין ימין בנפש [זכר ונקבה]:

Mishnah 5: He made the letter *Bet* king over life (chaim) and He bound a crown to it and he joined them one with another. And He formed with them Saturn (Shabbatai) in the universe, Sunday in the year, the right eye in the soul (Nefesh) [male and female].

משנה ו': המליך אות ג בשלום וקשר לו כתר וצרפן זה בזה וצר בהם צדק בעולם יום שני בשנה ועין שמאל בנפש [זכר ונקבה]:

Mishnah 6: He made the letter *Gimel* king over peace (shalom) and He bound a crown to it and he joined them one with another. And He formed

---

[5] I believe there are two sides to the doubles—that there is not one correct system of correspondences, but one for a particular purpose, and others for other purposes.

with them Jupiter (Tzedeq) in the universe, Monday in the year, the left eye in the soul (Nefesh) [male and female].

משנה ז׳: המליך אות ד בחכמה וקשר לו כתר וצרפן זה בזה וצר בהם מאדים בעולם יום שלישי בשנה ואזן ימין בנפש [זכר ונקבה]:

Mishnah 7: He made the letter *Dalet* king over wisdom (Chochmah) and He bound a crown to it and he joined them one with another. And He formed with them Mars (Madim) in the universe, Tuesday in the year, the right ear in the soul (Nefesh) [male and female].

משנה ח׳: המליך אות כ בעושר וקשר לו כתר וצרפן זה בזה וצר בהם חמה בעולם יום רביעי בשנה ואזן שמאל בנפש [זכר ונקבה]:

Mishnah 8: He made the letter *Kaf* king over wealth (*osher*) and He bound a crown to it and he joined them one with another. And He formed with them the Sun (Chamah) in the universe, Wednesday in the year, the left ear in the soul (Nefesh) [male and female].

משנה ט׳: המליך אות פ בחן וקשר לו כתר וצרפן זה בזה וצר בהם נוגה בעולם יום חמישי בשנה ונחיר ימין בנפש [זכר ונקבה]:

Mishnah 9: He made the letter *Peh* king over grace (chen) and He bound a crown to it and he joined them one with another. And He formed with them Venus (Nogah) in the universe, Thursday in the year, the right nostril in the soul (Nefesh) [male and female].

משנה י׳: המליך אות ר בזרע וקשר לו כתר וצרפן זה בזה וצר בהם כוכב בעולם יום ששי בשנה ונחיר שמאל בנפש [זכר ונקבה]:

Mishnah 10: He made the letter *Resh* king over seed (Zera) and He bound a crown to it and he joined them one with another. And He formed with them Mercury (Kochav) in the universe, Friday in the year, the left nostril in the soul (Nefesh) [male and female].

משנה יא׳: המליך אות ת בממשלה וקשר לו כתר וצרפן זה בזה וצר בהם לבנה בעולם יום שבת בשנה ופה בנפש [זכר ונקבה]:

Mishnah 11: He made the letter *Tav* king over dominance (*memshalah*) and He bound a crown to it and he joined them one with another. And He formed with them the Moon (Levanah) in the universe, Shabbat (Saturday) in the year, the mouth in the soul (Nefesh) [male and female].

משנה יב׳: [כיצד צרפן] שתי אבנים בונות שני בתים שלשה בונות ששה בתים ארבע בונות ארבעה ועשרים בתים חמש בונות מאה ועשרים בתים שש בונות שבע מאות ועשרים בתים שבע בונות חמשת אלפים וארבעים

בתים מכאן ואילך צא וחשוב מה שאין הפה יכול לדבר ואין האוזן יכולה
לשמוע: ואלו הן [שבעה] כוכבים בעולם שבתאי צדק מאדים חמה נוגה
כוכב לבנה שבעה ימים בשנה שבעת ימים השבוע שבעה שערים בנפש
שתי עינים שתי אזנים שני נקבי האף והפה שבהן נחקקו שבעה רקיעין
ושבע ארצות ושבע שבועות לפיכך חבב שביעי לכל חפץ תחת השמים:

Mishnah 12: [How to join/permute them?] Two stones (other versions: "two letters") build two houses, three build six houses, four stones build twenty-four houses, five build one hundred twenty houses, six build seven hundred twenty houses, seven build five thousand forty houses. From here onward go forth and consider (or calculate) that which the mouth cannot speak and the ear cannot hear. And these are the [seven] planets in the universe: Saturn, Jupiter, Mars, Sun, Venus, Mercury, Moon. Seven days in the year, seven days of the week, seven gates in the soul (Nefesh): Two eyes, two ears, two nostrils, and the mouth. For with them are engraved seven firmaments, seven earths, seven weeks. Therefore seven is beloved among all things under all the Heavens.

Chapter 5   פרק ה'

משנה א': שתים עשרה פשוטות הו"ז חט"י לנ"ס עצ"ק יסודן ראיה
שמיעה ריח שיחה לעיטה תשמיש מעשה הלוך רוגז שחוק הרהור שינה:

מדתן שתים עשרה גבולים באלכסונין גבול מזרחית צפונית גבול מזרחית
דרומית גבול מזרחית רומית גבול מזרחית תחתית גבול צפונית רומית גבול
צפונית תחתית גבול מערבית דרומית גבול מערבית צפונית גבול מערבית
רומית גבול מערבית תחתית גבול דרומית רומית גבול דרומית תחתית
ומתרחבין והולכין עד עדי עד והם זרועות עולם:

Mishnah 1: Twelve simples: HV"Z ChT"Y LN"S ATz"Q (*Heh, Vav, Zayin, Chet, Tet, Yod, Lamed, Nun, Samech, Ayin, Tzadde, Qof*). Their foundation is sight, hearing, smell, speech, taste, coition, action, motion, agitation (anger), laughter, thought, sleep.

Their measurements are twelve diagonal boundaries: The northeast boundary, the southeast boundary, the upper east boundary, the lower east boundary, the upper north boundary, the lower north boundary, the southwest boundary, the northwest boundary, the upper west boundary, the lower west boundary, the upper south boundary, the lower south boundary. And they extend continually until eternal eternity of eternities; and they are the arms (alternative translation: "the boundaries") of the universe.

משנה ב': שתים עשרה פשוטות ה ו ז ח ט י ל נ ס ע צ ק חקקן [חצבן שקלן] וצרפן [והמירן] וצר בהם שנים עשר מזלות בעולם טלה שור תאומים סרטן אריה בתולה מאזנים עקרב קשת גדי דלי דגים:

Mishnah 2: Twelve simples: HV"Z ChT"Y LN"S ETz"Q (*Heh, Vav, Zayin, Chet, Tet, Yod, Lamed, Nun, Samech, Ayin, Tzadde, Qof*). He engraved them, [He carved them, He weighed them], He joined [and per-muted/exchanged] them. And He formed with them twelve constellations (signs of the zodiac) in the universe: Aries, Taurus, Gemini, Cancer, Leo, Virgo, Libra, Scorpio, Sagittarius, Capricorn, Aquarius, Pisces.

[ואלו הן] שנים עשר חדשים בשנה ניסן אייר סיון תמוז אב אלול תשרי חשון כסלו טבת שבט אדר:

[And these are the] twelve months in the year: Nissan (March–April), Iyar (April–May), Sivan (May–June), Tammuz (June–July), Av (July–August), Elul (August–September), Tishrey (September–October), Cheshvan (October–November), Kislev (November–December), Tevet (December–January), Shevat (January–February), Adar (February–March).

[ואלו הן] שנים עשר מנהיגים בנפש שתי ידים שתי רגלים שתי כליות טחול כבד מרה מסס קבה קורקבן:

[And these are the] twelve directors (i.e., directing organs) in the soul: two hands, two feet, two kidneys, [the] spleen, [the] liver, [the] gall bladder, [the] (small) intestine(s) (masas), [the] stomach (kevah), [and the] bowels (qurqevan).

[המליך אות ה [בראיה] וקשר לו כתר וצרפן זה בזה וצר בהם טלה בעולם וניסן בשנה ויד ימין בנפש:]

[He made the letter *Heh* king [over sight] and He bound a crown to it and he joined them one with another. And He formed with them Aries in the universe, Nissan (March–April) in the year, the right hand in the soul (Nefesh).]

[המליך אות ו [בריח] וקשר לו כתר וצרפן זה בזה וצר בהם שור בעולם ואייר בשנה ויד שמאל בנפש:]

[He made the letter *Vav* king [over hearing] and He bound a crown to it and he joined them one with another. And He formed with them Taurus in the universe, Iyar (April–May) in the year, the left hand in the soul (Nefesh).]

[המליך אות ז [בשמיעה] וקשר לו כתר וצרפן זה בזה וצר בהם תאומים
בעולם וסיון בשנה ורגל ימין בנפש:]

[He made the letter *Zayin* king [over smell] and He bound a crown to it
and he joined them one with another. And He formed with them Gemini
in the universe, Sivan (May–June) in the year, the right foot in the soul
(Nefesh).]

[המליך אות ח [בשיחה] וקשר לו כתר וצרפן זה בזה וצר בהם סרטן
בעולם ותמוז בשנה ורגל שמאל בנפש:]

[He made the letter *Chet* king [over speech] and He bound a crown to it
and he joined them one with another. And He formed with them Cancer
in the universe, Tammuz (June–July) in the year, the left foot in the soul
(Nefesh).]

[המליך אות ט [בלעיטה] וקשר לו כתר וצרפן זה בזה וצר בהם אריה
בעולם ואב בשנה וכוליא ימניה בנפש:]

[He made the letter *Tet* king [over taste] and He bound a crown to it and he
joined them one with another. And He formed with them Leo in the universe, Av (July–August) in the year, the right kidney in the soul (Nefesh).]

[המליך אות י [בתשמיש] וקשר לו כתר וצרפן זה בזה וצר בהם בתולה
בעולם ואלול בשנה וכוליא שמאלית בנפש:]

[He made the letter *Yod* king [over coition] and He bound a crown to it
and he joined them one with another. And He formed with them Virgo in
the universe, Elul (August–September) in the year, the left kidney in the
soul (Nefesh).]

[המליך אות ל [במעשה] וקשר לו כתר וצרפן זה בזה וצר בהם מאזנים
בעולם ותשרי בשנה וכבד ימין בנפש:]

[He made the letter *Lamed* king [over action] and He bound a crown to
it and he joined them one with another. And He formed with them Libra
in the universe, Tishrey (September–October) in the year, the liver in the
soul (Nefesh).]

[המליך אות נ [בהלוך] וקשר לו כתר וצרפן זה בזה וצר בהם עקרב
בעולם וחשון בשנה וטחול ימין בנפש:]

[He made the letter *Nun* king [over motion] and He bound a crown to it
and he joined them one with another. And He formed with them Scorpio
in the universe, Cheshvan (October–November) in the year, the spleen in
the soul (Nefesh).]

[המליך אות ס [ברוגז] וקשר לו כתר וצרפן זה בזה וצר בהם טלה קשת
בעולם וכסלו בשנה ומרה ימין בנפש:]

[He made the letter *Samech* king [over agitation (anger)] and He bound a
crown to it and he joined them one with another. And He formed with
them Sagittarius in the universe, Kislev (November–December) in the year,
the gall bladder in the soul (Nefesh).]

[המליך אות ע [בשחוק] וקשר לו כתר וצרפן זה בזה וצר בהם גדי
בעולם וטבת בשנה ומסס ימין בנפש:]

[He made the letter *Ayin* king [over laughter] and He bound a crown
to it and he joined them one with another. And He formed with them
Capricorn in the universe, Tevet (December–January) in the year, the
(small) intestine(s) (masas) in the soul (Nefesh).]

[המליך אות צ [בהרהור] וקשר לו כתר וצרפן זה בזה וצר בהם דלי
בעולם ושבט בשנה וקבה ימין בנפש:]

[He made the letter *Tzadde* king [over thought] and He bound a crown
to it and he joined them one with another. And He formed with them
Aquarius in the universe, Shevat (January–February) in the year, the stomach (kevah) in the soul (Nefesh).]

[המליך אות ק [בשינה] וקשר לו כתר וצרפן זה בזה וצר בהם דגים
בעולם ואדר בשנה וקורקבן ימין בנפש:]

[He made the letter *Qof* king [over sleep] and He bound a crown to it and
he joined them one with another. And He formed with them Pisces in the
universe, Adar (February–March) in the year, the bowels (qurqevan) in the
soul (Nefesh).]

משנה ג': עשאן כמין עריבה סידרן כמין חומה ערכן כמין מלחמה
[וגם את זה לעומת זה עשה אלהים: שלש אמות שהם שלשה אבות
שמהם יצר אש ורוח ומים: שלש אמות ושבע כפולות ושתים עשרה
פשוטות:]

Mishnah 3: He made them like a plain (desert, wilderness), He arranged them
like a wall, He organized them like [armies in] a war (battle) [and also this
opposite of that made Elohim (God). Three mothers that are three fathers
for with them He formed fire (esh) and breath (Ruach; alternative: spirit)
and water (mayim). Three mothers, seven doubles and twelve simples].

משנה ד': אלו עשרים ושתים אותיות שבהם יסוד הקב"ה יה יהוה
צבאות אלהים חיים אלהי ישראל רם ונשא שוכן עד מרום וקדוש הוא:

Mishnah 4: These are twenty-two letters for with them founded HQB"H
(the Holy One blessed be He) Yah YHVH Tzevaot (of Hosts) Elohim
Chaim (God of Life) Elohey Yisrael (God of Israel) Ram ve-Nissa (High
and Exalted) Shochen Ad (Dwelling Eternally) Marom ve-Qadosh Hu
(lofty and Holy Is He).

Chapter 6   פרק ו'

משנה א': שלשה אבות ותולדותיהן ושבעה כובשין וצבאותיהן ושנים
עשר גבולי אלכסונין וראיה לדבר עדים נאמנים עולם שנה נפש:

חק שנים עשר ושבעה ושלשה ופקידן בתלי וגלגל ולב:

שלשה אש ומים ורוח אש למעלה ומים למטה ורוח חק מכריע בינתים
וסימן לדבר האש נושאה את המים מ"ם דוממת שי"ן שורקת אל"ף חוק
מכריע בינתים:

Mishnah 1: Three fathers and their descendants and seven storm troopers
and their hosts and twelve diagonal boundaries; and the proof of the matter: trustworthy witnesses [are] the world, the year, the soul (Nefesh).

A decree of twelve and seven and three and their clerk is in the dragon
(Teli; i.e., the constellation Draco), and the circle (of the year) and the heart.

Three (i.e., mothers): fire (esh) and water (mayim) and breath (Ruach;
alternative: spirit). Fire (esh) is above and water (mayim) is below and
breath (Ruach; alternative: spirit) is a decree balancing between them, and
the sign of this matter is this: The fire (esh) carries the water (mayim).
Mem is silent, *Shin* hisses, *Alef* is a decree balancing between them.

משנה ב': תלי בעולם כמלך על כסאו גלגל בשנה כמלך במדינה לב בנפש
כמלך במלחמה:

גם את כל חפץ זה לעומת זה עשה האלהים טוב לעומת רע טוב מטוב
ורע מרע טוב מבחין את הרע ורע מבחין את הטוב טובה שמורה לתובים
ורעה שמורה לרעים:

Mishnah 2: The dragon (Teli; i.e., the constellation Draco) in the universe
is like a king on his throne. The circle (cycle) in the year is like a king in
the country. The heart in the Nefesh (soul) is like a king in war.

Also, all things—this one opposite that one—made the Elohim (God)
(compare Ecclesiastes 7:14): good opposite evil, good from good, and evil
from evil, good discerns (reveals) evil and evil discerns (reveals) good. Good

is guarded (maintained) by the good ones and evil is guarded (maintained) by the evil ones.

משנה ג': שלשה [כל] אחד לבדו עומד שבעה שלשה מול שלשה ואחד
חק מכריע בינתים ושנים עשר עומדין במלחמה שלשה אוהבים שלשה
שונאים שלשה מחיים ושלשה ממיתים שלשה אוהבים שלשה הלב
והאזנים [והפה] שלשה שונאים הכבד והמרה והלשון [שלשה מחיים
שני נקבי האף והטחול ושלשה ממיתים שני הנקבים והפה] ואל מלך
נאמן מושל בכולם ממעון קדשו עד עדי עד אחד על גבי שלשה שלשה
על גבי שבעה שבעה על גבי שנים עשר וכולן אדוקין זה בזה:

Mishnah 3: Three: [Each] one stands alone. Seven: three opposite three and one a decree balancing between them. And twelve stand in war. Three lovers, three haters, and three life-givers, three killers. Three lovers: the heart and the ears [and the mouth]. Three haters: the liver, the gall (bladder), and the tongue. [Three life-givers: the two nostrils and the spleen. And three killers: the two orifices and the mouth.] And El Melech Ne'eman (God faithful King) rules over them all from His Holy Dwelling until the eternal eternity of eternities. One upon three, three upon seven, seven upon twelve, and all are fastened, one to another (literally, this one to that one).

משנה ד': וכיון שצפה אברהם אבינו [ע"ה] והביט וראה וחקר והבין
וחקק וחצב וצרף ויצר ועלתה בידו נגלה אליו אדון הכל [יתברך שמו
לעד] הושיבו בחיקו ונשקו על ראשו קראו אוהבו ונכרת ברית לו ולזרעו
[עד עולם] והאמין בה' ויחשבה לו צדקה כרת לו ברית בין עשר אצבעות
רגליו והוא ברית מילה ובין עשר אצבעות ידיו והוא [ברית] [ה]לשון
וקשר עשרים ושתים אותיות בלשונו וגילה לו את יסודן משכן במים דלקן
באש רעשן ברוח בערן בשבע[ה] נהגן בשנים עשר מזלות:

Mishnah 4: And when Abraham our father [may he rest in peace] saw, and looked, and quested, and understood, and engraved, and carved, and permuted (i.e., exchanged), and formed and succeeded [in his spiritual work], and thus Adon ha-Qol (the Lord of all) [blessed be His Name forever] revealed Himself to him and seated him in His bosom and kissed him on his head and He called him "His beloved" and a covenant was made with him, and with his seed (i.e., his descendants) [forever and ever]. "And he believed in YHVH, and He considered it to him for (i.e., he regarded it as) righteousness (tzedaqah)" (Genesis 15:6). He made a covenant (brit) with him between the ten toes of his feet and this is the covenant of circumcision (brit milah), and between the ten fingers of his hands and this is the [covenant of the] tongue ([brit] lashon). And He bound twenty-two letters to his tongue and He revealed to him their foundation (their Yesod; other versions write "His Sod"; i.e., "His Mystery"). He drew them with (or "in") water (mayim), He inflamed them with (or "in") fire (esh), He enlivened them with breath (Ruach), He burned them with the seven (planets), He guided (directed) them with the twelve constellations.

Pathworking for Preparation and Purification before Ritual

Some of the rituals in this book require a long period of preparation and purification. Because this may be very difficult for some readers to accomplish, we will go through the whole process of three week's worth of preparation and purification in just one pathworking.

Preparation

During the day before the ritual, do not eat a great deal and make sure you eat only pure, fresh food. Skip the evening meal. Before you go to sleep, wash yourself thoroughly, and, if possible, immerse yourself in a ritual bath.

In the morning, wash yourself thoroughly again, and during the day make sure to keep yourself pure. (You should be able to have at least one day of purity. It is important that you go through the entire purification with great care and attention so that you will be able to remember and visualize your feelings.) It is a good idea to go to a local synagogue and to give some money to charity.

In the evening, immediately before the ritual, sit down in meditation. Start with a prayer in which you ask forgiveness for your sins and request that the Holy One, blessed be He, grants you success in your ritual. Then close your eyes and imagine going to your ritual bath or other place of purification. Alternatively, you can imagine visiting a spiritual place, such as the River Jordan, for purification. You might even build a place on the astral plane that is entirely your own and can be used only by you for this and other spiritual purposes. (This is a very effective technique, because the astral place becomes more and more powerful every time you use it.)[1]

Whatever place of purification you choose, go there and purify yourself in the astral water, and cleanse your soul from the impurities of your worldly life. Then imagine going to a place where you can eat. If your astral place has a garden, go to it and eat the pure fruit which you find there. (Some rituals may require a special diet, and, if so, follow this outline.) After you have eaten, rest in your astral location, and imagine the sun setting and letting your astral self fall into a dreamless sleep. (In terms of time on the material plane, your sleep may last only a minute, but imagine that you have slept for an entire night.) Next, imagine waking up the next morning, and again purify yourself and have a pure, good meal. (If the ritual requires you to fast, then imagine drinking a fresh glass of water.) If there is a pure well or another source of pure drinking water, use this water for drinking and for purification in your astral place. After the meal, imagine the sun moving farther and finally setting again. Continue following this routine for as many astral days as are needed. If the required time of preparation is rather long, and if either you are not used to such long meditations or you simply want to shorten the process, you can do so by continuing to "fast forward" to the end of the first week. As you wake up again, imagine how you feel after one week of purification. Feel that most of the impurities of your worldly life have disappeared, and further deepen the process of purification as you go through the procedure again. After this day, continue immediately with the end of the second week, and then go the end of the third week, each time imagining that you are becoming ever purer.

After the meditation wash yourself thoroughly, and, if possible, immerse yourself in a ritual bath. Take a while to relax in the bath, for the meditation may have exhausted your concentration, and you will need to be in your best possible condition for the ritual.

Using this method, you can do any kind of purification or preparation on the astral plane that you may not be able to do on the physical plane, and the result will be just as effective as a result on the physical plane.

---

[1] A highly useful example for such an astral place, called the Inner Temple, can be found at my website: www.qabbalah.org (English) or www.qabbalah.de (German).

Illustration Sources

Page 128. Bowl against the Tormentor, Joseph Naveh and Shaul Shaked, *Magic Spells and Formulae* (Jerusalem: Magnes Press 1993)

Page 130. *Jacob Wrestling with the Angel,* by Julius Schnoor von Carolsfeld, originally printed in *Das Buch der Bücher in Bildern* (1908)

Page 142. Squatting man, from Dolores Ashcroft-Nowicki, *The Ritual Magic Workbook* (York Beach, Maine: Samuel Weiser, 1998)

Page 164. *Ezekiel's Vision,* Julius Schnoor von Carolsfeld, originally printed in *Das Buch der Bücher in Bildern* (1908)

Page 203. Moses receiving the Ten Commandments, from *Sefer Minhagim* (Venice: 1593)

Page 272. Rabbi Loew and the Golem, Mikolas Ales (1899)

Page 318. Woodcut of woman performing the Shabbat Blessing, from *Sefer Minhagim* (Venice: 1601)

Page 331. *Song of Solomon: Rose of Sharon,* Julius Schnoor von Carolsfeld, originally printed in *Das Buch der Bücher in Bildern* (1908)

Page 347. Woodcut of Havdalah, from *Sefer Minhagim* (Venice 1601)

Page 356. Woodcut of Tu B'Shevat, from *Sefer Minhagim* (Venice 1593)

Page 390. *Elijah Ascending to Heaven,* Julius Schnoor von Carolsfeld, originally printed in *Das Buch der Bücher in Bildern* (1908)

Page 424. Portrait of Chaim Samuel Jacob Falk, the Baal Shem of London, by J. S. Copley (Formerly in Cecil Roth Collection)

Bibliography

Traditional Sources

Abulafia, Abraham. *Ner Elohim.* Munich: n.p., Ms. 10, 172 b.

Agrippa of Nettesheim, H. C. *De Occulta Philosophia.* Antwerp and Paris: 1531.

Azulay, Abraham. *Or ha-Chammah.* Premysl: 1896.

Babylonian Talmud. Jerusalem: Tal-Man Inc., 1981.

Becker, Hans-Jürgen, and Christoph Berner. *Avot de-Rabbi Nathan.* Tübingen: Mohr Siebeck, 2006.

ben Chushiel, Chananel. Commentary on the Talmud. In *Babylonian Talmud: Masechet Moed Qatan and Chagiga.* Jerusalem: Tal-Man Inc., 1981.

ben Jacob Bacharach, Naphtali, of Frankfurt. *Sefer Emeq ha-Melech.* Amsterdam: 1648.

ben R. Amram Adani, David. *Midrash ha-Gadol, Leviticus: Midrash ha-Gadol on the Pentateuch.* Edited by A. Steinsaltz. Jerusalem: Mosad Harav Kook, 1997.

ben Samuel, Isaac, of Acre/Acco. *Meirat Eneyim.* Washington, DC: Library of Congress number BM525.I79. Quoted by Jellinek, Adolf. *Beiträge zur Geschichte der Kabbala.* Heft II, 1851–52.

ben Yehudah, Eleazar, of Worms. *Sodey Razayah.* Bilgoraj: 1936.

ben Yitzhak Sambari, Yosef, ed. *Sefer Diwrey Yosef.* Jerusalem: Yad Izhak Ben-Zvi Publications, 1994.

Berechiah, Aaron, of Modena. *Maavar Yabboq.* Venice: 1626.

———. *Seder Ashmoret ha-Boqer* (also published as: *Me'eirey ha-Shachar*). Mantua: 1624.

Chaim Vital. Jerusalem: n.p., 1998.

Cohen, Seymour J. "Iggeret ha-Qodesh." In *The Holy Letter.* New York: Ktav Publishing House, 1976.

Fisch, Solomon, ed. *Midrash Haggadol on the Pentateuch.* Manchester, England: Manchester University Press, 1940.

Goldschmidt, Lazarus, trans. *Sefer Jesirah - Das Buch der Schöpfung.* Frankfurt 1894, Darmstadt 1969.

Goodman-Thau, Eveline, and Christoph Schulte, eds. *Das Buch Jezira.* Berlin: Akademie Verlag, 1993.

ha-Roqeach, Eleazar, of Worms. *Perush al Sefer Yetzirah.* Mantua: 1562.

———. *Perush H" RA me-Germayza le-Sefer Yetzirah.* Edited by Shapiro. Przemysl: 1888.

Keter Shem Tov. Podgorze: 1898.

Margalioth, Mordecai, ed. *Sefer ha-Razim.* Jerusalem: Yediot Achronot, 1966.

———. *Sefer ha-Zohar,* 5 vols. Jerusalem: Mossad ha-Rav Kook, 1978.

———. *Zohar Chadash.* Jerusalem: Mossad ha-Rav Kook, 1978.

Margulies, M., ed. *Midrash ha-Gadol, Exodus: Midrash Haggadol on the Pentateuch.* Jerusalem: n.p., 1997.

———. *Midrash ha-Gadol, Genesis: Midrash Haggadol on the Pentateuch.* Jerusalem: n.p., 1997.

Qaro, Joseph. *Maggid Mesharim.* Jerusalem: Ora-press, 1960.

Qordovero, Moses. *Pardes Rimmonim.* Cracow, 1592, reprinted Jerusalem: Offset Press of Sh. Monzon, 1962.

———. *Pardes Rimmonim.* Krakau: 1592.

———. *Shi'ur Qomah.* Jerusalem: 1966.

Rabinowitz, Z. M. *Midrash ha-Gadol, Numbers: Midrash Haggadol on the Pentateuch.* Jerusalem: n.p., 1997.

Reform Synagogues of Great Britain. *Siddur: Forms of Prayer for Jewish Worship.* London: Assembly of Rabbis of the Reform Synagogues of Great Britain, 1977.

Scheuer, Rav Joseph. *Siddur Schma Kelenu.* Basel: Morascha, 2003.

Sefer Chassidim. Bologna: 1538.

Sefer ha-Gematria. Quoted by Abraham Epstein. In *Beiträge zur jüdischen Altertumskunde.* Vienna: 1887.

Sefer ha-Zohar, 3 vols. Wilna: 1882.

Sefer Minhagim. Venice: 1593.

Sefer Raziel. Amsterdam: 1701.

Selig, Gottfried. *Sepher Schimmusch Tehillim.* Berlin: 1788

Sheelot ha-Zaqen. Oxford Ms. 2396.

Shibche ha-Besht. Berditschev: 1915.

Shulchan Aruch ha- Ari. Lvov: 1788.

Theodor, J., and Ch. Albeck, eds. *Midrash Genesis Rabbah.* Jerusalem: Wahrman Books, 1965.

Tiquney Zohar. Mantua: 1558, Amsterdam: 1718.

Tzavva at ha-Rivash. Warsaw: 1913.

Vital, Chaim. *Etz Chaim.* Warsaw: 1891, Tel Aviv: 1975.

———. *Sefer ha-Chezyonot.* Jerusalem: n.p., 1954.

———. *Shaarey Qedushah.* Jerusalem: 1926.

Vital, Chaim. *Ketavim Chadashim me-Rabeinu.* Jerusalem: Hotzaat Chevrat Ahavat Shalom, 1998.

Zalman, Shneur, of Liadi. *Tanya* (also published as *Liqutey Amarim*). Wilna: 1912.

Zohar Chadash. Warsaw: 1885.

Modern Sources

Adler, Sulamit H., and Marc Verman. "Path Jumping in the Jewish Magical Tradition." In *Jewish Studies Quarterly* 1 (1993–94).

Ashcroft-Nowicki, Dolores, *Illuminations.* Woodbury, Minn.: Llewellyn, 2003.

———. *The Ritual Magic Workbook.* York Beach, Maine: Samuel Weiser, 1998.

Ashcroft-Nowicki, Dolores, and J. H. Brennan. *Magical Use of Thought Forms.* Woodbury, Minn.: Llewellyn, 2001.

Besserman, Perle. *Der versteckte Garten.* Frankfurt: Spirit Fischer, 1996.

Blau, L. *Das altjuedische Zauberwesen.* Budapest: 1898.

Etkes, Immanuel. *The Besht: Magician, Mystic, and Leader.* Hanover, N.H.: Brandeis University Press, 2005.

Fortune, Dion. *Esoteric Orders and their Work and the Training and Work of an Initiate.* Glasgow: Thorsons, 1995.

———. *Sane Occultism.* London: Rider, 1928.

———. *The Cosmic Doctrine.* London: SIL, 1995.

Ginzberg, Louis. *The Legends of the Jews.* Philadelphia: The Jewish Publication Society of America, 1909.

Idel, Moshe. *Golem.* Albany, N.Y.: State University of New York Press, 1990.

———. *Kabbalah & Eros.* New Haven: Yale University Press, 2005.

Kaplan, Aryeh. *Meditation and Kabbalah.* York Beach, Maine: Samuel Weiser, 1982.

———. *Meditation and the Bible.* York Beach, Maine: Samuel Weiser, 1988.

———. *Sefer Yetzirah.* York Beach, Maine: Samuel Weiser, 1997.

Matthews, Caitlín, and John Matthews. *The Western Way.* London: Arkana, 1985.

Meyrink, Gustav. *Der Golem.* Leipzig: 1917.

Montgomery, J. A. *Aramaic Incantation Texts from Nippur.* Philadelphia: University Museum, 1913.

Naveh Joseph, and Shaul Shaked. *Amulets and Magic Bowls.* Leiden and Jerusalem: E. J. Brill/ Magnes Press, 1985.

———. *Magic Spells and Formulae.* Jerusalem: Magnes Press, 1993.

Rappoport, Angelo S. *The Folklore of the Jews.* London: Soncino Press, 1937.

Regardie, Israel. *Foundations of Practical Magic.* Wellingborough, England: Thorsons, 1979.

———. *The Golden Dawn.* Woodbury, Minn.: Llewellyn, 1994.

———. *How to Make and Use Talismans.* London: Aquarian Press, 1970.

Schäfer, Peter. *Geniza-Fragmente zur Hekhalot-Literatur.* Tübingen: J. C. B. Mohr, 1984.

Schäfer, Peter, and S. Shaked. *Magische Texte aus der Kairoer Geniza,* 3 vols. Tübingen: J. C. B. Mohr, 1994–99.

———. *Synopsis zur Hekhalot-Literatur.* Tübingen: J. C. B. Mohr, 1981.

Schiffman, L. H., and M. D. Swartz. *Hebrew and Aramaic Incantation Texts from the Cairo Genizah.* Sheffield: JSOT Press, 1992.

Scholem, Gershom. *Die jüdische Mystik in ihren Hauptströmungen.* Frankfurt: Suhrkamp, 2000.

———. *Ha-Qabbalah be-Provence.* Edited by R. Shatz. Jerusalem: Akadamon, 1979.

———. *Major Trends in Jewish Mysticism.* Jerusalem/New York: Schocken Books, 1941.

———. *On the Kabbalah and Its Symbolism.* New York: Schocken Books, 1969.

———. *On the Mystical Shape of the Godhead: Basic Concepts in the Kabbalah.* New York: Schocken Books, 1997.

———. *Von der mystischen Gestalt der Gottheit. Studien zu Grundbegriffen der Kabbala.* Zürich: Rhein-Vlg., 1962.

———. *Zur Kabbala und ihrer Symbolik.* Frankfurt: Suhrkamp, 1998.

Schrire, T. *Hebrew Amulets.* London: Routledge and Kegan Paul, 1966.

Schwartz, Howard. *Gabriel's Palace—Jewish Mystical Tales.* Oxford, England: Oxford University Press, 1993.

Shelley, Mary. *Frankenstein or The Modern Prometheus.* London: 1818.

Stemberger, Günter. *Einleitung in Talmud und Midrasch.* Munich: Beck, 1992.

Trachtenberg, J. *Jewish Magic and Superstition.* New York: Atheneum, 1939.

Wandrey, Irina. *Das Buch des Gewandes und Das Buch des Aufrechten.* Tübingen: Mohr Siebeck, 2004.

Index